PECAN PIE

A HAP-PIE-LY EVER AFTER STORY

Katelyn Brawn

The Omnibus Publishing

Baltimore, MD

The Omnibus Publishing
5422 Ebenezer Rd.
POB 152
White Marsh, MD 21

www.theomnibuspublishing.com

Publisher's Note: This is a work of fiction. Names, characters, places, and incidents are a product of the author's imagination. Locales and public names are sometimes used for atmospheric purposes. Any resemblance to actual people, living or dead, or to businesses, companies, events, institutions, or locales is completely coincidental.

Book Layout ©2022 BookDesignTemplates.com

Cover Design by The Omnibus Publishing

Ordering Information: Quantity sales. Special discounts are available on quantity purchases by corporations, associations, and others. For details, contact the "Special Sales Department" at the address above.

Pecan Pie/ Katelyn Brawn. -- 1st ed.
ISBN 978-1-7335985-7-6   Library of Congress Number Contact publisher

The Omnibus Publishing is a division of Reading Pandas, Inc.

To Nannie and Honey, two women who did so much to form the person I am. I wish you were here to see this.

Everything has beauty, but not everyone sees it.

—CONFUCIUS

CHAPTER ONE

The concept of giving flowers as a romantic gesture is something of a mystery to me. It's like someone saying, "Here, darling, I've bought you this bunch of decaying sex organs of what may as well be weeds. Please love me forever." And women buy it, actually swoon over it! I consider it my life's work to find the perfect love story. In the beginning of my literary romance journey, I read every dime-store, smutty novel there was on the subject. Ripped bodices and quivering members every day. But let's be real; the girl who wants the quivering member doesn't need the flowers. That was my early teen years, hiding books under my mattress from my mother so she wouldn't find them and consider me scandalized. My tastes evolved later to the pages of Brontë, Austen, and Hardy. I ended up with more of a thrill from a stolen glance or touch of the hand than any steamy sex scene. If anything, the convoluted variety of stories has left me only more confused as to what constitutes a great love. One thing remains however. No flowers. Flowers are stupid.

My mother is one of the swoony women who believes, with her whole heart, that all problems in a relationship can be solved with daisies and violets. Shocking, because I consider her otherwise the world's most level-headed woman. No matter the size of the indiscretion, my father could apologize for anything with a well crafted arrangement. Julio, of the sole Harpersgrove flower shop, brings bouquet upon bouquet of flowers to our door after every argument. Mom can forgive anything with enough chrysanthemums.

Imagine my surprise this morning when Julio shows up at my front door with an absurd number of flowers. There was no need for Dad to continue the charade. The cat was already back in the house after their most recent fight. "Sure you have the right place Julio?" I ask as he heaves the pile into my arms.

"Oh yes Miss Southland," he whistles through the sizable gap between his front teeth. His S's turn to high pitched bird calls. "Your father called them in last night."

"Is he already apologizing for something new?"

"No Miss Southland, these flowers aren't for your mother. They are for you," Julio says, turning away and back to the bright yellow van he drives around town. Every woman holds her breath in anticipation when it pulls in front of their house or workplace. Every girl hopes that inside that beat up sunflower of a car is a gift for them. I don't get it. If a guy wants to impress me, he should buy me a book.

"Dad!" I call into the open house. No immediate response.

My brother, Jonah, rounds the corner and notices the flowers on my arm. "Have you seen Dad?" I sign to him with my free hand, shifting the weight of the vase to my hip.

"In his study with earbuds in," he responds with his hands. Pointing to the bouquet, he questions, "What did he do now?"

I place the flowers onto the counter so I can use both my hands to talk to my brother. "Julio said they aren't for Mom. Dad got them for me."

Jonah's dark eyebrows knit together. "What did he do to you?" he asks after grabbing a crisp, green apple off of the top of the fruit pile. He takes a loud, crunching bite, chewing with smacking lips. Decorum is not my brother's strong suit.

"I can't think of anything. I'm a little worried I missed something."

As if on cue, my dad appears in the kitchen doorway. His shiny, bald head reflects the light from the bulbs in the ceiling. He catches us staring, then he signs, "What?"

"Julio was here." I sign and speak. "He said that they're for me?"

What is he up to? What did he do? What did I do?

I motion to the flowers on the counter.

He pulls the buds from his ears, tucking them into the pocket with his phone. "Oh yeah?" he remarks, a few octaves too high.

"Yup," I snap, a little sharper than I mean to, but I'm agitated and uneasy. I fiddle with the fraying hem of my lavender sweater. I know I shouldn't be wearing pastels. They do nothing to help girls with round waistlines like mine. Unfortunately, it's the only clean thing warm enough to handle the arctic, premenopausal temperatures Mom keeps the house at these days.

"What are they for?"

Dad shrugs. "Can't a father do something nice for his daughter?" he asks. My weight shifts between my feet and I can feel the bones click in my big toes. I can't seem to get comfortable.

"Sure, except when he has a daughter who doesn't like flowers." I catch the blossoms again out of the corner of my eye and see red in more ways than one.

"What's going on, dad?"

Pinching the space between his eyes, the cool and casual mask drops and he replies, "Okay, the flowers were your mom's idea."

Now here I sit in my car, driving up the highway at speeds that are by no means safe. The flowers my parents thrust upon me to apologize for their betrayal mock me from the passenger seat of my old car. Mounted to the dashboard, my phone shakes against the rattling of my heater. My friend, Rosie, is on the screen as I try to explain what happened. Something about watching her head bob up and down with the shaking of the phone is making me queasy.

"They're the most selfish, inconsiderate people in the world!" I shout, blaring my horn at a minivan driving five miles under the speed limit in the fast lane. I'm definitely getting a ticket on this trip. If I do, it will be my parents' fault and they can pay the fine.

Rosie sits in her black pleather pants on the kitchen counter in the pie shop. Her short and curvy body can pull off a pair of leggings in a way that's a crime against nature. However, it skeeves me out when she sits on the counter. She makes food there for goodness sake!

Tossing a mix of berries in a large, ceramic mixing bowl, she says, "You've said that four times since you called me and I still don't know what's going on." Placing the bowl aside, she crosses her legs and gives me her full attention.

The entire group of girls I work with at Hap-PIE-ly Ever After are my best friends, but I'm the closest to Rosie. I function as the shop manager, running pretty much everything for our boss, Beattie. Rosie runs the kitchen. When she's not sewing a button on a sweater that I've popped, or hemming pants for our friend, Blanche, she bakes. She creates all the delectable pies that people travel from all over to try. Between the two of us, we keep the shop standing. The dream team.

Rosie's red lips purse as she waits for a real answer.

"My parents have exiled me."

"Start talking," I demand of my father as the front door swings open at the most opportune of times. Jessica Southland owns every room she walks into, no matter the situation. In the lifetime I've known her, she's never had a single hair out of place or a wrinkled article of clothing. She was a prestigious college professor until she decided to stay home to teach Jonah and me. My brother and I have been homeschooled all of our lives. It's what made it possible for me to graduate high school months ahead of any of my friends.

Mom switches her attention between us then settles on Jonah. She raises her slim fingers, finished with perfectly manicured nails, to sign, "Can you get the bags out of the car, please? Just a few groceries."

Jonah, oblivious as always to any tension, shrugs and heads to the door. He pulls his phone out of the back pocket of his jeans, which are at least two sizes too big. His hair flops over his eyes in sandy curls. It's only when he passes Mom that I realize how much he's grown. He can look clear over her head now.

She waits until the door closes before returning her gaze to Dad and me. "What's up?" she asks, her tone far too chipper for ten o'clock in the morning.

"Flowers are here, Jess," my dad remarks as he rubs the back of his neck. For all the skill and experience he has with Mom, my Dad hates confrontation with either of his children.

"Yes, Jess," I mock in a way I know my mother won't appreciate. "The flowers are here and Dad was about to tell me why. I, for one, know that flowers in this family are only given as an apology. What are you apologizing for, exactly?"

Her expression never breaks. She pushes her sleeves up her slender arms to bunch at her bony elbows. I'm the only member of my family that isn't a gangly piece of asparagus. Maybe I'm adopted.

"Why does it have to be an apology, Isabella? Can't we do something nice for our daughter?" Her words are almost identical to Dad's.

My fists cement onto my round hips, standing nose to nose with my perfect mother. Truth be told, she's the person I'm closest to in the entire world. Growing up, I could tell her anything. She never gave me a hard time about my weight. She did try to make me healthier and push me toward clothes that flattered me more, but never with an ounce of malice to it. I think the closeness we normally share is what makes the secrecy so unsettling.

"Dad already said that. Please tell me what's going on. You're scaring me."

Mom chuckles before tousling my hair like I'm five years old. "Oh, my dear, sweet Isabella, don't be dramatic. It's nothing bad."

Jonah chooses this moment to barrel through the front door. His arms lined and weighed down with grocery store plastic bags. I can feel my father cringe from across the room. Hopefully he'll refrain from chastising mom for not using the reusable totes. After watching a documentary about dying seagulls caught in plastic grocery bags, he had insisted we stop using plastic. Breathing heavy from his exhausting trip from the car, Jonah exclaims aloud, "Just a few groceries?"

I always wonder how he thinks he sounds, or what he would think if he could hear his own voice. While it's normal for us, we are not immune to the stares we get in public when Jonah speaks. Knowing my aloof little brother, though, I'm sure he wouldn't care anymore than he already does. I'm really the only self conscious one of the family. Of course it doesn't hurt that Jonah is the epitome of cool with his tall, lean body and fashionably shaggy hair and perfect face. I am an amorphous potato.

My mother, completely unfazed by his distress, says, "Put them away for me." No hint of a question. Mom has this way of demanding things of you that makes you believe they're your idea. To me and my father she voices, "Let's take this into the living room." Again, no question.

Mom smooths out her ivory skirt as she takes a seat. She pats the space beside her, inviting me to sit. Dad already took the armchair for himself. Unless my plan is to sit on the floor, the couch is my only option. I tuck one legging covered leg under me and pull the other knee up to my chest. When I say to my chest, I mean as close as I can get without my belly or boobs getting in the way. The resistance is like shoving together the same poles of two magnets. I'm trying my best to guard myself from whatever's coming. The lump in the back of my throat refuses to settle.

"Okay," I begin, refusing to let them push this off any further. "My most beloved parents, start talking. What is going on?"

As she is prone to do, Mom takes the lead. "First of all, your father and I want you to know how proud we are of you. All the hard work you've done to finish your studies early hasn't gone unnoticed. You've been incredible."

"And we're sure your college acceptance is coming any day now," my dad chimes in, considering himself a part of Mom's conversation.

"In keeping with that spirit," my mother continues, barely registering that my father had spoken. "A very interesting opportunity has arisen that your father and I have decided you need to pursue. It's going to make a huge impact on your future. We couldn't let it pass by. We had to accept it for you-"

"Whoa." I hold my hands up in a time out position, trying to pause her for a second. "You're like ten steps in front of me. What opportunity are you talking about?"

Now Mom looks to Dad to pick things up. He sits forward in his chair, resting his elbows on his navy blue slacks. "Peanut, have you ever heard of Baxter Industries?" *he asks.*

"Yeah, they make everything." *By everything, I mean from batteries and toys to firearms and genetically engineered food.* "What about them?"

"Well," *Mom begins again. This conversation is like a tennis match with its back and forth.* "The CEO and founder of the company, Lionel Baxter, is an old classmate of mine from college. He's currently in a predicament and reached out to me to see if I was still teaching."

"What kind of predicament?" *I ask.*

"He has a son who suffered some severe injuries in a horrible accident about a year ago," *Dad explains.*

I pull my knee a little closer to my chest, my back screaming at me in protest. It's a protective stance I'd taken on as a little girl to guard myself against things I didn't want to face. I have no idea what's coming, but for some reason "arranged marriage" keeps entering my mind.

"That's awful, but what does that have to do with me?"

"It's a great opportunity," *my mother says again, and I wish she'd stop.* "Mr. Baxter requires a live-in tutor to help catch his son up on his studies. I signed you on for the job." *The world drops to the floor and even if my life depended on it, I can't find any words. Mom seems to sense my aversion to the idea, possibly by my slacked jaw and bugged eyes.*

"It's the best possible thing for you. It's not good for you to waste all your time for the next few months." *Months?! Does she really expect me to go live away from my family for months, plural?!* "Working at that pie shop nonstop is not a good use of your talents or your brain."

This is not a new argument. She's always made it abundantly clear that she would prefer I get an internship somewhere rather than waste my life in a normal teenage job. I scrub my hands up and down my face, feeling like I've aged twenty years in the last five minutes.

"It feels like you're both speaking another language or something. This makes absolutely no sense. Why would you want to send me away? What did I do, exactly?"

"Oh, honey," Mom says, reaching forward and taking my hand. I have to resist the urge to pull away. "This is not about sending you away. It's about providing you with a chance that doesn't come around every day." This is beginning to sound a lot like when she made me try ballet for "the experience." I still have nightmares about it.

"In addition to paying you extremely well," Dad chimes in, his face hopeful and determined. "You already applied for the Baxter Industry's scholarship. This might not gain you any favor, but you never know. It's a lot of money."

"I don't even get a vote on this?" I ask. Until now, the Southland family has always been a democracy, not this dictatorial nonsense. My parents grow silent and my mother starts to run her thumb back and forth over her lower lip. It smudges her perfect, rose pink lipstick. I secretly enjoy that something about her is off balance now that she's completely knocked me off my feet. She squares her body to me, hands folded in her lap.

"Sweetheart, there are certain things you won't understand until you're a parent." And there it is. My mom and I have always had a very open and honest relationship, but there have been occasions where I've backed her into a corner and she's not been willing to submit. She'll say something along the lines of, "You won't understand until you have children of your own."

And that's it. The conversation is over. I run my fingers through my tangled brown hair, letting out an alien sound too generous to call a sigh. "I don't want this!" I exclaim to the floor, tugging on the roots. The tiny hint of pain keeps me grounded.

"Sometimes the things that are best for you are the things you don't want to do," my father muses in his very Confucius, all knowing voice

that makes me mad. Always the man with a resolution.

"The two of you made this decision without even consulting me. I have a job. I have friends and something resembling a social life. And the two of you pull the rug out from beneath me? This is not like you at all." They both look down to the floor. Probably formulating further ways to work around the issue of ruining my life. My mother sighs and shakes her head, looking, dare I say, disappointed?

"I honestly did not expect you to respond this way, Isabella. You have always carried yourself as a much more mature young lady than this." She tsks like I've forgotten to empty the dishwasher or something. This is my life! I pull away from her touch to put some space between us.

"You're really trying to call me immature, mother? Seriously? I feel like I'm trapped in the twilight zone!" I shout. Nervous energy pulses through my legs and I have to move to work the jitters out. Our living room is small, so I end up pacing in a small circle between their seats.

"Peanut, New York is only a few hours away. You should be home for Christmas," my father begins, but I can't hear anything else. All sounds have been replaced by a high pitched squeal and my stomach hurts. My knees weaken, like a newborn baby deer, as I settle onto the floor beneath me. A little dramatic? Maybe.

"I'm sorry, I'm sorry. Did you say New York? You're not simply sending me off, but you want to ship me to another state? That's not a quick trip to Baltimore, Dad! That's what, five, six hours in the car? And you want to sit here and act like I'm being ridiculous or immature? Well, I'm not going!" I exclaim, crossing my arms over my chest like a petulant child. If they want immature, I'll give it to them. My mother sighs from the depths of her lungs, only angering me further.

"Of course you're going Isabella, don't be absurd. This is not the kind of thing you turn away. You'd have to work at that pie shop for years to make the money you will in even just a few months tutoring the Baxter

boy. Remember, an Ivy League school is not cheap. Don't be a child about this. I need you to grow up and accept a gift when it's laid at your feet."

Tears prick my eyes. Every intense emotion I go through ends with me in tears. My mother has never yelled at me. At my father and occasionally my brother? Yes, but never at me. My words disappear at the back of my throat and I'm certain I'm about to lose it. Mom shifts her weight off the couch to sit beside me on the floor. Reaching forward, she takes my hands out of my lap and leans in close to whisper, "Honey, I'm not doing this to punish you. The last thing I want is to send you away for a bulk of the last year before you leave for college. But, I would do you wrong as your mom if I didn't make you carry this out."

"Why would these people even want a teenager to tutor their kid if they have all this money? Can't they hire a retired Harvard professor or some savant to teach him? Why do they need me?" My father holds my gaze with an unblinking intensity.

"Because they have already tried those things and none of it has worked. You're their last shot." Oh, good, they're shipping me away to work with an impossible psycho.

It would have been easy to lay my head on Mom's shoulder and tell her I understood, completely submit. But for the first time in my life, I don't want to do that. I don't want to be the good girl for the sake of being the good girl. I want my parents to see me. I want them to see the hurt and the anger that they caused. I don't want them to be able to settle into their decision with any kind of calm or resolve. I want them to know this is not okay. I pull myself out of her hold and push up to my feet.

"And how long before I leave for Alcatraz?" I huff, moving toward the living room window. This space is far too small for the three of us. They share another psychic communication with only their eyes and it makes me want to punch them both.

You need to be on your way in the morning."

CHAPTER TWO

Rosie shrieks, "What?!" back at me in horror from my phone's little screen. I pull over on the side of the highway to keep talking to her. I'm bound to have an accident or get a ticket at the rate I'm going.

"This happened yesterday? Bella, why didn't you tell me?"

"Don't you think I would have said something sooner if I had known? I'm pretty sure they were afraid I'd revolt if they gave me advance notice."

A motorcycle flies by me at the speed of light. I hate driving out amongst the non-Harpersgrove humans. I don't know these people who drive twenty miles over the speed limit and switch lanes like it's some well choreographed ballet to which I don't know the steps.

Rosie's shoulders scrunch up to her ears. The purple rose tattoo on her left shoulder peaks out of the collar of her shirt. "You mean like when you came by the shop yesterday afternoon?"

My cheeks flush red with embarrassment for forgetting about that point. My mind is one-tracked right now. I turn down the car heater as sweat begins pools on my upper lip. No one likes the sweaty fat girl.

"Well, it happened yesterday."

A red pickup slows to a stop beside my car. The driver is my father's age with salt and pepper hair that flips out from beneath his baseball cap. He mouths an exaggerated *You okay?* to me. I muster the best smile that I can and nod. He offers me the same back and peels away. Maybe the people outside my town aren't all bad.

"How did Beattie react when you told her?" Rosie asks, pulling my attention back to the little screen.

I rest my head back against the seat and stare at the small hole in the padding above.

"She was Beattie."

I stomp up to my room and pout. Planning the perfect retort to keep me cemented in place. I flip through my phone to find justification that this is some violation of child labor laws or indentured servitude. I'm not finding as much as I'd hoped for. Then I remember the pie shop and all the things I need to do there. They can't make it work without me. Definitely not on such short notice. How on earth will Beattie take the news? She relies on me to take care of the day-to-day operations. I'd be leaving her high and dry. Why didn't my parents think of Beattie?! I need to get as much in order at the shop as possible. I check the time: a little after eleven. I force myself to my feet and down the stairs.

My mother is working her magic over the stove, something delicious cooking up in the assorted copper pans. She's pushed her dark hair away from her face with a thick black headband. Around her waist she wears an ivory lace apron that is definitely more style over function. Sunshine beams from her face when she sees me. I suppose she thinks I'm finally ready to be "rational," ready to accept her "gift" with a smile.

"There you are!" she exclaims as she grabs the handle of one of the pots. "Are you hungry? Would you like some lunch?" I honestly think she's going to hand me the whole pot.

I resist the urge to give in to her tasty treats and pull my coat off the hook by the front door. "I have to go to work," I say, my voice flat as I pull the zipper up to my chin.

Mom's entire face falls and regret fills me for all of a minute.

"Izzy," she begins, pulling a childhood nickname from her back pocket. I'm pretty sure I haven't heard it in about ten years, around the time I found out there wasn't a Santa Claus. I caught my parents laying the presents out under the tree late in the night on Christmas Eve. It was awful. She'd tried to soften the blow then and I know she's trying to do it now.

"I know you're upset, but we have a lot to do before you leave. I want to make sure you're ready." My hand rests on the doorknob. I know I should walk through, but I can't let it go.

"I'm not going to be ready, Mom. Not in a few hours or even a few days. You guys threw out everything that makes our relationship strong. I can't catch my balance. Right now, I'm going to do the one thing I can do. I'm going to work and try to explain to my boss that I'm abandoning her, with no notice, for months." Her jaw hangs open and I know she has plenty to say, but I'm not willing to give her the chance. Before she can take a breath, I open the front door and step out into the brisk cold. Breathing the freezing air into my lungs sends a chill through my body.

I slide into my car and zip away to work. Just as I'm getting out, Lucy Wilcox, head cheerleader and local meanie, emerges from Curl Free or

Dye Trying Salon. Having never gone to school, I didn't have the normal unpleasant upbringing that the other girls experienced with Lucy. But knowing me didn't seem to be important to Lucy, she hated me anyway.

I have never been thin, not a day in my life. My waistline is wider than it should be and my boobs never fit right in any shirt. My butt and legs look thick like tree trunks in whatever I wear on my lower half. Don't get me started on dresses. My face is actually pretty nice, gray eyes and full pink lips, never a pimple. My hair falls in soft, light brown curls at my shoulders. I have that going for me.

Lucy doesn't give a damn about my face or hair, she only sees my less than desirable body. I've spent a significant amount of my life beating people to the punchline. I figure, if I make the fat joke first, it'll sting a little less when other people make them. I try to take the power back. But then there's Lucy. I'm pretty sure girls like her have a sixth sense ability to find exactly what you hate about yourself and make you feel much, much worse. I've never known how to fight that. She clicks towards me in her knee-high, heeled boots, outfitted in a skin tight sweater dress and expensive leather jacket. My throat closes when a grin stretches across her red glossed lips. She's like a hungry fox and I'm a lone, scared chicken.

"Well, well, well," she begins, her voice smooth as a cat's purr. "If it isn't Bubble Butt Bella." My grip on the strap of my bag tightens like I'm holding onto a security blanket. I try to channel the no nonsense attitude of my friend Goldie. She may be the one person alive who has no problem dealing with Lucy.

"Oh, Luce," I begin with a smile, fighting the urge to sprint to the shop or vomit. "You know the way to my heart. I love a good alliteration." For a moment I hope my five dollar word will throw her off balance. That's when I remember that Lucy is ridiculously smart.

"Yeah, fat ass. I know what an alliteration is, you socially awkward freak," she spits back at me. Her words burn. My tongue feels too large

for my mouth. I want to swing the moment back in my favor, throw some sharp jab back in her face, but the only word repeating in my head is "DANGER!"

"Begone, Satan," I hear from behind me. Goldie walks in strong strides toward us. I could have run away and lived to fight another day, but having my one girl army is better.

Lucy is undeniably pretty, but Goldie Rust is drop dead gorgeous. Her corn colored hair hangs in straight locks down to her knees. She wears it today in a thick, long braid that must have taken at least an hour to construct. Her skinny waist expands out into perfect hips and perky boobs. She has a face so flawless that sometimes it's hard to look at her for too long. She's as pretty as Lucy could ever be, but Goldie's kind and caring in a way that Lucy could never fathom. Lucy rolls her eyes and pops the gum in her mouth as she rests her weight against my car. I wince, wanting her to move, but my tongue is still paralyzed.

"OmiGod Rust," she says to Goldie. "Do you ever remove the cape and take a break from being the savior of your little freak friends?"

"Sorry, Lucifer, I guess I have a problem with bullies picking on my friends. Now why don't you get on your broomstick and fly away?" Lucy narrows her gaze at my friend, temporarily forgetting all about me.

"Goldie, you think you're so amazing because you're pretty. But don't forget that you're stupid, poor, and a bastard child. You will never be me."

Goldie licks her lips, thinking for a second before she answers. Then she leans in close to Lucy's face and hisses, "And thank God for that."

Beautiful face glaring into beautiful face. It's like Clash of the Barbies. I can see the muscles work in Lucy's throat before she shoves into Goldie's shoulder to get past her.

"Get out of my way, freak," she snarls at me. I'm happy to oblige. I'll have the perfect comeback next time. She stamps away to terrorize another

village or punch a small child in the face. Once the demon girl is gone from sight, Goldie turns to me with complete disapproval.

"You really have to learn to harness your inner power with that one, Bells," she says, her tongue clicking like a very annoying bell. Guilt fills me. I'm sure being everyone's knight in shining armor gets old for Goldie. I pull my arms into the sleeves of my coat, like a turtle sinking into my shell.

"I know. I tried, but I did not succeed," I admit with defeat and only a hint of a pout. Goldie smirks at that.

"Yeah," she begins, leaning her weight back against my car. It's too cold to be having this conversation outside, but Goldie doesn't seem bothered at all. "I saw you square your shoulders. Then you slumped forward and I figured you needed me."

She knows me all too well. Goldie will never be a damsel locked in a tower. She'd climb down her own hair to get away. Not only does Goldie work at the pie shop, she helps whenever she can at her grandfather's drugstore across the street. It's easy enough for her to bounce back and forth between the two when necessary. I know how strong Goldie is and how hard she works. That's probably why Lucy's comments hit me like they did.

"She shouldn't have said those things about you," I say, shoving my hands into the depths of my pockets, desperate for warmth. I feel the need to impart whatever kind words I have onto my people before I have to leave them.

Goldie shrugs and rocks her weight back on her heels. "She wasn't completely wrong. My mom and I are pretty poor, we still live with my grandparents, and my parents weren't married when they had me. I guess that makes me whatever the female equivalent of a bastard is. The stupid was a little mean, but Lucy is mean. What are you going to do?"

I wrap my arms around her middle, hugging her to me when the words aren't enough. She hugs me back, rocking back and forth with me and it feels like a goodbye.

"I thought the shop was closed today," Goldie continues, thrusting her chin in the direction of the door with a big, red "Closed" sign on it.

"Yeah it is. They're finishing up the new floor in the dining area. I need to take care of payroll." And figure out how to tell everyone that I'm leaving.

"Oh, well don't let me keep you from paying me! I'll let you get to it," she says with a laugh.

I have never moved faster to get inside out of the cold in my life. I'm sure there's permanent frostbite on every surface of my body. After a few failed attempts, I get my shaky hand steady enough to slide my key into the lock and walk inside. Bombarded with the sound of Whitney Houston belting from our speakers, I smile. Rosie must be here. I see her blonde head bobbing up and down through the small kitchen window as she rocks out at the top of her lungs. Rosie's a free spirit if I've ever met one and loves her work in solitude more than anything else. Our ever diligent baker, she practically lives at the shop. Rounding the corner out of the kitchen, she nearly drops dead when she sees me standing there.

"Damn it, Bella!" she exclaims. "Announce yourself! I could've had a knife and killed you."

I smirk as I take in her traditional Rosie costume. Slutty Sandy style, she calls it. I'll miss that familiarity. Pleather leggings and a low-cut black shirt make up her skin tight catsuit. She finishes the look with red ballet flats and a red rose nestled in her blond bun at the base of her skull. White makeup covers her olive skin and contrasts with her stark black eyeliner and flashy red lipstick. It seems like it would be too much for the everyday, but she always surprises me and pulls it off. My own leggings and tee-shirt make me feel underdressed.

"The floors look good," I say, taking in the finished product. To be honest, it's pretty much the same floor. A checkered black and white linoleum. But Beattie insisted that this was a better quality and would hold up much longer. Rosie nods, already on her way back to the kitchen.

"Yeah, they did a good job, but man they were loud," she says with a disapproving shake of her head.

THEY were too loud?

"I'll be in the back taking care of payroll if you need anything," I say, instead of pointing out her own noisiness. There's no reasoning with Rosie anyway. She grumbles something inaudible as I head back to the office. I know it's a little thing. I'm the manager of a shop with seven employees, including the owner and myself. But at seventeen, I'm already in charge. That's why I can't figure out why my mom hates this place so much. It's important to me; it should be important to her. Now she's taking it from me.

The next hour flies by as I run the payroll. I slide my black framed glasses to the top of my head to give my eyes a rest. I stand up just as the office door swings open. In walks our fearless leader, Beatrix "Beattie" Cod. True to her nature, her wild red curls stick out in every direction off her head. The hoop in her nose and lenses of her wire rimmed glasses glisten in the light coming from the desk lamp.

"What part of 'take the day off' did you not understand exactly?" she asks, her voice deep and smoky.

"Sorry. I forgot about payroll and I wasn't sure if you'd remember." Beattie smiles, crossing her arms over her chest, leaning her weight against the closed office door.

"I don't know if you've ever heard of these magical contraptions they make called cell phones? Revolutionary, you should think about getting one." She closes the space between us in only a few steps, picking up the neat and orderly stack of papers that I've left upon her desk. "The only reason I came in was to take care of this, thank you very much."

"Beat. Do you have a minute?" I ask, knowing it's now or never. Her eyes leave the papers, looking up at me from under her pale lashes. She motions to the chair across from her desk.

"Are you all right? You look a little pale." I force a smile to my lips, but I'm sure it comes out as some kind of twisted grimace.

"Yeah, yeah I'm fine," I lie and settle into the egg shaped plastic chair that sits opposite Beattie's desk. "I just —I just need to talk to you about something. I'm not sure where to start."

Beattie rests her elbows on the desk, balancing her chin on her folded fingers. "The beginning is usually a good place."

The look of overwhelming concern on my boss's face makes me want to break down and cry.

"I have to take a leave of absence for a little while," I croak out as fast as I can so that sobs can't consume me. Crying in front of Beattie is a no-go for me.

"Define a little while, please," she says.

"A few months, the exact amount of time is still a little unclear."

Beattie's eyes widen as her hands disappear from the desk down to her lap. "Bella, I need you to actually explain now," she says, jumping past all my barriers. "What is going on?"

I run my fingers along my ponytail and let out a loud puff of air before answering.

"My mother is shipping me off to a family as a tutor for their teenage son in New York."

"What?" she exclaims, her head shaking back and forth like it's an Etch-A-Sketch. "I mean it. What? It's like you started in the middle."

"Okay," I mumble, lowering my forehead to the cool wood of the table. "Shipping me off was probably the wrong way to put it. She signed me up for a job without my consent. Mom and Dad are making me take it."

Beattie nods, digesting what I'm telling her. She reaches back to the small mini fridge and pulls out two bottles of water, placing one beside my face on the desk. "Can they do that?" she asks.

I'm pretty sure my parents have no legal right to make me take the job, but I don't disappoint them. I don't let them down and I certainly don't disobey. I know that no matter how much I struggle against the idea, I'm going. But being mad? Yeah, that I'm allowed to be. "I always do what my parents tell me. I don't want to do it, but I know I will. I kind of hate myself for it." It's an utter lack of backbone beyond my normal scope. I may not be as brave as Godie or Blanche, but I'm not a coward. I've always been sure-footed, especially in matters of right and wrong. However, it flies away like a lost balloon when it comes to my parents' wishes.

"I could talk to your mom if you want? I know she's not a huge fan of mine, but I'd be willing to try for you," she offers. Beattie may not always know how to fix a situation, but she's always willing to try. It's one of her most lovable qualities.

I shake my head and reply, "That's very nice of you to offer, but it's not going to make a difference. I don't want her to give me any grief about coming back to work here when I'm home."

"But you don't want to go," she says simply. Another one of those stubborn tears springs to my eyes and I don't bother trying to wipe it away.

"No I don't."

CHAPTER THREE

Rosie responds, "Dude, that's rough," as she carries the phone from the kitchen out to the main dining area. The jostling of the camera is making me nauseous and the speeding cars aren't helping either. My brain pounds inside my skull like it's trying to escape through my eyes.

"Can you stop moving so much?" I beg. I roll the window down and throw the flowers out onto the highway's shoulder. Infantile? Maybe, but I can't look at them anymore.

"Say hello to everyone," she bellows and faces the phone out towards the small group of our friends. The camera settles long enough for me to see Rosie's definition of "everyone." Blanche and Elle, as well as Elle's boyfriend, Finn. Since those two got together they've been attached at the hip. It's exhausting.

"Hello, Hells Bells!" Blanche shouts into the face of the phone. I force myself to keep composure. It's going to be a very long few months if I break into hysterics every five minutes. Blanche and Finn must have come right from track practice as they're both decked out in their New Shiloh High School uniforms.

"What's up, buttercup?" she asks, plopping down onto one of the stools in front of the long counter at the front of the shop. I can tell from the camera view that Rosie is sitting on yet another tabletop. Her butt should not be where we put food. It takes everything in me not to chew her out for it.

"Living the dream, Blanche. How are you?" They don't need my drama.

Blanche groans, settling her elbows on the counter. "Avoiding the cutesy twins over there. They're making me ill."

Rosie turns the camera in the direction of the far booths to reveal Elle running her hands through Finn's hair. We're all glad to see Elle happy, especially with everything that's happened with her parents' divorce, but the two of them are a little much.

There's a moment of blissful silence, before Blanche opts to ruin it. "Could you order more of the raw sugar for the sugar shakers? Everyone seems to like it more."

"I would run that by Beattie," I say, my voice small and squeaky.

"Don't you process the inventory orders?" Elle asks, pulling herself from her boyfriend long enough to come up for air. I swear, one of them is going to end up with lockjaw.

"Yeah, I usually do. But for a while it would be best to direct those things to Beattie."

"Why? What's going on?" Blanche asks, grabbing the phone from Rosie. All I can see is a close-up of her freckled nose. Of course she's going to try to jump in and micromanage everything.

"Nothing is going on. I'm going to be away for a little while is all."

That stops everyone in their tracks and the camera pulls back to show my three friends sitting in a line scrutinizing me. I don't like this! I'm normally the one directing the show. The one with all the answers. Now it feels like I've been thrown onto a stage without knowing any of the lines.

"What are you talking about?" Elle asks. I can see Finn's head bobbing behind her and I kind of wish he would leave. I pound the palms of my hands on the steering wheel and balance my phone on its curve.

"I'm going to New York for the next few months," I grumble. I realize how tired I am with hours ahead of me in my journey. I need to get back on the road.

"What?" Blanche exclaims. She and Elle trade horrified glances. Rosie is perched quietly between them, letting them absorb the shock like she had a few minutes before.

Another car pulls up beside me, flashing its lights. They are either checking if I'm okay, or I'm about to be part of a drug deal. When I see a soccer mom inside the minivan, I assume the former and wave her on to tell her I'm okay. She smiles politely and pulls back onto the highway. I had no idea people out on the open road could be this nice.

"My mother signed me up for a tutoring job in upstate New York for the next few months," I admit to my friends after the nice lady pulls away.

"I'm still not computing," Blanche admits, her black eyebrows pulled close together. Elle stares back with a blank face equivalent to TV static and I realize that no one's getting it.

"I'm not going to be in Harpersgrove. My mom thinks it's a waste of time for me to hang around town and the pie shop since I'm done with school. She doesn't think it will impress anyone at college if I take months off to do nothing before I start." It's not like I've been frying my brain for the last twelve years or anything. I guess I don't need a break.

"So she's shipping you off?" Elle demands, slapping her palm onto the counter. "You're not letting her do that are you?"

Letting her? Who's letting? This is force! I'm a hostage!

I feel like banging my head into the dashboard. I'm sick of having this same ongoing battle with myself and everyone else. I want a break. A few more solitary hours in my car and being a few states away may not be the worst thing.

"I've already gone over it so many times. It's happening and I can't change that."

"You're taking a big leap assuming that we can live without you," Blanche chimes in with a pout. "I don't even know where the coffee filters are." That strikes me hard in the chest.

"I'm sorry, back up one second. Are you upset that Bella, your friend, isn't going to be around? Or is it Bella, the store manager, you're going to miss?" I bark at her, outraged and more than a little hurt.

Blanche and Elle fidget in their seats. Rosie slides off her stool and disappears into the kitchen before the firing squad lets loose. Blanche looks me square in the eye as she says, "They're the same person Bells."

I grip the phone a little harder, my finger hovering over the call end button before I blurt out, "I have to get on the road. I still have a long way to go."

Blanche moves forward like she's going to say something, but I end the call before she has the chance. They try calling me back almost immediately, but after two rings I hit ignore. Hopefully they get the point. I tap back to the home screen, then open my music. A moody cover of *All By Myself* comes on and I can't help the laughter that sputters from my lips. I take a few deep breaths in through my nose until my breathing settles back to normal and I can see clearly again.

I do what any normal teenager would do. Throw a royal hissy fit. I stomp up the stairs to my room after returning from my meeting with Beattie. I hope my parents hear every step. I refuse dinner, for maybe the third time in my life. There's too much to do anyway. I know I should get started, but I'm too mad to breathe let alone pack. Someone must have replaced my parents with aliens, making me a stranger in my own home. Mom and Dad are a lot of things, but never this crazy, irrational, or unfair.

A sharp knock on the door interrupts my mopey teenage thoughts and then it swings open. If it had been either of my parents they would have waited for a response, but Jonah never pauses. He rounds the corner of with a hand over his eyes and waits. One time he came in when I was fresh out of the shower. Needless to say, he's never made that mistake again. I grin in spite of everything I'm feeling and throw a balled up tee-shirt at him. He pulls his hand away and rocks back on his heels.

"You okay? You weren't at dinner and Mom and Dad are all tense. I figured something was wrong."

I sign so fast my fingers cramp.

"They're sending me away to New York to tutor some spoiled rich kid who's too injured or sick or something to go to school himself. They didn't ask me, they're forcing me. I've never been this mad at anyone before." *I pop the knuckles in my left hand, flexing my fingers open and closed. Jonah nods his head, a small smirk hinting at his lips.*

"I have a feeling you'd be out of breath if you'd spoken all that," *he voices with his throaty tone. It's always reminded me of the way an old man with a bad smoking habit speaks. I flop my head back on my bed and throw my forearm over my face, wishing I could wake up from this awful dream. I feel his weight settle at my feet and look up to see him sit-ting cross legged at the base, waiting for me. We used to spend Christmas mornings like this, me, sound asleep, and Jonah, awake early, sitting at the foot of my bed. Waiting. I wonder if we'll even have a Christmas at all together this year.*

"It's so close to Christmas and they're sending me away, like over five hours away. They didn't even ask me if it was okay." *I'll be gone for the next four years and then forever. Isn't that enough?*

"Tutoring," *Jonah begins.* "Does it pay well?"

"That's not the point, Jonah!" *I exclaim. What is with my family's sudden fascination with money? I don't think we have ever had a single conversation about it before.* "They didn't talk to me, they decided and did it. I have a life here. I have a job and friends, and they don't care!"

"You think maybe it's because they care? Isn't that what parents are supposed to do?" *he asks. That sounds much more like something my mother would say than Jonah.*

"Did they send you up here?" *I demand, getting as far away from him on the bed as I can. Of course my parents would use my lifetime confidant to betray me. It's like a damn Russian novel.*

"Did they tell you to come up here and convince me not to be mad at them?" *Jonah's face contorts as if I'd slapped him.*

"Yeah, Bella," *he says aloud, his voice raised an angry octave or two.* "That sounds like me." *He gets up off my bed, never turning back to look at me as charges through the door.*

The angry energy that had been so strong a moment ago fizzles into nothingness as he leaves. I will the tears to fall back inside, but they won't go. A stray one falls from my lid down to my pink polka dot pillowcase. I have always had an equal say in the affairs of my own life. My parents have always boosted the idea that the Southlands are a team. We make decisions together. I pushed the bullies in the sand that made fun of the way Jonah talked. Mom raised all kinds of hell when the other little girls in my very short lived ballet career poked fun at my weight. Dad is always the steadfast rock, there when we needed him. We're supposed to be a unit I can count on, but now everything's turned on its ear.

I barely get a moment to myself before the door opens again.

"Can I come in?" Mom asks, her hands gripping the door frame. If nothing else, she was respecting my right to tell her no and I find it tempting to make her leave. Even in my anger, though, I know I can't turn my mother away. I make room on my bed so she can sit down with me.

"I don't know how to do this with you," she says. "I guess I'm lucky. We've made it seventeen years and never had a real fight."

"What can I say? I'm a late bloomer," I grumble. She places her hand on my knee.

"Isabella, look at me please." Being ever the parent pleaser that I am, I obey. "You know your father and I are only doing this because it's what's best for you, right?"

"That's not enough Mom," I say for the first time speaking without anger. "I'm not a little kid anymore. You can't make decisions like this without talking to me. This isn't like you picked a new dentist for me. This is months of my life. The last months of my childhood."

"I don't want you to feel that way, Isabella. Your father and I are your parents above all else. If you can't see why we're doing this and agree with it, then I'm sorry. But you are going." Her voice wobbles but that classic Jessica Southland strength rings through loud and clear. I flip away from her to face the wall. The flame may have been suppressed, but the anger still simmers under the surface.

"Well then," I begin, trying to hold back the betraying emotion in my voice. "Please leave. I need to pack."

"Okay. Let me know if you need any help," she says before getting off the bed. I keep my eyes on the wall.

"I'll be fine. Go, please."

The door clicks shut and I want to pick something up and throw it. I want to throw everything, but that's not my style. I'm the quiet, good girl, to a fault it seems.

The night falls away too quickly and before I know it, we're loading up my car for the banishment.

"I told you I would drive with you, Peanut," my dad begins as he puts a suitcase in my back seat. "I don't feel right about you going all the way up there by yourself."

I wipe the sweat off my brow with the back of my hand. That's one of the many downsides of being so well insulated —you sweat even in the winter.

"No, it'll be good for me to go alone. Let me clear my head for a while." That was partially the truth. Mainly, I'm trying my best not to be mad. It's too consuming. I know that will be near impossible with one of my parents next to me in the car for hours. I'm not ready to forgive them yet. It seems unfair that they get to take a wrecking ball to my life and I'm supposed to be okay with it. I need some time. Jonah comes barreling out the front door, pulling the last of my bags behind him. I try not to cringe at the fact that he's dragging them on the ground.

"You know you're not actually leaving for forever, right?" He drops the bag at my feet. Thankfully there's nothing fragile inside. My heart aches that it's the last time I'll see him for a while. He and I have never spent any real time apart since he was born.

"Of course not," I sign back to him with a wide stretched grin, hiding my feelings so it won't be harder for either of us. "You can't get away from me that easily." He pulls me in for a quick, tight hug.

"I don't like the idea of you going alone either. I could drive up with you, take a bus or the train home. It would be like my own little adventure." When I don't immediately respond, he leans against my car and laughs. "You can pin a note to my jacket so I don't get lost."

"I need to do this on my own," I sign and I mean it.

He nods, a sad smile curling to his lips. I settle next to him and rest my head on his shoulder. Both my parents emerge from the house with items in their hands. My mother approaches me first and hands me an envelope.

"We put most of it directly into your checking account because it's not good for you to have a lot of cash on you. But we wanted you to have a little walking around money." I flip open the lip of the envelope and see enough twenties to gift wrap my car. Where exactly does she think I'm walking to?

My dad holds out his hand with the newest iPhone, something I had been saving months for to purchase. Clearly, my parents are making a last ditch effort to bribe me and I'm not of a high enough moral code to refuse.

"The guy at the phone place said it should be easy to transfer all your stuff from one phone to another," he explained, tapping on the screen. I find it unnecessary to tell him I could have done it all before he finished the sentence.

"Thank you." I tuck the phone and envelope into my purse. Gratitude without sass is the least I can do. Without pausing, or giving me a chance to refuse, my mother pulls me into a hug hard against her chest.

My dad practically yanks me away, impatient for his turn to hug me goodbye. The scratchy hairs of his black beard tickle my forehead.

"Make sure you lock the car if you stop anywhere. Only park in well lit areas. Don't talk to strangers." He continues to rattle things off that he's told me a thousand times before. He's talking to me like I'm a child, but it's not completely unwarranted. I'm sheltered on an Emily Dickinson *level. I nod against his chest and hug him a little tighter. Just because I'm not ready to forgive doesn't make me love him any less.*

"Positive you don't want me to go with you?" Jonah asks

I appreciate it, but I need to do this by myself. Besides, Mom and Dad would kill me if anything happened to you on your train ride back." His brow furrows.

"I'm not a baby Bella. I can take care of myself." Maybe he doesn't need me as much as I need him. I hug him one last time and whisper into his shirt, even though I know he can't hear me.

"I'll miss you."

CHAPTER FOUR

Driving is stupid. Driving long distance is torture. It's nothing but asphalt, the occasional tree, and many angry people in their cars bobbing and weaving in and out of each other. Every time I catch a glimpse of the dashboard clock, thinking another hour must have gone by, it's only been three or four minutes. I'm in hell, that has to be it. This is my purgatory and I am driving to my own personal hell. Merry early Christmas to me.

It's only when I actually enter the state of New York and get away from the highway that I see any beauty. I suppose in my suburban ignorance I always thought that there was nothing more to New York than the city. I couldn't have been more wrong. The area I find myself driving through is nothing but green, even at the start of winter. A huge mansion is plopped into the middle of this fine foliage about every half mile. Eventually I turn into the mouth of a long, winding driveway that leads to the house where I'll be staying. I can't see the actual house from the street, but the numbers on the intimidating pewter gate confirm I've arrived at the right place. I'm unsure of how I'm supposed to get in, but a loud buzzing sounds from outside my window. On the intercom screen, from which the sound emerges, I see the face of an older gentleman. I roll down my window and smile at the screen.

"Can I help you? I must warn you, we do not take solicitors of any kind," the man says. His voice is tired and frustrated, almost to the point that I feel like apologizing. The wrinkles in his forehead push over his eyes like a constipated Shar-pei. I angle my head out the window for the man on the screen to see me better.

"Hi, I'm Bella Southland. Mr. Baxter hired me to tutor his son," I shout, much louder than necessary, but the man is pretty old. I don't know how well he can hear. He peers over the rim of his glasses and down at me like I'm some kind of bug.

"You're the new tutor?" he accuses, a sneer stretching across his lips like there's some big joke I'm not privy to.

"Yes, sir, I am. It's kind of cold out here. Could we discuss this inside?" I ask, my body shivering against the chill.

"Does Mr. Baxter know how young you are? Have you been to college?" the old man hisses. He's interrupted by another voice in the distance.

"Good God, Colin!" the smooth, feminine voice calls out. "Let the poor girl in."

The old man takes his time, still debating whether to grant me entrance. He mumbles something under his breath and hits a buzzer, opening the gate. I inch inside, my tires crunching through the gravel driveway toward the house. When it finally comes into view over the crest of the hill, my stomach jumps into my throat. I shift my car into park before moving any closer. I lean forward to look up at the home resembling a castle straight out of a children's book. Of course, it's not actually a castle, but it definitely seems like an evil queen or wicked witch belongs inside. It's made of a dark black stone. The windows are devoid of light, which makes me wonder if anyone is inside. The landscape hasn't been touched in years. Every plant lining the house is either dead or working its way up the walls in suffocating vines. It's like salted earth. Could flowers even grow here? The grass is buried beneath layers of decomposing leaves. Everything is suffocating. I catch a small movement in one of the upper windows. As soon as my eyes start to focus the dark, heavy curtains close and all movement ceases. The only two things missing from the ominous scene are lightning bolts and storm clouds.

Suddenly, someone emerges from the front door, pulling me out of my fear. She's a tall, lean woman with long black hair in braids twisted behind her head in a bun. She smiles and waves to me as I get out of the car. A little sunshine is more than welcome right now. She greets me at the driver's side and extends her long-fingered hand with short, unmanicured nails toward me.

"Hello, Isabella, it's a pleasure to meet you," she says. I recognize her in an instant as the second voice from the intercom.

"Yes," I try to radiate back her level of brightness, happy for her kindness and find myself at ease. I take her hand in mine, "You can call me Bella. My mom is the only one who uses my full name."

"Ah yes, I understand," the woman releases my hand and clasps hers together at her waist. "I'm Lusta, the housekeeper here."

"It's nice to meet you. Thank you for backing me up there," I signal to the gate. She rolls her eyes and starts to help me gather my bags from the car.

"Oh, don't mind old Colin. He thinks because he's a man that makes him head of the house. Mr. Baxter made it very clear when he set us up here that I'm in charge. Colin only spends a day or two here every few weeks, making sure that we're all doing our jobs."

"I don't understand," I admit, pulling my laptop bag over my shoulder and dragging my suitcase behind me.

She carries my other two bags as we walk into a massive foyer. It shouldn't surprise me to find that the inside is as depressing as the outside of the house. From the black slate of the floor to the dark wood and iron that make up the staircase. It's super dark and super cold. The very definition of unwelcoming.

"Well, Colin stops by for Mr. Baxter every now and then to check on us and make sure we have everything we need. Then he heads back to the main house."

"The main house?" I question, not sure exactly what she means. I examine my surroundings. The light bulbs in the dazzling chandelier overhead are mostly burned out with two holding on for dear life. The darkness is maddening.

"The main house is about fifteen minutes from here. It's where Mr. Baxter and his daughter live," she answers, starting up the stairs. I hadn't known there was another child in the family.

"They don't live here?"

Lusta shakes her head, "No, Mr. Baxter set up this house for Conrad to convalesce privately until all his injuries healed. Then it was decided it might be better for him to stay. Pollie, Conrad's sister, still comes often to visit."

I think of how close I am with my own father. The idea of being away from him is hard enough. I can't imagine staying away by choice. I focus on catching my breath as we reach the top step.

"And their mother? Where is Mrs. Baxter?"

This place is a labyrinth with its long, unending hallways. I'm going to need a map and a Sherpa to get around. Lusta stops and turns back to face me, sadness written in her pale brown eyes.

"She died six years ago. Cancer. Mr. Baxter actually closed up this house after she died. It was her favorite. Nobody had been back until Conrad got hurt."

We stop in front of a heavy wooden door, dark like everything else here seems to be. Before opening it, I ask, "Can you tell me what happened to him? My parents only said it was an accident."

"That's a story for another time," she says, pushing into a bedroom bigger than my entire house. The windows stretch up as high as the ceiling and there's a fireplace on the far side of the room. It feels like stepping into my grandmother's home with curio cabinets full of Hummel figurines. A garish sleigh bed sits in the center of the room that looks more like a museum display than a warm place to sleep. Sitting in the middle of the bed is a little girl, about eight or nine, who looks very much like Lusta. She hasn't seemed to notice that we've entered. Her head of dark curls stays buried in the book in front of her, pinky finger in her mouth chewing on the nail. Lusta stomps on the floor.

"Lottie!" she exclaims. The little girl's head snaps up, pale green eyes reflecting back at us. "What are you doing in here?"

The little girl lifts her hands and signs, "I've been waiting for her."

Joy fills my spirit, but I do my best to contain it so as not to look like a crazy person in front of these strangers. My heart already misses Jonah. Lusta's eyes zero in on her daughter. She opens her mouth to shout again, but I lift my hands to sign first.

"It's okay. I think it's sweet." By the look on that little girl's face, you would think I'm a real life fairy. Lusta's jaw hits the floor. I take a step toward the bed, where Lottie shifts to sitting on her knees.

"Your name's Lottie?" I ask with my hands. Her head bobs up and down so fast I'm certain I hear her teeth crack together.

"Do you have a sign name?" I ask with my hands and mouth. I get the impression that signing isn't Lusta's strongest skill. Lottie's quick to raise her hands and show me her name. It's the sign for happy with an "L".

I smile brightly and respond, "That's a beautiful name. My name is," and I proceed to finger spell B-E-L-L-A before showing her my own sign name. Lottie beams with joy in her eyes. It makes me want to cry.

From behind, Lusta announces, "Lottie, it's almost time for dinner. Why don't you head down and see what Mr. Potter has made?" I can tell she doesn't want to go. She seems more hungry to stay and talk to me. But like any good girl, she knows better than to disobey her mother a second time. She hops off my bed and makes her way to the door, an extra skip in her little steps. Lusta and I both watch her go before she turns back to me.

"Well, that was a surprise!" Her eyes twinkle with unshed tears. This moment means far more to her than a few simple hand gestures. I giggle, covering my mouth to mask the sound.

"It was for me, too!"

"How do you know sign language?" she asks, sitting on the edge of my bed, gesturing for me to join her.

"Shortly after he was born, the doctors discovered my brother is deaf. The whole family learned the language," I explained.

"I feel like a terrible mother. Lottie had meningitis when she was three. It required strong antibiotics to treat it, which caused her deafness. She's almost nine and I can't speak her language. I'm getting better at understanding, but the actual signing is proving very difficult for me. She attends a school for the deaf, but I know that's not enough."

"You're not a terrible mother," I shake my head and do my best to offer my sympathy. "New languages are hard for adults. It took a while for my parents to get it down."

It definitely wouldn't hurt to have this woman in my corner. I'll be living here for the next few months and I can use all the friends I can get. "I could always help you if you want. In any downtime I have from tutoring Conrad?"

A little smirk hits her lips and disappears as fast. "Yes, let's hope you have more luck than the others have." Something about the way she says it makes my heart fall to my feet.

"What do you mean?" I actually want to say, *What kind of petulant monster am I dealing with?* Lusta scratches at the back of her head. This woman is like an unbreakable vault. She's clearly hell bent on keeping Conrad Baxter's history to herself, but I think I have a right to know.

"Ever since the doctors cleared him to start schooling again, Conrad has been difficult. You'll be the seventh tutor in less than six months."

I, of course, know that it's no accident that I'm here. My father even said that the elder Mr. Baxter tried everything else before hiring me. It shouldn't come as a surprise, but it does.

"Can you elaborate at all?" I appreciate that Lusta's loyal to her employers, but that doesn't stop me from pushing. I need to know what I've walked into.

"Lusta," a male voice calls out from a speaker. "His Highness's dinner is ready," the voice reports in a cool tone with a hint of a laugh. Lusta walks over to the intercom panel by the door.

"I'll be right down, Mr. Potter, keep your shirt on," she says with a grin in her voice. "Are you hungry, Bella? Mr. Potter is an amazing cook."

"I actually need to call my parents." I reach into my purse to get my phone.

"Of course. Come downstairs when you're done. We'll feed you." Before she leaves she motions to the intercom. "Should you get lost, locate one of these and I'll come rescue you."

"Thank you, Lusta"

When she's gone, I open up my phone contacts and swipe past my mother and father. I don't want to talk to them. I know how that conversation will go and I'm not in the mood to make them feel any better. But, they still need to know that I'm okay.

I click on Jonah. As a video chat buzzes in my hands, I set my phone onto the mantle of my own personal fireplace and take a step back. My brother's beautiful face flashes onto my screen and says, "You're alive!"

"Yeah, the drive was pretty easy."

"Mom's been waiting for you to call." He seems a bit distracted by something on his computer. I barely get a second of eye contact.

"Jonah, if you're watching porn, I'm going to kill you when I get home." I'm only half joking, but I'm desperate for a smirk or a grin, even a grimace will do.

An unencumbered laugh erupts from Jonah's mouth. I can't help but giggle. He reaches over and pulls his laptop around to show me the photosynthesis chart on the screen. "I'm doing my homework," he voices.

"Thank God." A wry smile spreads across my lips. "I'm not in the mood to talk to the parents right now," I explain. He nods, never judging and I love him for that.

"How's the house?"

"M-A-S-S-I-V-E," I slowly fingerspell, over emphasizing every letter. "Seriously, it may be bigger than the White House. Look at this," I pick up the phone and walk in a small circle around the room.

"Do you have a fireplace?" His eyes bug up to twice their normal size, a pen falling from his lips as his jaw hangs slack.

"Yes! And it's all mine!" I squeal aloud.

"Rich people," he utters. It's simple and perfect and the best thing he could have said to me in the moment.

"What are they like?"

"I've only met the housekeeper and her daughter. Both seem nice. The little girl is deaf, which is unexpected. But it's like I've brought you with me." Even though his face is only inches away, my heart misses him already. The miles seem to have multiplied.

"That's badass!" He reinforces what I love about him. "What about the cripple you're supposed to tutor?"

"Jonah Leonard Southland!" I shout at the screen. "I can not believe that you would say something like that!" Of anyone in my world, he should be the most sensitive. He shrugs.

"Well he is, isn't he?"

Truth be told I have no idea.

CHAPTER FIVE

My mother has always said that the kitchen is the heart of a home. No matter how much things spread out, it always comes back to the food and where it's made. The Baxter house is no exception. It takes me a couple wrong turns, and a few doors opening into closets, before I find the first floor kitchen. Pale green paint stretches up to an ivory ceiling decorated with gold embellishments. Four double ovens line one of the walls. I didn't think it possible to use that many ovens at once. Over the giant marble island at the center of the room hangs a full set of copper cookware and two side by side stainless steel sinks. Beside those sinks Lottie sits at a long breakfast bar, chomping on vegetables. She sees me and her face splits into a grin, broccoli stuck between her teeth.

"Ah, you found it all on your own," Lusta says from behind me as she emerges from a hidden pantry in a wall by the entrance. Lottie motions for me to come sit by her. I take a stool beside her, snatching a baby carrot off her plate. She giggles deep in her chest.

It's a laugh from the soul in its unselfconscious spirit. The way it echoes through the room warms me.

"Lusta!" A sharp, deep voice booms from the intercom at the far side of the kitchen. I swear the pots clank together while the room shakes with the sound. Lusta sighs and walks toward the tablet mounted on the wall.

"Yes?" she replies calmly.

"Is the troll gone?" the voice demands. The corner of Lusta's mouth turns up as she responds, "Yes, Conrad, I sent Colin home." I'm glad to hear that Lusta sent away the old curmudgeon. I hope he's not back again anytime soon.

Lusta pauses for only a beat before she continues, "Conrad, dinner is ready if you'd like to come down. Your new tutor is here. Maybe you'd like to meet her?"

The line's quiet for a good moment, but I can still hear him breathing.

"I'm not hungry," he barks before clicking off the line. Lusta sighs softly and steps away from the intercom before moving to a covered tray on the counter. She carries it to where Lottie and I sit.

"Go lay this in front of his door please." Lottie takes a moment to process before getting off her stool and taking the food from her mother. Lusta looks up at me with a knowing gaze. "I know the boy. He's hungry, but too proud to come down."

"He, um, he sounds a little abrasive." I grab another carrot off of Lottie's plate. If nervous and compulsive eating was an Olympic sport, I'd have the record for most gold medals. She hands me my own plate, full of veggies and whipped hummus. My stomach growls, ready for feeding.

"I told you he will take some patience. He's a good boy, Isabella, but he's lost right now. I remember the sweet child he was. When

48

Mrs. Baxter passed, we lost him and we haven't gotten him back yet." It's still not an answer, but I figure bit by bit I'll break through.

"Did His Majesty get his food?" a velvety, rich voice proclaims as a redheaded man emerges from the hidden pantry inside the wall. Is this the mansion from *Clue*? It seems unfathomable that a house in reality would have so many secret rooms and corridors. He stops when he sees me, offering a dashing smile of crooked, but pearly, teeth. He's about my father's age with broad shoulders and a general masculine beauty.

"And who do we have here?" he asks, placing the sack of potatoes hoisted on his shoulder on the kitchen counter. He wipes his hands on the legs of his beat-up blue jeans before extending his big mitt of a hand to me.

"I'm Bella Southland, Conrad's new tutor." It takes everything in me not to say victim. Mischief dances in his speckled green eyes.

"You're the new tutor? Well now, that's an interesting development." He squeezes my hand and adds, "I'm Patrick Potter, I do the cooking."

"It's very nice to meet you, and yes, I'm the tutor. I know I'm young, but I'm smart," I say, my head held high. I notice the streaks of silver that pepper his red hair as he turns in the light.

"She's going to an Ivy League in the fall," Lusta adds, bringing a stool around to sit in front of the sink.

"Did I tell you that?" I ask. Our conversation had been pretty limited and I didn't remember mentioning school to her.

"Mr. Baxter keeps me informed. He likes to know everything possible about the people he employs." She reaches into the bag of potatoes and begins to peel. How does Mr. Baxter know? My parents don't even know! Keeping the fact that I'd been accepted to Brown University, early decision, to myself had been difficult, but I was certain I was the only one who knew.

"Do you need help with that?" I look around for another knife to join her.

Mr. Potter and Lusta exchange glances as though they're not sure how to react. Mr. Potter pats me on the shoulder as he walks by me to stand beside Lusta at the sink.

"Oh, no, dear, that's not your responsibility. Why don't you sit down and have some food. Then you can go unpack your things." He motions to a pot of stew on the stove and I must say, the smell is more than enticing. My growling stomach agrees, but to me it seems disrespectful to eat while others work.

I begin to protest, but Lusta stops me with a raised hand. "Trust me, you will have plenty on your hands starting tomorrow with Conrad. Take it easy for tonight."

I head to my room, belly full of food, and change into more comfortable clothes. Most of the time I'd swear it doesn't get more comfortable than yoga pants and a sweatshirt. But right now my flannel pajamas beg to differ. The fluffy white clouds circle the soft blue fabric and wrap me up in their familiar embrace. I pull down on the thick, comfy quilt and crawl underneath, cold and exhausted. I turn away from the window and bury my face in the pillow. Before my eyes are closed, I'm asleep, lost in a dream like falling down a well.

I wake with a sudden jerk. The room is pitch black and my back is stiff, like I haven't moved in days. I blink against the surrounding darkness and try to figure out where I am. Someone must have turned out the lights, because I didn't do it. I grab my phone from the bedside table and slide my glasses over my eyes. The home screen of my phone tells me it's 3:00 in the morning. Apparently

Lusta was more than right. Sleep is exactly what I needed. I know it would be best to fall back to sleep, but it was the rumbling of my stomach that woke me. Another grumble sounds low in my belly and I sit up. My toes touch the cool, hardwood floor and a shiver zips up my spine. I grab my discarded sweater and zip it up to my neck to try and control the quivering in my limbs.

The house is spooky without any lights. Correction. The house is much spookier without lights. It's like being stuck in a Brontë novel, Charlotte not Emily. I should check the attic and be sure they aren't keeping anyone locked up there. Poor Mrs. Rochester.

I need a candelabra to navigate the halls. It seems like every inanimate object I pass springs to life as I walk by, scaring the crap out of me. I first see the light when I clear the last step to the first floor. The closer I get to the kitchen the brighter it becomes. Maybe Lusta or Mr. Potter needed a midnight snack as much as me. I wouldn't say no to the company. Rounding the corner into the kitchen, I discover the light is coming from the open refrigerator, casting the room in a soft glow. I can see a white knuckled hand on the rim of the fridge door, gripping for dear life.

"What are you doing down here?" a voice I have only heard once before over an intercom roars at me. All moisture flees my mouth and I become about two feet tall.

"Um," I stammer, finally able to squeak out some sound through my cottonmouth. I wish a brilliant thought would come to mind, but instead, "I'm sorry," are the only meek words I can utter. I hate sounding like a Dickensian orphan.

"It's three o'clock in the morning. Why are you here?" Conrad demands, his face remains buried in the cold and open fridge. I force myself to stand a little taller, act braver than I feel.

"You're in here."

"That's beside the point," he grumbles.

I start to walk toward the fridge, thinking it's ridiculous that he's hiding.

"Are you going to keep your head in there the whole night?" I laugh in an attempt to break the tension. "We can try being friendly, if not friends, can't we?"

"Stop!" he bellows, sending my heart plummeting to my feet. I hear him take a deep breath and close the refrigerator door. The room returns to its eerie darkness, save for the small amount of light coming from the moon and stars outside. He's wearing a black hoodie, pulled low over his face and with his head bowed. Even hunched over, there's no hiding his substantial height. His shoulders are broad like he could swallow me whole in his arms with space for Lusta and Lottie too. As my eyes adjust to blackness, I can make out a few details. The burn scars are undeniable. A cold sweat pricks the back of my neck, wondering what the rest of him looks like. How hard his recovery must have been. I can't fathom.

"So you're supposed to be my tutor?" he mocks. As I'm evaluating him, clearly he's doing the same to me. I lean against the door frame, trying my best to look aloof and much more comfortable than I am.

"That's what your dad hired me to do," I responded, proud of my ability to hide the quiver in my voice. Fake it till you make it, scaredy cat.

"That's so typical of him. Of course, I have no idea what kind of joke this is," he replies with a sour edge to his voice. With his hands lost in the pocket of his hoodie, none of his skin is visible. He's reminiscent of a comic book villain. All that's missing is a white cat for him to menacingly stroke.

"Why does it have to be a joke? I'm smart. Really smart. I'm going to Brown in the fall," I proclaim, saying it for the first time aloud to anyone. If Lusta knows, this jerk might as well too.

"How wonderful for you, but you have nothing to teach me," he scoffs.

"That's kind of insulting, considering you don't know me."

He reaches out, grabbing a box of cereal from the expansive island. He moves past me, back in the direction of the stairs.

"I intend to keep it that way."

I stand there staring after him, dumbfounded over what just happened. My blood boils in my veins. I'm sure I look like one of those beet red cartoon characters with steam whistling from my ears. I wish that my anger had made me less hungry, but alas my inner ravenous beast will not quiet. I open the refrigerator and try to calm myself down, but all I can think of is how much a few simple words have hurt my feelings. I grew up as a fat kid, I know I have thicker skin than this. I do my best to distract myself with the plethora of covered dishes in the fridge. My heart breaks when I see a pie dish waiting for me on the bottom shelf. I pull back the aluminum foil and rejoice at the sight of pecan pie, my absolute favorite. I doubt it can ever be as good as Rosie's, but I'm happy for anything that brings me close to home right now.

I consider hunting for a knife and a plate. There's half a pie left and no one has a need to eat that much, but I can't bring myself to look. I pull out one of the iron stools from the breakfast bar and plop down to eat the entire dish.

"Isabella. Isabella," a distant voice whispers in my ear as my shoulders jostle. My eyelids flutter open, one at a time to the crack of sunlight and haze of the early morning. I peel my face off the breakfast bar, mortified as the drool sticks to my skin. I feel so bad for the poor sucker who has had the misfortune of waking me up. I'm certain I look like an extra from "Night of the Living Dead", but Mr. Potter is very sympathetic as he stands before me. He rubs his hand in gentle circles on my back.

"Don't fret, Isabella, we've all fallen asleep in this kitchen at one time or another. Those stools are deceptively comfortable."

"I respectfully disagree," I groan against the stiff stretching of my back. "What time is it?"

"Quarter past six," he replies, laying some supplies on the counter in between us.

It makes me feel better that I've only been here for a couple of hours. Of course, if he hadn't woken me up I'm sure I would have slept much longer. The sides of my mouth turn far down when I run a hand through my knotted hair and feel the trace of pie crust crumbs left behind. I look down horrified at an empty pie dish in front of me. I can still taste the sugar on my lips.

"I'm sorry about eating all the pie," I mumble. Ever the plight of the chubby girl, always apologizing for eating. Mr. Potter sets an empty mug in front of me. He reaches forward and taps me on the tip of my nose in a paternal gesture that I find comforting.

"I won't tell a soul, I promise." Then, he gestures to the cup. "Caffeine does wonders. Can I get you some coffee?" I smile and cross my arms on top of the counter to settle my chin on.

"I'm more of a tea kind of girl." He grins a little brighter and grabs a water kettle off the stove to fill at the sink.

"That's my kind of girl." The water clangs a little too loudly inside the metal container. I sit still for a few moments while the water heats up and Mr. Potter goes about his morning work. He prepares the kitchen for breakfast then places a tea bag in my mug, pouring the steaming water overtop.

"Would you like some food? I'm happy to make you some breakfast." I hum an agreeable response.

Mr. Potter sets a full plate of food in front of me. I'm not sure how, but I'm going to eat every bite. I dig in with the ferocity of a vacuum cleaner, sucking up all the food in front of me. I take a long drink, finishing my tea, wincing at the heat.

"That good, huh?" Mr. Potter laughs. He takes my empty plate and plops a fresh tea bag in my cup, the water soon to follow. He read my mind. My cheeks flush with embarrassment, wrapping my fingers around the warmth of the teacup.

"Sorry, it was really good," I murmured, taking another long sip.

"Oh, never apologize for liking my food darlin'. I see it as a compliment." His face is bright and happy. I'm getting the distinct impression that he's always that way.

A while later, after Lusta weighs down my arms with a full year's worth of schoolwork that Conrad has yet to cover, I feel a little overwhelmed. All I want is to clear my head and wash away the pie crumbs.

I've never had my own bathroom before. The one connected to my room here is painted in a peaceful sea-foam green. It's far more appealing than the atrocious and depressing maroon of our bathroom back home. I have offered many times to repaint it to a color that doesn't look like death. Mom insists that it's chic and will not be budged on the matter.

All the fixtures here are bright white and remind me of the countless pieces of milk glass that line my grandmother's condo in Florida. There's a pile of fluffy white towels on the wicker stand across from the sink. I lift one to my nose and inhale, absorbing the smell of warm sunshine from the terry cloth. And just like that I start to cry. I cry for the things I'm missing at home. The idea of my friends' lives going on without me makes me feel crushingly insignificant because nothing for them has changed. I had a plan in place for holding onto the bonds I've made at home. I'm trying not to worry about them forgetting me, but distraction only takes me so far. I also cry for everything that's here. Mr. Potter, Lusta and Lottie all seem very kind, but there's a lot of pain here and plain, bitter loneliness.

After a blistering hot shower, I play my favorite game of "how quickly can I wrap myself in a towel before I catch sight of my body in the mirror?" I am the reigning champion. Opening the bathroom door to a puff of steam, the cool air of my bedroom instantly turns my skin to goosebumps. Grabbing my hairbrush, I move it through my hair, then braid it into pigtails before slipping on a pair of black leggings and a long gray sweater. The daunting pile of work that I brought upstairs mocks me from the nightstand. I know it's my job and I need to get it done, but I'm not in the mental place to bury myself in it just yet. I leaf through my big suitcase and pull out my old tattered copy of *Wuthering Heights*. Unlike many people, I haven't embraced the revolution of e-books. I could never abandon the smell and feel of a good old fashioned paperback. It's my totem. I head out into the hallway in search of somewhere cozy to cuddle up and disappear into my favorite book for a while. Halfway down the hall I run into someone I haven't met yet rounding the corner.

"And who the heck are you?" she asks when her sparkling green eyes meet mine. She seems about my age, but much, smaller. Her black hair hangs in tight curls at her shoulders. She's dressed in ripped denim jeans over black tights adorned with shin-high black biker boots. She's like a chipper, punk rock, cartoon mouse. Her stack of silver bangle bracelets clang together on her wrist as she skips toward me.

I'm a little taken aback by her bubblegum attitude, especially given her tough exterior. "I'm Bella, I'm here to tutor-"

Her squeal interrupts me. Excitement flashes through her charcoal lined eyes and you'd think I'd offered her a free trip to an amusement park. "No freaking way!" she exclaims with a snap of the gum in her mouth. "You're Conrad's new tutor? That's too amazing! You're like a regular person, not one of those uptight, East German, spinsters with a mustache. This is too awesome!"

"And, uh, who are you?" I ask, intrigued with this person who has no appreciation for personal space.

"OMG, I'm sorry. It's like 'who's this psycho hanging on me,'" she giggles, continuing to touch my arms.

"I'm Pollie Baxter, Conrad's sister." She shakes my hand with all the vigor of a professional linebacker.

"Nice to meet you, Pollie," I begin, but she doesn't seem very interested in what I have to say. She grabs my elbow and starts pulling me down the hall. I trip over my feet, but she never slows. We end up in a sitting room at the end of the hall. Pollie flops down on one of the couches and signals for me to sit beside her.

"What's your story?" she asks, pushing her black curls away from her face. A part of her reminds me a bit of both Blanche and Rosie. They have the same complete lack of boundaries and an "out there" attitude. She giggles, color springing to her bronzed cheeks.

"Sorry, I can be a little much. My therapist is trying to fix me. I'm excited to see someone new in this house. Maybe you will actually be able to get through to Grumpy Gills." Her eyes roll up and around in her skull.

I realize that this might be my chance to get more information. Pollie strikes me as the kind of person who doesn't need an excuse to start talking.

"Can you tell me about your brother? The information's been a little cryptic."

Pollie smiles softly, a knowing expression on her face.

"Let me guess," she begins, pulling her booted feet up onto the couch. "Lusta refused to tell you anything to protect Conrad's privacy, right?" I shrug. That was more or less the gist.

"Something like that."

"Come with me. I want to show you something." On the far side of the room she hands me a picture off the fireplace mantle. "This was Conrad."

The guy in the picture stands tall and muscular. His sandy blonde hair wisps on its ends. It frames his face in a way that gives him a beach vibe, even in the middle of a New York winter. His eyes are a piercing blue and his skin, sun kissed and warm. His lips are full, but serious. He fills out his private school uniform very well. Crisp lines are pressed into his navy blazer and khaki pants, and he seems uncomfortable posing for the camera with his stone like stature.

"Can you tell me what happened to him? I'm going a little crazy not knowing. It's lonely here in the dark." Pollie sighs and shifts her weight back on her heels.

"We should probably sit back down," she starts, sitting first. I follow her lead. "When we were little Conrad always smiled. A generally happy kid. Before we were ten years old, our mom got sick. Breast cancer took her life a couple of years later. Conrad took it hard. I mean, I did too, but his relationship with my mom was something special. They did everything together. They'd read books, really bonded over black and white movies, and the way they tended to her rose garden was next level." She must see the confusion on my face. "I'll leave that story for another day. After Mom died, Conrad started to change. Puberty's a bitch anyway, but her death didn't help. The boy he was kind of evaporated. He started getting into things that he shouldn't. The scariest was when he started racing. He used to race cars with guys from our school. Nobody could convince him it was dangerous, until the night of the accident."

I can tell how difficult it is for her, but I sit quietly and let her finish. I need to hear this.

"Conrad wasn't drinking like the cops kept trying to report. He was reckless, but not that stupid. He was racing a friend on a back road about two miles from here when it happened. Conrad was far enough ahead of the other guy that he already won, but he didn't slow down, that's not his style. He took one turn too fast and lost control. The car flipped a few times before landing on its roof. No one could get to him before the fire started. He was lucky that anyone got there at all before he was dead. The burns are bad. I won't sugarcoat that. He was in the hospital for months. When he finally got out, Conrad had to face a sentence for reckless driving and a bunch of other charges. My dad worked out a plea deal with the courts for him to serve his sentence under house arrest. The lawyers argued that his injuries were enough punishment." Her eyes glisten, but no tears fall. I feel for her. If anything like that ever happened to Jonah, I'd be catatonic.

"After Conrad got here he pushed himself away from everyone and everything." She sighs before starting again. "You have to understand. Conrad was the center of the universe around this town before the accident. He was our lynchpin. Captain of the lacrosse team, head of student council, and member of the honor society. He dated the most beautiful girls and he was all around the most popular guy, and then he shut down and shut everyone out. It's like pulling teeth to get him to see me."

"What about your dad?"

Pollie's face sours, pretty much the same reaction I've gotten from everyone here about Mr. Baxter. "My dad prefers to throw his money at problems and pretend it'll make them go away."

"I'm sorry."

She shrugs, pulling the sleeves of her sweater over her hands. "It is what it is. I know my mom would be super pissed if I didn't stick by her Connie." Something about his nickname makes me miss my dad. I can't remember the last time he called me Bella instead of Peanut. I need to call my parents.

"Plus, he is my brother and I do love him. I don't want you to take it personally, but he's going to be awful to you."

"He already kind of was," I mumble, my mouth flattening into a line. This seems to surprise her.

"Conrad's already talked to you?" she asks, the shock echoing in her voice. "Haven't you only been here for like a day? I figured he'd freeze you out for at least a week."

Well, that's comforting.

"How did it go?"

"It was an accident. He was getting something out of the kitchen last night and I interrupted him."

"You've already seen him?" Pollie's face blanches and my fear around seeing Conrad is only intensifying. I don't want to shriek when I fully see him like he's some Mary Shelley abomination.

"Not exactly, it was dark. The only light came from the fridge, but I did see an outline of him. And heard him insult me." That makes her giggle.

"Yeah, that sounds like Conrad. Sorry if I freaked you out a little, the scars are kind of jarring. You should be prepared if you ever do get the full view."

Light fills Pollie's face like a cartoon character with a lightbulb over their head.

"Hey, what are you doing tonight?" she asks as the spark in her green eyes grows.

"Are you serious? That would be a big heap of nothing."

"Awesome sauce," she squeaks, clapping her hands together. "A friend of mine is having a party and you should totally come with me! I insist on being your own personal welcome wagon to the neighborhood."

I hadn't meant my admission of nothing to be an invitation to something. I don't have a lot of experience with parties. I don't even have practice with school dances. I want to make excuses, to tell her how shy I am and how I won't know anyone. Then I think again. Maybe this is an opportunity. I've been so worried about my friends moving on without me, maybe it's okay for me to take some chances while I'm here.

"Okay, sounds like fun," I say, trying my best to hide my dread.

Pollie hops up and down a couple times in her seat, reaching out to grab my hand.

"Hurray! It will be a blast. Trust me, this will be better than being stuck here all night." She glances down at the face of her phone and says, "I can pick you up at eight, if that's cool?"

My heart beats a little too fast, but I hold my voice steady.

"Yeah, that sounds good. I will see you then." Her attention is already locked on her phone as she skips away from the room. As Pollie leaves, the door fills with Lottie's little body.

"What were you doing with her?" she signs, sitting beside me on the couch, her curls swaying as she does.

"Talking. She's taking me to a party tonight," I reply, turning to face her. Her fluffy brown hair is pushed back with a bright orange headband that matches the laces in her tennis shoes. She's far more put together than I've ever been. It's a little depressing.

"With Pollie?" she questions, her eyebrows popping up to her hairline. "She usually comes and leaves without pausing to say hello. Sometimes when she sees me she speaks so slowly like that will help me hear her." I can't help but laugh at that. Jonah has experienced that more than once in his life.

"Yeah, hearing people do things like that sometimes. I'm pretty sure they believe they're helping."

"It's silly," Lottie responds.

"I know, hearing people are strange that way," I smile. "What are you up to today?"

She shrugs, picking at the knee on her leggings. "I have a little homework. I usually help Mama on the weekends too. Maybe read." That peaks my interest.

"You like to read?" I ask, a grin growing across my face. Now she's speaking my language. Her little head bobs up and down with an enthusiasm that reminds me of myself. She reaches out and grabs my hand.

"Let me show you!"

Lottie leads me out of the room and down one of the many long and winding hallways to another door I've yet to see. She looks back at me before turning the knob and pushing the squeaky door open to reveal a beauty unlike any I'd ever seen, more books than I've ever since in one place. A library in a single home that would put the entire Harpersgrove Public Library to shame.

"This is incredible," I breathe. The ceiling is decorated with painted angels and gold accents. It warms me like a hug, while the smell of old books takes me home.

"I love it in here," Lottie signs back before scurrying across the room to pick up a book on the end table beside the lush purple couch. She pulls her feet up underneath her and disappears into a world that I have run to many times myself. Books can take us places we never imagined. I should go back to my room and tackle the mountain of work I have to do with Conrad. It's plenty to keep me busy for the rest of the day. But instead, I curl up with my beat up Brontë on the opposite end of the couch from Lottie. Reading in a room like this brings me the first real joy I've felt since I arrived.

Later, the adventures of Catherine and Heathcliff thoroughly explored, I find my way back to my room. Inside the huge closet, the sad number of clothes I own mock me and my lack of fashion sense. I let out a frustrated huff. The only thing I can think of to wear to a party full of rich kids is a tiara and I don't own one of those.

"Why were you talking to my sister?" a grainy voice booms behind me as my soul leaps from my body. I spin around, looking simultaneously for my intruder and something to hit him with. Upon finding no one lurking in any corner, I'm left confused.

The grainy sound that had accompanied the voice continued to echo around me. I follow it to the wall near the door where the intercom panel is mounted.

"Hello," I call out to the box, waiting for some kind of response. I am the crazy woman who speaks to inanimate objects.

"You have to hold down the button to talk," the voice barks back.

I narrow my eyes towards the rude little square and take a step forward. Obviously I know it's Conrad yelling at me, but what concerns me is how he knows I'm in my bedroom and what I'm doing inside. I push my thumb down on the round red button in the corner of the box.

"Hello," I say again.

"What were you talking about with my sister?" he snaps at me. Nasty little gargoyle.

"How did you know I was in here?" I demand. I can be a brat right back to him with as much gusto.

"There are cameras, but that's not important. What were you talking about with Pollie?" he orders.

"What?! Cameras?" I scream into the intercom mic, that fun feedback sound bouncing back to me. "What is wrong with you, you pervert?" I can't see him, but I can hear in his voice that he's rolling his eyes at me.

"Will you relax? I like to know what's happening in my house. Along that line, I will ask for a third time, what were you talking about with Pollie?" And again I ignore him as I dart around the room like a rat in a maze.

"There isn't a camera here is there?" The line falls silent and my skin flushes. "Conrad!" I shout.

"Calm down, it barely ever gets turned on." He speaks so non-chalant that I want to reach through the intercom to strangle him.

"Where is it?" I demand, scanning the room for anything that could possibly be a camera.

"It's in the corner, by the door. You need to calm down," he hisses, like he has any room to be agitated. Up in that corner a shiny black orb sticks to the ceiling. I stomp over to it and stand underneath, feeling like the fire's going to explode out the top of my head at any moment.

"Get it out of here!" I shout at the camera.

"It doesn't have sound," I hear from the intercom behind me, confirming that he does in fact have the camera on. I slam my finger onto the button with enough force that it actually hurts.

"I want it out of here now or I'm going home. I mean it, I will pack my bags and leave this second. You can't invade my privacy like this." I'm fuming, rage burning holes through my body. "And to answer your damn question, your sister asked me to go to a party with her. Of course, that's not any of your business." Conrad is quiet a moment before he responds.

"I don't think I'm comfortable with you hanging out with my sister." I reach around to the underside of the intercom box until I find a bunch of wires.

"Well," I begin, gripping the cables in my fingers. "Luckily it's not up to you. Get rid of the camera." I yank the wires free from the box as the crackling inside it silences. I feel powerful and in control. I scowl at the camera and pick up my phone. Grabbing my clothes, I return to the bathroom. No way in hell am I going to get dressed in that room until I know the camera is gone.

CHAPTER SIX

I emerge from the bathroom in the only dress I brought with me. It's gray and sweater like, short-sleeved and turtlenecked, something my mother demanded that I buy. As always, I layer the dress over black leggings. I pull on a pair of black boots that hug my robust calves, almost to the point of cutting off circulation. I don't normally put that much thought into what I wear. I like to think of it more as a uniform. Utilitarian. Concrete. Shopping for clothes at my size isn't fun, it's a chore. I've always figured that if I wear the same thing every day, people wouldn't notice me. Maybe it didn't matter what I wore because everyone would always see me the same way. Now I want to try something different, feel something different. And I have no idea what I'm doing. I like to believe that I don't care what people think of me, but I can't help wondering if that's only because my world has been so small and filled with the same people. There's a bit of fear attached to the unknown. A soft knock on the door interrupts my thoughts, followed by Lusta popping in with a step ladder.

"I hope I'm not disturbing you." She sets the ladder down under the corner of the room with the camera and starts climbing with a screwdriver in hand. "For the record," she begins, reaching for the orb in the ceiling. "I told him to make sure this was down by the time you got here. I was not aware that he hadn't listened to me. For that, I do apologize."

I take in Lusta's simple ensemble and perfectly applied makeup and wonder if maybe she can help.

"Lusta, do I look okay?" I ask, feeling suddenly naked in front of her. A smile stretches her flawless mouth as she makes her way back down the ladder.

"You look very pretty." The look on my face must betray me further because she sweetly adds, "But I don't think that's what you're asking." I cross and uncross my arms over my chest. It feels like I'm bursting out of my skin.

"I'm going out with Pollie tonight and I don't know what I'm doing, to be honest." The words fall from my lips before I can take them back. My eyes fall to the chipped yellow nail polish on my fingers. I have to fix that before I leave. Pollie's friends surely don't have chipped nails. When I finally gain the courage to look up, Lusta is watching me with a motherly kindness. I want to cry.

"Come with me," she says as she takes my hand.

Lusta leads me back to the first floor, past the kitchen to a place I haven't explored yet. She pushes a door open to find Lottie on the far side of the room. She sets her book aside and waves to me as we enter. Her bright eyes fill with intrigue that remind me what it's like to be a child. Everything is bright and new and worth seeing. There are too many days I wish I could go back to that time and stay. Lusta squares her shoulders to face Lottie.

67

"I'm helping Bella get ready to go out with Pollie," Lusta says. She motions for me to sit on the bed, moving to her vanity and rustling through the drawers. She plugs a curling iron into a wall outlet and turns to me with a brush and a makeup bag in her hands. She unties my hair, soft brown strands falling around my face. It's like letting go of a security blanket. She starts brushing the strands back toward her. The bristles scratch against my scalp, sending pleasant tingles down my spine. When I was a little girl, my mother used to have me take a hot shower whenever I was sad or had a headache. Then she'd brush my hair back, as Lusta's doing now. It's every comfort I need wrapped up in one act. I'm simultaneously grateful to Lusta for giving it to me and sad for how much it makes me miss my mom. I need to call her immediately after Lusta finishes helping me.

"We won't go too drastic," she assures me. I normally let my hair air dry after washing, then immediately put it into a bun or braids. I rarely, if ever, use any heat on it. A curling iron has such a distinct smell. I know it's the smell of burning hair, but it makes me think of special occasions. I can feel Lottie's eyes on me, watching every move her mother makes as she runs the brush through my hair. Lusta reaches over and picks up the curling iron and starts working on the ends of my hair.

"I wanted to try something new. I'm not exactly what you'd call a party person," I admit tragically. I hope neither Lusta nor the eight year old will judge me for my lame social standing. "I don't know how to do this."

"Mama says I should always be myself and if people don't like it they don't deserve my friendship," Lottie signs after pushing her curls away from her face. I can't help but wonder what after school special I've been sucked into.

"Your mom's a smart lady," I respond, instead of voicing what's in my head.

"What are you going to wear?" Lottie asks, rolling over to her stomach and kicking her feet behind her. I glance down at my sweater dress and look back to Lottie whose eyes flash wide with horror.

"Charlotte Louise," Lusta hisses at her daughter with narrowed eyes. Clearly, Lottie's body language is understandable even if her ASL isn't.

"You look just fine, Bella." That's incredibly underwhelming and doesn't make me feel any better. I bury my face in my hands and let out the groan of a strangled cat.

"This is the only semi nice thing I brought with me. I usually wear leggings and t-shirts for goodness sake!"

Mother and daughter share a look and a psychic connection that goes far beyond their language barrier. "Go see what you can find," Lusta instructs. Lottie hops up off the bed and bolts from the room. I want to see what Lusta's doing, but she holds me firmly in place. When she's through, my head bounces with the weight of curls before she pins a few sections back. Then she drowns me in hairspray. Lottie reenters the room through the aerosol haze with my new outfit. A pair of dark blue jeans, a black tank top and a thin sweater. Leave it to a child to make more sense out of my closet than I ever could. Are jeans fancy enough?

Below me, Lottie sits cross-legged on the floor pulling up my feet to measure different shoes against my soles. I wiggle my foot in her face to get her attention. "I'm a size nine," I sign down to her so she'll release my leg. She starts her new project of flipping through shoes.

Lusta moves in front of me, sitting on the bed and balancing her makeup bag on her lap. My skin is about forty shades lighter than Lusta's is. How could she possibly have anything that could work for me? She seems to sense my apprehension and offers me a comforting gaze.

"Don't worry, I won't make you look like a clown. I do makeup and hair for weddings on occasion. I was a cosmetologist before becoming a housekeeper." Her hands fly around my head in a rhythm unlike anything I have ever seen. She pulls out products I didn't know existed as she plucks and pokes and prods, dabs and stabs and slathers and smears. I feel like a Thanksgiving turkey when she's done, but the warm pride in her face tells me it's okay. I turn to look in the mirror, but she grabs my shoulders and twists me into the bathroom, the clothes draped over my arm. I realize there is no mirror in here! Who makes a bathroom without a mirror?

I tentatively touch my cheek in order to not to mess up any of Lusta's hard work, just enough to embrace my insecurities. I pull my fingers away and wince at the various powders that remain on my hand. I thought she promised I wouldn't look like a clown. I normally only wear jeans with an oversized sweater down to my knees. I'm not used to wearing clothes that hug me this close. I'm used to fraying hems from pulling on the edges of t-shirts that are too short for my torso while simultaneously tugging up the stretchy elastic waistline of my never ending line of leggings. This outfit is different.

"Is it okay?" I ask. The answer seems pretty obvious.

"You look lovely, Bella," Lusta says. Lottie signs, "Beautiful."

I steel myself against all of my fears before looking into Lusta's vanity mirror. The normal, inconsistent kinks and waves of my hair have been replaced with soft and natural curls. Lusta was true to her word in not making me look like a clown. Even with the makeup I still look like myself, but I've been put through a filter to take away the less appealing blotches and spots. Can clothes make you look taller? My body looks longer and, dare I say, leaner too? I had no idea clothing possessed this kind of transformative ability. A little pair of hands pull on my leg as Lottie attempts to shove my feet into a pair of loud, sparkly gold ballet flats. I eye her doubtfully. It's a little too much for me. "Trust me," she insists.

From the corner of the room, another one of those heinous little intercom boxes starts to crackle. I swallow the acidic feeling in the back of my throat. Conrad is everywhere.

"For the love of God, get the new girlie down here," Mr. Potter's deep voice hums through the speaker. My shoulders relax and my toes wiggle in the shiny shoes. Lusta struts across the room to the angry little box with its bright red light and pushes the talk button.

"What's the matter, Patty?" she asks and I smile at the familiar nickname.

"Palarma's car pulled up in front and if Bella doesn't meet her first she's going to come looking for her. She'll end up in here with me and I'll have to kill her," Mr. Potter rambles off in a hurried breath. I finger spell the name that Mr. Potter had said to Lottie.

"That's Pollie's full first name," Lottie replies. My hands begin to sweat. Mr. Potter calls to me again. Lusta tells him that I'll be right down.

"Breathe," she says to me as I release a breath from deep in my chest. "Now," she starts again, straightening her spine and motioning for me to do the same. Oddly, it makes me feel confident. I stand about a head taller than Lusta, but there's no doubt who the bigger person is here. "You're going to get your purse and meet Pollie at the front door. I demand that you have a good time."

I turn to Lottie and wag my eyebrows up and down at her. She giggles and signs, "Have fun," and I'm determined to do so.

I hurry back through the maze of hallways to my bedroom and grab my purse. I hesitate a moment at the copy of *Wuthering Heights* before sticking it in my bag. You never know when you'll need a good book. I check my hair in the mirror one more time, still not feeling like myself. If there's ever a time when I need hair and makeup to make me a little more solid, this is it!

Each step down the stairs pounds with my heart against the wall of my chest, but the dread is mixed with genuine excitement. I never take chances. I live in a world of very strict routines and boundaries. My only adventures are in the pages of books. I've always liked it that way, but this is a chance for an adventure all my own. Pollie waits at the bottom of the steps, painted into a high waisted leather skirt and low-cut gray tank top. It leaves very little to the imagination under her black leather jacket. Her own flawless makeup resembles Rosie's, with bright red lips and dark smoky eyes. Her black curls stand teased out at a volume that completely defies physics. Miss Baxter is a presence. Upon seeing my grand entrance she leans back and purses her lips, letting out a resounding "DAYUM GURL!"

I motion up and down at her. "Right back atcha," I respond.

"Is what I'm wearing okay? I wasn't sure." It suddenly occurred to me Lottie might not actually be the fashion genius I thought she was. Pollie pauses a moment long enough to cause panic inside me.

"Oh my God, yeah, you look amazing. Ignore me. I'm being a psycho." That doesn't instill much confidence in me. She grabs my hand and tugs me toward the door and never stops talking. The words have faded from decipherable to a loud buzz like a swarm of bees. Outside, I wince at the sharp chill of the northern air. I should have worn a coat. Pollie doesn't seem the least bit fazed. She walks around to the driver's side of a sleek silver Bentley that costs more than my parents make in a year. I stand dumbstruck for a moment staring at the majestic machine. I don't want to touch it for fear of leaving fingerprints.

"What's the matter?" Pollie laughs.

"Is—is this your car?" I fumble over my words in a way that I hope comes out more like my teeth chattering in the cold. It has to be her father's car. There's no way anyone, even someone as rich as Lionel Baxter, would give their barely-of-legal-driving-age daughter a car like this.

She pumps her palms up to the sky like she's raising the roof.

"Happy sweet sixteen to me," but her voice doesn't match the nature of her gesture. "My daddy's all about buying my affection."

She slips inside and I follow. The black leather interior smells like new, expensive shoes. I cozy into my heated seat, snuggling into the comforting warmth with my hands squashed between my thighs.

"Where are we going?"

Pollie flips a few tight curls away from her eyes as she peels down the driveway. I try not to grip the passenger door too hard even though I know I'm white knuckling it as I pray that I don't die in the expensive car of this complete stranger.

"A guy I go to school with is throwing a party. His house is pretty sick. He used to be a good friend of Conrad's." I think back to the pictures on the mantel. Different young men on each side of Conrad clad in navy sports jackets with a school's insignia on the lapels.

"Used to be?" I ask, forgetting about her stuntman driving and loosening my grip on the door.

"Yeah, I told you, he dropped everyone after the accident. Most people in his life tried, but there's only so much pushing away people will take, you know?"

"Sounds like it's what he wanted," I say, writing my name in the fog of the passenger side window. My "E" and "L"s swoop together in a swirly script and I can't remember the last time I wrote in cursive on a piece of paper.

It's quiet in the car for a moment before Pollie admits, "No one wants to be that alone."

I twist in my seat and I can tell I've upset her. Her eyes fixed on the road as ever, hands planted in the ten and two positions on the steering wheel. The corners of her scarlet mouth turned down. I wonder how I'm supposed to approach this. The last time I'd found myself in a prickly situation with a friend had been at the age of six when Rosie ripped the heads off two of my Barbie dolls in our first organized play-date. My mom forced me to play with the weird girl who wore her blonde hair in pigtails on top of her head and lived in a trailer with her flighty mom. I'm out of practice.

"Pollie, I'm sorry. I shouldn't have said that." She shakes her head, clicking her turn signal as we go to the right.

"You have nothing to apologize for." Her voice is gravelly and low. "You didn't know him before. He was never a prince, but there was still light in him. That's gone now. The whole thing destroyed his relationships, especially with Gatty."

"I'm sorry, what is a Gatty?" I ask as we turn into a swanky development of mansion after mansion. They must mass produce them here.

She laughs again, this one reaching all the way down to her toes.

"It is the nickname of the guy whose house we're going to. His last name is Gattman." Pollie pulls her car up next to a black Audi and turns off the ignition. "Ready?" she asks, the mask of security falling back over her face.

I steel myself against the screaming inside me and smile.

"Let's do it!"

From the moment I open the door the bass from distant music thumps deep in my chest. Dozens of people litter the front lawn, red solo cups in hand, all shouting over the music. It's cold and I can't help but wonder *why on earth are these people outside?* I can't feel my feet. Pollie struts with a confidence I can't help but envy. She slips her jacket off her shoulders, even though she's only wearing a tank top underneath and tosses it to some kid by the front door. The poor guy is weighed down with coats piled above his head and I swear I see his knees shaking. "Sorry," I whisper as I slink past him. I'd love to help him relocate some of them, but I have to stay glued to Pollie's heels. I've never been to any of Lucy Wilcox's parties back home, but I'm fairly certain they're never anything as insane or lavish as this.

If I thought the Baxter house was big, then this place is actually a castle. The room everyone has congregated in seems like it should host an epic ball full of gowns and an orchestra. Instead, it's filled with a mosh pit of drunk teenagers with a DJ tucked in the corner. It removes a bit of the romance. From the number of people in this room, it feels like a furnace. Sweat pools onto my upper lip and I wipe it away. I don't want anyone to see. I pull back fingers full of the makeup that Lusta had meticulously applied and I panic. I'm sure I have a splotchy red mustache, my skin is flushing crimson under the veil of foundation.

Pollie stops dead in front of me, her feet planted in place.

"Shit," she mutters. She turns on her heel and places her hands on my arms. "Act normal, she can smell fear." I have no idea what she's talking about, but I've forgotten how to be normal. I take to crossing my arms over my chest, up above my boobs. Pretty much the most alien pose I could have taken. I'm not exactly sure who Pollie is talking about as I scan the crowd. When I find her, it's obvious, because she's staring right at us.

My father has taught me throughout my life to never speak in absolutes. If an "I would never..." or an "I always..." crossed my lips, he would cast me a single look telling me to rephrase. The only absolute that I've ever used with any conviction is that my dear friend Goldie is the most beautiful human being ever to grace this planet. Now I know that this is not the case. The girl that Pollie seems so jumpy about is the reason cavemen drew on walls. Her shoulder length blonde hair shimmers like the sun at its highest point with curls on the ends in massive sausage spirals. Her eyes sparkle in a pale periwinkle. Her pink lips are plush and full, and she has a nose straighter than anything in nature. Outside of a bit of mascara I can see no trace of makeup anywhere on her face. People this beautiful don't exist outside the pages of romance novels. The corners of her mouth turn up as she slinks toward us, the crowd parting on either side of her. Beautiful people have power.

"Pollie Wollie, what are you doing here?" she asks.

Pollie digs her red fingernails into her palms. Damn, I forgot all about removing my chipped polish. Pollie starts tapping her fingers against her legs one at a time like she's playing a song on a piano.

"Parker," she begins, her voice high and musical. "I thought Gatty banned you from his parties because you can't keep your top on." Parker barely registers the insult as her weight shifts to her other hip.

"Gatty could never stay mad at me." Her attention switches to me and stays there. "And who exactly are you?" The words cut through me like a knife. I can feel the lingering stabbing dull in my gut. Pollie steps in front of me and speaks before I can.

"This is Bella. She's Conrad's new tutor." That piques Parker's interest and I wish I could hide behind Pollie's skirt like a little girl. Sadly, I stand a few inches too tall and too wide to even hide behind her whole body. Parker's tongue licks across her teeth before she takes a sip from her cup that I'm pretty sure is full of something other than ginger ale.

"You're joking right," she laughs as she thrusts her finger in my face. "What are you? Like fifteen? And you're supposed to tutor Conrad? My Conrad?" The last words hiss with a stinging bite.

"He stopped being your Conrad the minute you broke up with him. Back off," Pollie growls at a level no one else could hear but us. She grabs my wrist and carts us to nowhere in particular, just away. I swear smoke pours from Parker's ears before one of her friends pulls her away.

"I'm sorry about that," Pollie apologizes. I shrug, but hold onto my own hands when I realize they're shaking.

"It's okay. Honestly, she wasn't that bad." A lifetime of Lucy Wilcox has made me at least a little bit tough in the face of mean girls.

"That chick is poison. I never liked her, long before Conrad decided to date her. Parker was never good enough for him. She spends most of her time at her sister's college parties hooking up with frat guys. I didn't think she'd be here." Pollie doesn't have to explain it to me. I get it. If any girl ever hurts Jonah I'll end up going to prison.

"Pollie!" We both turn in the direction of the sound.

"Hey, wait here a second," Pollie says, "I need to talk to someone real quick." She's gone before I can process and protest and I am alone.

The panic starts to swim low in my stomach while obnoxious, drunk people bump into me from all sides. The music is too loud and it's too hot. I count to ten over and over, trying to settle. I can feel the makeup melting off my face and my hair starting to frizz. I need to calm down. It'll all be okay if I can get away from the sea of strangers for only a minute. I clutch my purse to me and shimmy through the crowd to the perimeter of the room. I can't see Pollie anywhere. A few people grumble as I push them aside. I break for the first door I see on the outskirts of the room, slamming it shut behind me. If I award myself only a moment of peace, I can get through the panic. I lean my weight into my palms against the smooth wood. It's like someone is chasing me and only the pressure of my body will keep them away. When my breathing finally evens out, I turn away from the door and press my back against it. The smell of old, polished wood fills my nose as my eyes open to an office decked in hunter green. Wooden bookshelves built into the wall, each jammed full of old cracked spines. Books that likely cost more than I can imagine. It's oddly nice to know that the absurdly rich spend money on the things that I would spend it on. There are a couple of overstuffed armchairs and a couch in the same color green as the walls, all finished off with a large wooden desk that looks almost presidential. It's quiet and serene and that's exactly what I need right now. I reach into my purse and pull out my glasses and my phone. There's one unread message from Elle.

How you doing, buttercup?

I take a deep breath, at least they care.

Tried to socialize, failed miserably. Now I'm hiding.

I tuck the phone back in my purse and eye the comfy looking chairs. I did bring my book for a reason. It's just for a few minutes; to get my feet back on the ground. If Pollie needs me, she can find me. I take out my worn paperback and snuggle into the chair, crossing my ankles and leaning back with a sigh. Solitude, my happy place.

"Did you really anticipate the party to be boring enough to bring a book?" a voice asks from across the room, causing me to jump from my skin. I'm pretty sure something equal to "Christ on a cracker!" escapes my lips. My heart pounds out of my chest. In the high backed chair behind the desk sits a guy about my age. His dark brown hair is thick and cut in a pretty fashion, parted and styled to the side. I'm certain he has more product in his hair than I've ever had in mine. His deep brown eyes watch me. A smile twitches to his lips and his fingers interlace together on his chest over a red and white checkered shirt.

"'Christ on a cracker'? Is that what you said?" His chest moving with laughter. I frown. He doesn't have to make fun of me. I shift in my seat, hoping the chair will swallow me whole.

"You scared me," I admit. His head cocks to the side and while the mischief is still in his eyes, he's softened slightly.

"I didn't know I was throwing such a lame party."

"You're Gatty?" I ask, folding my book closed over my thumb.

His eyebrow arches, intrigued. He leans forward over the desk with his elbows balanced atop it.

"You have me at a disadvantage. You seem to know me, but I haven't the slightest idea who you are."

My cheeks flush again. Damn it.

"I'm Bella Southland," I respond with an uncharacteristic wave. This level of cringe is a tragedy normally reserved for Greeks. "I came with Pollie Baxter."

His demeanor noticeably changes, everything stiffer. The way he is staring at me makes me uncomfortable. Guys don't look at me with such hyper focus. Usually it's a passing glance until Goldie walks by. I need to cut this tension.

"What kind of name is Gatty anyway?"

Thankfully, he grins before standing up from behind the desk. He's taller than his sitting position gave away. On the lanky side, like a cute string bean. He rests his palms back on the desk and sits against it, uncomfortably close to me.

"It's a nickname for my last name. What, you think it's no good?"

I shrug and play along. I'm already not dressed like me, may as well not act like me either.

"I mean, is your first name really that bad that 'Gatty' was the best you could do?" I tease, crossing my legs at the knee, not an easy feat because my thunder thighs do not like for my knees to be together. A playful look pops onto his face and it's unsettling because I don't know what it means. He sticks out his hand to me in a very professional and formal manner. I feel like he should have a tie clip and a pocket square.

"Bernard Ambrose Gattman III. An absolute pleasure to meet you."

I bite down on my bottom lip to keep from giggling.

"Gatty it is," I responded and take his hand in mine. His head tips back with a hearty, full-bodied laugh erupting from his throat.

"That was good," he says, finally coming up for air. I try not to blush any harder, proud of myself for my funny jab. He releases my hand and sits back against the desk. "Bella Southland, who came with Pollie Baxter, how is it I've never seen you before?"

Sweat pools at my temples. When did this become a job interview? "Well, I'm not from here. I arrived yesterday."

"Where are you from then?" The level of eye contact he is keeping makes me squirmy. He leans close enough that I can feel his breath on my skin.

"Um, I'm from a small town no one's ever heard of in Maryland. I'm here to tutor Conrad Baxter." The playful sparkle drops from his eyes. "Are you okay?" I ask.

"Conrad. How is Conrad?" he asks, his voice noticeably hushed.

All I can do is shrug my shoulders. "I don't know. The only times I've spoken to him, he's yelled at me."

Gatty chuckles, "Yeah, that sounds like Baxter." He catches my eyes again, his gaze focused so deep it makes me feel naked in front of him. But I don't look away. "Don't let him scare you off, he's harmless." Before I have the chance to speak the office door opens and Pollie's curly-haired head pops through.

"There you are! I look up and you're gone." She left my side when she promised not to, but I won't point that out.

"I needed a little air," I reply, trying to keep up my cool persona in front of Gatty.

"And *you're* avoiding your own party. Why?" she asks Gatty with her hip popped against the door frame. The music and loud voices seeping into my peaceful escape start to make me uneasy again.

Gatty's shoulders shrug up to his ears as he says, "Parker's out there."

Pollie's eyes roll all the way to the back of her head as she lets out a groan. "I cannot believe you boys are scared of one little girl." She bounces toward me, her heeled boots clicking against the hardwood. "Well, I'm taking back my date. You two are in here hosting book club while there's a perfectly good party going on and it's sad." She yanks me by the wrists out of the chair. For someone this tiny, she's got some serious strength. I manage a, "Nice to meet you," over my shoulder to Gatty who offers a wave as I'm lugged away.

Pollie spends the rest of the evening introducing me to people with names like Daffodil and Wednesday and I forget them as fast as she introduces me. These faces all blend together in their similarities. Same haircuts, same clothes, same makeup, same everything. I've never in my life seen a group this plastic. I'm sure I stick out like a sore thumb. The fact that I'm with Pollie, the only person with any identity of her own, surely doesn't help. Her wild, fluffy head of curls makes her stand out in this crowd. We dance to loud house music, with bass booming so hard, it's impossible to hear anything else. I take a cup of some mystery liquid that Pollie hands me, but I don't drink it. It's not that I don't trust her. I just don't want my first drinking experience to be amongst strangers. It should be with my friends. But I do keep the cup half full and in my hand at all times. At least Pollie will think I'm drinking it.

I'm trying my best to be a different Bella, a braver Bella, but I don't get it. This whole "party" thing doesn't seem fun. Everyone is jumping around, being drunk and stupid, and trying to have conversations when they can't possibly hear. Couples either sneak off into other rooms or very publicly lick each other in plain view of everyone. The only reason I'm still playing along is because every once in a while I catch Gatty looking at me. I never thought I'd be attracted to cocky confidence, something Gatty has in duplicate. My heart skips a beat every time I find him staring and I go back to dancing awkwardly with Pollie.

By one o'clock in the morning, I'm somehow both completely exhausted and filled with exhilaration. I've never had a curfew in my life. I've never needed one. I am the in-bed-by-ten type. Yet I can say with almost certainty that my parents would not be okay with my being out this late. I have to force Pollie's keys from her hands. She keeps insisting that she's fine, and she might be, but she's itty bitty and has been drinking. I am the opposite of itty bitty and haven't had a drop. The math adds up in my favor. It takes some convincing, but she finally drops the keys in my hand. The car costs more than my entire college tuition will. Wrecking it is not on the agenda for tonight. I plug the Baxter's address into the GPS and enjoy a few moments of static silence.

"Gatty seemed to like you." Pollie mutters, pressing her tiny forehead against the glass of the passenger side window.

"He was trying to figure out why some weirdo was reading in the middle of his party." I'm simply a puzzle to be solved.

Pollie shakes her head, her skin squeaking against the glass. "Nope. You got him to leave his Parker hiding place. He's interested, but you should be careful. Like I said, he and Conrad used to be friends."

"What is this thing with Parker?"

"She's a vulture." Pollie flips over in her seat to face me, tucking her hands under her cheek like a little girl. "Well, I guess she's the opposite of a vulture, because once the animal's dead, she flees."

"She's interested in Gatty?"

Pollie shrugs, "She wouldn't be Parker if she wasn't sniffing for something new. But Gatty doesn't like her, so I doubt anything will come of it. Parker is always looking out for Parker. She is always hunting for the next opportunity. Always ready with an escape if things go awry. She was that way when she dated Conrad and I'm sure she'll be that way with everyone. Her many future husbands won't see it coming." She snickers at the last part and, I can't help it, I do too. After arriving back at the house, car in one piece, Pollie and I walk arm and arm to the door.

"I hope you had fun. I really wanted you to have fun." she says as I fiddle for the keys to find the one for the house.

"I did. Thanks for taking me." It's not a lie. Surprisingly, I did enjoy myself. Especially after meeting Gatty. The way he looked at me made me feel special.

Pollie grabs the knob and opens the front door, no key needed. I'm from a small town where the biggest criminal element is sixth graders stealing candy bars from the drugstore, but we still lock our doors at night. Pollie hits a panel of light switches and the foyer springs to life. No sooner do the lights come on than a voice booms from the speakers on either side of us.

"Palarma!"

The fingernails of Pollie's right hand dig into my forearm like a cat being forced into a bath. The unfeminine grunt that escapes my lips is inevitable. She releases my arm as quickly as she took it and begins to stamp her foot against the marble floor.

"God damn it, Conrad!" she screams it into the open space, but of course he isn't here. There's a crackling moment of silence as the person on the other end of the speaker is silent.

"Pollie, you know these cameras don't have sound. You have to use the intercom panel if you wish to speak with me." Conrad's voice is calm and even and his choice of words remind me of an

Austen character. Pollie stomps in her heeled boots to the intercom and slams her thumb down on the round talk button.

"God. Damn. It. Con. Rad!" she shouts into the microphone.

"Don't be dramatic Palarma. Come up here please." His cadence remains unchanged.

"No!" she shrieks back, forgetting about the button. She groans and corrects herself before he can snap back at her. Jabbing the little plastic circle she hisses, "No! I'm tired and I'm going to bed."

Her brother doesn't hesitate a moment. "I will not have this conversation in front of her. Come up here now." Pollie thinks this over before shooting a sympathetic glance my way.

"I'll come up if you give me at least twenty minutes of face time with you." Ah, she's going to abandon me for selfish purposes. The line is quiet for far too long, but of course I know he's still there. He's always there. "Conrad," she eggs on, swaying between her feet. If he doesn't answer her I may be carrying her to bed.

"Fine," he snaps, his tone sharp and I jump back. "Get up here."

Pollie flips around with a cheesy grin plastered on her face but I can see the hurt that lingers in her eyes. She rises up on her toes and kisses my cheek. "Thanks for coming, Chicky, you're a blast." I don't think anyone's ever used such a word to describe me in my life, but I'll take it.

Pollie takes off up the stairs, her hip bouncing against the rail as she tries to keep from falling over. I could help her, but I have no interest in facing the wrath of her beastly brother. I should be exhausted, but I'm wired and wide awake. There's no sleeping for me right now. My stomach rumbles. It's bad for my metabolism to eat this time of night, but the kitchen calls to me anyway. I take my snack into the living room to watch TV, snuggling into an armchair that swallows me whole. Once it's on, the TV sound blasts from the speakers, scaring me a foot off of my seat. I frantically smash remote control buttons until it quiets down to a point that is barely audible. The last thing I want is to wake Mr. Potter, Lusta, or Lottie. I don't care if Conrad knows I'm down here. I pull my sweater a little closer around myself and shove a cracker piled high with cheese into my mouth. The sharpness of the hotsy-totsy spread causes my lips to pucker. Why would anyone buy this? Of course, it doesn't stop me from immediately pushing another into my greedy pie hole. I take a long gulp of milk, letting my gaze settle into the colors flashing on the screen. Black boxed captions roll across the lower edge, Lottie must use this TV a lot. The rhythm of my chewing mixes with the sound of my heartbeat and the feeling of this plush chair all around me. My eyelids feel heavy and I'm slipping away before I even finish chewing.

I wake with a start and it feels like someone is touching me. Everything is dark and I'm lost in time. Is it still night? When did I turn off the TV? I need to stop falling asleep in strange places here. Confusion overwhelms me as I grip for the plate I'd balanced on my chest, only to find a soft flannel blanket instead. I shift my weight onto my elbows and reach toward the light switch on the lamp beside me.

"Don't!" a voice snaps in the dark as my heart falls into my shoes. My eyes adjust to the darkness and I can make out the shadowy figure in front of me.

"Jesus," I shriek, recoiling back into the upholstery. "What are you doing, Conrad?" I'm still half lost in fuzzy unconsciousness.

"Go back to sleep, Isabella," he bellows with force, but his voice is low. I imagine it's how he'd try to comfort a small child. His black hood is pulled up over his head again, obscuring my view of any of his features. He's starting to remind me of a TV vigilante. I rub my eyes, cringing as I remember that I haven't removed my makeup. Maybe it's good that we're in the dark. I don't need him seeing me all raccoon-eyed.

"How did you know I was in here?" I ask him through a very unfeminine yawn. His right hand motions to the far corner of the room. Sure enough, on the ceiling is another one of those floating black orbs.

"Ahh," I mumble, settling back into my sleepiness. "Isn't the Big Brother thing a little bit weird to you?" He doesn't speak, but I do hear him take in a deep breath. He sounds more human tonight.

"Go back to sleep, Isabella," he says again. For a moment, I can see his eyes, soft against the dark silhouette of his face. He's not a monster. He's only a boy. It would be easy to reach over and turn on the light, finally see the mystery everyone's been hiding from me. But there's something about the fact that he asked me not to that keeps my hands in place.

"Thank you for the blanket."

He grunts something that I'm sure is his equal to a "you're welcome" and shoves his hands into the pockets of his sweatshirt.

"Go back to sleep, Isabella," he says a final time, causing my lip to pout. He's so bossy.

CHAPTER SEVEN

It feels like I barely settled back down before sunlight streams in through every window. I'm wrapped up like a caterpillar in a cocoon, snuggled in the warmth of the chair. The harsh sunlight beats on my face. All I can do is surrender to it. True, there's no pie in my hair today, but I know I look like a train wreck. Yesterday's makeup streaks my hands and I can only imagine how disastrous my face is. Beside me I hear mindless chomping. Lottie is chilling on the sofa with a salad bowl of cereal, her eyes glued to the television screen. When she spots me watching her, she waves.

"What time is it?" I ask with the hand that I allow to peek out over the cover into the frigid air. I like my baking temperature under the thick blanket.

"8:30. Why are you sleeping down here? You know you have a bed, right?" I sit up and pull the blanket down to my waist. It's as good a time as any to wake up.

"I had an interesting night."

No sooner do the words leave my lips than a thudding presence stomps into the room. Clad in an oversized shirt and athletic shorts that slip down her narrow hips, Pollie looks like a little girl dressed in her father's clothes. She rubs her sleepy eyes and sweeps her messy raven hair out of her face. For having such a small and delicate frame, she moves like an exhausted elephant. Every stomp sends a vibration through the floor. Her shoulders slump forward and her dark painted toes squish into the carpet as she collapses onto the couch. She throws her head onto Lottie's tiny lap, narrowly missing the cereal bowl.

Lottie looks up at me in horror. "What do I do?"

I try to keep from giggling, but it's almost too much to bear. A hungover Pollie buries her face into the legs of a disturbed Lottie. The little girl throws her hands over her head in an attempt to keep from touching the lush.

"Pollie," I begin, sitting forward in my seat. "You okay?"

"I'm never drinking again," she groans in Lottie's legs. "Alcohol is the devil, little one! Heed my warning!"

"She's telling you to make good life choices," I tell Lottie. It's best to leave out the particulars. Pollie sits up straight and flings her arms around Lottie's shoulders, running her fingers around each soft curl on the young girl's head. Lottie eyes meet me with a desperate plea to save her.

"Why don't you take your dish back to the kitchen?" I say. She jumps up so fast, milk spills onto both Pollie and the floor. Pollie's plump lower lip, still stained red from yesterday's makeup, juts out as she pulls her feet up onto the couch and swipes milk away from her legs. She rubs her eyes with the heel of her hand. I move to sit beside her on the couch.

"Pollie, are you still drunk?" I have to ask. I've dealt with Goldie drunk a couple of times but I'm not sure how to deal with anyone else's intoxication. She looks up at me with her round green eyes from under long black lashes like I'm a complete and utter moron.

"No, Captain Sobriety. For the record I wasn't drunk last night either. I was pleasantly warm."

"I'm pretty sure that's not a thing."

"Fine, I was a little tipsy, but I'm all good now."

Feeling the need to change the subject, I motion my hand in her direction as the shoulder of her white t-shirt slips down her olive skin. "How are you this tan? It's winter." I demand, hoping it has nothing to do with a tanning bed. A sad smile touches at her lips and disappears as fast. She pulls her phone out of her bra and starts tapping on the screen. She hands it to me with a picture displayed. The woman in it looks like an older version of Pollie. Black curls spring from a decorative hair wrap and the tanned skin of her cheek is pressed against that of a sandy blonde baby with chubby cheeks.

"That's my mom. She was Iranian," Pollie answered. That baby must be Conrad. I doubt Pollie was ever blonde a day in her life.

"You look a lot like her."

Her head tilts to the side as her eyes drift far away. "Thanks, a lot of people say that. Conrad looks like Daddy." Her gaze focuses on her knees as she sucks in a sharp breath. "Looked like Daddy."

Without another word, she takes the phone from my hands, tucking it back away to safety.

"I don't remember what her voice sounds like," she admits, and I'm not sure if she actually meant to say it aloud. "Like, I used to be able to focus hard and come up with it, but it's been a while since I could do that. How does that happen? How does a person get erased like that?"

The only person I've ever lost is my grandmother and she died when I was three. I can't for a moment imagine what it would be like to lose my mom.

"I'm sorry," is the best response I can muster.

When she turns back, a big toothy grin stretches across her lips. Only the memory of sadness remains on her face. I can tell the conversation is closed by the squareness of her shoulders.

"So," she begins, as though she'd never had a hangover or an emotional episode at all, "what're you up to today?"

"I need to try and tackle the 'teaching your brother' obstacle today." I've put it off for too long, considering it's the whole reason I'm here.

She rolls her eyes as she blows a rogue curl out of her line of vision. "Look, Chicky," she begins, draping her short legs across my lap. It's far too familiar a gesture, but I'm getting the feeling that Pollie has no concept of boundaries. "I'm not going to tell you how to spend your time, but teaching Conrad is never going to happen. You might as well figure out something else to do."

I laugh, tapping my fingers on her shins. "Well, I'm still going to give it a shot if it's all the same to you." She swings her legs off me and back to the floor.

"You do you, buttercup. I'm not a fan of wasting my own time." As she sashays away she calls over her shoulder, "I'm going to use your shower." I suppose that means I'm waiting to take one. I grab my purse off the floor and fish around inside the pockets for a hair-tie. Last night's delicate curls are now twisted into a bird's nest of knots and hairspray. When my hair's secured atop my head, I journey off in search of breakfast.

The kitchen is in the full bustle of morning. Lottie spreads her coloring books across the long breakfast counter, a colored pencil in each hand. Lusta is busy scrubbing the floor while Mr. Potter is busy washing the dishes from breakfast. I still live on homeschool time where you eat whenever you wake up. Schedules have never been my thing. Maybe they have the sugary cereals my Mom won't let me have. That would be zero work for anyone! Mr. Potter spots me lingering in the doorway.

"Good mornin' sleepy head," he sings, catching Lusta's attention. "Can I make you something to eat?" he asks as he dries off the final dish. I'm about to ask about cereal but my rumbling stomach betrays me as the leftover aromas of eggs and bacon fill my nose. Mr. Potter picks up the spatula he washed only a moment ago and waves me away from the sink. "I'll hear no argument, young lady. Go have a seat."

I take a stool next to Lottie. She looks up from her artwork and extends a yellow pencil to me and asks if I'd like to color. I dive happily into a picture of a butterfly. After a belly full of breakfast and a completed artistic masterpiece, Pollie appears in the kitchen dressed in fresh clothes.

"Hey Chicky, go get dressed and come out with me."

I'm about to protest, she already knows what I need to get done today. She puts her hand on my shoulder and leans down close to my ear where no one else could hear.

"It's not a good day for you to try with him," the corners of her mouth turn down in a deep frown. "Besides," she begins again, "I have a quest for us."

"What kind of quest?" I ask, rising to my feet as Lottie swoops in to finish off my French toast.

"You have to come to find out."

I look to Lusta for guidance. My new friend shrugs from underneath the table and says, "Sunday is the day of rest, you know?" Someone should tell *her* that.

I squat down to her level. "I'm here to work and I feel like I haven't done anything yet. Does it really seem like a good idea for me to go out again?"

"You arrived on a weekend. I think you can cut yourself a little slack. Go have some fun, then come back and review everything you need to tonight. Start fresh tomorrow."

I let my head fall back, staring at the ceiling. "I need to go take a shower."

Pollie claps her hands like I've given her a present as she turns her attention back to her phone. "That's fantabulous, it'll give me some time to respond to these DMs. My inbox is flooded!"

After a shower and a fresh change of clothes I'm ready to take on whatever mystery Pollie has for me. No sooner do I turn the knob to close my bedroom door then a voice booms from every direction in the hall.

"STOP!"

My body slams into the wall. "What?!" I shriek, rubbing my elbow. I spot the nearest intercom panel and jam my thumb into the mic button. "You have to stop doing that!"

"I told you, I don't want you hanging around with my sister." Conrad's voice bellows, dripping with authoritative finality. My jaw clenches to the point I'm sure my teeth will shatter.

"Well it's a good thing I don't answer to you, isn't it?"

There are a few *Isabella!*'s shouted over the crackly speakers as I make my way down the hall to the stairs. I'm equal parts too angry and too cocky to consider pausing. I rush down the steps terrified that I'll trip on the laces of my undone boots. I'm more afraid that Conrad will see me fall than worried about hurting myself. Pollie waits for me in the foyer, her black nails clicking against the shiny screen of her phone.

"You ready, Chicky?" she asks, her eyes never moving from the soft blue glow in front of her. I push my glasses up my nose and grab my coat from the closet beside the door.

"I was born ready."

"Seriously?" I squeak, unsure if it's out of joy or terror, as we pull into the parking lot of a pricey looking Christmas tree farm. Audis, Bentleys, and better line the lot. In every direction, families follow their guides out into the field to chop down the perfect tree. By the matching plaid outfits most are wearing, I assume it's also the ideal opportunity to snap a Christmas card photo, too.

"Yeah, I called Daddy after I got out of the shower and told him I needed a Christmas decorating budget. That house is far too dreary for my tastes and I demand some cheer."

I can't get my seat belt unfastened quick enough. I wonder if anyone would look at me strangely if I belly flopped into the snow to make an angel. There hasn't been a snowy Christmas in Harpersgrove since I was a very little girl. Seeing fluffy, white powder this close to Christmas makes me giddy. I can hear a soft giggle pour from Pollie as I bounce from one foot to the other beside her.

"I mean, I was hoping you'd be into it, but I wasn't expecting you to get this excited!" She locks the car and falls into step beside me, our booted feet swishing in tandem through the snow. We make our way toward a hipster lumberjack in pressed jeans and a t-shirt that reads, The Vending Machines. He moves his thick black framed glasses, which have no lenses, up on top of his head as we approach.

"Good morning, ladies," he says, the words run off his tongue like milk poured from a glass bottle. One hundred percent of his attention is on Pollie. Not that it's hard. I'm surprised anyone ever looks away from her. Pollie reminds me a lot of Rosie in that way. They both demand to be seen.

"Will you be needing help cutting down your tree today?" he asks with an over enthusiastic grin. "I have to wait for the other dude to come back, then I can go out with you." His skin flushes as he realizes the double meaning of what he's said. If Pollie noticed she's not letting on, she hasn't looked away from her phone since we walked up. I feel bad for the guy. I'm about to open my mouth to help him out when a voice behind me beats me to the punch.

"That won't be necessary, my fine fellow. I'll help them."

The familiarity of that voice flips me around so fast that I trip over my feet. Gatty stands behind us with a saw slung over his shoulder and broad smile across his mouth of perfect teeth. He looks like a fashion forward Paul Bunyan in a crisp red and green plaid shirt and tan khakis. The hipster lumberjack looks disap-pointed, but manages a "Suit yourself," and walks away.

"Hi," I utter. My cheeks burn hot even in the bitter cold air. Hopefully he chalks it up to windburn.

"Hey yourself," he says, taking a step closer. Even though my instinct is to step back or flee, somehow I manage to keep my feet planted. My heart thumps like a drum against my rib cage and I'm sure everyone is able to hear. I peer over his shoulder and see a pair of people, clearly his parents, decked out in similar outfits.

"Family excursion?" I ask, removing my hand only a moment from the warmth of my pocket to motion to them. He never looks back as he shrugs with an indefinable look in his eye.

"My father's corporate Christmas cards go out this week."

"Where's your tree?" I question at the obvious absence of one amongst his family. There is a crew among them lugging camera equipment, but no Christmas tree. He reaches up and scratches the back of his head and I notice a hint of something peeking from the cuff of his shirt. A tattoo? He doesn't strike me as the type, but that's probably because I associate tattoos with Rosie and Beattie. Gatty is a far cry from either of them.

"This was for a picture. Our family isn't the 'chop a tree down in the forest' type." Gatty answers. Pollie continues to click away on her phone. "But I'm happy to help the two of you out."

"Or, the seasoned professional," Captain Lumberjack chimes in from behind, "could be the one to help you." He doesn't take too kindly to Gatty's invasion on his turf, but Bernard Gattman is all too ready to defend his place.

"My man, you've gotta be in college right?" Gatty asks, sauntering away from me and right up next to the hipster. When Captain Lumberjack doesn't immediately reply, we both take his silence as confirmation. Gatty points over to Pollie.

"Well," Gatty continues, his arm now draped across the stiff shoulders of Captain Lumberjack, "she's sixteen. How about you avoid a felony?" Then, for added effect, he taps the attendant on the bridge of the nose with his index finger.

I can see the rage building up inside of Captain Lumberjack and centering in clenched fists at his sides. Gatty, used to certain privilege, knows the hipster won't hit him or even tell him off. I know that type of arrogance should be a total turn off. The testosterone levels here are off the chart. But for some reason that makes Gatty even more attractive to me. I can tell the attendant wants to punch Gatty in the middle of his perfectly proportioned face. But the status quo hits him first and his body tenses up to absorb the rage. Through a clenched jaw he mutters, "You already have a saw. Go cut down a tree."

Gatty turns back to me with a wide spread grin and says, "Shall we?"

I glance back to Pollie, attention still locked on her DMs. "Poll," I call back, hoping for a response. "You ready?"

"Do you mind picking one with Gatty? It's too frickin' cold out here." She doesn't wait for an answer, already halfway back to the car, her eyes glued on her screen and the keys in her hand. Gatty is laughing when I turn back to him. The saw drapes over his shoulder as he offers me his elbow. I take a deep breath and walk toward him, looping my arm through his. With difficulty, I try to ignore the electric charge that sears through me.

"I don't even know what size tree she wants," I say, making any attempt to break the deafening silence.

"We're talking about the Baxters here, Bella. Bigger is always better."

We walk for what feels like miles, but as I can still hear the Christmas music coming from the parking lot, we can't be far.

"You intrigue me, Miss Southland." Gatty says out of nowhere, forcing me to take an intense interest in the surrounding trees and the cold winter wind on my face.

"Why?" I'm able to mutter, the word coming out like a breath. I'm not sure he hears me until he stops and forces me to look at him. The air freezes in my lungs, making me painfully aware of how out of shape I am. I pray to whatever God is listening that I don't start wheezing in front of this cute boy. He shrugs as he finally picks a tree. It's massive, standing a full two heads taller than Gatty who already towers over me.

"We are a small little unit. Contrary to what you may have seen last night," he explains, kneeling down in the snow. He pushes his sleeves up his defined forearms revealing that indeed, an Asian character of some sort is tattooed on his wrist. I'm standing there alone to the side with no idea what my hands should be doing.

"New people aren't something we're accustomed to here. When a girl decides that reading a book is more fun than the party I dropped a ton of money on, I take an interest."

It's like I'm standing naked in the middle of this farm of trees. Even though Gatty focuses his attention down, on the trunk of the tree, it's like he's staring right at me.

"I don't really do parties," I say, fighting through a mouth full of cotton. It takes everything in me not to implode on myself, but I command the new, more confident Bella to take the reins. "I have my own crew. I'm not really one of the popular kids back home."

"I like you even more now." I can hear the grin in his voice when he says it. I've never thought of my social ostracization as a selling feature.

"You okay?" he asks after I've been quiet too long. He twists toward me on his knees, hands still grasping the trunk of the tree. It looks like he's barely made a dent in chopping it down.

"Do you need some help?"

"Think you can hold it steady for me?" he replies.

I wade through the snow that's deeper here on the hill to stand across from him, my feet planted on either side of the tree. I wrap my mitten covered hands over the center of the trunk, holding tight as Gatty saws back and forth, the vibrations sending chills up my arms. A few beads of perspiration form at his temples and I can't take my eyes off of him. I've never stared at a boy for any significant amount of time before. I'm always quick to divert my eyes before they see me. There's something calming about being in his presence that keeps me focused.

I hear a crack as the tree breaks free. Unfortunately it breaks free onto me with all of its weight falling into my hands. In this moment, I know the true limit of my strength. It is less than one Christmas tree. Falling backwards with my hands still clenched around the bark, I can feel the weight of every embarrassment of my life coming to the surface at once. Thicker girls don't always do unflattering things gracefully and I'm even less graceful than most. I hope the ground doesn't shake when I hit it. The pillow of snow at my back soaks through my leggings and into my hair. I close my eyes and let the humiliation sink in. If Gatty didn't think I was a helpless dork before, he must now. Before my eyes can reopen, the weight of the tree is thrown from me. Gatty's at my side with his hands on my shoulders, running up and down my arms checking for injuries.

"Oh my God, Bella!" he exclaims, panic contorting his face as he checks me for harm. "I'm sorry, are you okay? Did the tree hurt anything? God, are you bleeding? I'm so stupid! I didn't think it was going to fall back like that."

He's talking faster than I can process the words. I awkwardly grab his elbows. It's the only part of him I can reach, and I squeeze him there to calm him down.

"Gatty, " I start, "I'm fine, I promise. The only thing that hurts here is my pride."

The steel gray, overcast sky takes my attention. My cheeks burn too brightly to consider looking directly at him. It doesn't seem to matter though, because the next thing I know his face is entering my field of vision. I can't identify the look on his face. It's not one I've ever seen before. His eyes twinkle with a question that knits between them. Even though I can't define it exactly, I find myself answering "yes" with my whole body. His tongue juts out from his mouth, parting his lips as his left hand moves to rest across my body in the snow. I cannot breathe. His free hand reaches up to tuck some hair behind my ear and his fingers linger on my cheek.

Before I can process what is happening, he' leans down toward me, his eyes closing as he moves. But I don't dare close mine. I want to remember every moment of this. Gatty's hand reaches around the back of my neck to cradle my head and pull me closer. My eyes are still frozen open and I'm panicked. I have no idea what I'm doing. My lips part, but aren't moving. My breathing, forced and labored, comes out of my mouth like a whistle. My hands cement to my sides, fingernails cutting into my palms. My discomfort must be as obvious as I fear because Gatty stops attempting to kiss my dead fish of a body and his eyes open.

"You okay?" he asks, his thumb moving against my cheek as a giddy feeling rushes through me. I have to force it down to keep laughter from bubbling out of my mouth. My head bobs up and down a little too enthusiastically and I wish the ground would open and swallow me whole. I decide, humiliating as it might be, that honesty is the best I have.

"I, um, I don't really know what I'm doing." My voice trails off and I have to look away. I can't face the look of horror that must be flashing across his face. His hand moves back to my neck and tugs on my hair, forcing my gaze back to him. Imagine my surprise when I don't see him cringing at all, but rather smiling down at me. His lips move closer to mine as he breathes against my mouth, "Relax."

I let my arms loosen and my eyes close. I opt to follow Gatty's lead. I've seen the way other people kiss their boyfriends. It can get pretty intense, way too much tongue. I'm thankful that he doesn't take it there. He must sense my inexperience, because he doesn't try to put his tongue in my mouth. I don't think I could take it if he tried. When he finally pulls away, he's grinning like a fool.

"Better when you're relaxed, right?" I don't get the chance to respond before he hops to his feet and extends a hand to pull me up. "We'd better get back before Pollie thinks I kidnapped you."

I'm supposed to move right now and, what, act like nothing transpired? I kissed a boy! An incredibly good looking one at that. Now I'm supposed to move on with my life like it's normal? I have no idea how to do that. I give him my hand and hold my breath, praying that I'm not too heavy for him to lift, but he sweeps me off the ground in one swoop. My heartbeat thumps in my ears. Exhilaration pulses through me. Is this why skinny girls always have guys picking them up? I get it now if that's why. There's a rush.

The silence hums low around us and I've been giggling like an idiot to myself the whole time. I need to say something before he thinks I'm completely crazy. I thank him a little too loudly, certain

I'll die of embarrassment. I wish the tree would fall back on top of me and crush me dead. A teasing glimmer flashes through Gatty's eyes before he squeezes my side. A self conscious flare bursts inside me at the idea of him feeling my rolls.

"You are more than welcome," he responds, saving me from myself. His head nods back in the direction of the parking lot. "Let's get back."

"So," Pollie begins, holding onto the "O" for far longer than necessary. "Took you two a while to get back with the tree."

I *mhmm* as I watch the foliage whip past my window. New York is beautiful in the winter. I've never noticed if Maryland is this pretty. "And you know, the back of your coat's all wet and your hair's kinda messed up," she continues. She steals glances at me instead of keeping her eyes on the road.

"Bella!" she exclaims, unsatisfied with my mumbling. "Did you hook up with Gattman in the snow?"

My jaw hits my knees as outrage radiates off of me. "I did not!" I shriek.

"Oh yeah, sure you didn't," she teases. Shame seeps all the way through my body.

"Pollie! I didn't. I kissed him, but that's all." Something that was so monumental to me fifteen minutes ago seems like nothing right now. I miss the high of my first kiss already. This feels like slut shaming. I've heard Lucy Wilcox say awful things to Goldie and Rosie in the past, but that couldn't be happening to me this fast. I'm so lost in my own downward spiral, I don't notice that Pollie is laughing at me.

"O.M.G. Chicky, calm down! I don't think you're the kind of girl to screw a guy in the middle of a field filled with families. In fact, I'm a little surprised that you even made out with him."

I don't know what makes me feel worse, the possible slut shaming or the insinuation that I'm an ice queen prude. Of course, the answer is both. They're both worse. Why are these always the only two options for girls? Couldn't it be happy? Isn't my first kiss supposed to be a story I get to tell my children one day while staring out of a window, remembering the good old days and drinking cocoa? This memory will completely ruin that! Armed with a pouty lower lip, and arms crossed to boot, I grumble a standoffish response.

Pollie isn't fazed in the least. Her eyes roll back so far back in her head that I'm worried her retinas may detach. "Oh please," she sighs, shaking her head. "I'm saying that you're a girl and Gatty is…Gatty."

I'm not sure what that means.

"It was nice," I respond, my voice vanishing in my throat.

"That is not a word I've heard used to describe him much."

"I always imagine the perfect love story. I like living in that little bubble, no matter how unrealistic it is," I admit without the tiniest hint of shame that I would normally feel.

"What's the perfect love story then?" she asks me.

I roll my head to look at her. "Now that is the question."

Pollie, of course, takes the small end of the tree, leaving me to lug the heavy trunk through the door. She tells me that normally they get trees three times the size of this one, so we're lucky for the small size. I beg to differ. We are barely inside the door when a familiar voice booms through the speakers.

"Palarma! I told you no!"

Pollie drops her end, leaving me with all the dead weight. The tree crashes to the floor with a defeated thud. She struts over to the intercom panel and presses the red button.

"You are free to come down and try to stop me, brother darling, but Daddy already approved it."

"Palarma Amal Baxter, I told you no!" Conrad's rage vibrates through the speakers. He middle-named her. I only get middle-named by my parents when I'm in serious trouble.

"Stop me," she sings into the mic before skipping back to pick up her part of the tree. To my surprise, Conrad doesn't respond. With pride, Pollie starts whistling "Jingle Bells".

Even though I know he can't hear her, I'm sure Conrad knows what's happening. We take the tree into the living room. To my surprise, multiple boxes of decorations line the walls in tall piles.

In the corner by the television, surrounded by a sea of tinsel, Lottie fills the tree stand with water, then she hops out of the way, allowing Pollie and I to place the tree inside.

"Where did all this come from?" I ask Lottie.

"Mama knows where to find anything," she responds and I doubt there's anything in this world Lusta can't find, or do for that matter.

Pollie dives head first into one of the hard plastic tubs, popping out with sparkle in her hair and on her cheeks. Her plump lower lip pouts out as she turns to Lottie.

"Where is the box of ornaments?" she says, obnoxiously slow.

Lottie, ever the cool cat, turns to me and asks, "What does her royal highness want?"

"She's looking for the box of ornaments." Lottie's brow creases as she circles the containers. She snaps her fingers against the side of her leg and signs, "It's still in the attic." Her little face is crestfallen. I suppose she's already made the trip enough times that she can't stand to do it again.

"Where's the attic? I'll get it," I say. Lottie doesn't get a chance to respond before Pollie hops to my side.

"Chicky, you're a doll! It's up all the stairs, the door right by where we first met." And, with no other instruction, she dives head first into a box full of tinsel.

The stair climb has me huffing and puffing like a wolf from a nursery rhyme by the time I reach the door. Through it a dark stairwell leads to another door at the top of the flight. It's on the climb up those stairs that the smell overcomes me. The floral perfume hits me like a wall with its natural sweetness. I grip the handle of the second door and swing it open. My breath catches at what's on the other side. I'm not a girl that's impressed by flowers, but this is the kind of thing that can change someone's mind.

The room is a rooftop greenhouse, overflowing with roses in every direction. Full pink and red ones to closed purples and peaches and every variety in between. I've never seen something this beautiful in all my life. I breathe in, letting the aroma settle into my lungs and tears flood my eyes. I lift my arms up like I'm dancing in a snowstorm and start to turn in a circle, the beauty consuming me. That is until I turn all the way to my left.

I stop dead, the world halting on a dime as my arms collapse to my sides and my eyes bug wide. On the opposite side of the room stands Conrad, no veil of darkness or black hoodie, only the boy everyone's prepared me to see. On the right of his body, he's the guy from the picture that Pollie showed me. His sandy blonde hair brushes in waves across his forehead and against his ear. A blue eye peeks out from behind thick, black eyelashes against tan olive skin much like his sister's. The left side is something profoundly different. He lost his hair on that side, including his eyelashes and brow. His lips, plump and pink on the right, are glassy and milky on the left, as is most of his skin. That delicate, blistered look makes him appear fragile, a stark contrast to his angry, growling voice. What I had not expected were the things missing. I had wondered in the kitchen that first night if he had lost fingers and I can see now that he has. Two from his left hand, the pinky and ring finger. The place where his left ear should be is a gnarled ball of flesh and it seems he's lost some of his upper eyelid too. When he blinks his eye doesn't close all the way. He looks weak and breakable on that side, but he stands strong and tall like nothing's wrong in the slightest.

His eyes scan me from left to right like reading the pages of a fascinating book. I'm learning at this moment that when Conrad Baxter looks at you, he consumes you. He memorizes you like you're the only thing in the world. It's beautiful, all encompassing, and terrifying at the same time. For a long while he says nothing and neither do I, too frozen in my spot to move. Then, when he finally breaks the silence, his voice is raspy, like someone who hasn't spoken in days. "You finally see the monster," he hisses with venom spewing from his words. "Was it everything you were promised?"

From deep down inside me I harness newfound confidence. I square my shoulders, trying to seem bigger than I am against his massive frame. "I've seen worse."

This is a total, utter, and complete lie, but something flashes across his face. A hint of amusement, maybe?

"What makes you think you have the right to come up here?" he sneers as he stalks past me. He's a guy with a lot of pride. I can tell by his labored walk that he's forcing himself to be as normal as possible. I fold my hands in front of my stomach, setting up a barrier between us. I feel like a little girl chastised by her father.

"Pollie asked me to grab more decorations. I thought this was might be the attic."

He scoffs like my stupidity is too much for him to process. A breathy chuckle spills from his mouth as he mocks me, "And you believed that the attic smelled like roses? I know how potent that smell is when you open the door." He picks up a watering can and heads back in my direction toward a tea rose plant popping in pinks. "Or did you think we accessed our attic through a greenhouse? That wouldn't be very efficient would it?"

The sarcasm drips from his words like the little stream of drool that trails from the side of his mouth that he can't easily control. My instinct is to start crying. Every part of me wants to cry. That's how I react to bullies, the Lucy Wilcoxes of the world. Not this time. I plant my feet and dig my fists into my hips like a superhero, narrowing my eyes at Conrad.

"You don't have to be an ass." If I didn't know better, I'd take the flick of his eyebrow as him being impressed, but I'm certain he's still mocking me.

"The precious princess has a mouth. I didn't think wholesome little girls like you spoke with such words." He's laughing now and I can tell it's affecting his breathing, but he can't seem to stop himself. A thought crosses my mind and the words are out of my mouth before I can pull them back.

"Just because you have a disability doesn't mean you get to be a jerk!"

His laugh ceases with a wheezing cough as the room falls to a booming silence. When his breathing settles, he eyes me with a renewed fire that in essence extinguishes mine. Any bravery I felt a moment ago is gone now. His jaw flexes beneath his skin as he hisses through his teeth.

"What makes you think for a second you know what I'm entitled to? You don't know a damn thing!" The volume of his voice raises and his pitch drops. It's like I'm being pulled through a black hole, sucking me in deeper and deeper.

"What are you still doing here? Do you want to gawk at the deformed beast?

Even in his injured state, I can't help but be aware of Conrad's intimidating physical presence, like a baited bear.

"Well, I want you to get your money's worth at the freakshow!" he shouts as he uses his good arm to pull his shirt over his head then casts it aside onto some of the roses. He lifts his arms and bellows, "Take a good, long look!"

Although I don't want to see it, my eyes won't pull away. From the months he spent immobile after the accident, his body should have withered away to nothing. Somehow the right side of his chest and stomach look normal. They've lost a bit of their definition, but it's nothing compared to the left. The damage starts at about his belly button where the glassy, translucent skin takes over. It's a solid, hard mass in which every muscle is indistinguishable from the one beside it. I have the sudden urge to touch him and see if his skin feels as much like marble as it looks. Luckily, I'm still holding onto a piece of my sanity and keep my hands at my sides. Tears brim and I can't stop one from rolling hot down my cheek. He growls at my emotion and pulls his shirt back over his head.

"Now you're going to cry? I don't need your pity."

I swipe my eyes with the back of my hand. "Don't flatter your-self," I snarl, taking back my ferocity. "I don't pity you in the least. You did something stupid and dangerous and you're paying the consequences. I couldn't feel sorry for you if I tried!"

My throat burns from the unfamiliar harshness of my words. He puffs out his chest in a feeble attempt to keep the upper hand, but I can tell he's standing a little less tall.

"Then why are you crying?"

I take brave steps toward him, my heels hitting the dirt dusted floor with the force of military boots on a battleground. I'm only inches from him when I stop. I measure only to the level of his heart, if he even has one.

"Because I'm angry! I'm angry at you for being a jerk and at me for reacting. Mostly I'm angry that you thought for a second that I was weeping for you. I will never cry for you, Conrad Baxter."

I demand to have the last word and storm away before he has a chance to say anything. I almost expect some dramatic, soap opera worthy moment where he runs after me, calling my name, but this is reality. He doesn't say a word. I hurry down the stairs, forgetting about the box of decorations. In the living room, Pollie and Lottie know something's wrong.

"What happened?" Pollie asks.

"Your brother happened," I growl.

I see the concern etched on Lottie's little face and I know I should feel awful for leaving without explanation, but I can't take it. I spot my bag on the floor beside the Christmas tree and grab it. I don't stop moving until I'm in the safety of my car. I catch a glimpse of curtains rustling in an upstairs window, but I refuse to give that guy another moment of my attention. I zip out of the driveway, spinning gravel under my tires and peel away. I need to put some distance between me and Conrad Baxter. I want to call the girls and scream, but I know that won't help anything. Seeing my friends in my safe space of the pie shop will depress me and probably make me cry. I tap the map app on my home screen and say, "Find pie near me." I need some comfort of home.

Della's Diner of Deliciousness does not give off the warm and welcoming aura as Hap-PIE-ly Ever After does. It tries too hard to be a fifties diner with its chrome decor and waitresses pulled right from the cast of *Grease*. I half expect to hear "Beauty School Dropout" spill from the speakers of the jukebox.

An older woman named Maude with a pronounced mole and a smoker's cough approaches my table with a glass of water. She places the smudged cup with cloudy ice in front of me and I try not to cringe. If this is the water, I'm a little terrified to see the food.

"Did you decide what you want, sweet pea?" Maude rasps.

"A piece of pecan pie please." Maude scribbles it down on her pad and shuffles away with my menu under her arm. I pull my phone out of my pocket, knowing that seeing the girls will make me sad. But my homesickness can't be fixed by this depressing diner. I need my people. I decide to video chat Rosie, certain she'll be at the shop. The camera jostles like a student made "found footage" film before Rosie's face comes into frame.

"Bells!" she exclaims with a toothy grin. "How are you doing, cupcake?" I can feel tears at the back of my eyes, but they don't surface. As much as I'd like my friends to jump in their cars to come here and save me, I don't really want to be the girl who only calls to cry.

"I'm hanging in there." This new brave facade doesn't have to be strictly for people I've just met. I can use it on my friends too. "How did the Christmas decorating go?"

She hops off the table and says, "Allow me to show you."

When she opens the door, it's exactly what I needed to see. Colored Christmas lights line the front door and the seams of the walls. Our normal alert bells hanging on the front door have been replaced with a set of jingle bells. A wreath with a red bow rests on the door beneath them. Sparkly gold and white garland hangs in symmetrical loops from the ceiling clear across the shop. In the far corner sits a modest sized Christmas tree decorated in blinking lights and chains of construction paper rings.

"What do you think, Hells Bells?" Blanche exclaims. She jumps into frame, her freckled forehead filling my screen. "We did pretty good, didn't we?" The pride radiating from her fills my heart.

"You did great," I say as I settle my hands in my lap. "Is it just the two of you?"

"Nixie's hiding around her somewhere," Rosie responds as she flips the phone around to face her. Blanche sits beside her at the counter.

"Yeah, Goldie and Elle are out on a double date because they're all cool and have boyfriends now," Blanche groans with a shake of her head.

"Who is Goldie dating?" I ask.

They both roll their eyes at my question. "Check this," Rosie says, holding her hand up to the camera. "Dubuque Reyes."

My entire face puckers up like I sucked on an especially sour lemon. Everyone in Harpersgrove knows Dub Reyes. He's one of the Lucy Wilcox crowd, on the football team and generally a brute. I remember he once pushed Rosie in the mud when we were in middle school.

"Why on earth would she do that?"

They both shrug.

"How's it going Bella Boo?" Rosie asks.

I want to keep things light and telling them about the horror that is Conrad would be the opposite of that. I go the other way.

"I kind of think I might have met a guy..." my voice trails off as my friends erupt into a hurricane of giggles and shrieks.

"More words please!" Rosie squeaks.

"What guy?" Blanche demands, and they both go back and forth until their voices reach a pitch only dogs can hear. Suddenly, the camera jostles and Nixie comes solely into view.

"These two need to remember how to breathe. Talk to me now," she says as she settles beside Rosie. "There's a guy, and?"

"The day I got here, I went to a party."

"You go to parties now?" Rosie demands.

"Okay, I'm not a freak at a circus sideshow," I snapped, kicking back in my seat.

"Calm down Sassy Pants," Blanche chimes in, tilting the phone in her direction. "We'll be quiet."

I proceed to tell them the tale of Gatty, from the party to the Christmas tree lot. They listen intently like a group of cats watching a goldfish in a bowl. The only break in concentration comes when my pie arrives. As Maude sits the plate down in front of me, Rosie shrieks through the phone's little speaker.

"What in the name of all that is good and holy is that?" she demands, her finger jabbing at the screen.

"It's pie," I answer, picking up my fork and spearing through the caramelized pecans into the gooey center.

"If that looks like pie to you, then I have failed," she barks, her eyebrows knitting close together in a fierce scowl.

When the bite hits my tongue, I have to admit that it's less than appetizing. To a novice, I'm sure it would be fine. However, to a palate refined by Rosie's baking skills, I know that the filling is too sweet and watery. The pecans are crystallized hard enough to crack a tooth. Rosie's arms cross over her chest as she waits for an answer. Somewhere in the distance I feel Maude's eyes laser onto me waiting to see what I think of the pie.

"It's fine," I say through a forced grin as I try to chew on the rock hard pecans. My mother will kill me if I break a tooth. Rosie's eyes narrow as she zooms the camera view closer to her winged eyes.

"You lie through your teeth young lady! Take me to the baker at once. I want a word!"

Before I can respond to her absurdity, someone collapses down across from me in the booth and smacks my phone flat on the table. Impossible beauty stares back at me as Parker settles back in the seat with overwhelming judgement.

"Well, look who it is," she sneers, flipping her perfect blonde curls behind her shoulder.

"What's happening? The screen went blank! Send a dolphin call if you're in danger, Bella!" Nixie's muffled voice yells from my phone.

"Good God, calm down!" Blanche snaps back, and it would make me laugh if it weren't for Parker now staring at me. Man, if looks could kill.

"What can I do for you, Parker?" I ask, my sweaty palms moving to my lap, fingers flexing over my knees. The voices on my phone have grown silent. I'm not sure if they hung up or if they are still there, listening as intently as me.

"What's your deal? Why is everyone obsessed with you?" I can promise no one has ever been obsessed with me. My confusion must be obvious. Her lips pinch tight with a huff.

"You're all Gatty wants to talk about today."

Well that can't possibly be true, there's so little to say. I can't help the little thrill that runs through me though. Of course, it's ruined by the realization that if I'm "all he can talk about" then he talks a lot to Parker.

"And Pollie brought you to our party when she knows we're a closed group."

I tug on the arms of my sweater and take another bite of my pie. "She was being nice," I mumble through the mouthful. Parker seems amused and the pie turns to ash in the pit of my stomach.

"What is it about a fat, poor, ugly nobody that has everyone fascinated? Because I am clearly missing something."

Her words are cruel and cold. It feels like I'm drowning in the open room when a familiar sound anchors me.

"What did that heffer say?!" Rosie shrieks, her voice echoing off the table. They didn't hang up. "Bella, pick us up so we can see this piece of trash."

I reach down and pick up the phone to see the fierce scowls across the face of my three friends. Rosie is removing her earrings like she's getting ready for a street fight and Nixie is crying. Blanche, ever the voice of reason, says, "What's your plan exactly, Rose? Punch the chick through the phone?" Blanche looks back to me. "Turn me around so I can see her."

I face the phone outward on the table between Parker and me. I'm surprised Parker is still sitting here, waiting for some kind of punishment. Blanche turns her protective rage on the blonde bombshell.

"Hey rich bitch," she snaps. "Why don't you leave and score your ecstasy or cocaine somewhere else and leave Bella alone?"

Drugs? I mean, it did seem strange to me that someone like Parker would be in a roadside diner. The place definitely doesn't sport any Michelin Stars, but my mind never would have made that leap. Parker flinches and I get the feeling that Blanche is right. Her face returns to its cold, stony expression before she shifts herself out of the booth.

"Later, Chubs," she whispers. Her words are like ice in my ear. Without a thought, my arms rush to cover the rolls around my midsection, hiding myself away.

"What did she say?!" Rosie shouts and I can't bring myself to look down. I'm going to start crying soon and I don't want them to see. All three of my friends are on their feet. Tears stain Nixie's face, her lower lip quivering. She resembles more of an angry, orange kitten than a blubbering mess.

"Don't listen to that girl, Bella," Nixie sniffs as she swipes at her eyes. "She's jealous of how great you are." It's very like Nixie to jump to my defense by telling me I'm beautiful, or special, or perfect.

"Thanks ,Nix," I mumble while swallowing the emotions crushing my throat. When I thought a call to the girls might make me cry, I hadn't expected this. I take another big bite of the unsatisfactory pie and hate how comforting and humiliating it is. I'm overwhelmed with the fear that everyone in the diner is watching me. Folks always seem to stare at heavier people when there's food involved. It doesn't matter if it's the same or even less than skinny people eat, they only gawk at us. I push the plate away as fresh tears brim my eyes because all I want to do is shovel the rest of the piece in my mouth.

"Bella," Rosie's soft voice calls out to me from the phone. I can't make eye contact with her. Rosie is curvy in all the good ways. She can't understand what it's like to curve everywhere and I can't take her pity.

"I need to get going, guys. I'm sure the people at the house will be looking for me." I don't wait for them to respond before I click to end the call. I hate good-byes.

After paying my bill and bidding farewell to Maude, I return to my car. Nestled into the cozy warmth, I wish the seat would swallow me up. I'm about to start the engine when my phone starts to ring. Instead of the girls calling me back, I'm surprised to see my father's perfectly bald head appear on the screen. I'm a bad daughter and hit the ignore button. It's too much right now. Guilt swims through me the second I make the choice. I open my phone type into a quick text message. *I'm fine, can't talk.* My father's voice will break me right now. He responds almost immediately with *I love you Peanut.* I barely get my phone back in my purse before the sobs take over.

CHAPTER EIGHT

When the house comes into full view, I feel like making a dramatic U-turn and head back to Harpersgrove. Let the Baxters keep my things. I never liked my clothes much anyway. Realizing that I'm acting like a child, I punch the code into the gate and wait for it to swing back. Disappointment settles in at the lack of decoration outside. I had hoped to see lights on the outside trees or around the front door and windows. I guess Lottie and Pollie gave up on the Christmas-ification when I left. I don't blame them. I didn't exactly leave them in the holly, jolly spirit.

As I turn the door knob, I can feel the warm glow of Christmas before I see it. The foyer and living room overflows with small white Christmas bulbs. They line the doorways, wrap around the railing on the stairs, and fill bowls on the enormous table.

I follow a string of lights into the living room and beam at what I find there. The fireplace on the far wall is draped in holly garland and red and white stockings hang from Santa Claus hooks. A glittery pair of reindeers sit in one corner of the room, surrounded by ornate boxes covered in red and green foil wrapping paper. The tree stands at its full height in the opposite corner. Lights sparkle against silver garland; the tree appears covered in newly fallen snow. I expected the ornaments to be something impersonal, like from a catalog. It's a pleasant surprise to see handmade, popsicle stick reindeer, cotton ball Santas, and cardboard picture frames filled with photos of grinning, toothless children and adoring parents. There are plastic toys and glass icicles in every shape and size the mind could imagine. I could stand here for days and keep finding new treasures hidden inside.

"Our mom didn't have Christmas as a kid." Pollie's voice startles me from behind. I whip around to see her curled up on the couch, staring at the tree like I am. "It became her favorite thing after she married my dad. She always went full out with the decorating."

"I can see that," I say as I move around the tree.

"I mean, you'll never see a nativity scene on the grounds of any of our houses," she continues, coming to my side, her fingers tracing the memories on the pine needles. "But, man, did that woman love Santa Claus!" She lets out a laugh that stretches all the way down to her toes. "I'm pretty sure I've seen *Rudolph the Red-Nosed Reindeer* more times than anyone in history. Con and I still watch it every year." The mere mention of her brother sobers our mood. We both shift our attention back to the soft glow of the lights.

"Look," Pollie says, breaking the tension. "Whatever he did, I'm sorry. He's not a bad guy, just a little beaten up and bruised." I appreciate that she didn't use burned as her metaphor. I don't think I could have taken it.

"It's not your job to apologize for him, Pollie."

"Of course it is, I'm his sister. I'm sure if you were in my shoes you'd be doing the same for your brother." I decide that it's best not to mention that Jonah would never say what Conrad had. I know the point she's trying to make.

"I don't want you to leave," Pollie blurts out, her eyes never straying from the tree.

"I can't exactly go anywhere." I can only imagine the hell my mother would raise if I came home early. She'd have a coronary.

Pollie throws her arm over my shoulders, squeezing me into her side. "You're a person with free will and a car. If you wanted to quit, you could. Yeah, you'd stop getting paid and your parents wouldn't be too thrilled, but you could leave if you wanted to. I'm saying that I hope you don't."

I suppose she's right. There's nothing forcing me to stay. I could get in my car and peel away screaming in the opposite direction. Away from this town and Parker and especially Conrad. Of course, that would also mean running from Lusta and Lottie and Pollie and Gatty. I can't do that. Not yet, anyway.

"I'm staying," I say definitively, letting my fingers trail the edges of a skiing snowman ornament. "The job was to tutor and tutor I shall."

"I'm glad to hear you say that," Pollie says. Reaching down into a cardboard box, she pulls a silver star tree topper out of it. "I thought it was only right that you add the last detail."

I reach up on my tiptoes and secure the star in its place. Not an easy feat when you stand a foot shorter than the tree. We both take a few steps back and admire our handiwork.

"Now it's perfect," Pollie remarks with a smile. "I think it's time for me to head home. My dad's going to think Conrad threw me in the dungeon." I wonder for a moment if this place actually has a dungeon.

After Pollie and I say good night, I head back upstairs to my bedroom, pulling off my shoes as I go. It's only a little past seven, yet I'm drained to the point that I might fall over. I open the door and jump from my skin at the sight of Conrad sitting on my bed.

"What in the literal hell?!" I shriek. This is the opposite of the relaxing moment I need. He looks uneasy, rising to his feet and holding a package against his good side. His familiar black hoodie has made its return, but he's left the hood down this time.

"Relax," he says. "I need to talk to you for a minute."

I'm amazed how little his physical appearance shocks me this time. I thought it would be something I could never get used to. But I'm mad and I barely notice it at all.

"What? You didn't yell at me enough earlier?"

He sighs and rubs the palm of his bad hand against the shiny surface of his head. He winces, only a moment, as though it's a surprise not to find hair there.

"You caught me off guard," he explains, taking a step toward me. I instinctively step back and he stops, a breath exasperatedly wheezing its way out of his lungs. "You have to understand, I don't let people see me like this!" he exclaims, his voice booming. It hits me in steady jabs in the pit of my stomach. "That's why people don't come here. That's why I don't go out. I don't want anyone to see me. Not the people I know and definitely not strangers. But I didn't have the right to speak to you the way I did and I'm sorry for that."

"Wow," I'm able to squeak out past the lump in my throat. "Did Pollie lay into you that much? That was some speech."

Color floods the good side of his face. "It wasn't Pollie," he mutters, his eyes casting back down to the floor. He lets out a low roar. "The little one can be pretty intense."

"Lottie? You talked to Lottie?" His lips purse up towards his nose.

"Who needs words? She stood with her fists on her hips and scowled at me until I cowered." I try, I really do. There's no helping the laughter that comes at the thought of Lottie conquering the mighty creature that is Conrad Baxter.

"You laugh," he continues, the red blush spreading further down his neck. "But it was worse than any look of disapproval from a parent." I can tell he's thinking of his mom by the way his eyes glaze over. Wanting to lighten the mood, I motion to the package he's balancing against his hip.

"What's that?"

"My mom taught me when I was a kid that if I ever did wrong by a girl I was required to apologize with flowers. You know I have plenty of those." The antiquated ritual of giving flowers to women rears its ugly head once again. "I got the feeling you might appreciate this more."

Intrigue gets the better of me and I reach for the present. Our fingers brush in the exchange and the heat left behind reminds me of a stolen moment in an Austen novel. I tear at the paper with painful scrutiny, like a member of the bomb squad going at an explosive. The soft leather covers of three books fall into my palms. I hand the discarded paper over to Conrad who backs away as soon as he can. I read the covers on the spines to myself. *Daisy Miller*, *Under the Lilacs*, and *The Chrysanthemums*. My stunned silence quiets the room.

"You got me flowers."

His hands are folded behind his back and he scuffs his foot on the floor. It makes him look like a shy little boy. The threat is all but gone.

"How did you know I'd prefer books?" I manage to ask.

"The cameras," he winces and says, "I saw you in the library with Lottie." The damn cameras again. Of course, this time I can't say that their result is completely displeasing. "You looked happy. At home."

I hug the books to my chest. They're stories I've read before, but these copies are much more than books. They're an olive branch.

"Thank you for this Conrad," I say with a genuine smile. His hands dig down into the pocket of his sweatshirt and he rocks back onto his heels.

"So, school," he starts and I can't help the way my eyes go wide.

"Wow," I laugh, trying and failing not to be smug. "That must have been some look she gave you."

"You have no idea," he says.

"Can we start tomorrow?" His body curls in, betraying how uncomfortable he is, so I don't torture him with a long speech.

"Tomorrow," I respond instead.

As he passes me to leave he pauses at my side and whispers, "Take it easy on me okay? It's been a while." I know he means schooling, but for some reason my mind lingers. Maybe he means more?

When I'm alone once again, the daunting task in front of me settles heavy like a suffocating cloud. We're starting tutoring in the morning and I've never been less prepared for anything in my life. I grab the stack of books and folders that I have to work with and spread them out on the bed. It doesn't matter if it takes all night, I'll be ready.

The next morning at breakfast, it feels like the only sleep I got was a blink of my eyes, but I'm invigorated. I have an outline, a plan, and color coded folders to boot!

As I munch on my pancakes at the breakfast bar, Lusta and Mr. Potter rush Lottie through her morning routine to get her off to the bus for school. It's a complex ballet that they've clearly perfected over time. Just as Lusta settles down to sit, someone clears their throat at the kitchen entrance. Conrad's frame fills the entire doorway. The favorite black hoodie is back with the hood pulled as far over his forehead as it can go. His hands ball into fists at the sides of his gray sweatpants that expose bare feet. It's too cold for that. Lusta seems overwhelmed at the sight of him as a grin stretches across her face from ear to ear.

"Well look who's up and about this morning!" she says, hurrying over to him and placing her hands on his arms. I can tell he tries to hide it, but the flinch that runs through his body at the contact is impossible to miss.

"Do you want breakfast?" Lusta asks, pulling Conrad forward, his jaw working back and forth under the skin of his cheek. "Mr. Potter will make you something." Mr. Potter in turn raises his eyebrows in protest, but a fiery look from Lusta shuts him up immediately. Lusta's maternal and protective nature where Conrad is concerned is rather endearing.

Conrad's shoulders stiffen every time Lusta touches him. His eyes squint in pain when her hands move.

"No," he says sharply. He deftly maneuvers himself out from under Lusta's grasp; his breathing visibly evens out when he's free. "I wouldn't want to put Patrick out."

The twitch that pulses through Mr. Potter is undeniable. I get the feeling he doesn't like being referred to by his first name, at least not by a teenager.

"I'd prefer we get this all over with, Isabella." Conrad's tone is pushy, in his normal way, but there's a hint of pleading in his words. I push back from the counter with my breakfast in hand and tell him to lead the way. I'm just as eager to get this started.

I suppose I should have assumed where we would go. It's not like I had discovered a classroom in any of the forgotten spaces here. I did not anticipate however, how difficult it would be to eat pancakes in the greenhouse.

"Would you like to go back to the kitchen?" he asks as he opens his laptop.

In very unladylike fashion, I fold and shovel the remaining half of a pancake into my mouth. I die a little inside as a look of shock mixed with disgust freezes on Conrad's face. Most people have the decency to look away. I try to brush it off, but that familiar sizzling feeling of complete embarrassment settles in my stomach, my cheeks warming. I've never chewed so fast in my life.

"See, all done," I murmur, picking up my own tablet and one of the many textbooks we have to get through. "I was thinking we'd start with calculus. How does that sound to you?"

"Like a thrill from which I may never recover," he mutters flatly, pulling something from his pocket. It's a pair of thick, coke bottle glasses that remind me of something my grandfather would wear. They sit unevenly because of the state of his ears. If I didn't think it would upset him, I'd laugh.

"This side doesn't work well. These are supposed to help," he says, motioning to his left eye with the creeping milkiness along its edges.

"And do they?" I hug the book to my chest. It's like I need a physical barrier to ask him any personal questions.

"We are about to find out." I avert my eyes to give him some semblance of privacy as he tries to conform. Opening the calculus book, I look upon Conrad as much as I dare.

"I know it's been a while since you've done much schoolwork. I honestly believe that math can be a 'use it or lose it' subject. If anything gets confusing, let me know and we'll slow down."

A groan like that of a sleeping dragon rumbles in this throat.

"Thank you, Miss Southland," he says in a mocking tone that I less than appreciate. He was the one to ask me to go easy. I slam my book shut. This will not be the way we start. He takes note and apologizes, blaming it on old habits.

"Why haven't you worn your glasses yet?" I ask, steering the conversation in a different direction. He's still acclimating to the world behind lenses. His eyes squint, pushing the glasses up and down his nose.

"I don't know. I figured I'm already deformed. I didn't have to look like a nerd too." I peer up at him over the edge of my own black frames. My eyes narrow as I digest his use of nerd as an insult. I always considered it a badge of honor.

"Not that you're a nerd," he corrects, half-heartedly.

"It's okay. I definitely am, but I don't see it as a bad thing." An unspoken question flashes across his face. I close the book against my finger to mark the page. I need to stand up in defense of nerds everywhere. I feel like the unofficial ambassador of awkward teenagers. "I'm smart, stupid smart. Smart to a level that people find annoying and I'm proud of that. If that makes me a nerd then you may as well tattoo it on my forehead."

His eyes swim with amusement.

"You're a lot cockier than I would have pegged you to be," he chuckles.

"My mom always says it's not bragging if it's true," I respond.

The laugh rippling from him spreads through his body, gaining momentum as it works its way up to his mouth. The sound is thick and rich like a decadent piece of chocolate.

"I like that a lot," he says when he finally stops for air. "Sounds like something my mom would have said."

I want to know more things about his mother. It's clear Mrs. Baxter directed a lot of what makes Conrad who he is. Yet even with his nudging the door open a little on the personal side, I find myself unable to push open and step through. We're not there yet.

My stomach is full of pancakes and I'm overwhelmed with the need for a nap. Back home I would have done that and faced my work when I woke up. Such a thing won't happen here. I get the strong impression that I'm locked into a "it's now or never situation" with Conrad Baxter. If I don't push forward we will never get started.

"Calculus," I began again, handing a pencil to him. He doesn't take it. He stares at the plastic in my hand like it's a torture device.

"What's wrong?" I ask. He lifts his injured hand with its remaining fingers.

"I'm left handed, or at least I was." He takes the pencil with his right hand and awkwardly handles it like someone who's never seen a writing utensil before. "I probably shouldn't have fought the doctors on occupational therapy. I guess I need to learn to do it with the other side." I can't imagine it's as difficult as Conrad seems to be making it. After a few painful minutes of him trying he throws the pencil down in frustration.

"This is absurd," he barks causing me to jump.

I pick the pencil up and place it in my non-dominant hand. "How about I do it too?" His body stills. I start penning the names of the different subjects we needed to tackle and it was tougher than I'd ever admit out loud. We could easily tackle something else that doesn't require writing at all. He picks up his own pen and stares at it like an alien probe before smashing laptop closed.

"This is a colossal waste of time. There's too much to do and there's no point. I'm sorry, Isabella," and with that he stomps out of the greenhouse. I take a deep breath, looking to the flowers around me for guidance. He told me that his mother had been the one to teach him about flowers. She probably had something to do with these.

"Any advice, Mrs. Baxter?"

CHAPTER NINE

When I regain a bit of my pride, I trudge downstairs to find Mr. Potter in the kitchen. Once again he's peeling potatoes. No group in history has eaten more potatoes than these people.

"What's up, buttercup?" he asks when he sees me. "How goes the book learning?" I sit down at one of the breakfast bar stools and pout with my chin on the counter.

"It doesn't go at all. We hit a bit of a road block."

Mr. Potter's eyes never move away from the potato in his hand as he calls out into the void for Lusta. His tone is bright and bubbly. Dare I say smug? She appears from the hidden pantry in the wall with cans of corn stacked in her arms.

"You owe me ten bucks," he sings out to her. Lusta curses under her breath and the cans rattle and clank loudly onto the counter. She reaches into her back pocket and pulls out a crisp Hamilton to give to Mr. Potter who's giggling like a schoolgirl.

"Here, you dirty little leprechaun," she mutters. He laughs and plants a loud, smacking kiss on the top of her head.

"What's happening here?" I ask, wagging my finger between them, feeling left out of a punchline where I'm at the heart. An unsettling and queasy feeling sets in my stomach that usually comes with being the butt of a joke. Lusta rolls her eyes at Mr. Potter and he returns to his pot of spuds.

"He bet me that Conrad wouldn't make it an hour."

"You bet against me?" I ask him. Hurt settles in my chest.

"Oh, darling, no. I'd never bet against you. But I know Conrad."

"Give him time, Bella. It's a big step for him," Lusta says.

"You want something to eat?" Mr. Potter asks as he puts the potatoes atop the flame to boil. "I can whip you up something." For one of the first times in my life, I shake my head to refuse food.

I pulled out the copy of *Daisy Miller* that Conrad gifted to me in his apology from my bag. I head into the living room to settle into my favorite armchair, very aware of black orb hanging in the corner of the room. I wonder if he's watching me. Part of me feels overexposed, like I have nine chins and a wart on the end of my nose. The other part of me feels a comforting calm at the idea that anyone would take the time to look in on me at all. I've had more attention cast my way in my short time here than I have in all seventeen years I've lived in Harpersgrove. Am I something strange to these people or have I been so sheltered that no one ever saw what was there?

I open the front cover of the book, my insides warming at the comforting sound of the cracking spine. It's the same in every language and it grounds me. I let Henry James carry me away for the afternoon into a story I haven't read in years. But it's as

129

familiar to me as though I'd read it yesterday. When Lottie gets home it feels like I'd only just begun to read, but an examination of the pages reveals I'm three quarters of the way through it.

"Welcome home," I sign to her when she flops onto the couch beside me. "Long day?" I ask.

"Third grade is kicking my butt," she responds, pressing the power button on the TV remote.

"The struggle is real, my friend," I try to appear sympathetic, but worry my face will betray me. Luckily, she's not listening. Her eyes are glued to the television and half glazed over. Pollie arrives a short time later, ready with gossip I'm not prepared to hear.

"Well, you were the total talk of Dayton Ivy Academy today," she muses as she drapes her arm around Lottie's shoulders. Lottie goes stiff as a board.

"What do you mean?" I ask, tugging the ottoman closer to me.

"Well," she begins, releasing Lottie from her grasp. The little girl bolts away so fast that she leaves a cartoon dust trail in her wake. "Anyone who can pique the interest of Gatty and incur the wrath of Parker Boyd will be the mysterious talk of my school for days."

"What are people saying?" I try and fail to act cool. I wonder if this is what it's like to be a normal teenager. I never wanted to be a gossip girl, but I find myself sitting on the edge of my seat sucking it in like it's oxygen.

"Depends on who you talk to," she says. "There were a bunch of questions about you since you're here to work with Conrad. And Gatty and I fielded most of those questions."

The silence of what's left unsaid hangs thick in the air. She won't meet my gaze. "But Parker put her opinion in too. She said that she can't understand why a fat, poor girl is getting so much attention. You must have been doing something at the party to get guys to care about you." My blood chills. It doesn't take much of an expert to break down what she means. Pollie doesn't look at me and I'm glad. I can't imagine what my face looks like at the moment. The pain that burns through me consumes from the tips of my toes to the ends of my hair. My hearing cuts out into a loud, high pitched whistle as my vision narrows to pinpoint.

"Shit. Chicky, don't cry," Pollie exclaims as she flips off the couch onto the floor in front of me. I shake my head, a few of the tears breaking free and streaming down my cheeks in angry streaks.

"I don't understand why she would say things like that. It's not true!"

Pollie puts her hands on my knees and squeezes. "Oh, Bella, you didn't do anything, nothing at all. Parker is an awful person who doesn't want anyone to steal her spotlight. It's not about you, I promise."

"It's not fair," I murmur pathetically, lip quivering. I'd just had my first kiss and somehow now I'm the super slut? I wish Goldie was here. She'd kick Parker's butt from here to Tuesday.

"You're right, it's not." Pollie's words are simple, but they say everything I need to hear right now. She tells it as it is. There's no sugarcoated effort to make me feel better. Then the doorbell rings. It's the first time I've heard it since I've been here. Not a lot of guests stop by. I head to the door to answer and fall back when I see Gatty standing on the other side. Thank God my hand grips the door handle so I don't completely collapse. He leans his shoulder into the frame, his dark hair hanging in his eyes. He's stupid pretty. I may literally die.

"Hi!" I shriek, wincing at the sound as it escapes my lips.

"Hey, you." His voice comes out creamy and smooth. I'm about to become a puddle of goo at his feet. I still can't figure out why he's interested in me.

"What are you doing here?" I ask him, my grip increasing on the door. He rocks back on his heels, digging his hands into his pockets.

"I wanted to see you, but I never did get your number. I've also never been here. I was curious, considering how much Conrad loved it when we were kids. I thought about coming sooner to see him, but..." His voice drifts off and I know I could ask him about the accident, but I won't.

"Mind if I come in?" he asks, taking a step forward.

Without thinking, I move out of the way to clear the path. This is not my home. I should get Pollie or Lusta and ask if it's okay, but there's no time. Gatty's already brushing past me into the foyer. His hand grazes mine and I try my best to tuck my blushing cheek into my shoulder.

"Wow," Gatty exclaims from behind me. I turn to see him taking in the surroundings. He opens his mouth to make some other remark, but before he has the chance an all too familiar voice echoes from overhead.

"No!" Conrad's voice booms from the speakers. Gatty takes a noticeable, and understandable, leap back.

"Out!"

Gatty looks at me, confused. I can offer nothing more than a shrug and say, "You know, it's not that cold. Let's talk outside." I reach for him his elbow, forcing him along. Even though I know he's rooms and floors away, I feel Conrad's eyes on me the whole time.

When the safety of the closing door clicks behind me I breathe a little easier. My arms break into goosebumps and I know the little red dots on the backs of them show through my pasty skin. I rub my hands up and down them to try and combat it. Without pause, Gatty shrugs out of his leather jacket and opens it to me. My core heats up as I turn around and slide my arms inside. I have longed for that feeling portrayed in a hundred teen movies, where the girl gets swallowed up in her beau's oversized jacket. Alas, my body will not be swallowed by any jacket. Even though Gatty seems much bigger than me, the lapels don't come close to touching.

"Thanks," I say with a warm smile. "What's up, Gatty? I'm pretty sure you didn't come just to see the house."

He pushes his hands through his hair before returning them to the depths of his pockets. "I'm not sure if Pollie told you what Parker was saying today," he says and my heart falls to my feet. Nervously, my fingers tuck hair behind my ears in a repeated motion, the leather of the jacket squeaking as I do.

"Um, she may have mentioned something," I lied, unable to say that I'd heard it all. Gatty's face and shoulders fall.

"I was worried I wouldn't get to you first." He kicks his heels against a pillar on the porch. "I'm sorry. I hope you know that I didn't have anything to do with that."

I'm not sure of anything except this is not the kind of attention I ever want again.

"I didn't think you did." Regardless of my uncertainties, I don't want to doubt Gatty. He reaches forward and grabs the sleeves of the jacket, tugging me forward until I'm standing right in front of him.

"Will you let me make it up to you?" he asks, his breath hot against the apples of my cheeks. I feel my entire body soften. What is it about the closeness of a boy that turns me into a wobbly blob? Goldie has been dating since infancy and she never gets nervous around boys. She makes boys nervous. Maybe that's the difference. Pretty girls have things to be confident about, but what do I have? Which, in my mind, leads to the question, *what does this impossibly good looking and popular boy see in me?* It's like a riddle that I don't understand.

I can't seem to summon words. The high pitched whine that sounds through my head whenever he's around is all I can hear. A sly half smile stretches across his perfect teeth as the tip of his index finger traces down my stomach. I can't help the noticeable shudder that runs through my body. I'm not wearing any kind of shapewear under my clothes. Every roll and dimple is on display and I don't want him to feel them.

"You okay?" he asks as he studies me.

A *mhmm* leaves my lips like steam escaping a kettle. Deep inside I feel the need to tell him the truth. Be a little braver and speak my mind.

"Um, maybe you could not touch my stomach?" My voice dips to such a weak level that academics will study for decades. Not exactly the courageous moment I'd hoped for. I wish I could crawl out of my own skin to get away. I take in the scuff marks on the toes of my shoes just to have somewhere else to look. I feel his smooth fingers trace my cheek as he urges my gaze up to his own. His dark eyes are soft and sweet and understanding.

"Are you really worried about that? I don't care about that."

Usually people say things like, *You're not fat, you're beautiful,* as though those things are mutually exclusive. I like that he didn't do that. "Can I take you out to dinner?"

Instinctively, I look back at the house and immediately wish I could take it back. Conrad doesn't own me. I don't need to seek his permission to leave the house. I'm not his prisoner.

"Sure, that would be nice," I say with a genuine smile. He must find it at least somewhat endearing as the skin by his eyes crinkles from his widening grin.

"You want to go grab your purse or whatever you need?"

"Oh, you want to go now?"

He chuckles softly, leaning back against the column. "Well, people do normally eat dinner in the evenings. Would you like to go?" My stomach rumbles with hurried anticipation. Stupid chubby tummy.

"Do you mind waiting out here for like five minutes?" I ask, pulling his jacket off and handing it back to him.

"Yeah, no problem. I'm not exactly interested in angering the monster." He laughs it off, but I feel an underlying aggression in his words. I know it had been some time since they'd seen each other and sure, their relationship had to be strained, but they had been friends once. Good friends, from how it seemed. I head back through the front door and no sooner does it close behind me than Conrad's voice booms through the speakers.

"Come up here, Bella."

I roll my eyes at his commanding tone. I can tell Pollie is trying her hardest to ignore what's happening in the foyer. I make no move to the intercom panel, only stare into the camera with my eyes narrowed.

"Please. Two minutes of your time. I'm in the greenhouse."

Even though I can't see her, I sense Pollie smiling from the couch. I rock back on my heels, pausing, before trudging up the stairs to push through the door of the greenhouse. "What?" I say flatly, as I try to control my labored breathing.

So. Many. Steps.

Conrad's busy pruning a bush of tightly wound red colored buds. He struggles to hold the shears in his good hand. His eyes narrowed with fierce concentration on the plant and I don't think he heard me.

"Conrad, what do you want? I'm about to go out."

He doesn't stop gardening or look up at me.

"Don't go out with Gatty."

"Oh my God. Don't go out with Pollie. Don't go out with Gatty. What is it with you?" I demand. "I'm not trying to invade your life, but you can't keep me in a little box like an inmate."

He still doesn't look back at me, but his shoulders noticeably tense before he says, "I shouldn't have said you couldn't go out with Pollie and I know you aren't a prisoner here." Every word out of his mouth sounds like the end of a conversation. "Gatty's different. You don't want to go out with him. Trust me."

"Why?" I ask, taking a nibble off the bait he's dangling.

He snaps off one of the roses and extends it to me. I take it from him and hold it at my side. I'm not sure what I'm supposed to do with a single rose.

"Trust me. Don't go."

I abandon the rose on the wooden table beside me and march over next to him, giving him no choice but to look at me. His blue eyes are as sharp as ever. The weight of the sadness inside them drowns me.

"Because 'I said so' is not a reason Conrad," I say, my voice softer than I expected. Those sad eyes hit me a little too hard. "You have to let me make my own choices all for myself."

"He was my friend, Bella. I know him." The bite of those final words hits me in the chest. I almost consider telling him I won't go. After all, Isabella Southland always follows orders. But the thing is, Conrad doesn't know better than I do. He isn't so other worldly that he can tell me what to do. I break my gaze and take a step back, my thighs creating their own friction as my knees bounce back and forth.

"I'm a big girl Conrad, I can take care of myself." As I turn to leave, he reaches out and grabs my elbow with his bad hand. We lock in place there for a moment, both shocked by the contact. When he finally lets me go, it's only to pick up the flower he'd given to me.

"I know you can. Be careful." He places the flower back in my hand. That same finality rings in his voice and he returns to the roses. My knees buckle from the slightest contact. I expected his skin to feel glassy on mine, but it's normal, other than the trail of electricity it left behind. I considered leaving the flower there. I take it anyway, placing it on my bedside table in my room for safe keeping. I grab my coat and purse from the closet and wish I had time to change but I've already left Gatty waiting long enough. Outside, he's in the exact spot that I left him, scrolling through his phone and leaning back on the pillar. He pushes his foot against it and moves toward me.

"I was beginning to think you were standing me up," he says with a chuckle. I hoist my bag up on my shoulder and walk with him toward his absurdly expensive car. I internally groan at the extravagance. Gatty can clearly see the amusement on my face as his head tilts to the side, studying me.

"What's going on in that noggin of yours?" he asks.

I slide into the heated leather interior and shake my head.

When we arrive at the restaurant, I realize I should have taken the extra five minutes to change my clothes. I'm under dressed in black leggings and oversized tunic. The messy bun atop my head isn't doing me any favors either. I unzip my coat and hand it to a man in a tux working the coat check.

"I wish you had told me we were coming somewhere fancy. I would have dressed nicer."

Gatty waves me off like I'm being ridiculous as he hands over his own jacket and a large tip. He places his hand on the small of my back, urging me forward.

"Don't be silly, you look great," he says.

An elegant woman wearing a slick black dress with perfect hair stands behind an ornate desk next to the coat check. She looks up and her eyebrow raises ever so slightly at me in harsh judgement. I want to crawl inside myself and die. I think being naked would be better than what I'm in right now. When her attention moves to Gatty, her entire demeanor shifts.

"Mr. Gattman," she begins, because, of course, she knows him. "What a pleasure to have you and your-" she eyes me with the same superiority as her brain lingers too long to find the right word to describe me, "guest dine with us this evening." The way she says the word "guest" tells me everything I need to know about how she sees me. In her eyes, I don't belong.

"Thank you, Josephine," Gatty says with that same heart stopping smile. I wonder if all rich kids call adults by their first names. My mother would have pinched me if I referred to anyone even five years my senior as anything other than Mr. or Ms. Whatever.

Josephine picks up two red leather bound menus and what seems to be a wine list. She can tell we're teenagers, can't she?

"Please follow me. Your father's table is ready for you."

"Your father has a table?" I whisper to him once Josephine's back is turned.

Gatty smiles down at me and says, "He should. He does own the place."

The hostess seats us at a table angled in proximity to the string quartet. Josephine picks up the folded napkin in the shape of a pyramid off my china plate and snaps it free of its form with a simple flick of her wrist before draping it across my lap.

"Would you like to start with something from the wine list, sir?" she asks. She can't be serious. I'm about to laugh her off and ask for a Coke when Gatty answers instead.

"My usual bottle will be fine, Josephine, thank you," he says nonchalantly, like it's something he does all the time. I can't help the way my jaw hangs open, like I've witnessed a drug deal in a church.

"It's okay, Bella, I promise," he mocks with a tilt of his head and a boyish smile. I want to tell him that I'm not comfortable with it. Even if he chooses to drink, which I really don't think he should since he's the one who drove us here, I'm not going to partake. That's what I want to say. As Josephine returns with the opaque green bottle however, my voice gets lost somewhere deep in my throat.

"Could I get a glass of water too?" I croak, the weakness makes me cringe. Gatty eyes me for a moment as try to make myself smaller. Josephine disappears again and Gatty pours the wine. The red liquid glugging into the glass speeds up my heart. I need to find a way to hide my revulsion before he figures out I'm a total loser. Gatty lifts his glass to me, motioning for me to do the same.

"To our first official date," he proclaims.

He brings the glass to his mouth and takes a few big gulps which, from my small understanding, is not how one is supposed to enjoy wine. I take a deep breath and raise my own glass. At the last second I can't go through with it and suction my mouth around the edge, the wine only splashing against my skin. I bring the goblet back down and lick away the remnants. It seems impossible that anyone could trick themselves into believing they like this swill. I can feel Gatty's eyes on me, staring. He's waiting for my approval. I let a "yum" roll through my lips. It's more like what I imagine aliens would sound like if they put on a play about how humans react to food. I would like to crawl under the table and never come out. Gatty reaches across the table to take my wine.

"Bella," he begins, placing my glass beside his own. "You don't have to drink that."

A young man with a pencil thin mustache comes to the table with our water. I grab mine before he can place it on the table and gulp it down. I'm shockingly dehydrated.

"Thank you," I'm somehow able to get out in between slurps.

"Not a big drinker, huh?" he says in a way that I know isn't a question.

"Am I that obvious?"

He finishes off his wine before moving onto mine. I guess I'll be the one driving us home.

"It's refreshing really," he says, placing the empty wine glass at the edge of the table for someone to retrieve. I've never put much thought into drinking before. I didn't go to school parties the way other kids did and my close group of friends don't drink. We're more of a hot tea and pie group than a *shots!, shots!, shots!* kind of crowd.

"My parents don't drink, my friends don't drink. Never really appealed to me I guess," I answer, flipping open the menu. I may not do alcohol, but I definitely do food.

"Not many big ragers at your school?" he asks.

"I'm homeschooled. My school is me, my brother and my mom. Not exactly a rave." When he doesn't say anything for a minute, I notice. Peering over my menu, I see him staring at me like an animal in the zoo.

"What?" I ask, feeling very overexposed.

"You? You're homeschooled?" he questions, setting his menu aside. This revelation requires his full attention. I nod and he folds his hands under his chin. "Fascinating. I never would have thought that in a million years." That plucks a nerve deep down inside me. People have a lot of assumptions about homeschooled kids that irk me.

"Why is that?" I ask. "How did you think I was able to drop everything and come up here to tutor Conrad in the middle of the school year?"

He purses his lips as though the thought had never occurred to him. "I guess you're right. You just don't strike me as the home-school type."

There it is. I close my menu, on the defensive, ready for a fight. "And what is the homeschool type exactly? Some kind of inbred, religious fanatic?" His grimace says that's exactly what he thought.

Typical. "Have you ever met a person who's been homeschooled before meeting me? Actually had a conversation with someone?"

"Nope. Educate me," he says; his easy candor annoys me to my core. I wish I had another way out of here. My walls are all the way up. That little smirk is back at the corner of his mouth. Right now I find it less endearing. I wish my heart were listening because she still flutters at the sight. Traitor.

"Why were you homeschooled?"

"Well, it's simple, really. My mom is an educator and knew she could do a good job. My brother is deaf and she was worried about how he'd be accepted."

Gatty chooses to leave it at that and I'm grateful. Jonah's not a little boy anymore, but I still find myself getting defensive where he's concerned.

"Deaf huh?" he says instead and I nod. "Does that mean you can sign?" he asks as he throws his hands into random signs that mean, "Angry apple". I try to hide my amusement as I sign back a simple "yes".

Gatty claps his hands together and exclaims, "Damn! Okay you need to teach me something."

Gatty refuses to let me see the bill at the end of the meal. He tells me not to worry about it, which means it was a lot. I stopped fighting since there's no way I could afford it anyway. Walking back to the car, I start to mentally tally the number of drinks Gatty had. He ended up finishing almost the entire bottle. While my experience with drinking may be limited, I'm fairly certain that his steak and asparagus couldn't have soaked all that up.

"Do you want me to drive?" I ask. My voice thickens at the awkward question. He looks at me like I'm precious, but naive, and unlocks the car.

"Trust me Bella, I'm good. I know when I've had too much. I'm not even buzzed."

I think back to his party and how fast I took Pollie's keys from her. There wasn't even a second thought. I shouldn't be hesitating now. "Are you -are you sure?" I ask, my voice meek and soft. "I didn't have anything to drink and I don't mind. I'm a good driver."

That sly smile that turns my knees to jelly slides across his lips. He leans in to kiss me on the cheek. "You're adorable. I promise I'm fine."

I know I should push harder, insist that I drive or take an Uber or something. I should not get in this car. Every lesson my parents have ever taught me rushes through my brain. It's also not lost on me that I'm currently tutoring a guy who was disfigured in a car accident. But I don't listen to a single one of those instincts. As much as I want to deny it, it's because I want Gatty to like me. I get in the car. Guilt overwhelms me on the quiet drive and my sweaty palm grips the door handle. I brace for impact, but nothing happens. It makes me nervous that he definitely seems to have done this before. When we pull into the circular driveway, I realize how hard I was holding onto the handle and flex my fingers. I'm ready to have my feet on land again.

While Gatty seems fine, I wish that did something to loosen the knot in my stomach. I'm about to get out of the car when Gatty reaches out and takes my hand. I turn back to him and there's a fire smoldering in his eyes. I'm frozen as he leans in toward me and brushes his lips against mine.

"I had a great time," he says. I don't get the chance to respond before his hands are in my hair and his tongue is in my mouth. I can still taste the wine on his lips. I brace my hands against his shoulders as I try to get my bearings. This is much rougher than the kiss at the Christmas tree farm. Is this the progression of such a thing? Of course, it could be the wine, or is it just a sign that he's really into me?

He pulls back and runs the pad of his thumb against my lower lip. "Good night, Bella," he whispers, his voice husky. I find myself unable to respond in any verbal way and pull on the handle of the car door. I don't know why I'm not beaming while I make the walk from the car to the house. Gatty waits with the headlights still on me as I head inside. Haven't I been waiting my whole life for a boy to pay me this kind of mind? I never thought it would be a boy as good looking, or cool, or rich as Gatty. He's like a modern day Prince Charming. Where's the spark I felt at the party or Christmas tree lot? What happened?

I settle my weight against the cool wood of the front door. I hate that I don't feel better. I start in the direction of the stairs, but something in the living room catches my eye. I pause on the bottom step and gawk as I try to process what I'm seeing. Lottie sits on my favorite armchair and Conrad rests on the ottoman across from her. Between them is a chessboard. The small lamp beside the chair is their only form of illumination. Both show Bobby Fischer-like intensity on the game board. Lottie rubs her chin like a grandmaster about to score her winning move. It feels more like a dream than something that's actually happening. I look at Conrad and notice that he has a translucent plastic tube in his mouth. The tubing winds down to a machine on the floor.

It crinkles as he breathes. Upon spotting me, Conrad's eyes go wide and he pulls the plastic from his mouth.

"Hey!" he exclaims, attempting to tuck the tube under his leg and hide it from me. Lottie hops up from her seat to grab the tube and shoves it back between his lips. He tries to swat her away, but it won't do any good. Lottie will get her way.

"The fire messed up his lungs. He has to do this every night," she signs.

I figured it was some kind of nebulizer treatment, which makes a lot of sense. I make a simple sign of understanding to Lottie. Conrad shakes his head vehemently. He pulls the tube back out and says, "No, no, you two. No super secret spy language." Lottie narrows her eyes at him and jabs a finger in his direction until he finally replaces the mouthpiece.

"You're a pain in the ass, kid," he mutters around the plastic.

I make my way in to join them. Lottie scoots over and pats the space beside her on the armchair. Thank God it's oversized. I don't have to embarrass myself by wedging in. My attention settles back on Conrad. His sandy colored hair drapes across the right side of his head and flows too long over his ear. If he cut some of it off, the burns wouldn't be as noticeable at first. His bright blue eyes catch mine. Nothing else about his expression changes in the slightest. He just holds me with his gaze.

"Did you call ASL a super secret spy language?" I ask with a grin. His expression never falters, not even a bit.

"Have fun with the ass hat?" he finally says, his voice flat and monotone.

"Sure, it was a wonderful time." My voice oozes with sarcasm. I settle back in the chair and pull a pillow over my stomach like a security blanket. He raises his head to his full height, broad shoulders stretching against his black t-shirt. I notice that his ever present hoodie is missing.

"That was convincing," he laughs around the tube but his eyes betray his curiosity.

"I don't know. It was weird," I answer, feeling my shoulders work their way up to my ears. The amusement is gone as his brow furrows and he pulls the tube from his mouth again. Lottie immediately hops up to protest, but Conrad raises a hand to stop her.

"Relax, Little Bit," he says with nothing but affection. It warms my heart. I feel like he'd be kind to injured woodland creatures too. Lottie finally moves a piece on the board.

"Are you all right?"

The depths of those blue eyes may drown me. I force myself to take a breath and choose my next words wisely. "Yes, Conrad, I'm fine. It wasn't bad. It was weird."

He puts the tube back in place and moves his own piece on the board. Lottie huffs in annoyance and goes back to studying the game like it holds all the world's answers.

"This is rather sweet," I say, motioning between the two of them. "The last thing I would have expected to see when I got home."

His focus shifts to Lottie as he waits for her to make her move. "She doesn't force me to talk. We can just be. She's my favorite person in the world these days."

I can see where he might take comfort in such a thing, but the revelation still makes me sad. I know what it can be like to feel isolated. I wish he didn't feel the need. Lusta appears at the doorway and motions to her daughter. "Time for this little one to get ready for bed."

Conrad doesn't say anything, reaching across the table to touch Lottie's hand. Her little eyes peek up to see her mother and her face falls with disappointment. She looks back to Conrad and her lower lip juts out in a pout. He reaches down to turn off the breathing machine. "Tomorrow," he says, and she understands.

Lottie reaches over and hugs me goodnight before moving around the table to Conrad. I'm more than a little surprised when she wraps her arms around his shoulders and plants a soft kiss on the injured side of his face. His eyes close slightly when she does it, as though it's the most agonizing yet life affirming act in the world. He pats her on the back before she skips away to her waiting mother.

"She's a good kid," he says, moving the board out of the way and hoisting the machine up next to him on the ottoman. "This thing is so compact, I'm surprised you even noticed it." His voice is dry, but I can tell this is his attempt at breaking the tension. Conrad humor.

"Must be a pain," I offer. He shrugs it off.

"Tomorrow," he begins, "I was thinking we could work on history? Reading and typing seem like they'll be easier for me right now. Besides, I don't think I could handle watching you try to write with your left hand a second time."

"You want to do school again?" I ask with equal parts joy and astonishment. I thought I was going to have to give him a day or two before I brought it up again.

"Isn't that's what you're here for?" he snaps as he winds up the long tube of his nebulizer. His left hand struggles to grip it but he is finally able to secure the plastic. I would have offered to help, but Conrad doesn't react kindly to assistance he hasn't explicitly requested. I sit on my hands and wait.

"Well, yes," I say. "Honestly, I thought that after this morning you might need a break."

"I'm fine," he hisses. "I'll see you in the morning," he says, and stamps away before I can say a word. When I'm certain enough that he's out of earshot, I pull my phone out and dial Rosie. I need my girls.

Rosie's boobs are the first thing to pop up on the screen.

"Hold on, kid!" she shouts as the pans clank against each other. "Hey, Belly Bells!" The ever present smear of flour is brushed on the front of her low-cut, black shirt. Her red lipstick smudged a little around her lips like she's been madly kissing someone, although I doubt that's the case.

"Are you busy?" I ask, hating to be a bother no matter how much I need her. Rosie waves me off like I'm being ridiculous.

"Nah, same ole, same old, you know? What's up?"

She's moving at twice her normal speed like a zippy cartoon character. "Guess what? I had an espresso!" she shouts, waving a coffee mug at the camera, and that explains a lot. Rosie doesn't sleep, maybe two or three hours a night if she's lucky. Caffeine is a big no-no for her. Blanche appears from the sidelines, her head of jet black hair cuts across the screen as she grabs the cup from Rosie's hand.

"Damn it, woman!" she exclaims, immediately dumping the cup into the sink. "We told you no!"

Rosie sucks in her top lip, leaving her bottom in the biggest pout I've ever seen. It brushes the tip of her nose. "I'm not a child you mean girl!" she shouts. The phone shakes, making me a little seasick. I pull my feet up onto the chair. The more in the fetal position I am the more comfortable I become.

"I did something stupid you guys," I blurt out.

"Are you okay?" Blanche asks before the conversation can go any further.

"Yeah," I immediately reassure. I should have phrased it a little differently.

"Did you lose your "V" card?" Rosie pulls from nowhere and I swallow my tongue, coughing against the shock.

"Excuse me!" I shriek, color heating my skin. "That isn't even close to true!" Thank God the cameras in this house don't have sound. I don't want anyone hearing this nonsense.

"How did you jump there?" Blanche retorts, pinching Rosie on the arm. "Bella's never even kissed a guy before." I flush a little deeper at the fact that this isn't a secret or even a surprise.

Rosie shrugs, rubbing the injured spot on her arm. "I dunno, she said she made a mistake and that was the biggest thing I could think of for her."

"Well, that's not what happened." I make doubly sure no one is lurking around to hear.

"Tell us what happened," Blanche says, bringing us a sense of calm. I let out a long breath that blows up into my eyes and fogs my glasses.

"Well, I have been kissed now. Let's start there." The words aren't completely out of my mouth before questions start squawking from their lips. Like a bunch of hens, I swear.

"Stop! I told you that I met a boy. Just listen for a second."

They quiet and lean back against the kitchen wall and let me talk. I spill about Gatty and the Christmas tree lot all leading up to dinner tonight. Nothing is sitting right with me about the fact that I got in that car. I need to know what to do, because God knows I have no idea.

"Well," Rosie begins, her lips pressing together. "It's not cool that he drove you if he'd been drinking, Bella. Did you tell him it made you uncomfortable?"

I pick at a loose hangnail on the side of my thumb. "Not in so many words. I did offer to drive." In my mind that was as good as expressing my discomfort.

"Guys are simple creatures, Hells Bells," say Blanche. "You have to spell things out for them."

"But shouldn't it be common sense that you don't drive after you've had almost a whole bottle of wine?" I fire back. This is the part that bothers me most, that he saw nothing wrong with doing either.

"It's common sense to us," Rosie adds. "But these guys live in a totally different world. Maybe this kind of thing is okay when you have money to fix everything?"

I nod along like I understand. It seems crazy to me. And all the money in the world couldn't fix Conrad.

"Next time you see him," Blanche takes back the conversation, "Tell him straight up that you are not okay with what happened and it can't happen again going forward. He will appreciate the honesty and if he doesn't, he's not worth your time anyway."

"Okay." I already feel a little better.

The call falls silent for a long moment before Rosie says, "Bella? You like him?" She always sees right through everything else. I let myself objectively mull it over. I don't know his super well. It's only been a few days, but up until tonight I got butterflies every time I saw him or thought about him. I like that feeling. I smile softly. "Yeah, I think I do."

"Hells Bells," Blanche's soft voice calls out. "Are you okay?"

Emotion in my body is always felt with tears. Damn it.

"Yeah," I answer as I wipe away the stubborn puddles. "I miss you guys. Rose, I would give anything for a slice of your pecan pie right now. Like, in ways I can't even describe." My stomach rumbles as if to affirm this, never satisfied.

"How does one ship a pie to Belly Bells? I feel like pie should be the one thing I'm able to do for you!" A genuine smile stretches across my lips, all I need is my friends to balance me.

"It's okay, Rose, I'm okay."

Her blonde eyebrows knit together. "Unacceptable! I shall find a way to get you pie. To the internet!" she exclaims, hopping off the counter and out of sight.

"Bella," Blanche begins. "I had no flippin' clue how much you do around here girl! Where do we order napkins from? Help us, Bella! We're dying!" She dramatically throws her head back to the wall.

"Well, Beattie should be able to give you all that stuff," I say.

"Beat is currently packing up her car for her bimonthly trek up the east coast to visit her other shops."

"Because everyone wants to head further north in December," I scoff. "Okay, get something to write with. This might take a minute."

CHAPTER TEN

"You look tired," Conrad says to me the next morning as we muse over the influence of Alexander Hamilton on our modern political world. I'm half tempted to put on the Broadway soundtrack and tell him this is everything he needs to know. However, he doesn't strike me as the show tune type. Maybe later. An unfeminine yawn spills from my mouth and I feel zero embarrassment because that would take energy I don't have. "It was a long night," I offer.

My friends are beautiful, amazing, kind, phenomenal women that I would die for. However, attempting to teach them how to run the pie shop was like teaching a squirrel to drive a car. They flailed around until midnight trying to grasp all the tasks I do on a regular basis.

"You got home at eight thirty," he laughs, adjusting his glasses against his lopsided ears. I'm sure my hearing deceives me, but I think Conrad Baxter is trying to tease me. I close my thumb inside my book and take a moment to choose my words wisely.

"You know, Mr. Baxter, my life doesn't stop when you leave the room."

His glasses slide back down the bridge of his nose and I catch those depthless blues over the rims. There's a twinkle I haven't seen before. "I would never say it did, Miss Southland."

His voice is deeper and huskier than I've heard it and the air around us in the greenhouse is thick and static. He takes pity on me and breaks eye contact first. I doubt he's unaware of his hypnotic powers.

"You know," he says, "they turned this guy into a musical." A toothy grin stretches across my face.

"I mean, I know that, but how did *you* know that?" I chuckle, setting my book aside. Most of my musical theater knowledge comes from Rosie. She is basically a Broadway encyclopedia, but I enjoy it enough all on my own. The last thing I would ever have pegged Conrad as was a connoisseur of foot tapping showtunes. He narrows his eyes and picks up his phone. After a few taps on the screen the familiar beats of the title track fill the empty space around us.

"You insult me, madam," he utters, but I can see that same touch of a smile on his lips. Glee, real blissful glee, rushes through me. "You are full of surprises, Connie."

I don't mean to call him by a nickname. It's out of my mouth before I know it. It's true that I don't know him well enough to assume to take such liberties. He seems to me like the type that's on a full name basis with everyone, even his relatives. Sometimes I'm shocked that he doesn't insist on being called Mr. Baxter. He flips his book over on the wood pallet we've been treating as a desk with his good hand before centering his attention on me. His mouth doesn't smile, but his gaze beams as the apples of his cheeks flush. It's all about the subtle changes with Conrad.

"What did you call me?" he asks, his eyes switching back and forth between mine, studying me.

"I'm sorry, I shouldn't have-" I begin, but he raises his hand to halt me.

"Stop," he starts, a chuckle in his voice. "I'm not going to cut you up and eat you, Bella. You can call me that if you want to. I don't hate it."

"Yeah?" I sigh, relieved that he's not mad. "You don't strike me as a nickname kind of guy." A deep laugh echoes inside him as his chest rumbles. He runs a hand through his remaining hair.

"Well, most of the time you would be right." He's silent for a moment before he says, "My mom called me Connie. I miss the way it sounds."

He's cracked the door open again, and choosing to be brave, I push it open. "Would you tell me about her?" I ask, trying to look cool and calm. Maybe if I fake-relaxed well enough, he'll relax too.

"You want to know about my mom?" My head bobs up and down a bit too vigorously, like a dashboard puppy dog. A sweet smile floats across his face. "She was beautiful. Pollie looks so much like her it's crazy."

"I saw that in the picture she showed me."

Conrad picks up his phone and starts scrolling. "Mom was funny, or at least she thought she was. She was obsessed with knock-knock jokes. If she heard one it became mandatory for every person in her life to hear it too. And she had this terrible laugh, like an asthmatic goose. It was one of my favorite sounds in the world."

He hands his phone to me and on the screen is an adolescent Conrad with braces and overgrown sandy hair. Standing in a grass stained white and hunter green lacrosse uniform, he drapes his arm over the shoulder of his mother as she plants a kiss against his cheek. "I'm only ten in that picture and already so much taller than her. She tried to convince me once when I was really little that she was a garden fairy. Part of me still wants to believe it's true."

"She sounds like a wonderful lady."

He takes the phone back and studies the picture on the screen like he's trying to memorize it. "She was. Whatever she saw in my dad was a mystery, of course. God knows my grandparents still don't like him for taking her from them." He sits the phone down on the makeshift desk between us.

"Is it because they're far away?" I ask.

"I like to think it was more because Dad's an asshole," Conrad says coldly, his jaw working back and forth under his skin. "But her parents live in Texas, we live here. I don't think that thrilled them either. I haven't seen them since her funeral."

"Tell me more about her." It spills from my mouth like he's at a job interview.

"She had a serious obsession with Santa Claus and everything about the American Christmas experience." His normally tense shoulders relax with refreshed ease the more he talks about her.

"Your sister told me something about that too."

"Yeah, one year she actually got my father into a Santa Clause costume." We both giggle like little kids who heard a dirty joke. "I know you've never met him, but that is a feat for anyone."

"I would have liked to have seen that," I say as I catch my breath. Conrad shakes his head, lost in thought, but still smiling.

"I'm pretty sure he made a point to destroy all photographic evidence that he ever did something fun."

"What else?"

His shoulders shrug up to his ears. "She was my mom. She was everything."

And that's all I need to know.

The Hamilton soundtrack serenades us through the rest of our morning. We finally break for lunch around one o'clock. My stomach is an empty, bottomless pit that demands to be filled! Conrad tries his best to convince me to go get food and bring it back up to the greenhouse, or even meet in the library. But I refuse to let him keep company with only his flowers any longer. The people he lives with seem like a good group to help start pulling him out of his shell. He pulls that black hoodie back over his face and I can't help how much it annoys me. Lusta and Mr. Potter know what he looks like.

In the kitchen, Mr. Potter shucks cobs of corn over a trash can at the table. "Well, hello there. What can I do for you?" he asks. Conrad stays behind me like a child hiding behind his mother and I am having none of it. I grab him by his arm, his bad arm at that, and pull him beside me begrudgingly. He complies.

"Connie and I were hoping you'd be so kind as to feed us some lunch," I say as I link my arm through his, testing the limits of our budding friendship. I think I may have overstepped a line or two.

Mr. Potter giggles, "Connie?" The death glare that Conrad shoots back is enough to make our faithful cook drop it. He lifts the ear of corn in his hand in the direction of the refrigerator.

"I made chicken salad today. Feel free to help yourselves. Lusta bought some new type of fancy bread. It's in the basket."

I unwind myself from Conrad's arm and push him towards the table. As I'm assembling our sandwiches, a loud, automated ringing sounds through the kitchen. Lusta appears from nowhere and hits the screen of the tablet mounted to the wall. The face of the horrid little man who tried to deny me access to the house on my first day appears on the screen.

"Lusta," he clips, dressed in classic butler attire, ripped from a "Clue" game board somewhere.

"What can I do for you?" she asks. I'm trying to eavesdrop but I'm as subtle as a rhino wearing fluorescent orange spandex in an aerobics class. I hope I don't cut open my hand trying to halve these sandwiches.

"I need you to deliver a message to the boy from his father," the gruff old man commands.

"I'm sitting right here, Colin."

Conrad sits as straight as an arrow in his seat at the kitchen table. His feet planted firmly on the floor, palms lay flat on the table. I'd swear he was a statue from his stiff posture. Everything stops and the kitchen falls silent. Colin coughs, caught off guard.

"Oh. Mr. Baxter, I apologize," he sputters, trying to regain his bearings. "I didn't realize you were there."

"Clearly," Conrad barks, the sharp tone of his voice causing me to wince. "What is the message?"

Colin speaks as if reading from a script. "I am sorry, sir. Your father regrets to inform you that he will not be able to attend your scheduled dinner tonight." Conrad laughs humorlessly as his posture relaxes and he sinks back in his chair.

"Colin," he begins, shaking his head back and forth. "Please tell my father that I'm ready to give up on this ridiculous charade whenever he is. Hang up, Lusta!" We all know it's not a request. No one moves. No one breathes. Even Mr. Potter, who doesn't always have the highest opinion of Conrad, looks at him with sympathy. Conrad is the first to move.

He stalks toward me, expression blank, like when I first met him. He reaches down and takes one of the quartered sandwiches from my hands. "Thank you for lunch, Isabella," and I know that this means our day is over.

His hand touches mine when he takes the plate from me. Even that small amount of contact makes my heart swell and I want to cry. He's a big, hulking guy, the type built to protect. All I want is to wrap my arms around him and shelter him like a hurting little boy. That's all I see right now. He offers me nothing more as he takes his food and breezes out of the room, right past Lusta, who's hurting for him as much as I am.

"That bastard," Mr. Potter curses under his breath, returning corn in his hands. The husks rip with far more aggression than is necessary.

"It's not like he actually expects him to come," Lusta sighs, running her hands through her braids, tugging hard on the roots.

"That's not the point. He's his father." Mr. Potter slams the last ear into the bowl of silk covered corn.

"What just happened?" I find the courage to ask. It's like they both forgot I was here.

"The elder Mr. Baxter hasn't visited since we moved Conrad here after leaving the hospital," Lusta says, rubbing a hand over her makeupless face.

"Wasn't that months ago?" I ask Mr. Potter. He looks ready to explode as his fist bounces in rhythmic punches on the glass table. Lusta finds it in her to stay calm.

"Lionel Baxter continues to promise every week that he'll come to dinner. Then he has Colin call on the day of, to cancel."

"Can't even call himself, bastard," Mr. Potter barks. For all his callousness against Conrad, it's clear that he cares, maybe even as much as Lusta.

"That's terrible. Poor Conrad."

The room falls back into silence as I chew on the sadness. It's unfortunate because Mr. Potter makes a banging chicken salad. One should never eat good food while sad, it's a waste.

The sound of the ringing doorbell cuts through our silence and I'm grateful for it. "I'll get it," I offer through a mouthful of food as I head to the front door. A mix of joy and surprise chokes me as I open it. That classic, curled, rust colored head with smoky eyes and paint splatter overalls stands before me.

"Surprise!" Beattie says, holding her hands up in the air. My body refuses to stop coughing, but who needs air? Beattie is here! She smiles and grabs a familiar white "Hap-PIE-ly Ever After" pie box from the ledge beside her.

"Rosie called. She considered it imperative that you get this pie, said it was life or death."

I make no move for the pie but instead fling my arms around her neck, crushing her against me. She laughs, one of those full body laughs that flows through all the parts of your body. She plants a smacking kiss on my cheek.

"Aw, I missed you too, nugget."

My hands keep moving from her cheeks to her shoulders like I'm trying to memorize her. She's a reminder of home and I need every piece that I can drink up.

"I can't believe you're here!" I start hopping up and down, which is never a good plan for someone with my bust size, but I don't care. Beattie is here! I grab the pie with one hand and her elbow with the other. In that one motion, everything comes crashing down. That glorious, sweet, beautiful pie, hits the ground with the full force of a nuclear bomb.

"Do not tell Rosie!" she exclaims.

I try not to think about the ooey gooey goodness in a pile at my feet. I take Beattie's hand and start pulling her toward the door. "Come in!" I exclaim. She puts on the brakes, sputtering us both to a stop and I look back at her confused. She grins wide, bigger than I've ever seen Beattie smile.

"Did you really think I'd only bring one gift?" Reaching around behind the giant pillar and she pulls not something, but someone out from behind it.

"Jonah!" I cry, taking a flying leap at him. Lucky for me, my little brother catches me with an unencumbered laugh, proud for all to hear. I swear he's grown five inches since I left home. His brown hair flops in his eyes as he puts his hands on my upper arms to push me away enough to see him.

"You should leave more often," he says, a devilish grin on his face. "No one's ever this happy to see me!"

"The girls seemed to think you needed some company," Beattie explains. I don't know how to put into words the total sum of the joy of every Christmas and birthday I've ever had. That's what I'm feeling now.

"Thinking of you up here all sad and alone was too depressing for me to handle. I volunteered to come," Jonah exclaims. I give him a questioning look and he raises the backpack in his hand. "With a semester's worth of homework from Mom."

I grin to the point my cheeks hurt and grab them both by the arm and pull them into the house. They have their moment of awe like I did when I arrived. They stare up at the ceiling and gawk at the sheer size and grandeur around them. I wait for Conrad's voice to boom overhead and throw the outsiders into the cold but it doesn't. I lead them into the kitchen to meet my new friends.

"I swear, Bella, since you've arrived there's been more action in this house than ever," Mr. Potter says. He wipes his hand on his jeans before extending it to Beattie. "Patrick Potter."

"Beattie Cod," she says and she meets him with an aggressive handshake. "I'm Bella's boss back home."

"And who is this young man?" Lusta asks from behind.

I tap Jonah on the shoulder and sign to him, "This is Lusta. She's Lottie's mother, the girl I told you about."

Jonah nods in understanding and signs to Lusta, "It's nice to meet you." She looks at me confused and a little panicked and I shake my head at Jonah.

"She doesn't sign."

"Well, we need to do something about that." Then, to Lusta, he holds out his hand and says, "I'm Jonah Southland, Bella's brother."

"Oh! What a treat!" she exclaims, shaking my brother's hand. "What brings you two up here?"

"I have business to attend to in New Jersey and Bella's friends thought she could use a little company." Beattie says. "It'll only be for a few days. I'll pick him up on my way home."

"We're happy to have him," Lusta says. She squeezes Jonah's hand a little tighter. She seems lighter and happier with people around.

"Absolutely," Mr. Potter continues. "We will take good care of him, my ginger sister." I know Beattie. That is not a term of endearment to her. Normally, she would have given him some crap, some mocking line, but for my sake she doesn't.

"Miss Cod," Lusta begins, breaking the silence. "Please tell me you'll stay for dinner." My boss visibly shudders at the formal address. "Beattie, please," she corrects. "As much as I would love to, I need to get back on the road." She looks at me and smiles.

"You sure you can't stay a little longer? Mr. Potter makes great food," I offer as some kind of incentive for her to stay. Bribery may be wrong, but it can be effective.

She places her hand on my cheek, rubbing her thumb across my skin. "As true as I'm sure that may be, I have driving to do."

"Thanks for bringing Jonah here," I say.

"I was happy to do it," she says. "Walk me to the car? It was very nice to meet you both," she says to Lusta and Mr. Potter.

Mr. Potter, being his normal self, raises his baseball mitt of a hand and bellows, "Bye-bye ginger sister!" Lusta shoots him a look, equal parts exhaustion and annoyance.

"Why are you like this?" she mutters to him.

"How are you really doing?" Beattie asks once we're outside.

I try to find the right words. "I miss being home, but it seems to be getting a little better every day."

She nods, "Well, I miss you, that's for sure. I've already fired Goldie two times this week. And I had to leave Rosie in charge of the shop. I'm pretty sure I'm having heart palpitations."

I giggle and pat her on the shoulder. "Rosie will do fine, she's smarter than she thinks. Plus, I'll make sure Elle double checks everything."

"Not as smart as you, not that anyone is," Beattie says as we reach the car. "I guess it's good for me to get used to what life will be like when you're off rocking the ivy league."

Something about the way she says it feels like a punch in the stomach. There's too much finality to it. Her fingers curl around the edge of the door. "If you need me, you call me. Okay?" I nod and step away, allowing her to pull backwards out of her spot next to my car. I wave to the back of her vehicle, fighting the instinct to sprint after her as she heads down the driveway. I wait for the gate to swing open and turn back to the house. The curtains in one of the upstairs windows flutters and my stomach flips. There's nothing he doesn't see. I step inside, shaking off the chill of outside, and make my way back to the kitchen. Lusta and Jonah sit across from one another at the kitchen table. He's molding her hands into proper gestures to make the correct signs.

"What's happening here?" I say, sitting down beside Lusta.

"I don't like the notion of a parent who can't communicate with their kid," Jonah signs back to me. His eyes are fixed and determined. My parents and I were able to learn American Sign Language together with Jonah. It's hard for him to imagine a world where he couldn't speak easily with our parents.

Lusta groans, hands motioning between us. Already defeated, her eyes flipping back and forth between the two of us. "There's no way I'll ever be able to sign like that."

"Yes, you will," I encourage. "It takes a long time and a lot of practice, but you can do this." I look up to Jonah and ask, "What are you teaching her?"

"I figured the alphabet is the best place to start. Then at least she can fingerspell," Jonah signs with a shrug. I should have thought of that. For God's sake, there are YouTube videos that can teach the alphabet! "We're still on 'B,'" he sighs as he straightens out Lusta's fingers.

When we're about halfway through the letters, the front door flys open. Lottie skips into the kitchen, flinging her backpack against the wall. She grabs a juice box from the fridge and a bag of chips from Mr. Potter. She goes through all her normal motions, until she sees us. Her gaze narrows on Jonah.

"Who's this?" she signs.

Jonah starts to sign before I can answer."You must be Lottie," he says with a grin that would make any little girl blush. Lottie's eyes expand to three time their normal size as she crushes her juice box against her chest.

"This is my brother, Jonah," I sign, trying to throw her a bone about what's going on. "He came to visit me."

She places her snack and drink on the counter, her skeptical eyes never leaving Jonah. "Nice to meet you," she signs before grabbing her food and dashing away. I hear her stomp up the stairs, getting as far away as she can.

Jonah turns to me and asks, "Was it something I said?"

"Your devilish good looks are too much for an eight year old." He puts all his attention back on Lusta and her lesson.

"This room is bigger than our house!" he declares.

"Signing please!" I demand with my hands. "You're basically screaming." One time when we were little, my mom took us to the mall to buy shoes. A little boy down the aisle from us started throwing a full blown, nuclear level temper tantrum. Jonah turned to me and shouted, loud enough for everyone two stores over to hear, "Bella, we'd get a beating if we did that!"

His subtlety has not evolved in the years since.

"Why haven't I met this guy yet?" he asks, flopping himself onto the bed.

"He's not exactly social," I explain, hoping he'll drop it, but I know my brother better than that.

"Maybe I can do school with you tomorrow?" he asks.

My eyes narrow and I pinch his big toe, making him squirm. "This is not a circus, Jonah Leonard."

He pulls his foot away from me. "Don't you full name me I-S-A-B-E-L-L-A," he takes the effort to slowly fingerspell my first name. "I am aware that he's not a sideshow. I would like to meet him. I'm only here for a few days."

"I can ask him, but I make no promises. He's not exactly warm and fuzzy."

"Are any of us?" he asks with a smile.

He doesn't know the half of it.

On my climb to the greenhouse, I hear soft, acoustic music from inside. I push through the door, which creaks loudly on its hinges, to find Conrad sitting cross-ankled on the floor reading. Upon noticing my entrance he throws his book behind a planter and rips the tube of his nebulizer from his lips. Smooth.

"You have no sense of boundaries do you?" he scoffs, but his smile betrays his amusement.

"Were you doing homework?" I tease. "Like actual schoolwork? Am I that good?"

He crosses his arms over his broad chest. "I admit nothing, deny everything, and demand proof," he says with a cock of his eyebrow. Proof? Okay, I can do that. I get up and move in the direction of the discarded book. He laughs and sticks his leg out to block me before reaching down and picking up the copy of *Sophie's Choice* that he chose from his English reading list.

"Okay, you caught me. I figured I'd get a head start on you." His cheeks pink with embarrassment as he tucks the text away and takes in a deep crackling breath through the mouthpiece.

"I've already read it twice," I say with a giggle. Books are my thing, after all, and this is a classic.

"I can't win!" he exclaims with a laugh, and it's nice to see him light, like a normal teenager.

"Listen," I start, changing the position in my seat to sit on my hands. It feels safer that way. "I'm sure on the security cameras you saw that we have a guest with us." He takes no immediate move to make it easier on me. I hate asking for things.

"I assume from the super secret spy language that he's your brother?"

"Right, secret spy language." I can't wait to tell Jonah about that. He'll get a kick out of it.

"Super," he corrects, pointing a finger in my direction. "Super secret spy language. It's an important distinction."

"I should have asked you if it was okay for him to be here," I admit, my voice lowering almost to a whisper. "I'm sorry. I was excited to see him."

He takes another breath before sitting the nebulizer aside. "You don't have to apologize. You're forcing me to get used to having people around. Maybe it's all part of my extended education. You know, before you got here Pollie would only stop by maybe once a week, if that, and I barely ever saw her."

That surprises me, especially considering how much I've seen her here. "I'm sure that doesn't have anything to do with me." I lie, since I'm the thing that's changed.

"Of course it does. It's okay, I've done a lot of work to make it that way," he says, adjusting his position on the floor. "You're making me get back into the world, at least into the realm of other people. What's one more in the house?" Before he returns to his book he mutters, "Except Gattman."

I choose to ignore the Gatty comment and focus on the positive. "Well, I appreciate it." Of course that isn't all I have to ask. "I was wondering if you'd be okay with him joining us for school for the next couple of days?" The words sputter from my lips before I lose the nerve to say them.

The sides of his mouth turn down as a groan escapes him. "You push too much, Miss Southland."

"Pleeeeeeeease," I sing with my fingers clasped together in front of my chest. "He's rather awesome, my little brother. He reads lips well and he talks. It won't be all spy language. I promise."

"Super secret spy language," he corrects, that familiar half smile coming into view. "Fine," he lets out in a huff. "You're making me soft, Isabella. What will this do for my reputation?"

"I think you'll survive," I laugh.

CHAPTER ELEVEN

The next morning, bright and early, I explode through the door into Jonah's room. I take a flying leap onto his bed, before cringing in a moment of regret, hoping I don't break the legs. Jonah buries his face in his pillows like an ostrich in the sand.

"Go away," he mumbles, his voice swallowed by the fluff.

I place my hands on his cheeks and turn him to face me. His eyes blink against the morning light. I place my index finger on my chin and say slowly, "You wanted to join us for school. We do school in the morning." Then with a smack on the mattress, I exclaim, "Up!"

"I hate you," he mumbles before flopping over onto his back. "Give me ten minutes?"

"Downstairs in the kitchen," I sign, heading to the door. I woke up extra early with a spring in my step, having Jonah here. I skip down to where the entire gang awaits.

The morning ritual is well under way. Lottie shovels cereal in her face while Lusta mercilessly pulls her hair into braids. Mr.

Potter flips pancakes while whistling and dancing to his own beat. Everything is in order except for one blaring difference. Conrad sits at the table with a full plate of breakfast and no black hoodie.

"Good morning, Isabella," he says around a mouthful of food. Mr. Potter hands me my plate and I join Conrad at the table.

"Well this is a nice surprise, Connie."

He spears a giant bite of eggs and pops it into his mouth. "I thought I'd start embracing this more social life that you've thrust upon me."

"What a welcome change," I mock. The playful banter settles into silent chewing. Lottie grabs her lunch from Mr. Potter then runs around in a circle to kiss all of us goodbye. When Jonah steps into the doorway she freezes.

"Off to school?" he signs to her with a lopsided grin. Her body goes rigid before she sprints around him. Jonah chuckles before taking his own plate of food. My brother halts in his tracks after making eye contact with Conrad. Ever the gentleman, Conrad stands up and extends his good hand to my brother.

"You must be Jonah," he says with a rigid spine. Perfect posture must be a Baxter rule. I have never held my breath tighter than in the long moment I wait for Jonah's reaction. *Please don't be weird!* If a psychic sibling connection ever intends to happen, this would be an ideal time.

Jonah cocks an eyebrow and stares at Conrad like his hand is toxic before he takes it in his own. "You must be His Highness."

So much for not being weird. Shooting daggers at him with my eyes seems to make him correct himself. "I mean Conrad, of course."

"I thought I told you to change?" I ask with my hands when Jonah joins us at the table. It's not time yet to switch to speaking. I

169

need to get my brother to stop embarrassing me first. He glances down at his clothes and looks at me like I'm crazy.

"What's wrong with what I'm wearing?" he asks out loud.

"Nothing, by my calculations," Conrad says with a smile. "Your sister tells me you'll be joining us this morning," he says more to Jonah.

"That was the plan, if that's okay with you," Jonah says. It's like having a normal conversation where Conrad isn't burned and Jonah isn't deaf. I know the two aren't very used to that.

"Fine by me," Conrad responds. "Should we get to it?" Conrad asks, pushing away from the table.

Jonah inhales his food at lightning speed, done before I've had even a few bites. I doubt he even tasted it. He grabs his plate, and Conrad's, and heads to the sink. Mr. Potter looks like he's seen a ghost as a child proceeds to clean his own dishes. Even Conrad seems surprised. It can't possibly be that strange.

"Jonah and I will meet you in the greenhouse in a few," I say as I reach forward and touch Conrad's arm. I can feel his muscles tense under my touch, but he doesn't pull away. He offers me a simple sharp nod before leaving.

"What's happening?" Jonah asks when he turns around after shutting off the water.

"Thank you," I say before anything else.

"For what?" he asks, balancing his elbows on the bar.

"I don't know. For not gawking, for not saying anything about the way he looks. For being here at all."

His lips press into a thin line to keep from laughing. "Hardest. Moment. Of. My. Life. I knew you'd be mad at me if I made any jokes. I resisted."

I take a deep breath and fight the urge to punch him. "Go get your school stuff and I'll meet you in the hall upstairs."

"How did it happen?" Jonah asks not even five minutes after we set up in the greenhouse. Apparently he'd used all the chill he had and couldn't take anymore. The kid at the carnival can only hold out so long. Conrad only looks at me briefly from behind his thick glasses before answering.

"I'm assuming you mean the burns," he asks, even though it doesn't come across as a question.

"You don't need to answer him," I begin with my voice and hands. "He's an idiot."

"I'm sitting right here," Jonah exclaims and I'm surprised to see Conrad laugh from the corner of my eye. The two of them sit across from each other with me in the middle so that I can interpret as necessary.

"It's okay, Bella," Conrad says, touching my shoulder. "I don't mind telling him. I'm sure it's a question anyone would ask."

I let him talk, but that doesn't mean I don't shoot my little brother a murderous look of displeasure. Conrad balances his elbows on his knees. Across from him Jonah does the same.

"A little over a year ago, I was street racing with a friend in the car my father bought me for my birthday. It was late and we were on a back road full of sharp turns and without any street lights. Ideal for two young men looking for danger. In other words, I was stupid. I took a turn a little too fast. By a little, I mean enough to flip my car. I don't totally remember what came next, but others have pieced it together for me." His breathing becomes a little ragged and I want to stop this, but I don't think Conrad is actually telling this story to Jonah. I think it's to me.

"The car rolled several times. I remember the first one and that I held my breath. I didn't come to again until after the car stopped rolling. That's when I smelled it."

"What?" I hear myself say it before I realize I'd thought it.

He never skips a beat.

"The gas and then the fire. Thankfully, I blacked out pretty soon after. A few days later, the police told me that my friend in the other car bailed and left me there. Two men that lived in a house across the street pulled me from the car. I still wake up sometimes in a cold sweat because I think I can remember burning. Remember the feeling and the smell of my skin on fire."

"What happened then?" Jonah asks.

"I spent months in the burn unit. I'll spare you the gory details of what it's like to be there." I shiver at the thought. Conrad's entire focus centers on me, making sure I'm okay. I smile the best I can.

"Let's talk about Sophie and her choices!" I exclaim, sucking the tears back in. Jonah chuckles and goes back to his history book. We fall into the world of the written word for a few blissful hours. Later that afternoon, Conrad decides to take a nap. After informing me that I've missed my calling as a drill sergeant, of course. Apparently in all his years of schooling, he's never been educated by anyone as strict as me. I tell him that I'm only using the Jessica Southland teaching methods that I grew up with, but he doesn't hear me as he's already off to bed.

After Jonah takes a shower, I use the opportunity of the two of us left to our own devices to show him around the house. The room I'm most excited about is the library. Jonah may not share my love of reading to the same extreme, but I doubt any person could see this room and not be impressed.

I expect to find it quiet and empty. To my surprise, Pollie sits on the couch with a book open on her lap. Her normally springy curls are separated into two braids that run down beside her ears. With her pigtails and uniform she looks like a backup dancer from a nineties era music video. Normally Pollie would greet me with a "Hey Chicky," but standing there barefoot, in ripped jeans and a "Too Many Jennifers" tee-shirt is Jonah.

His soft brown ringlets are still dripping from his shower. I look back at Pollie who has a defined twinkle in her eye. She hasn't met him yet. I wave to my brother to get his attention and sign and speak. "Jonah, this is Conrad's sister Pollie." I take the time to deliberately fingerspell each letter. "Pollie, this is my brother Jonah. He's here to visit me for a few days."

"Nice to meet you Pollie," he says, his voice as clear as I've ever heard it. He crosses the library in a few, long strides and extends a hand. Her eyebrow cocks up near her hairline before she takes it in hers.

"Nice to meet you." Unfortunately, she tucked her chin into her shoulder, so there's no way he could read her lips.

"You have to make sure you're looking at him when you speak," I say to Pollie. "Or he won't know what you're saying."

She straightens up and says again, "It's nice to meet you."

I interrupt their moment and motion around the room. "Isn't this place incredible?" I say aloud. Privately to Jonah I sign, "Focus, Casanova."

"It's pretty amazing," he says, sitting down beside Pollie on the couch. "What are you reading?"

"I was actually going to ask your sister about this," she begins, lifting up her textbook for me to see the cover. "How's your Latin?" she asks, her eyes full of despair. I'm pretty sure she'll give me a kidney if I tell her what she wants to hear.

Jonah jumps in before I can. "Id est bonum," he says. I'm pretty sure it means "it's all right," but for all I know, it could be "insecure penguin." Latin is not my strongest language.

To Pollie however, it doesn't seem to matter. She nudges her textbook over to him with a sweet smile and says, "Any chance you want to do my homework for me?"

Jonah scoots a little closer and I'm increasingly aware that I've become a third wheel. Typical.

"I'm not going to do it, but I'll help you."

"That would be amazing!" Pollie exclaims, clapping her hands together. The two squish closer together and I feel completely out of place.

"Is this what brings you here today, Pollie? Homework?" My conversation with Conrad about Pollie coming to see me more than him has been bugging me.

"More than homework actually. I wanted to see if you were interested in going out with me tonight."

I cock my head to the side and ask, "Isn't it a school night?"

She bites her lip to stop herself from laughing. Coming from someone younger than me, her patronizing nature around my naivety is a little irksome.

"It'll be okay, I promise."

I think about how out of place I'd felt at the last party.

"I don't know, I'm pretty tired," I lie, fingers tracing the spines of the books on the shelves. A night here would be a party much more my speed.

Pollie begins to pluck at her braids. Her hair falls in soft curls and my brother definitely notices. In fact, I'm not sure if I've ever seen him look so intently at a girl.

"Listen," Pollie begins, running her hands through her freed hair. Jonah isn't even pretending to look at her Latin book any longer. His hand hovers above it as he gawks at Pollie. "This is a much smaller and laid back thing. A few people at my friend Jamie's house. I'll have you home by eleven." She sounds like the pushy boyfriend from an 80's teen comedy that tries to pressure his girlfriend.

I look over to Jonah and sign, "Have any interest in going to a party tonight?" I hope that he says no and guilts me into not leaving him.

"With her? I think I'd go just about anywhere with her."

"Seriously?" The underside of my eye starts to twitch like an S.O.S. in Morse code.

"Sure. I'd love to see more of how the other half lives."

Through a clenched jaw, I ask Pollie if she would mind if Jonah joined us. She beams, clapping her hands together. "Oh, Chicky, that would be excellent!" She leans over and kisses Jonah on the cheek. "I'd love for you to join us."

His entire body freezes and pink color spreads up his neck and across his face. The Southlands are blushers.

"Okay! Game plan! I'm going to freshen up. Then Jonah and I will do my homework and then we'll go. Sound good to you guys?"

As cartoon hearts spin around my little brother's head, I know he's down for anything. "Yeah, that's great. Text me when you're ready and we'll go."

She skips from the room and Jonah melts into a puddle on the couch. "She kissed me!"

I shrug like it's no big deal even though we both know it is.

"I mean, she did, but in the same way you'd kiss our grandma. It was very sweet." I flutter my eyelashes at him and he doesn't appreciate it.

"Don't you have a party to get ready for?" he mocks. Clearly I'm the winner of the little bicker battle. Sisters rule after all.

"Yeah, about that," I say, switching gears back to annoyance. "You were supposed to be my 'get out of jail free' card."

The corners of his mouth turn down. "I feel like I should be offended."

"Don't be dramatic. I thought we'd hang out tonight, just the two of us." Jonah picks up Pollie's Latin book and starts flipping mindlessly through the pages.

"It's been just the two of us our whole lives. This will be fun."

After finishing her homework with Jonah and leaving me to fret over what to wear for far too long, Pollie shows up in the doorway of my bedroom with a garment back draped over her arm. "Jesus, Chicky, did you leave anything in your closet?" she asks, motioning to the mountain of clothes on my bed.

"I was trying to find something suitable to wear."

"Ask and you shall receive," she says, tossing the bag on top of the pile smothering my bed.

"What is that?"

She shrugs, fingering through the endless line of cardigans laid out on the bedspread. "A little birdie told me you might need an outfit."

"Is that birdie named Lusta?"

She pulls an invisible zipper across her lips and shakes her head. Leave it to Lusta to know what I need more than I do. Inside the bag is a solid back dress with black leather panels down the sides. I search for the rest of the material. There's no way this can be all of it. The sound of my heart pounding is overwhelming.

Pollie's hand covers mine. "Trust me, it's going to look great."

I shoo Pollie out of my room so that I can try on the dress. I slip out of my clothes and step carefully into it. My heart starts to race like I'm being swallowed by a giant snake. While it's in my size, I struggle to get myself into the Bodycon silhouette. I'm shocked when it zips rather easily up my back, the end of the zipper settling between my shoulder blades. The panic that had consumed me moments before has nowhere to go and my hands start shaking. A million images rush my mind from the best to worst case scenarios as I dread what I'll see in the mirror. I hold in a deep breath, and my stomach, when I turn to my reflection.

The rolls that I normally try to hide from myself and the world, ripple through the fabric. The panic reroutes its way from my hands to my lungs. My breathing comes in shallow puffs. I thrust my hands into my hair, frantically searching for some way to make this better. I start shifting through the pile of clothes I've created on my bed looking for the control top tights that I brought. Maybe they'll suck things in a little. Upon finding them I shimmy into the shiny black nylon, tugging them higher and higher until they rest right below my bra line. The tights make a huge difference and if I don't sit or breathe all night, no one will notice that I'm not thin. It sounds stupid, even in my own head. I turn to the side again and cringe at the sight of my flabby arms. A cardigan hides all sins. With my pale and makeup-less skin, and messy top-knot of muddy brown hair, I'm definitely not a vision. I scrub my hands over my exasperated face. I can do this. After a battle with a brush and an eyelash curler, I leave my room at least slightly put together. Bursting into the hall with too much excitement, I run face first into Conrad.

"Sorry," I yelp when I see him, but then feel strange by the way he's staring at me. Oh God, my rolls must be even worse than I thought. *Suck it in, Isabella! Suck it in!* I cover my stomach with my hands.

"What?" I whine when he doesn't look away.

"Nothing," he says, adjusting his thick glasses. He dog-ears the page of his book he's on and closes it. We will be having a serious conversation about that crime another time.

"You look different," he says, motioning to me.

Different is never the word a girl wants to hear in reference to her appearance. I take another long self conscious look down at my attire. I might be better off switching back to my leggings and sweater.

"Is different bad?"

The dress is a little short, but the tights should help with that. He pushes his glasses up on top of his head. I love seeing his full face without his hair blocking half of it from view. Burns or no burns, he's a handsome guy.

"It's not bad at all." he mutters, clearing his throat. His eyes scan the cover of his book with an intensity that could burn holes through the pages. I must look pretty nice. "Only, it looks more like something Palarma would wear than you."

I have to admit that he does, in fact, have a point. From the black color to the leather, this is a very Pollie-esque outfit. I shrug, trying my best to focus on the fact that different isn't bad.

"Change is good isn't it?"

His right shoulder shrugs up to his ear. "I don't mind you the way you are," he says. He moves his glasses back into place and opens his book. Before he gets too far past me, he adds, "Have a good night Isabella."

"You too, Connie."

Downstairs in the living room, Pollie and my brother sit shoulder to shoulder on the couch watching TV. When she sees me, Pollie lets out a high-pitched whistle. "Look at you!" she exclaims.

"What are you wearing?" Jonah demands, gawking at me.

With Conrad I, was shy and self-conscious but with Jonah I'm annoyed. "It's a dress. Girls wear them sometimes," I respond, sticking my tongue out in an expert demonstration of maturity.

"Mom would kill you if she saw you in that." He can be really obnoxious sometimes. I reach forward to grab him by the chin and focus his attention on my face.

"Then it's a good thing she isn't here." These are not the kind of thoughts I would ever voice out loud. Something about the distance from home has made me more brazen. I kiss him on the tip of his nose and he giggles like a little boy. I can't help smiling.

I'm just about to take a seat in my favorite chair when Lottie skips into the room. She comes to a screeching halt, her attention hyper focused on Jonah.

"Hi Lottie," I say to her, trying to break up a little bit of the tension. She's not biting.

"Oh! I've got this!" Pollie proclaims, flipping around in her seat to face Lottie. In slow, deliberately fingerspelled letters, Pollie signs, "H-I L-O-T-T-I-E." This makes Lottie scowl harder and I can't understand why.

"Good job!" my brother cheers, giving the sign for "applause".

"It's the alphabet," Lottie signs sharply, her face contorting. "I learned that before I even went to school."

I narrow my eyes, more than the tiniest bit perturbed at her attitude. Shouldn't she be happy that the people around her are making an effort?

"What's wrong with you?"

Lottie doesn't answer me, simply continues to scowl.

"Well that's enough of that," I mutter under my breath before turning to Pollie.

"Hey, can you two give me five minutes?" After giving their nod of approval, I walk over to Lottie, still hovering in the doorway. She looks up at me with fierce and angry eyes and I motion her toward me with my index finger. Together we walk into the foyer and she plops down on the bottom stair.

"Okay," I begin with my hands, settling in for the story. "What is going on with you?" She glares at me for a long moment, no attempt to uncoil her arms from around her. Then, in one fluid motion, she angles herself toward me and starts signing so fast that her fingers may fly off completely.

"I have been deaf my whole life. Nobody has ever even tried to learn sign language. Then he," the expression of disdain on her face nearly snaps her in two, "comes here and everyone wants to learn! Next thing I know, Mr. Potter will be doing it, too."

"But isn't it a good thing everyone is starting to learn it?" I ask. Angry crocodile tears drop over the rim of her eyelids.

"But they didn't want to learn for me, they only started to learn because of him," and that angry face is back. Maybe I'd read the situation wrong yesterday. Perhaps it wasn't a girlhood crush that Lottie had with Jonah. It was jealousy.

"I don't think," I begin, pausing to not make the situation worse. "I don't think your mom didn't want to learn. I don't think she knew where to start. My parents went through months of classes to learn. With it just being your mom and her work schedule, I don't think that was an option for her. It must have been hard for her to know where to begin. That's all Jonah gave her, a place to leap from."

Lottie's stubborn little face continues to frown, but I can see her eyes softening. "And Pollie?" she signs back. I bite my lip to keep from smiling too big.

"Well, she probably learned the alphabet to impress Jonah."

Finally, the anger breaks a bit and she wipes away the last of her stubborn tears. "You're probably right."

"Look at the bright side. Now you can start showing your mom new signs since she's figured out her letters." I say. But from the anxious look on her face I can tell that's not everything.

"Lottie, is there something else?" She fiddles with her fingers in her lap, before she explains.

"Being deaf, here in the house, it's what makes me special. All the kids I go to school with are deaf and sign, but I'm the only one here. I guess I wasn't thinking I'd ever have to share that with anyone."

"Listen to me," I sign slowly, making sure she absorbs what I'm about to say. "You are incredibly special and being deaf is only a small part of that. You are by far the coolest little kid I have ever met in my life. I promise you it isn't because you're deaf. It's because you're awesome. You're smart, funny, and wise beyond your years. Being deaf is another layer, but not everything."

She beams, her smile stretching across her perfect, straight teeth as she wraps her arms around my shoulders. She leans back far enough to sign with one hand, "I'm glad you came here."

"Me too."

A poppy song blasts from Pollie's speakers as we zoom down the winding country roads. Jonah stretches out in the back seat playing on his phone while Pollie and I talk.

"Where are we going?" I ask, having to shout over the boom of the bass.

"Well," Pollie begins, content with shouting. "It was supposed to be at my friend Jamie's, but her parents opted to cut their trip short. It's been moved to Gatty's."

"Are his parents ever home?" I ask.

"Of course, but they go away a lot."

"Without him?"

"Without him, without each other. Relationships can be complicated, Chicky, at least that's what my dad always says." She turns the music up and the conversation is over.

As we make our final approach up the hill to Gatty's house, I worry that Pollie only told me it would be a small gathering to get me to come. We find the house eerily quiet. No crowd spilling from the front door, no one taking our coats, and no music thumping through the walls and floor. The party seems to be happening in a room down the main hallway. About fifteen people are paired off and talking with glasses of wine.

"Did we wander into a cocktail party?" Jonah mocks. He's right of course. This strikes me more like a scene out of *Mad Men* than a teen party.

"See," Pollie says, pinching me softly in the side. "I told you it wasn't a big party."

A tall thin girl with narrow features and way too much mascara walks up to us and groans to Pollie. "Girl, I'm glad you're here. This is a drag. It would have been much better at my house."

"Well, Jamie darling, maybe you should watch your parent's schedule a little closer. It's great that Gatty could host at all on such short notice. Be nice." Pollie reaches out for my hand and pulls me into the conversation. "Chicky, this is my friend Jamie Torrance. Jamie this is-" but she doesn't get a chance to finish as Jamie interrupts.

"Oh, I know who she is," she sneers, her face is cold and unreadable as her eyes scan my body. I have no idea what she means until my mind jumps back to the rumors Parker is spreading around her school and I want to be sick.

Jonah must sense my apprehension because he puts his phone away for the first time since we left the house. "What does she mean by that?" he asks.

"Don't worry about it," I responded. I have neither the will nor the energy to explain any of this to him. It's when Jonah protectively puts his arm around my shoulders that the energy in the room shifts.

"Hey bro, want to get your hand off my girl?" Gatty demands, moving towards us in focused, powerful strides.

Jonah, not the least bit fazed, says, "Do you know this tool?"

I knew we should have stayed home. Before things can come to any sort of blows, I step in between the two.

"Gatty, this is my brother Jonah."

I can almost hear Gatty hit the brakes in brain, switching gears just as fast. "No way, the deaf guy? Nice to meet you man."

Jonah eyes him with dumbfounded awe. To me he signs, "Who the hell is this guy?"

"Mind if I steal your sister for a minute?" Gatty asks before I can answer. His lips brush my ear and a pleasant chill runs through me. Electricity sparks through every neuron in my body as he places his hand on the small of my back. "Let's go find somewhere to talk."

From the corner of my eye I can see Jamie chuckle. I'm sure she probably thinks it's a code for us to run off and hook up. That should bother me and in any other instance it would, but I need to get out of this room. I let him lead the way, his hand sliding from my back to link our fingers together at our sides. I feel bad for leaving Jonah, but Pollie has already commandeered him into meeting her other friends. A few moments and hallways later we're back in the same office where we met. He flops down on the leather couch and pats the seat beside him. I sit down, crossing my ankles and resting my hands on my lap. My posture is perfect and I'm incredibly uncomfortable.

"What's up?" he asks.

I'm even less subtle than I thought. My tongue jets out of my mouth to lick my lips and I twist to face him a little better.

"I know that Parker said all those terrible things about me. I guess I didn't expect anyone to believe it or throw it in my face. And I really didn't want my brother to know anything about it."

He doesn't address my concern, not even a moment of pause, before he says, "No, I don't mean tonight. I put my number in your phone at the restaurant and I haven't heard from you. What gives?" He seems annoyed. Is he actually mad at me? I remember that my friends told me to be honest. That's what I intend to be.

"Right, I wanted to talk to you about that," I say. I wish I could take my eyes off my hands and look at him directly. Sometimes there's only so much courage a person can muster, in a single moment.

"It made me uncomfortable that you drank and drove me home. I know you said you were okay to drive, but I didn't like it. I know that probably makes me sound like a child to you, but that's how I feel." I blurt it out at such a hurried pace that I worry he didn't catch it all. The silence that grows between us in those next few moments deafens and seems to last for years. I feel two fingers under my chin as he lifts my face to his. His expression is full of compassion and the corner of his mouth turns up.

"Is that all?" he asks, his voice soft and sweet. Tears burn the back of my eyes. I'm overcome by my own bravery and how well he's taking it. "Bella, you should have told me then," he chastises.

He makes it sound so easy.

"Well, I did offer to drive," I begin, sitting up a little straighter and his hand falls away from my chin. "You insisted you were fine. I should have pushed it, but I didn't know what else to say. And... I wanted you to like me." He runs his hand through his parted hair, messing it up.

"I'm sorry I made you feel unsafe. I promise I wasn't drunk. I get it now. You aren't comfortable with any drinking and driving at all. It won't happen again." I force a smile that doesn't feel honest.

"I appreciate that, thank you for taking it seriously."

"Feel better?" he asks. Tension continues to pulse through my body as I summon another pinched smile.

"Yes, thank you."

"Good," he begins, shifting a closer to me on the couch. "Now that's that out of the way," the tip of his index finger runs over my knee. "Think I could kiss you hello?"

Maybe that's the best way to relax and turn my brain off for a while?

"Because looking at you in this dress, you are so hot."

My cheeks flame over his words. I'm still adjusting to the concept of any man outside of my family telling me that I'm beautiful.

The term hot is a real shock to my system. He places his hand on my cheek, his fingers moving through my hair to the back of my head, pulling me toward him. His eyebrows lift in a question as his mouth nears mine. I am unable to form a coherent word, but I can nod my head up and down. That's all it takes before his lips connect with mine and I have to remember how one breathes while making out. I try to focus on relaxing and enjoying it, but I think my brain might be broken. I let my hands roam to his shoulders as his arms wrap around my back to pull me closer. My heart flutters, my eyes close and I try to lose myself to the moment. He's adept in what he's doing. He must have a lot of practice.

Nope! I refuse to let my insecurities ruin this for me. I let it all drift away and tell myself to remember this moment. Remember how it feels to be so wanted. I stop fighting, stop worrying that I'll be awkward, and follow Gatty's lead. His tongue teases at the seal of my lips, begging for entrance. I let myself take a deep breath in through my nose before letting my lips part. A growl hums in Gatty's throat as the grip of his fingers digs into the skin of my back, sending a pulsing flicker to the pit of my stomach. His right hand moves back behind my head and he eases me back against the couch. Due to the narrowness of the seat, I have no choice but to split my legs and let him settle between them. His movements become more hurried, more aggressive. He switches his hand to my knee, pulling my leg up higher, sliding me further down the couch. I'm lost in the kissing until his hand starts to move up under my skirt. I snap back to reality with such abruptness that it leaves me breathless.

"Whoa, whoa, Gatty," I start, trying to catch my breath, but his mouth is still sealed over mine. I work my arm down to place my hand over his as he reaches the top of my hip under my clothes. "Slow down Gatty, slow down."

"What's wrong?" he asks half hearted, switching to kissing and licking against my neck. I didn't even know that was a thing! His fingers brush against the sensitive flesh of my upper thigh and it takes all my willpower to stay focused.

"You're moving too fast. I need this to slow down," I pant. I'm trying and nearly failing to keep my wits about me because of whatever voodoo he's doing to my neck. "Way down," I insisted and pushed his hand away. He groans and settles his forehead against my collarbone.

"What's the problem? I thought you weren't mad at me?" he sounds frustrated.

I lift his head to mine. "I'm not mad. It's that I'm not ready to move that fast."

He looks confused as his head cocks to the side. "You're not a virgin, are you?" The way he says virgin makes it sound like a filthy word. I didn't know that being a virgin was something to be embarrassed about.

"Well, I mean, I am, but that's not what this is about. I've only known you for like a week. I can't have sex with you." It's crazy to me that I have to argue my point.

A sly smile spreads across his lips as he kisses my cheek. "You know, it doesn't have to be sex. There are plenty of other things we can do." There is zero subtlety to his words, and while I may be inexperienced, I'm pretty sure I can connect the dots to what he means. I place my hand on his chest and push him back.

"No," I say simply. "I'm not ready for any of that."

He groans loudly and lifts his weight off me. He raises to a sitting position and mumbles under his breath.

We sit side by side in an awkward silence for what seems like forever. When I can't take it anymore, I pop up to my feet and run my hands through my hair a few times, hoping I don't look too tousled. I reach out for his hand and I'm thankful that he takes it. "Come on, let's go back to the party."

I approach Pollie and Jamie, in a very passionate, but hushed conversation, only the end of which I catch.

"Don't be a bitch, Jamie, she's my friend," Pollie is whistling, her voice hoarse. "Besides, you know Parker made up all that crap."

I'm frozen in position next to them, my arms cemented at my sides. A cruel smile slithers onto Jamie's face. She looks me up and down again with her harsh judgement. I'm all too aware of my kiss-swollen lips and messed up hair.

"Oh yeah, I'm sure she did," she snickers as she walks away. Pollie turns to me as she pushes her curls away from her frazzled face. Every insecurity I've ever felt comes bubbling to the surface. Like there's a piece of spinach stuck perpetually between my teeth. My dress is suddenly way too tight and short and my hair is too done and I'm wearing too much makeup. Even though none of those things are actually true.

"Do you know where Jonah is?"

"He went to get something to drink," Pollie says. Seeing a red solo cup in my brother's hand fills me with dread and irrational anger. Meeting him halfway across the floor, I motion to the cup, ready to let loose my big sister rage.

"Relax, it's water," he signs.

"Would you hate me if I wanted to leave?" I blurt out.

Jonah's eyes squint. "Did something happen? Did that guy do something?"

"Jesus! No!" I exclaim. "I just don't want to be here. I'd rather spend time with you back at the house. That's what we should have done in the first place."

"Yeah, let's go. These people make me uneasy anyway. Did you talk to Pollie already?"

I shake my head. "Not yet. Can you request a ride and I'll meet you out front after I talk to her." I'm suddenly so exhausted I can barely keep my eyes open.

When we split, I go back in search of Pollie and find her on the couch, thankfully by herself, perusing her phone. "Hey Poll, Jonah and are going to get going."

Her entire face falls. "I'm sorry this sucked so bad. Do you want me to come with you? I promise not to drag you to anymore of these things. I thought if they just got to know you a little better they'd realize that Parker was just being a jerk."

"It's all good, I want you to stay. I don't belong here." I let those words sink in because they're true. I can like Gatty and even date him, and I can hang out with Pollie and be friends with her. But as far as these people in their friend group? I don't need them or their acceptance. I'm not from their world, and from what I've seen, that's a good thing. Money isn't everything.

Pollie still looks guilty about letting me go by myself, but over in another corner Jamie calls out her name and I encourage her to go. I'm fine. I'm sure Jamie intends to make fun of me some more, but I don't care what she thinks. It's a shocking revelation, because usually I care what everyone thinks about everything.

These aren't my people and they never will be. It doesn't matter if they like me. I smooth my hands over the dress that I know I'll never wear again. Conrad was right, it isn't me.

Before I can head out the door, an arm reaches out and grabs me. Gatty pulls me against him, his breath heavy with the sweet and sour smell of wine. I'm ready for sweatpants and a cup of tea. Leather and liquor are not made for me.

"And where are you going?" he asks, holding me a little too close.

"I'm going to head home. I've got a headache." Again, not a lie, as the smell of booze is enough to turn my stomach. When I start to pull away he brings me back a little harder and wraps his arms around me, pinning my hands to my sides.

"No, you're fine. Stay and hang out with me for a little bit. I barely got to see you." The way he's whining makes me think he's drunker than I realized.

"Gatty, I will text you in the morning. Maybe we can do something this weekend?"

People on all sides are starting to stare and I don't need to be a spectacle. He's about to protest further when a kid in a striped button down walks up to him and proceeds to rub his nose and raise his eyebrows. Clearly it's another code I don't understand, but Gatty does.

"Yeah man I'll be right there," he replies before turning back to me. "Sure I can't convince you to stay?" He wiggles his eyebrows up and down while his fingers wander down my side again. He better not try to put them up my skirt.

"I'm sure." No sooner am I out of his grasp than he's fleeing into the next room with his friend. I grab my coat from the hall closet and join Jonah outside.

When we get back to the house we end up collapsing on the couch watching bad TV and giggling like little kids. I opt to head to bed first, thoroughly exhausted and emotionally spent. I crest the top stop, my arms stretched out from my sides, sighing at the pleasant popping sound between my shoulders.

"Are you all right?" I hear from beside me. I almost fall back down the stairs. Instead, my hand smacks the wall like a cat clawing for balance. The sound of the slap reverberates through the air in a strong echo.

"Damn it, Conrad! I'm going to put a bell around your neck!"

I can hear the snicker in his voice as he emerges from the shadows, he's good at that. Total comic book character. Of course, I'm starting to wonder if he's actually the villain, or a reluctant hero.

"Sorry you're so easily startled. Are you all right?" he asks again, that same deep tremble in his voice that hits me in the pit of my stomach.

I nod, regaining my bearings and say, "Of course, why wouldn't I be?" I never fully settle down around Conrad. My brain can never take a break. He always has me on my toes. He nods in the direction of one of the cameras in the ceiling.

"You weren't gone very long. I want to make sure you are okay." Again with the eye in the sky. But there is something endearing about the fact that he's looking out for me.

"Yeah," I say instead. I'm ready to get out of this dress and into something more comfortable. He blocks my route, unconvinced.

"It wasn't that much fun. I don't fit in with your crowd," I admit to him.

"Neither do I," he shrugs. I guess he has a point, but he once did, at least. I yawn in spite of myself, cringing for being rude, but in the ever classy Conrad fashion he moves along. I whisper a quiet good night to his back and head off to sleep.

CHAPTER TWELVE

The next morning, Jonah beats me to breakfast. It looks like Lottie woke up on time as her hair is already done and no one is moving at a panicked, hectic pace. The two each have a bowl of sugary cinnamon cereal and are deep in the middle of a life or death stare-off. Before I can ask, Mr. Potter hands me a steaming mug of tea. He's watching the two of them like a finals match at Wimbledon.

"What's going on?" I ask, blowing away the curls of steam. The fogginess they form on my glasses needs to go away. I have to see what's happening. Mr. Potter's broad shoulders shrug up to his ears as he takes a sip of his coffee.

"Hell if I know," he replies, his attention switching back and forth between them. "They both showed up about twenty minutes ago and have been staring at each other since. It's fascinating."

Mr. Potter does have a point. It's a rather extreme battle of wills and neither seems interested in being the one to break.

"Pass the honey, please," I ask, settling in to watch too. It's better than television. Completing our trifecta of voyeurs, Conrad enters the kitchen as well. Normally it would be a quick trip for him to either snag something from the fridge or to hustle me along, but not today. Today, he accepts a cup of coffee from Mr. Potter and leans next to me at the counter.

"What are we watching?" he asks.

"A David and Goliath battle of wills," Mr. Potter answers.

"Who's who in this scenario?"

"Both, they're each both," I respond honestly because it's true.

Lottie's phone starts to flash on the table in front of her. She hops up from her seat, eye contact never breaking from Jonah. Before she turns to leave she signs to him, "I'd say it was nice knowing you, but my mother told me I shouldn't lie."

The sly and cruel smile on her face cuts like a slap. Who knew she could be vicious?! I can tell my brother is biting the insides of his cheeks to keep from laughing. Jonah appreciates sass the way Gatty appreciates wine.

Conrad leans close to my ear and asks, "What did she say?"

I wave him off, trying to pay attention.

"Stupid super secret spy language," I hear him mutter.

No sooner has Lottie cleared the doorway, skipping as she goes, than my brother breaks into a fit of laughter. "Oh man! I like that kid," he exclaims aloud.

"What was that?" I squeak, my jaw hanging so low I'm afraid he won't be able to read my lips.

"Can someone clue in the people who don't speak the super secret spy language?" Conrad demands.

I roll my eyes, unaffected by his tantrum. "She was being super sassy," I rattle off, hoping that will placate him. To my brother, "Seriously, what just happened?"

194

He's still laughing so hard that tears pool in his eyes. It forces him to take a deep breath and level out enough to form a coherent sentence, he signs, "I don't know! I came down to get some breakfast and she was sitting there, staring at me with this evil glare. Man that last little jab! That was gold!"

"She's always sassy. It's her main personality trait." Conrad grumbles beside me. He sips his coffee, wincing at the scalding heat. Serves him right. "I'll meet you in the greenhouse," he says, pivoting out of the kitchen, continuing to sip the drink that's too hot. Boys never learn.

I opt to take a quick shower before heading up to the land of the roses. As I climb the steps to the greenhouse, I can hear Conrad arguing with someone. The growl in his voice sounds like a lion's roar and I'm not sure I want to go up. I crack the door just enough to see. Conrad sits on one of the stools opposite Jonah, who somehow looks more irked than Conrad. I wouldn't have thought that possible.

"This is absurd," Conrad barks, throwing his arms up.

I swear I can hear Jonah roll his eyes. My brother is not a fan of theatrics. "You are a frustrating ham sandwich of a human being," my brother barks back.

Conrad sits up, his face a beautiful combination of appalled and admiring. "Did you call me a ham sandwich?"

I'm not ready to break in on this yet. I turn and sit on a lower step, balancing my chin on the top one, wishing I had popcorn.

"I barely have two hands. Don't you need two hands for this?" Conrad whines as my brother tries to manipulate his fingers.

"Oh boohoo," Jonah exclaims, less than moved by Conrad's lamenting over his disability. My brother pities no one. "I've seen people work the whole language with one arm. You have more than they do. It's like when a person has a stroke. Sometimes it's a little hard to understand what they mean but eventually you get the gist and can fill in the blanks. You're like that!"

Conrad is silent for a long moment before he says, "I'm a ham sandwich who's had a stroke?"

"You're impossible is what you are!" Jonah yells to the ceiling. I figure that's enough alone time for the guys. I have no interest in cleaning up anyone's blood. I push off the stairs to a standing position before exploding through the door.

"Hello, beautiful boys!" Conrad eyes me like I'm some curious alien. Maybe I come on a little too strong.

"Beautiful boys?" he laughs, his eyebrow arched up at me. He looks down at himself, motioning his arms up and down. "You've seen me right?" He's nowhere near as grotesque as he imagines. In fact, after a little while, the burns aren't that noticeable.

"Yes, drama queen, I've seen you," I say with a scoff of my own. My words hang a little too heavy in the air for a moment before I cough to break the thick tension.

"What are you two up to?"

Conrad's panic is nearly audible before Jonah turns to me and says aloud, "House painting, World War II, exploring our hopes and dreams. You know, normal guy things."

"As entertaining as I'm sure all those topics are, what school related thing would we like to tackle this morning?" I put my glasses in place and flip open my tablet.

"I don't know about you two, but I have calculus to do," Jonah says before pushing his soft wavy hair from his face. All the men in my life need haircuts. I remember the last time I tried to tackle math with Conrad. It did not go well. I'm about to tell him we don't have to work on the same thing as Jonah. But I don't get the chance.

"Yeah," Conrad says, "we still need to get through calculus ourselves, don't we, Isabella?" Zero fight. I start nodding a little too enthusiastically, but can't seem to stop myself.

"We do, we do indeed," I exclaim like a secondary character in a Rodgers and Hammerstein musical. I wonder if that's the kind of reference Conrad would get.

"Sine, cosine, cosine, sine, 3.14159!" my brother shouts.

In this one moment, he brings to light the true level of our family nerdom with one of many rhymes my mother has instilled in us over the years. She heard it on some nineties sitcom and it is good at helping you remember the first few digits of Pi. I look cautiously at Conrad, trying to hide my suffocating shame. His face splits into a grin before his body explodes into ground shaking laughter. He grips at his bad side with his good hand. I start to worry that laughing like that is making it hard for him to breathe. Unfortunately, I've started laughing so hard myself that my vision blurs with tears. I'm of no help to anyone. On the right, I hear that familiar laugh of Jonah's and now the three of us are no good. When the roar dulls down to a hum, Conrad pulls an inhaler from the pocket of his jeans. He takes a few long pulls on it, coughing after each one.

"Where on earth did that come from?" he asks as his laughter fully subsides.

"It's something our mom taught us. It's Pi," I shrug. "She's full of those devices."

"Why didn't my dad hire her?" he asks. The room falls eerily quiet. I'm about to start defending myself when Conrad starts giggling again.

"Oh God, if you could see your face right now!"

I reach over and snap the rubber band on his wrist. "You think you're so funny, Baxter?" I shout, but a tremble of laughter betrays me. I'm no good at playing the tough guy. "I will have you know that I am quite smart!"

"Oh trust me, I know," he mocks. "Off to Brown in the fall."

As soon as the words leave his lips my heart drops to my shoes. My family doesn't know about school yet. I'm terrified to take my focus off of Conrad, but I am overwhelmed by Jonah's presence.

"My lip reading must be off. Say that again?" Hurt radiates off of him in waves as he settles forward, elbows on his knees. Conrad goes as white as a ghost, knowing that he's tread somewhere he shouldn't.

I turn completely to face my brother and sign, "I was going to tell you..."

"But you decided to tell him first?" my brother interrupts with his hands, gesturing to Conrad.

"I got the letter a few days before I came here. I didn't get a chance to tell anyone and then I was mad," I try my best to defend myself. But how can I really? My brother has always been my greatest cheerleader and I didn't share this major thing with him. Jonah's having none of it.

"You're mad at THEM! What did I do? Why didn't you tell me?" His gestures are big and overemphasized. The way his jaw sets under his skin reveals how hurt he really is.

"I don't need you to be sorry. This is a good thing, but damn it, hurts that you didn't tell me."

An apology isn't strong enough, but it's all I have. "Jonah, I am so sorry," I signed again. "You're my best friend. I should have told you."

"Brown!" He exclaims aloud, a smile twitching to his lips and he blinks the anger away. "Damn it, give me a hug!" I hop up to my feet and circle my arms around his waist. When we finally pull apart he takes a deep breath and signs, "I need a minute, okay?"

Jonah turns away and hustles down the stairs. I wait until I can no longer hear his footsteps before turning back to Conrad. An uncomfortable grimace stretched tight across his lips. His spine is pin straight with his hands pushed between his legs like a little boy in trouble.

"I didn't realize he didn't know. I can't apologize enough," he says again, finally allowing himself to shift in his seat. I sit back down on the stool beside him and hold my head in my hands. I'm suddenly completely exhausted.

"There was no way for you to know." He's not omniscient. I would have assumed my family was aware too.

"Can I ask you why you didn't tell them?" he questions, his voice smaller than I've ever heard it.

"I'm excited to go," I say. It shocks me how easy it is for me to be honest and open with Conrad. "I've worked really hard for it and an Ivy League school isn't something that just happens. My mom has been a huge part of that. I don't think it would have happened without her. But I needed a minute where it was only mine. I needed it to belong to me, before it became 'ours.'"

"I completely understand that." And I don't need anything more. At that moment, Conrad and I are the same. I love my mom, but I've always been under the thumb of her expectations. I have a feeling that before the accident it was like that for him and his father.

"Okay," I say, trying to giggle it off ad he's kind enough to let me. "That's enough of the gushy stuff. Are you serious about trying to tackle some math? Because that's an excellent plan."

"Math was always one of my better subjects." His smile fades but his voice remains light. "Screw the crappy hand, let's do this."

I shall never admit it, and will deny it if anyone ever asks, but it is entirely possible that Conrad Baxter is better at math than me. He caught me in a couple of small mistakes, but decided to take the high road and not roast me for it.

After an hour of humbling on my part, I insist on a switch to English and bring up *Sophie's Choice*. I know at least I have more expertise in this arena. I begin to realize that Conrad has been holding back on me. His questions are insightful and his comments come with defenses. It's nice to have a true academic conversation with someone other than Jonah or my mom. I can only hope this is what college will be like. No one has ever seemed as interested in learning as me. Eventually, Jonah rejoins us, but only to gather his books. He doesn't look angry, but I still can't get my bearings. When I can't take it anymore, I reach out to touch his arm.

"Please don't be mad at me. I can't take you being mad at me."

"I'm not mad Bella, I'm just a little disappointed." He shakes his head back and forth. He looks like a parent. I want to slap him. I groan and stomp my foot on the floor like a little girl.

"Don't use a Mom line on me, please!" That makes him laugh.

"You don't have to defend your choice to keep it a secret to me. But maybe plan to tell our parents by the time you come home. You know Mom's feelings are going to be hurt." In the pit of my stomach, I know he's right. I love my mom, I don't want to hurt her. I need to call her.

"If you're not mad, why are you packing up all your stuff?" I whine out loud. Jonah sits back on his abandoned stool and takes my hands in his. A soft, almost angelic smile touches his lips.

"Beattie is on her way here," he says aloud, his monotone voice hitting me deep in my chest. I don't want him to go. It wasn't enough time, not that any length of a visit would have been. It may not have been an epic visit, but a little taste of home was incredibly necessary.

Jonah's bag sits by the front door as we wait in the kitchen for Beattie. An ever present pout purses my lips as I rest my head on my brother's shoulder. Mr. Potter appears in the doorway, making a deep and dramatic bow as Beattie rounds the corner rolling her eyes. Mr. Potter huffs in disappointment and says, "I didn't get to introduce you."

"I think everyone here knows who I am," she scoffs, patting him on the arm like he's a little dog doing his best.

I stand up from the table, forgetting completely about Jonah. I wrap my arms around Beattie's shoulders and breathe in the comforting smell of lavender and coffee. "Hi," I murmured into her ear and I felt her smile against my cheek.

She pulls back and squeezes the tops of my arms. "How are you doing?" she asks, looking up at me.

I glance around at the little unit of people who have adopted me. Lusta and Mr. Potter stand over the sink peeling potatoes —always with the damn potatoes. Lottie twirls the end of one of her braids around her finger, chewing on the eraser of a pencil as she tackles the terror of multiplication tables. Then I think about Conrad, sequestered somewhere upstairs. Probably with his roses, maybe reading a book, or doing a little more calculus. His eyes are trying to focus through his coke bottle glasses. An easy smile falls across my face. "I'm doing pretty good," I answer and tap my forehead against hers.

I close the passenger side door of Beattie's car and lean to the window that he's rolling down. "Are you sure you have everything?" I sign, my face drooping with sadness.

Jonah's head tilts to the side after he locks his seat belt in place. "Could you please not look at me like I ran over your puppy?" he asks with his hands, a smile in his eyes. "You knew this was a quick visit and you'll be home before you know it." He reaches out and places his hand over mine, the cloud of our breathing mixing together in the frosty air. "I love you," he says aloud, squeezing my fingers as he says it.

Something in his face shifts, his eyes desperate but focused. "Can you give me one second?" he says aloud to Beattie before getting out of the car.

He pulls me hard against him and holds me there. "Don't let these people change you or the way you see yourself unless it's for the better," he says into my ear. "I know what those girls were saying at the party, about you and that guy. I know that's not you. You are phenomenal and strong and more yourself than anyone I know. Don't let them decide who you are."

I squeeze him as tight I can, hold him for as long as I can, before he gets back in the car. Sometimes I wonder how the universe determines what souls they'll put together in families. Time and time again throughout our lives Jonah has proven that soulmates are a real thing and our souls clearly always belonged together. I smile, more at peace now to let him go than I was a moment ago. I pick up my right hand from the car door and push down my ring and middle fingers, extending the other three, giving him the sign of "I love you". I speak his language and he speaks mine. "Let me know when you get home safe, okay?"

He squeezes my hand one more time before I step back from the car. With smiling faces, Beattie and Jonah both wave before beginning their way down the driveway and away from New York, back to Harpersgrove. I miss them already.

I fall into a pretty regular routine over the next few days. I wake up early to watch the dramatic ritual of getting Lottie off to school. Sometimes Conrad joins me, other days he waits until after I've showered and made my own way to the greenhouse to see him. We spend a few hours on English, History, and Physics; everything but calculus. He can work on that all by himself. In the late afternoons, I go off on my own, to either my favorite chair in the living room or to the library in search of a new book while Conrad studies on his own.

I eat dinner in the evening with everyone. Conrad even joins from time to time, sometimes Pollie too. It's a lot of fun, like our own adopted and blended family. Mr. Potter and Lusta sit at the heads of the table, like two proud parents. Lottie, Pollie, Conrad and myself in the middle, as the children. Of course, there's never a shortage of potato dishes.

We talk about our days. Conrad stays silent, I interpret for Lottie, and Pollie's voice causes Mr. Potter a headache. I volunteer every night to do the dishes. I'm more than happy to contribute and Conrad sticks around to talk to me. He never offers to help me, but he smiles more than I'm used to. I'm enjoying that happy face on him. After all the chores are done and the schoolwork complete, I make my way back to my bedroom to call my friends, Gatty, or Jonah, and then head off to sleep. Rinse and repeat.

One evening Conrad and I are in the kitchen completing our post dinner activities. He finds it very concerning that I would consider *Wuthering Heights* the perfect love story. He picks grapes out of the fruit bowl in front him, popping them into his mouth in rapid succession. I swear boys are like human vacuums, we just ate our weight in roast chicken!

"Whatever souls are made of, his and mine are the same" is the most romantic quote in all of literature," I defend myself.

"Isn't Heathcliff some kind of stalker in that book?" he asks with a mouth full of fruit.

"Nooooo," I groan. My head falls into my hands, absorbing dish soap and my agony. "He's passionate and brooding. It's completely different."

"Oh God, are you one of those girls who thinks *Romeo and Juliet* is really romantic?" he asks, a sour expression spreading across his face that I'm pretty sure has nothing to do with the grapes. I slam the dishwasher shut, but he smiles back at me the way I'd grin at an angry baby.

"I am not some stupid little girl. I'm aware that Romeo is some emo little punk and they were two kids wrapped up in their own drama. If that happened today everyone would have smacked them upside the head."

Conrad sits forward, focusing his attention onto me. "And what do you consider romantic in Shakespeare?" he asks.

I shrug, running through my knowledge of the Bard, which is more limited than I care to admit. "I dunno. I like *Antony and Cleopatra.*" I hate how unsure my voice comes across, almost like I guessed.

"Doesn't that end in suicide too?"

"At least she does it in a cool way," I justify, placing my hands on the breakfast bar across from him.

"Death by snakes is cool?" he laughs, clearly mocking me. I scrunch up my nose, furthering my status as an angry baby. I'm sure he's about to tell me that I'm precious.

"Can you think of a more badass way to go?"

"You know," he begins, pushing himself slightly away, "The local theater company is putting on a production of *Antony and Cleopatra*. It's the week after Christmas. You should go," he says to me, encouraging me out in the world. What kind of friend would I be if I didn't do the same?

"WE should go!" I exclaim, wondering why I hadn't thought of this before.

"You're hilarious, Bella," he says flatly, crossing his arms over his chest.

"No, no, hear me out," I begin, ignoring the air rushing from his nose like a bull ready to charge. Danger Bella, danger. "It would be a perfect outing for you. I know you don't want people to see you. We can get seats in the back, get there right before it starts, and then leave at curtain call. It's perfect!"

He takes a deep breath before pushing up to his feet. "No," he snaps. It's so dismissive that I can't help but be annoyed.

"Come on, it's a good plan. You can't just shut me down, you have to at least give me a reason."

"No, I don't. Let it go, Bella," he hisses, his voice low and dark.

"Look, I know that you're afraid to have people see you, but I can help you-" I start again, unaware of the storm I've unleashed.

"And you're here to save me Bella?" he howls. "OH, the poor broken monster. You're here to rescue me?" His palm slams into the counter and the sound ripples through the silence. "Do you honestly think I'm afraid? If I had any interest in going out there I would do it! I don't need some socially stunted, homeschooled girl to come rescue me. I am no damsel in distress." His voice drips with malice, it feels like he slapped me.

"I never said you were a damsel in distress, that's not fair." I say, trying to defend myself, but I sound like a scared little mouse.

"Not fair? Not fair!" he yells, the veins in his neck straining against his delicate and glossy skin. Slowly, he prowls in my direction until my back is against the refrigerator and he's only inches away. My fingers flex back and forth against the cool metal of the stainless steel appliance. "What do you know about fair? I watched my mother die from cancer. One stupid little mistake turned me into this creature. My father can't stand to look at me. He hides me away and you want to talk to me about what's fair?"

His head settles forward, his shoulders inched up to his ears. Every breath ripples through his entire body like a fallen angel whose wings are waiting to emerge through his skin. My hands settle on my stomach, trying to calm my frantic nerves. Conrad stands over me like a dark cloud, engulfing me in his rage and crippling sadness. His jaw clenches until I'm sure his teeth will shatter. Those blue eyes, the eyes I had seen magic in before, fill me with dread now. He is such an overwhelming presence. The silence crackles between us until I can't take it anymore.

"I'm sorry," I let out before dashing around him. I hear him call my name as I sprint out of the kitchen, but I can't stop my moving feet. In one motion I grab my purse and coat from the hall closet and flee out the front door without bothering to close it.

Once I'm safely inside my car, I see Conrad's figure fill the doorway. For a moment, I think about giving in and going back inside the house, but I can't. I wipe away my tears and focus on the driveway ahead of me. In my rearview mirror, I see the front door slam shut. Rolling through the gate, I realize I have no idea where I'm going. If this were home, I would make a beeline to the pie shop and drown my sorrows in pecans. I consider heading to Della's Diner of Deliciousness, but I don't think my heart can take subpar pie. I wish I knew where the main house was. Pollie is the closest thing I have to a friend.

But there's only one address nearby saved in my phone and it's not hers. I'm not sure how he'll feel about me dropping in on him upset and unannounced. I don't know what else to do. I tap on Gatty's address and let my phone navigation guide me. The only thing that matters right now is putting some distance between me and Conrad Baxter.

CHAPTER THIRTEEN

When I pull up to Gatty's house, my eyes are red and puffy from crying. I'm sure the little bit of makeup I had on is gone and my skin gets blotchy when I'm upset. I'm not sure if I should call him first or go ahead and ring the bell. I've never been here without Pollie. I finally take a moment to squash my fears. I already got myself here.

"Grow up, Isabella," I mutter and get out of the car.

At reach the front door, the frosty air burns my lungs with every icy breath. I need to get into shape. My body is not quick to recover from emotional turmoil mixed with an uphill walk. I lift the heavy door knocker etched with elegant filigree, when a sense of impending dread prickles the back of my neck. I should have called. As the door opens, I'm surprised to see a short, middle aged woman in a knee length gray dress.

"Yes, can I help you?" she asks with a warm smile.

"Um," I shakily began, "I'm here to see Gatty." Having never seen staff here before, I'm a little off balance. She eyes me up curiously as she opens the door the rest of the way. I can't read the expression on her face. I'm too exhausted and embarrassed to try.

"Mr. Bernard is in his bedroom, second door on the left at the top of the stairs," she says. She directs me to the staircase and I grip the banister before making my way up the steps. I'm still not in a hurry to get anywhere and I'm chubby and out of shape. I end up taking the steps one at a time like a little girl learning to climb. When I'm at the top, the beat of my heart thumps in my ears and I try to steady my breathing.

At Gatty's door my fingers linger above the doorknob. I should knock. I've already shown up unannounced. I should knock, but I don't. I place my hand on the gold, swirly knob and press down. The heavy mahogany door swings open. My brain tries to catch up as the room fills with light. The dark silhouette of my body stretches across the floor and up the side of the bed to where Gatty is laying. But Gatty isn't alone.

Unclothed and on top of him, Parker's pale hair falls across his naked chest. The moment before they notice me in the doorway seems to last a lifetime. His hand is tangled in her hair, her body moves against his. I don't know what to do.

Parker sees me first, her eyes narrowing to slits as she glares. Gatty's jaw hangs open, his eyes bugging wide. My hearing settles into a high pitched squeal and I forget how to move, my fingers white knuckled against the door knob. Reality slaps me as Parker screams, "Get out, you freak!"

I blink once, twice. I slam the door, flipping my back onto it, frozen in place. New tears replace the ones I've already shed. It's not like I should feel betrayed. Gatty isn't my boyfriend. We've made out a few times, been on one date, and talked on the phone. That's it. If he wants to see other people, I guess that's his business.

But why did it have to be her? And if it shouldn't be a big deal, why does it hurt this much? I have to get out of here. Embarrassment and overwhelming shame flood my entire body as I push away from the door to make my escape. No sooner do I step away then the door behind me flies open and Gatty emerges in only a pair of running shorts.

"Bella, wait. Let me explain," he slurs, grabbing me by my arm before I get to the stairs. He pulls me back and blocks my exit. The smell of booze wafts off him to a point that I think I might gag. I vehemently shake my head and push my glasses up to wipe away my stubborn tears, hoping he's too intoxicated to notice.

"You don't need to explain anything to me," I say, trying to sidestep him. He blocks me again, grabbing my shoulders to keep me in place and himself steady.

"No, no, let me say this. It's not a big deal. You said you weren't ready," he tries to justify. His dark brown hair falls across his face as he turns a little green. When I look at him, I feel nothing at all outside of my own stupidity.

"I tell you I'm not ready to sleep with you and that means you jump into bed with Parker?" I shout, pulling myself from his grip. His hands move to my wrists.

"Don't be mad. This is something Parker and I do sometimes. It just lets off some steam. It doesn't have to mean anything. You said you weren't ready. What else was I supposed to do?" His words hit me like a punch to my stomach.

"Is that a serious question?" I hiss, trying to get around him, but he squeezes me harder, to the point that it hurts.

"Calm down," he murmurs pointedly. He starts walking me back toward the wall and every defense signal in my body starts firing. I need to get out of here, but I can't seem to get my feet to listen. When my back is against the wall, right next to his bedroom door, he pushes himself against me. With his knee against my hip keeping me in place, his hands move from my arms to my sides. The air is sucked from my lungs as the tip of his nose runs across mine. "Relax," he whispers, menace dripping from his alcohol fueled words.

My fingernails with the chipped yellow polish dig into the skin of my palms when he pushes me back harder and starts kissing my neck. His fingers trace the waistline of my pants through my shirt.

"Calm down and let me show you how good it can be." The way he says it kickstarts something in my body. The way he says it makes me realize I am not safe. My heart is in overdrive. I place my palms on his chest and try to push him away.

"Gatty, stop!" I exclaim, hoping he'll hear the seriousness in my voice. He doesn't budge an inch. He takes my hands away from his chest and pins them to my sides and crushes my body with even more force. Between the fear and physical inability to move his body weight, I cannot breathe.

"Don't be a baby," he yells, using his knee to keep one of my arms down and free up his hand. "It's gonna feel good." The tears don't start until he aggressively nips at my neck, forcing me to cry out which only seems to egg him on.

"Please stop," I cry as he shushes me and I wonder where Parker is. She can't possibly hear this going on and think it's okay. "Gatty, stop!" I yell again, thrashing my shoulders against him as his free hand moves to the waistline of my pants and his fingers skim the inside lining. Oh God, this can't be happening. It can't happen like this! It's not supposed to happen like this! I took an online self defense course that's proving useless right now. I can't remember a single thing I learned. I try to raise my knee to push him off, but he's so much bigger than me. I seal my eyes shut, so tight that I see stars and cry. "*Please, please stop!*"

Then his weight is gone, his hands off me. When I can dare to look, it's Conrad pushing Gatty into the opposite wall.

"Oh my God," I gasp. Conrad is here.

"Baxter!?" Gatty exclaims. Conrad presses his forearm against Gatty's throat. His eyes are wide as they roam over the burns. The burns Conrad didn't even bother to cover with the black hoodie.

"How dare you touch her," Conrad hisses. He pulls back and throws Gatty into a wall. I swear the entire house shakes. Conrad's breathing is ragged and wheezing. His muscles quiver either from anger or exhaustion.

Gatty reaches up to push his arm away. "Get off me!"

"How dare you touch her!" Conrad screams louder and swings his uninjured fist into Gatty's jaw. I almost feel the punch against my own face. I can't move. I can only hug my arms around myself and pray for it to all be over. Conrad's chest puffs with rage as his nostrils flare like a charging bull and his fists ball at his sides.

"What the hell, man?" Gatty exclaims, gripping his injured jaw. "What's your problem?"

"What's my problem? What's my problem?!" he shouts. "You're assaulting Bella while she screams for you to stop, and you want to know what my problem is?" Then Conrad punches him again.

Gatty let him have the first two, but that seems to be enough. He raises up to his full height and pushes his palms into Conrad's chest, shoving him away.

"Look dude, I know you're crippled now and I really don't want to kick your ass. But you touch me again and I will."

Conrad doesn't hesitate to crash his fist into Gatty's face.

"I can handle everything you've done to me, but you will never hurt Bella," Conrad huffs, his breathing becoming more labored. This is too much for him. A scream bursts from my lips as Gatty takes his shot and slams his fist into the good side of Conrad's face and I want to help him more than I want my next breath. I have to stop this. I finally open my mouth to speak when Conrad looks ready to charge, but a sound behind me stops us all.

"Conrad?" Parker's gasps. Her thin, naked body is wrapped in Gatty's bedsheet. Her palm is clamped over her mouth to hide how she gawks at her ex-boyfriend in horror.

Conrad's jaw flexes against his skin as he growls at Parker.

"Of course." His face is pained and rejected and hurt, but he refocuses on Gatty. He raises his fist again and from deep inside myself I find the strength to move. I reach up and grab his elbow before he can strike.

"Connie," I say, my voice small again. Those deep blue eyes search mine for something I can't define. "Can you take me home now, please?"

My tears are gone, I'm all cried out. I want to leave. There's already a bruise forming on his cheek. He reaches down to take my hand, squeezing tight. Gatty and Parker remain silent and all of my attention is on Conrad. He leads me down the stairs and through the front door. He extends a hand, demanding my keys and I don't fight him on the matter. I've used every ounce of bravery and energy that I have. I feel like a shell now. I rest my forehead against the cool glass of the side window, focusing on my breath fogging it up. I know I'm still alive. We pull to stop in the circular driveway and settle into the dark silence around us. He cuts the engine of the car and sits back in his seat, both of us stare out the windshield in complete silence.

"Are you okay?" he finally asks. I don't have the words. I nod and it seems to be enough.

He's the first to get out of the car, rounding my side, opening my door and offering his hand again. If it were anyone else, I can't imagine I would let them touch me after what Gatty had done. But Conrad makes me feel safe. It's amazing how quickly feelings can change.

We pause inside the front door. I don't move, I don't speak. The house seems quiet and I'm glad. He takes my hand again and leads me up the stairs. I trail slowly behind but he lets us go at my speed. He leads me down the hall in the opposite direction of my room. To the west side of the house that I haven't visited. We pass the door for the greenhouse and keep going. He leads me all the way down the hall and opens the very last door and inside there's a neatly made bed with a plaid sheet set, an uncluttered desk with his laptop open, and a dresser closed and orderly. On either side, doors open into a bathroom and sitting room.

This is Conrad Baxter's bedroom.

He lets me enter first, gauging if it's okay. He won't make me do anything I don't want to. I take three strong strides into the room and he follows me. I hear the door close behind us, but I don't turn back. I'm terrified that if I look at him now, I'll break into sobs that I can't stop. I don't know if I can take that last little bit of my sanity being stolen from me. I expect him to do something. Talk to me, touch me, move me around to see him, but he does none of that. He stands behind me and though I can't see him, I know he's keeping a distance so I feel safe. He never makes a single move, but he came for me. He rescued me. Conrad did the hardest thing in the world for him to do. He went out and people saw him; people he knew, and he did it for me. God only knows what would have happened if he hadn't been there. God and my worst nightmares.

A shudder runs through my whole body as I remember the feeling of Gatty's hands on my skin. I wince at the soreness across my neck and dread looking into the mirror to see what he left behind. It could have been worse but that doesn't mean it wasn't bad. While he didn't get as far as he wanted, it doesn't mean what Gatty did wasn't traumatizing, earth shattering, or life changing. My soul aches.

A sob ripples through me as I turn around and Conrad is right there, ready to save me again. I collapse into his chest, my glasses smashing up my face before he pulls them away and casts them aside. My hands grasp the front of his gray t-shirt like I'm falling and he's the only lifesaver I have. His arms encircle me protectively. His good hand digs into my hair and cradles my head. His other arm wraps around my shoulders, holding me to him. The sounds that echo from me are alien as I cry, soaking his shirt in my tears. My arms move from smashed between us to wrapping around his back, interlocking my fingers to hold him tighter to me.

I hope, when in such desperate need of comfort, everyone can find someone to be for them what Conrad is for me right now in this moment. He doesn't try to kiss the top of my head. He doesn't try to tell me that I'm all right or that I'm safe. Conrad doesn't speak at all. He holds me tight and balances his chin on the top of my head and lets me cry. After my body has wrung itself dry of tears, and my limbs are numb from exhaustion, I pull my face away from Conrad's chest enough to tilt my face up. I won't let go, I can't. He leans back far enough to see me.

"You came for me," I'm able to chirp out before the quivering in my mouth makes it impossible for me to speak. He nods. His eyes swim with concern and apology as his hand moves from my hair to my cheek, sweeping away tears from under my eyes with his thumb. His palm stays there as I feel the weight of my head settle into his hand, but it's okay. He's got me.

"I'm so sorry I didn't get there sooner, Bella."

I place my hands on his cheeks; my heart breaks at the flinch that runs through him when I touch his scars. I wish I could take them away.

"Listen to me," I begin forcefully, a sniffle betraying my strength. "You were my hero tonight. I can't imagine what would have happened if you hadn't been there."

Conrad looks away, but doesn't pull from my hands. He merely places his own over my wrists, holding me there. He stands more than a head taller than me but he seems like a broken little boy. He needs me.

"You never should have been there in the first place. I had no right to speak to you the way I did, Bella. I regretted the words as soon as they were out of my mouth. I have anger built up inside me and I put that on you. It wasn't your fault. I'm so very sorry. I followed you to apologize. When I got to Gatty's house and saw your car I sprinted to the door. The housekeeper said everyone was upstairs. I didn't pause to think what that meant. When I got there and I saw his hands on you...I don't know. Something snapped. I had to get you away from him." He's sobbing, crying uncontrollably, his forehead against mine. He starts to wheeze and I remember how much stress he's put his body through. I ease him back toward his bed.

"You need to sit down," I command. I scan the room for his nebulizer and lug it over to him. His breathing starts to settle after a few puffs. I take a seat on the bed beside him, allowing plenty of space between us. We sit in silence for a few minutes before I find the courage to speak again.

"You're right," I begin, my voice buzzing through my lips as I stare at my hands. "You shouldn't have spoken to me the way you did. You really scared me and you broke my heart a little. No, you can't snap at me like that, but you can talk to me. I want you to talk to me."

He takes a few long inhales before he speaks. "You were also right. I am afraid to be out there. I am terrified for people to see me like this." He stares up at his ceiling, his expression blank.

"Did you see the way she looked at me?" he says, his voice small. "It's like I was the elephant man." I know people seeing him as a monster is the thing he fears most.

"She's an idiot. I can't stress this enough Conrad." I pause for emphasis and to make sure he hears me. "You are not a monster. I see you." Fresh tears spring into place, blurring my vision. I let the moments drift away in comforting silence. My heart settles into rhythm with his and a thought occurs to me. Something I can't believe I hadn't seen.

"Conrad," I whisper. "You said to Gatty that you could handle everything he'd done to you." His body freezes as he waits for me to say it. "The friend who left you when you were hurt was Gatty, wasn't it?"

The air leaves him in a deflated rush and he lays flat against the mattress. "I know I should have told you but I didn't know how much I should interfere."

He did try to warn me not to go out with Gatty. Maybe I should have listened. I doubt that even Conrad could have ever predicted this. Tension swims between us and we sit there silently, staring at each other.

"Will you stay here with me tonight?" he requests, his cheeks pinking up after the words leave his mouth. "I just- I don't want to be alone. I think I'll have nightmares about what happened tonight if you're not here. I don't think I'll sleep."

Before I can respond, he grabs his pillow off the bed and lays out on the floor with a blanket. He reads my mind and my discomfort before I know it's there. Exhausted, I rest my head against the pillow and stare up at the ceiling.

"I'm not going anywhere," I whisper, before I fall to sleep.

CHAPTER FOURTEEN

I wake to the feeling of warm sunlight touching my face. The events of last night flood my mind as I open my eyes to find Conrad seated in his desk chair. His hands are folded behind his head and he's watching me like I'm the most fascinating creature in all the world. I cover my face with my hands to hide my embarrassment when his eyes crinkle at the corners with a playful grin. My chin tucks down to my breastbone, my gaze traveling down his jean covered legs to his crossed bare feet.

"It's funny," Conrad says in a deep smoky voice, "I woke up about an hour ago and didn't know what to do."

I push myself up to a sitting position, stretching against the tight feeling in my back. "What do you mean? What time is it?" I ask. My mascara left a trail on his pillow.

"It's almost three o'clock. Last night was pretty heavy. I woke up and had a moment where I thought I'd imagined the whole thing. Then I looked up from the floor and you were here." Those deep blue eyes lock on mine and I swear I swallow my tongue.

"Snoring away," he laughs and my jaw flies open and I flop to my side. I hide my face with my hands as his laugh echoes through his whole body.

He's still giggling when I feel his hand on my shoulder, urging me to roll back. When I do, pouting all the while, he sits beside me on the mattress. The ever present lines around his normally frowning lips and narrowed eyes are smoothed. Playful mischief dances in his expression, finally making him look like a teenager. It's when he turns his head a little further that I see his bruised and swollen jaw. The injury roams up the good side of his face.

"Oh my God! Are you okay?" I shriek. He winces when I touch him. It's like I can feel the throbbing in my own cheek, but I realize the pain I'm actually feeling is in my neck.

Conrad notices and his fingers brush across one of the more sensitive spots on my skin. I dread seeing what it looks like.

"Are you?" he breathes.

"Does it look bad?" I ask.

He shakes his head, "No, just a little bruised. God, I'm sorry."

"It is not your fault, but yours really looks like it hurts." I feel guilty. He wouldn't have been injured if not for me.

Conrad shrugs, his hands returning to behind his head.

"Gatty was pretty drunk. He definitely didn't have his full force behind him. This is a piece of cake compared to spending months in the burn unit.," he says with half a smile. "We should probably get up."

My spine stiffens remembering that I am, in fact, lounging on Conrad's bed. My hands roam through my hair, matty and knotted. I'm sure I'm a vision to behold. My shirt's twisted and riding up my stomach. I try to avoid full panic as I put it back in place.

I searched the room for my glasses, lost somewhere last night. The world is fuzzy on all its edges. He chuckles and picks them up from his bedside table and extends them to me. The world comes back into focus. Conrad's expression is unreadable and it's making me uneasy. I rub my hand up and down my arm and wait for him to say something. "We should probably talk about what happened last night."

I've never had the we-need-to-talk conversation. The feeling is as awful as I imagined.

"Oh-okay," I say shakily, pinching at the skin on my arm.

Honestly, I'm not the tiniest bit sure what happened between me and Conrad last night, but things have definitely changed. Maybe talking about it isn't a bad idea. I, however, am a coward and can't handle the quick beating of my heart under my skin. I scurry to the door.

"I'm going to take a shower. Then let's get something to eat and talk," I yammer, pulling the door shut before he has a chance to say anything. I barely make it three steps before an arm reaches out and starts pulling me down the hall.

"Pollie, are you okay?" I ask as she pushes me through the door of my bedroom, slamming it behind her. Her mouth is pursed tight, her eyes narrowed and her cheeks flushed.

"Are you mad?" I ask, nervous dread pooling in my stomach.

She lets out a huff, "I'm confused," she mumbles simply, her arms crossed over her chest and her hip popped to the side. The shirt is untucked from her school uniform and her hair is down and frizzy. It's the most disheveled I've seen her. I walk around and sit on my bed. I may have slept for an absurd number of hours, but I'm still exhausted.

"What's wrong?" I ask as I lean back on my elbows, letting my gaze lift to the ceiling.

"Oh my God, Bella!" she shrieks, running up to me and gripping my shoulders. "What happened to your neck?"

A shiver runs through me. I still haven't seen it. I turn my head to the side to see myself in the mirror. I feel my skin go green and my stomach flip. I wiggle my way out of Pollie's hands and shuffle off my bed to my reflection. My lower lip trembles as I gingerly inspect the golf ball sized angry purple bruise across my skin. Pollie touches me and slowly turns me around to face her. The anger previously on her face is gone and replaced with genuine concern.

"Chicky, what happened?" she demands, her voice forceful.

Instead of answering I ask, "Why were you mad?" I try to stop the quivering in my lips, but it's fruitless. I'm destined to be an eternal sappy mess.

Pollie's mouth opens and closes a few times. Her fingers flex against my shoulders. She's debating whether or not she should tell me. Finally she licks her lips and says, "Gatty came to school today with his face all busted up."

The sound of his name nearly makes me throw up. It's a good thing Pollie has a hold of my shoulders.

"Gatty said that Conrad showed up at his house and beat him up, because Gatty and Parker started dating, and Conrad is jealous." A humiliating feeling sits heavy in my stomach like a rock. They're dating now?

Pollie moves her fingers to my cheeks, squishing them together in a way that, under different circumstances, would be funny, but right now breaks my heart.

"That's not the real story though, is it?"

The sob, and the entire story, break free from inside of me. I tell her everything. All the while her hands stay on my cheeks, her thumbs stroking back and forth against my skin, soothing me. I leave out what happened with Conrad and me after getting back to the house. I still don't know what any of it meant and I think it's okay for that part of it to belong to us. When I'm finished, she rests her forehead against mine, focusing herself and her thoughts.

"Are you okay?" she finally asks. "Do you want to go to the hospital or the police?" The police?!

"Why would I want to go to the police?" I yelp, worried for Conrad's safety.

"Bella, Gatty assaulted you. Just because Conrad stopped him doesn't mean it didn't happen. Look at your neck!"

"I'd rather not," I say definitively and turn away from her. The concept of going to the police had never even for a millisecond occurred to me. Is that something I'd even want to pursue? I shake my head. Too many thoughts already occupy a space too small and I'm pretty sure my head will fall off if I add anymore.

"I need to take a shower. A long, hot shower." I feel Pollie step back. "Do you think you can help me cover this when I get out?"

She offers a sad smile and nods. "We can work a little makeup magic, but scarves are probably going to be your best friend for at least a week. I have a few in my room if you'd like to borrow them."

"That would be nice, thank you," I say, backing my way to the bathroom. I want to be alone.

After a steaming hot shower, my skin pinked and my eyes cried out, I pull on the one and only turtleneck that I own and a pair of leggings before heading down the kitchen. Walking down the hall, I keep fiddling with the navy blue collar. I am not a turtleneck person. It's like being continuously strangled by a person not really committed to the cause. As I'm about to head down the stairs, Conrad steps out in front, startling me. I trip over my own feet and into his chest.

"You Baxters need to use your words," I utter.

"Sorry," he says and lets go of my arm.

"Pollie came to see me," he adds with a rock back on his heels. "Are you okay?"

I kind of wish they'd stop asking me that.

"Are you?" I ask instead, nodding toward his puffy jaw and repeating the sentiment he'd given me earlier. We're both hurt. He shrugs.

"I was on my way downstairs to get some ice. Of course I don't have a plan on what to tell Lusta." A considerable predicament given Lusta's very protective nature, especially where Conrad is concerned. I purse my lips and cross my arms over my chest.

"Bear attack. Always go with bear attack."

As always, Mr. Potter is busy peeling the day's potatoes at the kitchen sink, humming along with a classic rock song playing from his old school radio, systems and all. Pollie is seated at the breakfast bar with Lottie. They're hunched over a binder pointing back and forth at things on the page. I'm honestly not sure who's helping who. From the hidden pantry in the kitchen wall Lusta calls out, "I was wondering if we were going to see the two of you today! I was about to send up a search party."

She emerges from the door with an armful of fresh carrots, stems and all, and a grin stretched across her cheeks. It only takes one look at Conrad though before that smile vanishes into a blank look of shock. "What happened to you?" she demands.

"Don't freak out Lus, it's okay. It looks worse than it is," Conrad soothes, opening the freezer in search of ice.

The silence is thick and static as Lusta waits for an answer. Conrad closes the freezer, presses a bag of peas against his jaw. "You got me, I slipped in the shower last night and hit my face on the wall. It already hurts less than it did."

She opens her mouth to push further, but Mr. Potter beats her to the punch. "Who's hungry?" he cheerfully chimes in. "I made corned beef!"

We fill our plates and sit next to each other at the glass table. The food lands ashy in my stomach. Everything is off.

He reaches out and touches my hand after we've finished and asks, "Can we talk?"

My stomach flutters. Nervous energy and raw emotion flood my body climbing the stairs to the greenhouse. I strongly consider turning around and running back down. Somewhere deep inside I remind myself that I'm being brave. Bella is brave now. I shake it off and keep climbing. Conrad sits down in his usual spot and I take mine. He pushes his glasses up through his sandy colored hair, freeing his face from the unkempt curls that normally block it. I like him this way.

"Well," he begins, a heavy silence falling around us in his pause, "last night was really emotional for both of us."

I feel too exposed for this conversation. My hair has dried in knotty clumps that I can't work my fingers through. This is one of those times I really wished I were one of those girls who could wear a hair tie on their wrist, but alas, my arms are too fat.

"Yeah, you could say that again."

He scratches the back of his neck, adjusts in his seat and taps his toes, even more fidgety than I am. "I'm really glad I was there to help you through all that," he says.

"I'm really thankful you were. It meant a lot to me what you did," I respond.

I'm pretty sure I know where this is going.

"This new friendship between you and me, it's important. I've had a really rough time since my accident and having you around has made it a lot better."

"I'm glad," I offer, suspecting that I should be contributing more to the conversation.

"But," there's always a 'but', "I hope I didn't cross any lines last night. I felt like you needed me and I needed you too, but I don't want to jeopardize our friendship." He wants to be friends. Of course he does, that's all I want, too. But if that's true, why does it sting a little now?

"Totally. I totally understand that. I wouldn't want anything to ruin our friendship either," I say with a smile even though my words completely lack conviction. His body relaxes and he gives me a sharp single nod, some of his sandy curls falling across his face.

"Good, I'm glad we agree."

The next few moments of uncomfortable, awkward silence pass like years before I come up with something to say.

"So, friend," I begin, putting a little too much emphasis on the word. "A thought occurred to me a few days ago. I want to mull it over with you."

"Do tell," he says.

"I know you're worried about people seeing you in public, and I am by no means saying this needs to be tomorrow, but I have a thought that might make it a little bit easier." He crosses his arms over his chest, closing himself off a little, but he still holds me with his gaze. I haven't lost him yet!

"I know you're really attached to your hair," my voice trails off as I motion to his head. The silence settles in when his body goes stiff and rigid. I decide that rushing through the remainder of what I have to say is the best option. "I know you really like it and it is good hair. But your face and head are split down the middle with the burns, and the hair draws your eyes right to it and it kind of makes you look like a Batman villain. Your hair is a light color. If you cut it to a buzz, it might blend together enough that so that people don't automatically see the scars." I'm basically panting after rattling it all off in one breath.

For a while he sits still as a stone and just as quiet as one. When he finally opens his mouth to speak, his voice is full of conflict. "There are clippers under the sink in my bathroom."

I squint my eyes, expecting this is a test or a trick.

"Yeah? You sure?"

His attention focuses on the floor between us. "Go get them before I change my mind," he says. He doesn't have to tell me twice. I hustle to his room and back with the clippers, a brush and a towel. I cross the threshold of the last step, holding up the clippers, and say, "You ready for this?"

He very unenthusiastically collapses back down on the stool and groans, "Are you sure you know what you're doing?"

I shrug, fiddling with the power button on the clippers and absorbing the vibrations as they run through my hand.

"I promise to let you keep your other ear," I joke, but immediately regret the words. I'm pretty sure it's overstepping. He stares at me a moment too long, his face twisted in confusion, before booming laughter roars from low in his stomach, all the way out of his mouth. That kind of laughter is contagious and before I know it, I'm laughing too.

"I would not expect something that vicious to come out of your nice, little mouth!"

I try my best to settle the flutter of giggles in my chest. "I grew up in a household where we made a lot of deaf jokes. I forget sometimes that not everyone laughs about that kind of stuff."

Conrad takes the towel from my arm and wraps it around his shoulders before swiveling away, his back to me. "Let's do this thing," he proclaims and I can't help but chuckle again.

A low moan rumbles behind his lips when I run the brush along his scalp, careful to avoid the border of sensitive skin that runs down the middle. His eyes flutter open and closed and while I don't need to keep going, I do. I like the look on his face.

"I'd give you a week to stop," he finally mutters after I've been at it for a solid five minutes.

"What was that?" I ask.

His eyes open, staring upside down into mine, but he doesn't move. "It's something my mom used to say," he explains. "Near the end she had a lot of pain in her hands and arms. I used to rub them for her. When it helped she would smile and say 'I'd give you a week to stop'. Seemed fitting."

I set the brush aside, letting my fingers run down his sandy curls. I pick up the clippers and look back at his eyes. "Ready?" I ask, a playful smile on my lips. He lets out a huff which I take as confirmation and I click the little machine to life. I run the blades across his skin, taking the first clump of hair with it.

"Hang in there," I mock. His all-consuming stare could bring anyone to their knees. I tilt his head forward, breaking his gaze and letting me focus again. I move the clippers in slow and very careful motions, making sure not to leave anything behind. When he's good and fuzzy, I pull the towel from his shoulders and say, "Ta-da!"

"It would be more impressive if I had a mirror," he says, rolling to his knees before standing up to his full height. I see I was correct. It obviously doesn't make the burns go away, but it does take a half second longer to see them. Mission accomplished.

"Does it look all righ?," he asks self-consciously.

I smile brightly. "It looks great."

He runs his hand across the peach fuzz left on his head and a little boy's giggle hiccups from mouth. "I don't know if I've ever had this little hair. I feel like a cue ball."

I wrap the brush and clippers in the towel and say, "Well, it suits you."

"Are you excited about going home?" he asks, completely changing gears. Conrad has a talent for twisting the conversation away from him. I shake my head, unable to process what he means.

"What?"

"Christmas, Bella. I'm assuming you're going home for a few days for Christmas," he explains, smirking at my idiocy.

"Yeah, of course. It'll be nice to go home."

While I do desperately miss my life in Harpersgrove, there's an ache in my heart at the idea of not seeing the holiday here. I've helped put it together, it would be nice to see it through.

"What will you do for Christmas?"

"Oh you know, I'm sure Lusta or Potter will make me something nice to eat."

My shoulders slump, "That's the saddest thing I've ever heard!" I exclaim. A part of me wishes I could snatch the words back. I don't want to make him feel any worse than he already does. I hate the idea of him spending such a big day without anyone.

He chuckles without any sunshine. "Well, I know Pollie will stop by at some point during the day." He's smiling, but his eyes are sad. His mother loved Christmas. It may be a hard time for the Baxter family overall.

"I don't want you to be alone," I mumble, unable to say nothing.

He shrugs, but I sense gratitude radiating off of him. "I'm okay with being alone these days. Christmas is just another day on the calendar." He pats me on the arm, moving past me to the door. "Did the towel do any good? Because my entire back itches. I'm going to go take a shower."

Before he opens the door to leave he turns back to me one more time with one of those refreshing smiles that makes him look his age. "Thanks, Bella," he says.

I smile back and respond, "You're welcome, Conrad."

CHAPTER FIFTEEN

Pollie explodes into my bedroom the next afternoon. "I require you!" she exclaims.

"Who's that?" Rosie giggles from the phone in my hand. She and Blanche are video chatting with me from the shop.

Pollie hops up on my bed beside me. Her splotchy bleached jeans look like they were painted on and her white top hugs her in all the right places. She pushes her black curls away from her face before waving to my friends. "Hello, friends of Chicky!" she says excitedly, pushing the sleeves of her leather jacket up her arms. Her makeup is more dramatic today than I'm used to, with smoky eyes and red lips. She's like a cheery biker.

Both sets of eyes on the other side of the phone widen at the screen before Rosie exclaims, "Did you replace me?" Her voice squeaks and pinches in a way I have never heard. It's anger. It's jealousy. It's incredibly un-Rosie.

"I think she replaced me, too!" Blanche whines.

Pollie casts me a sideways glance but doesn't move. I doubt anyone actually intimidates her. I look her up and down for a moment, trying to figure out what my wack-a-doodle friends are seeing. Pollie's black hair and olive complexion do remind me a bit of Blanche, but I have to say that her loud and out there personality and style are all Rosie, right down to the red lips.

"Okay, Captains of Rudeness," I begin, "This is Pollie. She's Conrad's sister and she's not replacing anyone. I am allowed to have friends outside of you guys, you know that, right?"

"No you're not," Rosie harrumphs, slouching further against the wall. I don't grump when she spends more time with Goldie than with me. What a baby.

Blanche, the far more reasonable of the two, shakes her head at her toddler counterpart and waves back to us. "Hi, Pollie, I'm Blanche and the sourpuss here is Rosie"

"Oh!" Pollie exclaims, her hands clapping together. "Is this the darling little pie shop you were telling me about?"

Rosie's eyebrows arch up to her hairline and I can see Blanche ripping her lip with her teeth trying not to laugh. "Yes, and it is utterly darling," she says with a devilish grin, her arm motioning to the kitchen in which they sit. "Nothing but flour and the smell of fruit filling here."

"You say that like it's a bad thing," Rosie says defensively. She's in a foul mood.

"You guys are nuts. I'm going to hop off. I'll see you in a few days."

"Bye Bella, love you!" Rosie exclaims as she clicks off the call before Blanche can say anything.

"I like your friends, even if they were making fun of me," Pollie laughs, more self-aware than I was hoping. I wanted to explain that they weren't truly making fun of her. It's their way. In fact, poking fun means they like you.

"I can see the panic on your face," she begins, giggles growing as she covers her mouth with her hand. "It's all good. I like ladies with some sass."

"Well, my friends definitely have that. You'll have to come visit me and see it sometime. The girls would really like you."

"Oh Chicky, that would be a dream!" she exclaims, bouncing up and down on my bed. "We'll plan something for this summer. I'd love a small town getaway." I put my arm over her shoulder and squeeze. She's too pure for this earth.

"Now, you popped in here for something urgent. What can I do for you?"

"Right! Christmas is in a few days and I have crazy amounts of gift shopping left to do. My question is, would you like to go to the mall with me so I don't get kidnapped?"

"Is getting kidnapped an actual concern of yours?" I ask.

"Hmm." She looks down her body and then back to me. "I don't know. I am small and cute!"

"I would love to go shopping with you," I answer. I do need to get pretty much all of my gifts.

About two hours into shopping, I realize I've made a horrible mistake. I have always shopped with purpose. Get in, get what I need, get out. Pollie is not that way at all. It's maddening. She blames her indecisiveness on her father and brother being near impossible to shop for, but I don't buy it. I've shopped for the men in my family many times. Men are not difficult.

Needing a break from the insanity, I dip out of the expensive store, leaving Pollie debating between two completely identical ties for her father. Down the far end of the strip of stores is a cheap and tacky novelty shop. It's the perfect speed for what I need to knock off my list. I fill nearly an entire cart before Pollie comes to find me.

Her expression is that of a child that's just found a wonderland from a children's book. "What is this place?" she gawks, in awe at the brick walls, colorful tee-shirt displays and even more colorful employees. "How did you find it?"

I pick up a mermaid scale tee that Nixie would love and drop it in my cart. "We have one a lot like it back home. My friends and I have spent a lot of money there."

Suddenly something catches her eye and she's off like a flash to the back of the store. Her feet start tapping in a gleeful little dance as her dark eyes widen to take in the long row of utterly hideous, but hilarious holiday ties. "How did you meet all those girls? I mean, you didn't go to school with them. How did you connect?"

"Well," I begin, "Blanche I didn't meet until she came to work at the pie shop because she doesn't live in our town. Rosie and I had a couple play dates when we were really little, but didn't become friends until she started work at the pie shop. She's a little bit intimidating until you get to know her."

It seems funny to me now because I know how completely harmless she is. When I used to pick up groceries for Mom, Rosie would be standing in front of the Rust's store, usually playing with a yo-yo and snapping gum in her mouth. I would pretend to be immersed in the flower shop's window display until she decided to move on, usually with Goldie at her side.

"Nixie's mom is our town's librarian. I always spent a lot of time in the library, either doing homework or just reading. In the summertime Nixie and her sisters would always be there. She and I bonded over our shared love of *The Babysitter's Club*."

"Aren't there two more?" she asks and I'm impressed that she remembers. It's not that I think our conversations are one-sided. I can't comprehend how anyone can process information they're hearing while typing with such singular focus on their phone.

"Yep, Elle and Goldie. The three of us attended exactly one Girl Scout meeting together before forming a united front to tell our moms that we weren't going back."

"And how did that go over?" Pollie asks. She scoops up three different ties and puts them in her basket. It will be a very tacky Christmas for Mr. Baxter.

"Elle's mom freaked, but I think it was more at the defiance than at the actual not wanting to be a Girl Scout thing. Goldie's mom is a little more on the laid back side. She was cool with it. My mom," I begin, remembering that I haven't reached out to her. The guilt hits me a little too hard in the chest. "My mom worried that I wasn't socializing enough. That's why she wanted me to join in the first place. I asked to be friends with the two girls who were on my side without having to be in the actual Girl Scouts and that's where it all started. We've been together ever since."

"That's a story that I like. With my friends, it's more like we're comrades in the same struggle. Our parents work a lot and travel a lot and even when they're here, they're not really here. I was super lucky. I had my mom who was crazy involved and great and loving, but we couldn't hold onto her. Most of the people I grew up with were raised by nannies. A lot of playdates, well past the point where we should have had them, were to give the staff a break and let us entertain each other." I'm not sure if she realizes I'm still here and listening until she turns to look me dead in the eye. Her green eyes hold me with the same intensity that her brother is famous for. "It's no excuse and a lot of them suck because they're bad people, but we're not all like that."

I'm lost, truly lost, until it clicks.

"Pollie, what happened with Gatty is not your fault. I know you're nothing like him."

Tears rolled down her cheeks. "I made you go with me to those parties. You never would have met him or been anywhere around him. You wouldn't have gotten hurt and Conrad wouldn't have gotten hurt…"

I place my hands on her shoulders, trying my best to summon that intense Baxter stare and say, "None of this, absolutely none of this is your fault. You wanted me to have a good time and brought me out with your friends-"

"Who were also jerks to you," she groans, shielding her face with her perfectly manicured hands. She's traded in the black nail polish for a dark forest green, more Christmassy I suppose.

I gingerly wrap my fingers around her wrists and lower her hands. "They weren't fabulous, but that's okay. They don't know me, and this may shock you, but I'm a pretty tough cookie. I've dealt with my fair share of bullies."

I throw my arm over her shoulder and pull her toward the wall of tee-shirts, surely there's something there she needs. "Remind me to tell you about Lucy Wilcox sometime."

When we are ready to check out, we both have a full shopping cart, checking pretty much everyone off of our gift lists. Well, with one exception for me. I still have no idea what to get Conrad. That is, until we make our approach to the register. The sweet, studded and pierced young lady behind the store counter compliments Pollie on her leather cuff bracelet. Pollie gushes on and on about the girl's denim vest, continuously reaching out to run her finger down the lapel. It's a rather intimate moment that I feel like I'm intruding upon. I look around one last time, allowing Pollie to check out in peace without my hovering over her shoulder. That's when something shiny catches me.

On the far side of the store, in a glass case, rests a vast array of fancy glass items. Inside is a glass rose ornament in a deep, scarlet red. It glitters as it turns on its hook and maybe it's a little gaudy and a little feminine, but I have to get it for him. It's calling to me. I ask the girl at the counter, "Excuse me, can I get something out of this case?"

Pollie has an extra spring in her step when we leave the store. She keeps looking down at her palm and the numbers written there. She pulls her phone out of her purse and starts plugging in the digits.

"And what is that?" I ask, playfully nudging her with my elbow.

"A phone number," she sings, hugging her phone to her chest.

I wish I could be more like that. Unabashedly confident enough to ask someone I like for their phone number without a sliver of self doubt. I want to tell Pollie as much, but I realize she's no longer beside me. Her feet are cemented in place a few feet behind. She's quiet a moment far too long before she says, her eyes never flinching from where they focus, "I think that's enough shopping for one day. Let's head back to the house. We can get takeout and watch a movie."

She tries to forcefully pull me by the arm and instictively I know something's wrong. My body stubbornly chooses to freeze instead of fight or flight. I'm about to ask what it is when I let my eyes drift to where she's looking. A few stores down, Gatty stands at a juice kiosk with some of his minions, howling with laughter at something he's said. I nearly drop my bags as my hand flies to my neck, guarding the sensitive flesh there.

Pollie pulls on my arm again. "You don't have to see him, let's go." I'm ready to move, but my feet don't seem to hear me. They lock me in place because he's staring back at me. The smile that had been plastered on his laughing lips was replaced with a thin line and his eyes ablaze, albeit puffy and swollen from Conrad's fists.

"I can't be here," I hear myself say before Pollie's arm circles behind my back and she leads me away.

CHAPTER SIXTEEN

I don't remember driving back to the house. I don't remember Pollie unloading everything from the car or me collapsing in the living room chair, Pollie right beside me, her arms around me as I cried. I don't remember anything until he comes into the room.

"What happened?" Conrad demands of his sister, sitting on the ottoman across from me. He balances his elbows on his knees, unsure if he should reach out to me or not. For a moment I'm glad for the distance.

Pollie runs her hand up and down my arm and it amazes me how someone so small can comfort me like that. I feel like I should put her in my pocket, not have her be my strong man in the storm.

"We ran into Gatty at the mall," her soothing voice begins as she tucks a few loose pieces of hair behind my ears. "Spooked her a little bit." She makes me sound like a pony.

Fire rages in Conrad's eyes as he clenches his jaw to keep from yelling.

"Did he touch her, talk to her?" he demands, completely bypassing me. "What did he do?"

"I'm right here, Conrad," I say. "You can ask me directly."

Pollie wraps her arms around me and hugs me tight. "I'm going to leave you two alone," she whispers in my ear before rising to her feet and grabbing her shopping bags.

"Pollie," I begin before she can leave the room. She looks back to me, that comforting lightness returning to her eyes. "I really did have a good time today."

She smiles brightly back at me. "Me too, Chicky."

Conrad hasn't moved an inch, sitting as still as a statue. "Are you all right?" he asks me sternly after a long moment of heavy silence. Gatty threw me off guard and, yes, he did frighten me a bit. I realize it was more shocking than anything else.

"I am, I really am. He was far away. We made eye contact for a second and then Pollie pulled me away. I'm okay, I promise," I conclude, reaching out and gripping the wrist of his left hand.He opens his mouth to speak when the doorbell rings.

"I'll get it," I say.

When I open the door, every happy feeling settles in my toes along with every drop of blood in my body as Gatty stares back at me from the other side.

"What the hell was that back there?" he demands, hand flying up in the air. New tears burn hot at the corners of my eyes, but I refuse to let them spill. I won't give him that.

"Wha—what?" I'm able to breathe out.

"What was that back there at the mall? You went psycho! All my friends saw you," he hisses, keeping his voice low, but I can tell a fire simmers inside.

"I didn't do a thing," I murmur, hating myself for my weakness.

"God," he groans, ripping his hand through his perfectly parted hair. "First you come on to me, then your boyfriend beats me up for no reason, and then you freak out when you see me? What the hell is wrong with you?"

I had to have heard him wrong. There is no way those words, in that order, just came out of his mouth. I step out onto the porch and pull the door shut behind me.

"Came onto you? What on earth are you talking about?" My fingernails dig into the sensitive skin of my palms, keeping me grounded.

"Come on, Bella, you showed up at my house in the middle of the night. I may have been with Parker, and a little drunk, but I know what you were there for. Who am I to deny you that?"

Without a second thought, my hand darts to the scarf around my neck and pulls it free, revealing the angry purple bruises he left behind. "Does this looks like something I wanted you to do to me, Bernard?" I hiss as my feet find their ground. His eyes blank and widen with shock. "And when I screamed and cried for you to stop and let me go, you think I wanted you to keep going? What kind of animal are you?"

His head shakes and he tries to stand a little taller to regain the power he's lost. "It didn't go that way," but his voice is devoid of its strength.

I take a brave step toward him, refusing to back down.

"You pushed me against the wall and wedged your knee against me. I couldn't move. Your response when I begged you to stop was to tell me to relax. Then you bit me and forced your hands on me."

Sorrow and rage grip me from the inside. I can't go on, but I won't allow myself to cry. My body starts to shake with fear, with rage, with pain, with fury. My body hums with the mixture of it. Horror screams through his eyes as it comes back to him in a tidal wave.

"Did I—Did I," he stammers, but he can't get it out.

"No, you didn't." I cross my arms over my chest, protecting my heart. "Conrad stopped you before you could." I shudder at the memory and hug my arms to me, my knees wobbling as the courage begins to fade. I'm not sure if it's the memory of it that makes me the angriest or the fact that I have to spoon feed the events to him.

"Is that true?" Gatty says over my shoulder and I look back to see Conrad filling the doorway with his overwhelming presence. His relaxed body leans against it like he's holding it up and his entire being is centered on me.

"Bella, why don't you go inside and let me handle this jerk?" he says, his voice low and serious. A menacing growl echoes deep in the pit of his stomach, like a jungle cat ready to pounce. For a moment, I consider how easy it would make everything. I'm practically shaking in my shoes standing here with Gatty. I want to go inside, go away and let someone else handle it. Then I think back to something Conrad said to me during our fight. Conrad told me that he didn't need me to save him, that he wasn't a damsel in distress, and I realize that neither am I. Not fighting my own battles wouldn't make the dragons disappear. It would only make them harder for me to fight in the future. I shake my head.

"No, Connie," I begin, holding myself a little tighter. "Thank you, but I've got this."

Conrad pauses mid stride between us and the door. Conflict pinches his face before it fills with admiration and he gives me a nod, turning back to the house. When the door clicks closed behind him, I return to Gatty who's gone almost as pale as I am.

"What're you going to do? Are you going to press charges, have me arrested? Go to the cops?" He begins to ramble and I swear he's shaking. I raise my hand to stop him. I have no time for his little boy antics.

"You don't get to ask questions right now," I bark, taken aback at the power in my own voice. "Why did you do it? Did you even like me at all? What was all this?"

He kicks the heel of his shoe against the stone pillar behind him. "I liked you," he mumbles like it should be the answer to every question. I clench my jaw tight and wait. "I was frustrated and a little pissed off."

"Why?"

He closes his eyes for a moment before he continues.

"I've never been with a girl like you before and you're nice and cute. The guys said that girls like you were always up for it. Girls like you are grateful." I can hear a low buzzing in my ears and the objects in my periphery become fuzzy. I'm pretty sure that the "it" he's referring to is sex, but what does he mean by 'girls like me'?

"What is that supposed to mean?"

His nostrils flare like this is painful for him to talk about. Too bad.

"Bigger girls like you."

It's like a punch in the stomach. The air is knocked from me. I let myself channel every skill and ability my friends possess which I have ever envied. Blanche's fierceness, Goldie's strength and Rosie's self-assurance. I stare up at the overcast sky, letting those ideals seep into my brain before I'm ready to be the bravest I've ever been. My torso, arms and legs all shake with unbridled rage. I need him to hear me and take me seriously.

I'm ready for battle.

"Girls like me should be grateful, huh?" I begin. "Let me tell you about girls like me. Girls like me spend our lives being told how beautiful we'd be if we were thinner or that we're so pretty in spite of being fat. I know who I am. I am a girl who has never been and never will be thin a day in her life -and I am beautiful." I make a point to accentuate those last three words. "And I'm not beautiful in spite of my size. It's only a single part of what makes me beautiful. I'm curvy and voluptuous and gorgeous in a way that is all mine. How dare you think you're doing me some favor and that I owe you my body because you looked my way."

I take another step forward and he freezes in a blank state of terrified awe. I'm not the quiet, mousy girl with a book he met at his party. This warrior inside me is new to both of us.

"There's not a girl on this earth who owes you anything. You are God's gift to no one, Bernard Gattman, and I feel sorry for you if you think otherwise. Grateful?" I spit as my face twists in disgust. "Grateful because some spoiled rich boy looked my way? No! You showed me your true colors and you are dirt, lower than dirt. Grateful? If anyone should be grateful, it's you. I'm smart, funny, kind and pretty. You were lucky I gave you the time of day."

Horror streaks through my brain and I realize something I never wanted to. "The rumors," I breathe out. "The rumors that Parker spread about me around your school. She didn't start those by herself, did she?" My voice vibrates with its sheer volume and rage, not from an ounce of fragility. I watch his Adam's apple bob up and down.

"Maybe I didn't deny it." I'm sure it's more than that.

"You are such a piece of trash!" My stomach is sick and sour. I feel like I'm going to be ill, but I will show him zero weakness.

He stands staring at me like a little boy caught in a lie. I was hoping for something profound to come out of his mouth. An apology or epiphany maybe? But that would have been asking too much of Gatty and his simple mind. Life isn't a John Hughes movie where everything gets tied up in a neat little bow at the end. Most of the time, I'm sure that the bad guy learns nothing and things go along as if nothing happened. He shoves his hands back into the pockets of his jeans and says, his voice small and low, "Are you going to go to the police?"

"Jesus!" I exclaim, throwing my hands up in the air, looking around me like there's some audience to back up how bananas this is. "Is that really all you took from what I said?! Good God, no. I'm not going to the police, provided you never contact me again and you stop spreading lies about what happened. I never want to see you again. I never want anything about you to be a part of my life."

He doesn't look back up at me, simply offering a small nod with, "I can do that."

It's the last time I'm ever going to see him, God willing, and there's a little bit of bravery in me. Conrad may not need a knight, but we all need a friend who has our backs. I have Conrad's.

"How could you leave him there?" The sound bites through my teeth, the back of my throat constricting. Gatty's shoulders slump forward.

"What are you talking about?" he demands, his voice weak and small, completely exhausted. Good.

"Conrad. The night of the accident, you left him there. You ran away! He could have died. He *would* have died if those other people weren't there to pull him out of the burning car. You were supposed to be his friend."

I can see the mistiness flood Gatty's lower lids as he pulls all of his energy together to stop his lip from quivering. His betrayal of Conrad breaks his heart and infuriates me down to the pit of my soul.

"He told you about that?" Gatty grunts, trying to hold onto his composure. I'm sure the last thing he wants is to cry in front of me.

"I figured it out all on my own." Which is mostly true. Conrad simply confirmed my own findings. Gatty's fingernails scratch into the flesh of his arm. Whether it's comforting or punishing, I can't tell.

"I was scared. I didn't think. I needed to get out of there."

I march right back to him, as close as I dare. "He was your best friend and you left him there to die because you were afraid?"

"I-I had a couple of drinks. I didn't want to get in trouble. My parents were on my case for about a hundred different things and my dad would have killed me." His voice trails off and anger shoots like an inferno up my body.

"Did you ever think, even for a second, if you had put your friend's life before your worries that maybe you could have gotten him out of there before the fire started?" Bile stings the back of my throat and I fight every urge to spit on him. "Did you ever think that if you hadn't run away like a coward, you could have spared him the last year of agony and the pain he'll have for the rest of his life?"

"I think about it every single day."

Taking a few paces back I feel the safety of the door behind me, my hand locating the knob. He doesn't deserve a second more of my time or attention.

"Get out of here Gatty!" I exclaim, moving myself inside. I press my palms flat against the door and flip the lock. Not that I think he'll try to break his way in, but it still makes me feel more secure. Conrad is at my side.

"Are you okay?"

I don't get the chance to answer as my stomach rolls inside me. I clamp my hand over my mouth and bolt in the direction of the kitchen, refusing to stop until my head is safely over a trash can where I can purge the vile sourness inside my stomach. Mr. Potter rushes to me, but Conrad is already there.

"I've got her," I hear him say and Mr. Potter steps away.

Conrad's hand settles on the middle of my back and he rubs in slow circles as my stomach twists and flips. "Let it out," he urges softly as my throat burns. When I have nothing left, Conrad puts a damp rag on the back of my neck. I stand up not wanting to ask for help. I want to be strong. He offers anyway, leading me to the living room, letting me sit in my chair. He takes the ottoman.

"That was the most courageous thing I've ever seen, Bella," he says simply after he sits.

I honestly thought he'd be mad that I asked him to go inside and let me handle it. His hand rubs against his wounded jaw as he explains, "When you didn't come back right away, I got up to make sure you were okay. When I saw him out there, I wanted him to get away from you. I thought you needed me to help you." The way he says it isn't condescending or patronizing. "Then you looked back at me and I knew you had it. Whatever you said to him was brave. It probably would have been easier to let me try to kick his ass again, but you stood your ground. You're amazing."

I want to speak, but "thank you" doesn't seem right. I scootch myself forward to the edge of the seat, place my hands around his shoulders and pull him in to hug me, hard.

We stay like that for a long while, it could be five minutes or fifty, I'm not sure. The front door swings open and Lottie and Lusta emerge, their arms full of grocery bags. Conrad and I break apart as they enter and I wipe my eyes so as to not raise alarm. It doesn't work. Lottie immediately unloads her bags onto Conrad's lap before sitting beside me.

"What's wrong?" she demands with her fingers.

I offer a simple, "I'm fine" before Lusta sets down her own bags.

"Isabella," she says to me, crossing her arms over her slim chest. "Have you seen the news today?"

CHAPTER SEVENTEEN

The news is filled with nothing but a sheet of white with a snow storm threatening to blanket the entire mid-atlantic region, mainly my home state. I immediately call my father with a deep seated feeling of dread. My fears are realized when he tells me there's no way I'll be able to safely make it home for Christmas. The disappointment far outweighs the sadness.

No pretending that Santa Claus ate the cookies Mom and I made the night before. I wouldn't get to wake Jonah up at five in the morning declaring that Santa had come, and have him whack me with a pillow before falling asleep next to him until a more reasonable hour. No opening the group gift from my parents. Last year it was a headlamp, because what self respecting teenager doesn't need one of those? No prayer before Christmas dinner, even though we aren't a religious family. My dad likes to say that since it's Jesus's birthday the least we can do is offer up some thanks for the day off.

I wouldn't watch continuous reruns of Christmas movies while we waited for extended family to come for dessert and presents. My Nanna never failed to buy me an ill fitting ugly sweater at least two sizes too small, but it's okay. I know she means well. Those are the things I will miss. The presents are nice of course, but it's the little things, the traditions and memories you make along the way that really matter.

After my dad and I end our call with promises of a better New Year, I consider wandering into the kitchen for food or friendly comfort, but I open a group text with the girls instead. I'm met with a flurry of sad emojis at the news that Snowpacolypse is delaying my Christmas homecoming. We collectively talk Rosie out of commandeering a dogsled team to rescue me. I shift the conversation to their holiday plans and live vicariously through their joy. Eventually, we sign off, and I turn on the TV.

I'm only pulled from the haze of white hair and sassy quips by the sound of the front door opening and closing. Pollie's bouncy black curls round the corner into the living room toward me. Her skin is blotchy from exertion like she just ran five miles and she seems oblivious to my existence as she mumbles to herself.

"You okay, Pol?"

Her eyes blink hard twice as she leaves her head and enters the present. "Yeah, yeah I'm good."

"I thought you went home?" I ask, clicking off the television. Her hands move from her pockets to her hips to behind her head, incapable of staying still. I rise to my feet, taking a cautious step toward her, like she's a sleeping bear I'm attempting to rob.

"Something is wrong with you," I state.

"No, I'm fine, just tired." It's not hard to tell that I don't buy it. Pollie is the kind of person to ooze carefree ease, even in the most stressful of times. She rolls her eyes and sticks her tongue out at me.

"I had to go take care of something, which I did. Con texted me and asked me to come back. Here I am."

I want to push. I know she's hiding something, but she doesn't give me a chance as she moves past me toward the kitchen. She hops up onto a seat at the breakfast bar next to Lottie and they instantly dive into an intense game of rock, paper, scissors.

"How did the call with your father go?" Lusta asks, taking an open chair at the table next to me.

I shrug. I can't take getting completely worked up again. Aloof seems the way to go. "There's no way I can make it down there. He promised we'll do something nice once the snow clears."

She reaches across the table and takes my hand in hers. "I am very sorry. I know how hard it can be without your family during the holidays."

I keep hold of Lusta's hand, but Pollie nabs my attention from the corner of my eye. She seems to be having some psychic conversation with her brother. When he catches me staring, he averts his eyes and becomes very interested in the pattern of the tiles on the floor. He rattles off some excuse before fleeing the room.

"I have an idea!" Pollie exclaims once her brother is gone.

"Oh, do you now?" I ask, sitting back in my chair. Her head bobs up and down, her curls trying desperately to keep up.

"Yep! And it's a brilliant one," she says proudly, her elbows up and fingers dancing. "We need to celebrate this glorious holiday together. Christmas Day is tough because my dad demands my attention for the day."

"I go to my mother's house in Rhode Island," Mr. Potter chimes in from the walk-in pantry where only his head of bright orange hair appears.

"Lottie and I drive to see my sister in Connecticut," Lusta adds with a wave of her hand.

"Exactly!" Pollie exclaims, happy to have everyone on the same page. "But Christmas Eve..." her voice trails off as though she's already laid out an entire plan at my feet. When I don't say anything, she sighs and continues, "We need to have a full out, no holds barred, zero expense spared, Christmas Eve blowout!"

I'm know she's expecting fireworks and rounds of applause, maybe flowers and a tiara; however, the rest of us wait for more information.

With a dramatic roll of her eyes, Pollie groans, "Good God people. Do you have absolutely no vision? We can get all dressed up, exchange presents, and have a special dinner. Maybe even sing carols! Have a good old fashioned Christmas party! We can dig my mom's old china out of the attic and use the fancy dining room table. We can keep a fire going and open presents around the tree, it would be fun!"

We sit in silence for a moment, no one wanting to talk first. Lottie and her mother trade a knowing glance before Lusta smiles and says, "Well, we're in!"

Mr. Potter sighs from the walk-in before proclaiming, "Fine! But I have creative control over the menu and will require some assistance putting it together."

"Maximum of two potato dishes," Lusta amends and I bite my lip to keep from giggling.

Everyone settles on me, and since I'm fairly certain this entire extravaganza is meant for me, it's not like I have many options.

"It sounds like a hoot, but I don't have anything fancy to wear."

Pollie grins widely before leaning across the kitchen table and crooning, "Oh, Chicky, that's what you have me for."

"There is no way on God's green earth that I can afford this place, Pollie," I whisper as a very fancy lady hands us each a glass of champagne inside the nicest store I've ever been to. I don't belong here.

Pollie smiles and whips out a credit card. "Then thank God it's on Lionel Baxter," she says before tucking it away.

"I can't take money from your dad outside of my paycheck."

We're seated in our own private area and Pollie sips on her drink. I'm too nervous to touch mine. Pollie laughs, finishing off the last gulp before handing the glass to another saleswoman walking by.

"Trust me, Chicky, I spend lots of money here. My father won't think twice. You said you didn't have a dress and this whole thing was my idea. I am happy to be of service"

There's one nagging insecurity that wiggles its way into my brain, especially whenever I go shopping. "Pollie, does this place even sell things in my size?" I ask. It's the nightmare of every plus sized girl shopping in non-speciality stores.

"Ye of little faith. Do you think I wouldn't make sure of that before I brought you here?" she asks. "Would it put you at ease if I tried on my dresses first?"

I want to scoff and say something like *Yeah sure, you'd look like a supermodel in a burlap sack, let's see how you look in amazing designer dresses!* But I've come to know Pollie and I don't think she'll do anything to make me feel uncomfortable, at least not intentionally. I smile and say, "Let's see whatcha got."

As I suspected, Pollie looks amazing in everything she tries on, a vision in each and every dress. Eventually, she's trapped between two. One is low in the front and silver, the other is a dark hunter green and nearly backless save a velvet strip that runs horizontally across the middle.

"How fancy is this dinner of yours?" I ask. She stands pouting between the two equally beautiful choices.

"One should sieze every opportunity to be fabulous!" Pollie answers, nodding in my direction like she'd dropped some deep philosophical wisdom on me. Realizing this doesn't answer my question, she rolls her eyes and continues, "Conrad and Mr. Potter are wearing suits and I gave Lusta an extra Christmas bonus to buy something for her and the munchkin. The answer is FANCY!"

"I've seen you in something like the silver dress before. I would go with the green," I offer.

Pollie holds it up to give it a good once over before nodding approvingly. "Yes, yes, big hair, dark eyes, pale lips. I can see it now!"

I laugh at Pollie's vision and undying optimism as one of the perfect saleswoman makes her way back to us, pushing a rack of dresses beside her.

"Your turn, Chicky!"

"Miss Baxter called earlier today and asked us to pull all the dresses we had in your size. These were the best choices."

God, do I hope something actually fits.

The woman pulls the first dress from the rack in a dramatic fashion, the long skirt twirling in the air. It's very pink, almost obnoxiously pink, like Pepto vomited all over the nice fabric. They went to all the trouble to pull them for me, I feel inclined to at least try it on. I hang the dress on one of the ornate gold hooks in the corner of the dressing room. The mirrors on all sides make me feel more than a little exposed. I am able to see my reflection any way I turn. It's daunting. I pull my sweater over my head, choosing to leave my leggings on. They will at least keep my stomach in a bit. The dress is empire waisted. The flowy silk skirt billowing out from under my boobs is covered in itchy tulle flowers that spread under my arms and behind my back. I look like a nursery rhyme gone terribly wrong.

"How's it going?" Pollie calls to me.

I'm lost in giggles at my many reflections. I whip open the curtain and Pollie gawks mercilessly at the monstrosity.

"Throw on some pearls and long gloves and I'm ready to play Miss Piggy," I giggle and strike a pose worthy of my favorite swine.

Pollie waves me back into the dressing room. "Take that off before it destroys my eyes!" To the fancy lady, she demands, "Burn that, like as soon as she takes it off."

The woman's skin brightens under perfectly applied makeup. In a hushed and hurried tone she says, "My apologies Miss Baxter." Turning back to the rack she hands me a lilac dress that looks like it was cut straight from the pages of a Jane Austen novel. What is with the empire waists? My boobs are big enough without drawing more attention to them.

I try on the dress, sucking my stomach in, hoping the overly fitted bustline will squeeze up over my belly. "This one makes it hurt to breathe," I wheeze, pressing my fingers against the place that pinches.

"That's okay, come here. I think I found a winner!"

I stick only my head out and Pollie waves for me to come forward. She frowns when she sees me in all my glory.

"Nancy," she says to the fancy lady. *Ha! Fancy Nancy!* "You guys are losing your touch." Fancy Nancy hangs her head in defeat.

"It's all good though, I have the champion right here. I know it." Pollie picks up a dress that she approves of. It's a golden, slip dress with a pale yellow, long-sleeved shimmery overlay on top. At its center it's fitted with a silver, very blinged out, belt, done in sparkling roses. It truly is a beautiful dress, but something seems wrong about it.

"Are you sure it's my size?" I ask, nervously chewing on a hangnail on my thumb.

Pollie drapes the dress over my arms. "Trust me, okay?"

Once I'm back inside the dressing room, I peel myself out of the pinchy purple ensemble. I also pull off my leggings, certain that I'll need all the room I can give myself to squeeze into this golden cocoon. I take in my nearly naked reflection.

My beige bra and black and white polka dot underwear don't scream Victoria Secret model, but they're cute. My bra has a bow and everything. Looking at myself straight on, I have this whole hourglass thing with the wide hips and chest. It's totally a desirable look. It's when I turn to the side that my opinion changes and it's why I'm nervous about this dress. I carry my weight in my stomach. Two perfectly round rolls hover above and below my belly button, which I haven't really seen in years. It looks like an uppercase "B".

I turn from left to right, examining my figure from all sides. I pull my ponytail free. My hair cascades down my shoulders to rest in gentle curls on the tops of my breasts. I can't help the negative thoughts that cycle in, back to my last encounter with Gatty. He said that girls like me tend to be grateful for whatever attention we can get from guys. I hold eye contact with my reflection. He was wrong. I smile at myself and take the power back. My fingers rest on my hips. I pop up a toe and run a hand through my hair, posing and kissing in the mirror like I'm a social media model. Have I always looked like this? Have I just been hiding it all under bulky sweaters and elastic waist leggings? Because the girl in the mirror right now can totally rock a fitted dress, tummy and all. She owes nothing to anyone.

I unzip the back and step in, sucking in again as I pull it up over my hips. I'm worried that my arms will rip the delicate sleeves, but they don't. They slide on easily, the straps resting in the right places on my shoulders. I reach behind me, my fingers catching the zipper, and pull it up. Moment of truth. My eyes roam from the flare at my feet, up my legs to where it hugs at my hips. Then to the way the silver belt pulls in my waist. The gold slip dress is cut in a sweetheart neckline that shows the right amount of cleavage while the sheer yellow cuts up high to my collarbone. Even from the side with my two rolls, it looks and feels like this dress was made for me. My many reflections seem to approve and it overwhelms me. I look epic, gorgeous, regal, amazing. Words I've never used to describe my appearance.

"You're killing me, Chicky!" Pollie crows from the other side and I swear I hear her feet stomp against the floor.

I wrap my fingers around the velvet curtain. With one quick, dramatic pull I whip it open. A jolt of pleasure jumps up my spine at the way both Pollie and Fancy Nancy's jaws drop at the sight of me. Both of Pollie's hands fly over her mouth.

"Oh my God!" she shrieks, the sound muffled by her hands. "You look like a princess."

"It's perfect," Fancy Nancy adds with an approving nod.

"Does the yellow look okay?" I ask sheepishly. "I'm really pale and I don't want to look like a giant blob."

"Nooooooooo, trust me girl. Yellow is totally your color."

I look back into the dressing room at the mirrors and really drink in my reflection. Maybe Pollie is right. This might just be my shade.

After seeing the astronomical bill for the dresses, I insist on treating Pollie to dinner.

"Mind if we stop to get wrapping paper on the way back to the house?" I ask when the waitress drops our drinks off to our table. "I need to wrap all my gifts before tomorrow."

Pollie's whole face pinches tight, like this just occurred to her. "Good call, Chicky. I need to do that too," she says, taking a long sip of her cherry coke, made with real cherries and to her exact specifications. Pollie is apparently super serious when it comes to food preferences. I hope they don't spit in anything.

In the basket of condiments by our booth's window, something catches my eye. It's a salt and pepper shaker set, with a Queen Elizabeth II salt shaker and a Buckingham Palace guard pepper. I sit them in front of me and it's like a sign that the girls are with me. I pull out my phone and snap a picture.

"What are you doing?" Pollie asks, eyeing me quizzically.

"My friend Elle collects funny salt and pepper shakers. She'd love these," I answer as I shoot a text off to Elle with the picture.

"I should start collecting things," Pollie muses, staring into her glass with disappointment. They must have made it wrong.

"So, Christmas Eve is our big party and you said Christmas Day is with your dad," I say. "Why isn't Conrad going? He's still part of your family, isn't he?"

I feel more defensive of Conrad lately than I do of Jonah. It's easier each day for me to understand Lusta's protective and mothering nature toward him. Pollie releases her straw and sits back against the booth, bouncing the back of her head a couple times against the cushioning.

"Of course he's still a member of the family. But like so many things in the Baxter world, Christmas isn't really about family. It's about business. If my father wasn't making me, I don't know if I'd go to the big party he throws. I have to go. He's my dad and it's the only time I'll get to spend with him even though it sucks and it's not personal."

I consider leaving it there. It's clear that this upsets her, but I can't do it.

"You didn't really answer my question, Pol."

She holds intense eye contact as she mercilessly gnaws on the inside of her cheek. "No, he'd rather not have Conrad out in front of his business associates."

"He doesn't want to see him for Christmas?" I ask, remembering Colin calling to cancel for Mr. Baxter. The man couldn't even be bothered to reach out to his own son.

"Even before the accident, they were never close. It was more of a thing he could ignore because Conrad grew up our 'mother's son', but after she died…" her voice trails off. Some memories are too hard to voice. "My dad is not good at emotions. That's not a good excuse, but it's not a skill he's ever learned and he doesn't know what to do with Conrad."

"So he pretends Conrad doesn't exist?" I practically shout it but, remembering I'm in public, attempt to sink down low enough into my seat that no one can see me.

"I didn't say I agreed with it," Pollie snaps. "I've told my father as much, but he keeps saying how it's for the best until Conrad is better. Better! Like Conrad one day is going to wake up and have his old face and body back. My dad is a smart man. I know he's aware that isn't how this works. You think I don't want to spend Christmas with my brother? You aren't the only reason I wanted to have this dinner. I want to be with him too."

"Was it your idea?" I ask, thinking back to how Conrad had hurried away before Pollie could reveal the grand plan.

She shrugs as she goes back to blowing bubbles. "I mean, the doing something Christmas Eve was my idea, but as for the actual party? That was all Conrad." She smiles at that last part.

I rest my chin in my hand, elbow on the table, and allow a cheesy grin to overtake me. "That doesn't sound like the Conrad I know."

Pollie chuckles, "Oh, Chicky, Con was like our school's own Jay Gatsby. Parties were legendary. He wore old school suits to all of them and would hire entertainers. There was expensive food, copious amounts of alcohol. Conrad knows how to throw a party. It was a big part of his life. I'm sure he misses it."

It's near impossible for my brain to wrap itself around the idea of Conrad being like that. It's not just the secluded way he lives, but his brooding nature doesn't exactly spring to mind the idea that he would be the life of the party. Not exactly what I think Mr. Fitzgerald had in mind when he wrote his novel. Of course, if the end of the book teaches us anything, it's that Jay Gatsby was very much alone. Maybe Pollie's right on track with her assessment.

"You know who Jay Gatsby is?" I tease as the waitress returns with our food.

The tip of Pollie's pointy shoe kicks lightly into my shin. "I do occasionally read my school assigned books, thank you."

I lean forward, elbows on the table. "Name two more."

She copies my pose, her eyebrow stretching up, crinkling her forehead. "No," she states firmly.

"I'm intrigued by the idea of Conrad in a suit," I muse.

"Oh yeah, I bet it intrigues you."

I swirl a fry around in the ketchup on my plate and say, "I kind of hate myself for it, but I couldn't help thinking about Gatty when I was putting on that dress. He told me he'd heard that girls that look like me are easy. That we're grateful for any attention."

She stops mid-bite of her burger, her face flooded with outrage. "He said that to you?"

My head shakes back and forth and I try not to cry. "I don't know. It hit me really hard while I was standing in that dressing room barely clothed." I take a sip of my drink for something to do with my mouth other than talking.

Pollie puts down her burger and presses her hands flat on the table. "Okay," she begins. "I did something that maybe I shouldn't have done. Or maybe I should. I don't know." She scratches her head through her miles of curls and I wait. I don't think I can move. "After the thing that happened at the mall, I drove to the Gattman's house."

My world drops around me and the sounds of the diner are replaced by nothing but deafening silence.

"You did what?"

Pollie's face pinches as she begins to ramble, "I know you don't want to go to the police and that's totally your call and I respect it. But he doesn't just get to get away with it."

I press my fingers into my temples and balance the weight of my head in my hands. "Pollie, what did you do?"

Her chest rises and falls with her quickening breath. She fidgets in her seat. "When I was helping you cover the bruises, I told you we should take some pictures, remember?"

I don't answer, but of course I remember. It felt like being in a true crime television episode.

"I showed those to Gatty's parents."

"Palarma!" I exclaim, and I do not care who hears me.

"I know, I know, I'm sorry. I didn't have the right to do this without your permission. But guys like Gatty seem to get away with everything. I couldn't let him get away with this."

"I'm sorry, is this about me or about Conrad?" I snap. I don't think she could look more shocked if I'd slapped her.

"That's not fair. Yes, I want justice for Conrad, but this is not about him. This is about you and the fact that no one just gets to hurt you."

My teeth grind together and I struggle internally, debating between strangling her and hugging her.

"Tell me exactly what happened, please."

"Mrs. Gattman opened the door and she knows me. That part was easy. I told her I needed to speak with her and her husband. I told them that their son hurt a friend of mine and I showed them the pictures. His mom got really upset, but his dad stayed quiet. He didn't seem surprised. I told them that you weren't ready to go to the police yet, but that they needed to handle their son or we would take action."

"Oh my God, Pollie! What were you thinking?" I demand, my forehead bouncing against the table.

"I know, but listen. His dad thanked me and told me he would take care of it. I don't know what that means, but it has to be better than nothing right?"

Is it? Is it better than nothing? It felt good to have a friend willing and ready to defend me. I think Pollie would fight the world to make this better.

"Look," I say after a silence that lasts too long. "Don't ever do anything like that again, to anyone. You don't get to make those kinds of choices for people, no matter how good your intentions are. That's my story, not yours, and I get to decide what to do with it."

Tears fill Pollie's eyes. I mutter, "Thank you," and refuse to say more. It's true, she did what I couldn't. What I wasn't ready to do. Maybe this isn't the kind of thing you should be allowed to keep to yourself. The longer we sit here, the more I realize that if the tables were turned, or if it had happened to any of my friends back home, I would have done the same thing.

CHAPTER EIGHTEEN

You've got this Isabella. I try to assure myself in my attempt to descend the stairs with arms piled higher than I can possibly manage. All of my gifts are in the main box in my hands. The tape, ribbon, and various wrapping papers are on top. I've made a serious error in judgement.

"What are you doing?" a booming voice demands from behind me. I hear his footsteps pound down the stairs.

"I've got this!" I exclaim. It's a lie, but a girl must have her pride.

"You're going to fall, Bella. You've got nothing," Conrad retorts, taking the box out of my hands. I scoop the wrapping paper off the top, even though he still would have been able to see over it if I hadn't.

"Thank you," I grunt before we make our way down.

He chuckles, "You're welcome."

I lead him to the living room and he places the box on the floor in front of my comfy chair.

"What are you doing?" he asks.

"You must leave now as I am about to wrap presents," I command, pointing my finger at full arm's length away from the room. Instead of doing as he is told, he plops down on the couch beside me, laying his chin on the armrest.

"You got me a present?" he asks, a smile in his voice. It's equal parts endearing and heartbreaking.

"Of course I got you a present. Did you get me one?"

"You will have to wait until tomorrow and see." He tries his best not to smile, but those deep blue eyes betray him. He gets up to give me my wrapping privacy, but before he goes he turns back and asks, "May I ask why you're doing this here rather than in the privacy of your own room?"

In response, I turn on the TV, already cued to some cheesy made for television movie. "One simply cannot wrap Christmas presents without a proper Christmas movie."

The evening and next morning pass in a blur of Christmas cheer as Pollie and I watch three different versions of *A Christmas Carol*. We bake sugar cookies with Lusta and set the main table in the dining room, making it ready for our Christmas Eve dinner. Lusta sings Christmas carols at the top of her lungs while she vacuums around us. All in all, not a bad way to spend the lead up to Christmas. I can't say that I could have done any better back home.

In the afternoon, Pollie starts nagging me to get ready. "We are on a strict schedule young lady," she snips, pushing me toward my shower. For someone so small, she is incredibly strong.

"Okay, okay, dinner doesn't start for hours. Don't you think we have enough time?" I demand, trying to dig my heels into the ground. It's not that I don't want to shower, but I already have a mother.

Pollie stops pushing and looks at me like I'm an idiot. "Are you even a girl? Sometimes I don't know! By the time you're showered and clean and I'm showered and clean, I'm going to do both of our hair and our makeup. Trust me, the time will fly."

She pushes me the rest of the way in and after throwing a towel at my head, pulls the door shut behind her. Through the door I hear her call out, "Tick-tock, Chicky! Tick-tock!"

I emerge from the steamy tub and realize I don't know my next instructions. Am I supposed to dry my hair? Should I leave it wet? What clothes am I supposed to put on? It has to be too early for the dress, right? I need to find Pollie.

In the hallway, I run into Conrad. "Where are you rushing off to in such a hurry?" he asks as I zip by him.

I fluff my hand through my hair before it splats, cold and wet back against my neck. "Your sister plans to make me beautiful for this evening," I laugh and curtsey, my hand dipping to the floor, my knee touching as well.

"Well, you're already beautiful, she doesn't have to do much," he says, like it's nothing. When Gatty said those same words to me, I thought they couldn't be sweeter because I had never heard them from any man outside my family. But with Conrad, I know how genuinely he must believe it. Conrad Baxter is not one to deliver a compliment if it isn't earned or true. He sees the look of awe on my face and he starts to blush. "Or you know, whatever," he stumbles, clearing his throat.

"I better go find Pollie before my hair dries incorrectly and she makes me wash it again." I'm not sure that's a thing, but I'm not willing to risk it. "I'll see you in a bit." I hurry away before he can respond. I don't want anything to ruin this moment.

In Pollie's room she flits around like a hummingbird in a slip dress. I didn't know people still owned those. Her hair is up in giant curls that remind me of women in old cartoons. She's one eye into her winged liner and hasn't blended any of her contouring. This state of dishevelment is not the Pollie I know.

"Finally!" she exclaims, grabbing me and pulling me inside.

"Finally? Really?" I mock as she yanks me toward the vanity, pushing me down in the chair. She starts running a comb along my scalp and I hum at the pleasant sensation.

"Well, it seemed like a long time. Have you decided what you'd like me to do with these locks?"

A memory comes to mind of a story that my father told me about his wedding day to my mom. He told me that he didn't care what she did with her hair or makeup, but he wanted to see the girl he fell in love with and not a stranger. I don't know what makes me think of it, but it gives me a smile.

"I want to look like me. Maybe a slightly bumped up version of me, but still me."

"I know exactly what to do," she says, resuming her combing.

She brushes and curls, buffs and polishes every inch of my hair and face. I feel like a new model car. All the while I face away from the mirror. Pollie is all about dramatic effect.

After what seems like a few hours, she sets her box of magical makeup tricks aside, admiring her work with pride.

"Take a look," she says, unraveling her hair from the giant curlers. My hair rests at my shoulders in rounded curls, pulled back at the top and cascading in swirls from the crown of my head and down my neck to join their sisters at my shoulders. Little wisps of hair frame my face like a soft brown halo. My makeup is simple and understated, a rosy hue at my cheeks and on my lips. I look like an enhanced version of me, the HD version of me. Exactly what I asked for.

I turn back to her and say, "You're an artist, my friend."

Back in my bedroom, I pull the garment bag out of the closet. The dress is as beautiful as I remembered. The sparkles in the sheer, yellow fabric capture the light and shine against the gold underneath. Pulling on this dress makes me feel like a superhero stepping into uniform. I look like a storybook princess from the top of my head with my soft crown of curls, to my professionally applied makeup, all the way down to pretty fingers and perfect dress. I stepped into the glittery gold heels, too high for my general liking. It's amazing. I look like me, but nothing like me. It's different, but lovely. I feel lovely.

There's a knock on the door, and much like my brother, Pollie doesn't wait for an answer before entering. The giant bun looks perfect atop her head and her makeup looks much better now that it's blended out. Her eyes are dark and smokey and her lips pale. She wears giant diamond hoop earrings and a big glittery bangle on each wrist. The dark green of her dress hugs her in all the right places, down to the floor where her silver pumps poke out.

"Chicky," she gasps, her hand flying to her mouth. "You are breathtaking!"

"Me!" I exclaim, taking in her movie star persona. "You look like you're ready for the Oscars!"

She rushes to me and I try not to be jealous of how quickly she can move in her shoes. "You're like that part in the rom-com where the small town girl gets a makeover and you realize that she's as beautiful as you always expected her to be. She just had to take off her glasses. You're a dream, Chicky!"

"Pol, I really don't know if I can walk in these," I admit,.

She links my arm in hers and we take our first steps forward. "Don't worry, I've got you."

After a shaky and nearly disastrous trek down the stairs, we make it to the kitchen without any injuries. The room is alive with activity as every available inch of counter space is covered with a different dish. More surprising are the three people I've never seen before hustling back and forth in tuxes.

"Who are these guys?" I whisper to Pollie. They seem to know what they're doing, which is even stranger.

She shrugs her shoulders. "This is a fancy affair. We shouldn't have to serve ourselves. I hired some people," she says, leading me away from the kitchen and toward the dining room.

Mr. Potter catches my eye first with his red hair brushed back from his face and styled like a guy from a boy band. His face twists in anguish and his body, decked out in a slick black suit, seems to be itching to get out of the room.

"I don't like strangers touching my things," he whines to Lusta, who reaches up to smooth the fabric of his red tie. She's wearing a tea length dark purple dress, with black crinoline underskirts making her look like a bell.

"Breathe and try to enjoy yourself Patty. It will be a fun night, I promise," she soothes, the two of them lost in their own little moment.

Before I can say anything to them, Lottie pulls on my hand. The olive green dress she's wearing is embroidered with bright pink flowers. Her hair is pulled back into a tight ponytail and curled. She looks precious, like a doll.

"You look wonderful!" she exclaims.

I lean down and tap her on the tip of her nose saying, "You look perfect." She smiles gleefully and skips back to her mother.

Mr. Potter walks toward me and wraps his arms around my shoulders, hugging me tight saying, "You look sublime."

I give my best royal curtsey. "I do feel kind of like a princess," I say with a smile.

Mr. Potter rests a hand on my cheek and offers me his best fatherly gaze. "Oh, darling girl, you've always been a princess. Now you're just one in a costume." Those are possibly the kindest words anyone has ever said to me.

I'm speechless as I stare back at him, absorbing his words. I don't have long to think before Lusta breathes, "Oh my," and I notice that all eyes have focused on the door.

Conrad fills the entryway, decked in a navy suit that fits him perfectly, paired with a crisp white shirt and a pale yellow tie that matches my dress. He looks like a gentleman. No more comic book villain in a black hoodie. It really does take the eye an extra moment to realize there's anything different about him at all. He looks like a handsome young man to me. The guy in the pictures from before the accident, but better. We may all be looking at him, but he only seems to see me.

"Wow," he says, almost inaudible. "You look amazing."

I stretch my arms out to show off my dress. "What? This old thing? Just something I had lying around," I joke, but those deep blue pools hold me steady.

"Haven't seen this guy in a while," Pollie adds, fiddling with his tie and Conrad smacks her hand away.

"I was thinking the same thing," Lusta agrees.

We each take a seat at the ornately decorated table, full of small Christmas trees, ornaments and fluffy white snow. Lusta and Mr. Potter sit at the heads of the table, Pollie and Lottie across from one another, and I sit across from Conrad. The three tuxedoed gentlemen enter, a bowl of soup in each hand.

"For our first course," Mr. Potter begins. "A baked potato soup with bacon and chives."

"Knocking out one of your two permitted potato dishes with the soup?" Lusta teases.

"Hush, you," Mr. Potter responds.

I'm suddenly panicked at the idea of eating anything in this beautiful dress. I know how people look at chubbier folks when they eat and, God forbid, spill something on themselves. I take small, careful sips off my spoon, mortified at the slurping sound. I hear him laughing before I look up and see Conrad ignoring his soup and staring. He sets his spoon back down by his knife and picks his bowl up to his mouth.

"Gah!" Mr. Potter gasps, cradling his head in his hands. "Good God lad, you're not a heathen. Use a spoon!"

"Sorry Potter," Conrad chokes. It takes everything in me not to start laughing too. Mr. Potter's stern expression says I shouldn't.

Lusta lifts her bowl off the table and announces, "A fitting way to toast our evening, with potatoes."

"I'm honored to be here with this hodge podge family. Thank you for letting me be a part," Pollie adds, lifting her own soup.

"I'm grateful to be around people who love me," Lottie adds with her hands before raising her own bowl, and even though I'm the only one who speaks her language, I can tell she's understood.

"Thank you all for making Christmas special for me when I couldn't be with my family," I continued, holding up my bowl. "I'll never be able to express how much it means."

Mr. Potter opens his mouth to speak, but Conrad starts speaking before he can.

"I'm an ass," an interesting way to start. "I know that and it isn't a secret, but not a single one of you has given up on me or turned your back on me when everyone else has. Thank you."

"Damn," Mr. Potter mutters as he lifts his bowl. "Can't top that! Merry Christmas everyone!" he calls out and we respond in kind before raising our bowls to our mouths.

"How is this better than using a spoon?!" Mr. Potter demands and a howl of laughter sounds around us.

Conrad raises his bad hand with its two remaining fingers and explains, "Do you really wonder why I don't eat with you folks that often? This isn't conducive to holding a utensil and I haven't mastered it with the other hand."

"Raising the bowl it is then!" Pollie responds in solidarity, continuing to sip from the lip of her own bowl.

Course after course graces our place settings. After a hearty dessert of chocolate cake, the waiters take our plates away and I have a feeling Mr. Potter is grateful for their presence now that they are cleaning. No one likes to do dishes.

Lottie hops up and down in her chair and repeatedly signs, "Presents! Presents! Presents!"

"I think Lottie is ready for gifts," I relay to the others while the last of the plates is removed from in front of us.

Lusta smiles and shakes her head, "That needed no interpretation. She's been excited for it all day." Lusta extends her hand out to her daughter and they make their way into the living room.

Pollie and Mr. Potter follow. When only Conrad and I remain in the dining room, I feel over exposed. A hand enters my line of vision. Conrad is waiting, fixed on me with his good arm extended. "Shall we?"

I lay my fingers delicately in his hand. I do my best to ignore the tingling electricity that shoots between our skin as he tucks my arm in the crook of his elbow. Against his side I realize this is the closest we've been since the night in his bedroom and the notion engulfs me. Our steps are so small that I'm not sure if he's trying to delay reuniting with the others or if he's taking pity on me and my newborn baby deer legs in these heels. I don't really mind whichever one it is.

In the living room, Mr. Potter and Lusta have set themselves up on the couch, Pollie is in my normal chair and Lottie is on her knees in front of the tree, bouncing up and down like a yo-yo.

Pollie motions to the ottoman that she pushed out. Conrad and I sit hip to hip on the plush seat. I cross my ankles and fold my hands in my lap in an attempt to make myself as small as possible. His right arm goes behind my back and rests on the far corner of the ottoman and all synapses stop firing in my brain. His hand is right by my butt. I could tell him to move it so I can focus, but I really want him to keep it right where it is. It's a paradox.

Gift after gift we unwrap, and "ooo" and "ahh" as everyone admires their treats. The punk Marilyn Monroe t-shirt I bought for Pollie is definitely a hit . She immediately slides it on over her elegant dress. Reminds me of a little girl who demands to wear every article of clothing she receives on Christmas morning.

Only two gifts are left under the tree by the time Lottie has lost interest in playing Santa. She cares only for the knitting loom that Pollie's given her. I stamp on the floor a few times to get her attention.

"Hey," I sign, when she finally looks up. "Could you get the last two gifts?" She groans before sliding the boxes across the floor.

"This is from me," Conrad says. My fingers brush across the perfectly wrapped green paper and red ribbon. My experience with boys wrapping gifts has been Jonah, and his skills are equivalent to a chimpanzee. Needless to say, I'm a little more than surprised at Conrad's near perfect execution, especially considering the state of his left hand.

"And that's from me," I say, nodding to the gift on his lap.

He needs very little encouragement before ripping through the paper. Self doubt floods me as he gets closer and closer to the box. Maybe what I got really is too feminine. It spoke to me, but that doesn't mean it will to him. Maybe I should have opened mine first. While I'm overthinking all of this, Conrad gets down to the box. It takes him a moment to finagle opening it and pulls the glass flower from inside. He casts the wrapping aside and cradles the rose in his lap. His eyes never move from it. His face is blank and unreadable and shame floods over me and my stupid gift. I gave a teenage guy a crystal flower, of course he doesn't like it. I'm sure he's trying to figure out some way to tell me without hurting my feelings, but I don't want him to have to do that.

"I'm sorry. I know it's kind of a weird thing for me to buy you, but when I saw it in the case, it looked too perfect, and I bought it without really thinking..." my voice trails off and my fingers knot together and my knuckles crack.

His mouth opens and closes a couple of times, false starts to speak before he finally croaks out, "Thank you for this, Isabella. This is the nicest thing anyone has ever given me. It makes me think of my mom." He sets the rose down carefully before he turns and pulls me into a crushing embrace. "Thank you," he murmurs into my hair. Then he pulls back to say, "All right, I've had my turn, now it's yours,"

Under the pile of discarded paper is a brown wooden box with an elegantly engraved filigree at its seams. I hand him the wrapping and slowly lift the lid of the box. My jaw drops as I process what's inside.

"I still think you're crazy for thinking it's the ultimate love story, but I doubt anyone would appreciate it more," he says. I gape at what is inside. My trembling fingers reach into the box and pull out the oldest book I've ever seen in person. The brown leather cover is slightly split at the spine and the pages have all yellowed with time. I feel like I need gloves to be handling it.

"Connie," I begin, my voice unsteady. "Is this-? Is this what I think it is?"

The proud smile on his face gives it all away. "*Wuthering Heights* by Emily Bronte, first American print," he answers.

"Conrad!" I will not faint, I will not faint, I will not faint. "This is amazing! How?"

His finger traces the edge of the box.

"It was in the library and I think it deserves a better fate than sitting on a dusty shelf forever. I'd rather it be in the hands of someone who loves it," he responds, his fingers brushing mine. I push away my timidness around touching him and grasp his hand in mine, interlacing our fingers and squeeze.

"Thank you, Conrad," I say, pouring every ounce of sincerity I possess into my words. He opens his mouth, but Pollie beats him to the punch.

"Ladies and gents, the evening is not yet complete. For what would a super posh, elegant Christmas party be without a little dancing!" A hush settles over the group, but Pollie is not the slightest bit dismayed. She cues up the melodic sounds of an orchestra playing Christmas carols on her phone. The remaining members of our crew trade nervous glances as we try to decide what to do. No one seems eager to pop up and start the waltz.

To my complete and utter surprise, Conrad is the first to rise to his feet. He reaches his hand out to me. "Miss Southland."

"No, no, no. You don't want to do that."

Conrad never falters, as he waits for me with his hand still outstretched. "Bella, if I didn't want to, I wouldn't ask." My skin tingles with a pleasant mixture of exhilaration and fear.

I raise up to the tops of my heels, my ankles wobbling, and Conrad chuckles.

"Please take those stupid things off before you hurt yourself."

Thank God! I think to myself. I kick my shoes off and under the ottoman, bringing me down to my proper and comfortable height, right at Conrad's chest.

I stare at the pale yellow tie around his neck and heat flushes down mine. I crinkle my toes down into the carpet and admit, "Conrad, I don't know how to do this."

He places the knuckle of his right index finger under my chin and raises my gaze to his. Placing my left hand on his shoulder, he lays his right on my middle back. "Don't worry, I've got you."

I do my best to follow Conrad's lead. He never gets frustrated, no matter how many times I step on his toes. Which I do. A lot. Mr. Potter and Lusta get up to join us and I'm only the tiniest bit envious at how effortless they are in their movement. I keep trying to look down at my feet, but every time I do, Conrad lets go of my hand and lifts my face again to his.

"Stop thinking so much. You can do this," he says in such an authoritative way that I have no choice but to believe him. I allow my body relax and allow him to lead me in a circle around our small, makeshift dance floor in the middle of the living room. For a moment, everyone and everything else fades away. It's like we're in the middle of a grand ballroom or even an open field of flowers. It's just us. A girl in a yellow dress and a boy in a blue suit dancing to a song that beats the same in them both. Conrad's gaze intensifies, his hand drops from my middle back to my waist and he pulls me a little closer. Before I know what's happening, he's placing my hand around his neck, his fingers interlacing behind my back. I'm close enough now that I can feel his breath on my skin.

"Bella," he begins, moving closer. I close my eyes, giving myself over to the moment, ready for it to happen, when a little set of hands step in between us and push us apart.

"You have to leave room for Jesus," Lottie tells me before crossing her little arms.

"What?!" I demand with my voice.

She looks at me like I'm stupid as her little hip pops to the side. "We took a dance class at school and the teacher said you always have to leave room between you and your partner for Jesus," she responds with such authority I feel the compulsion to apologize for my own ignorance. Slowly she pushes me out of the way and wiggles in between Conrad and I. "Besides, it's my turn to dance with him."

Conrad never skips a beat, bowing down to scoop Lottie off the floor before twirling her around the room. She lets out a laugh so joyful that for a second, it's worth it that she ruined my moment. Pollie comes up beside me and links her arm through mine and we both watch Conrad twirl the happy little girl around.

"Chicky!" Pollie begins. "What was that?"

"What?" I ask.

She reaches over to pinch me through the glittery sheer of my sleeve. "Don't you dare pretend. Conrad almost kissed you," she blurts out, her hands clapping together. "If you marry him, you'd be my sister and that would be super cool because I've always wanted a sister."

I seal my hand over her mouth and kiss her forehead. "Nothing happened, Poll. Let it go."

"Fine," Pollie groans. It seems physically painful for her. I doubt she's ever let anything go in her life. She reaches down and fluffs my skirt. "Chicky, we need to get some shots of you in this dress. This is an evening that needs to be remembered and remembering requires documentation."

Normally this is the kind of thing that would make me cower in the corner or demand to take a selfie. I have never been big on other people taking my picture. They always seem to get me at the wrong angle, which has always been every angle. But it doesn't scare me anymore.

"Let's do it!"

"Strike a pose darling," she says in her best French accent. I place my hands on my hips and start making ridiculous faces and poses. She giggles, snapping picture after picture. It's impossible to miss Conrad watching me over Lottie's shoulder. He's barely moving with her as he stares at me, an unreadable expression deep in his eyes.

"You're a natural Chicky," Pollie muses, admiring her work.

Do I look chubby in the pictures? Yes. I will always look a little chubby in pictures, but in these particular shots, I'm doing it with fabulous flair! Maybe that's what's making the world of difference. If there's one thing I'm really learning, it's that my worth isn't measured by the size of my waist. I alone make that call.

Pollie continues to go on and on about the pictures, but I barely hear her. My world is singularly focused on Conrad. I'm moving before I realize it and I am without a plan when I find myself next to him.

"Yes, Bella?" he asks, his voice dripping with amusement. He refuses to bail me out of my awkwardness.

"Wanna go for a walk?" I blurt out at a volume far too loud for how close we're standing. God, I wish I could crawl into a hole and die with my own embarrassment.

He reaches out and takes my hand, cupping my palm in his.

"Lead the way, Miss Southland."

Christmas Eve in upstate New York is not the best day to go wandering around outside. The scenery is beautiful. We received a touch of the storm that hit Harpersgrove. The perfect amount of snow coats the ground and dusts the trees. I try my best to think of warmer climates to keep from shivering because I like being out with him, even if I'm freezing. As usual, Conrad sees right through me. Without a word, he shrugs out of his suit jacket and places it around my shoulders. As I'm pulling it closer around me I ask, "But won't you be cold?"

"Nah, I was on fire once. I'm pretty sure I'll always be warmer than most people," he jokes with an evil grin.

"Conrad Baxter! That's not funny!" I shriek and he begins to laugh. He clutches his side, trying to keep from doubling over.

"No, it wouldn't be funny if you said it. I have free reign."

I tuck my free hand into the pocket of his jacket and touch something hard. Without thinking, I wrap my fingers around it and pull it out to find a pair of pearl cluster earrings in my hand.

Conrad stumbles when he sees me holding them. "Well, you weren't supposed to find those."

"Sorry," I yelp, shoving them back inside like that will erase my seeing them.

"No, no, it's okay. They were my backup in case you didn't like the book," he says.

"You were going to give me these?"

"I told you, I don't like things that are important to sit around here like ghosts. My mom would have wanted someone I care about to have them. I thought two gifts might be overkill, that's why I held onto them. When you responded well to the book I kept them in my pocket. Since you found them, you should have them," he says, closing my hand around them.

I shake my head. "The story was even better than the earrings." Looking up into his face, battered and scarred through a war he continues to fight, I can say, beyond a shadow of a doubt, that he is the most beautiful creature I have ever seen. Beauty is about so much more than what's outside. He loves his family and defends his friends, likes Broadway musicals, can kick my butt in calculus, and makes my heart flutter by walking into a room. I've cared about him the whole time, but its evolved into something else, something more.

"Conrad," I say, closing the gap between us. "I-"

He cuts me off, "No, Bella."

His jaw clenches against his smooth, shiny skin. He places his hands on my cheeks and rests his lips against my forehead. He doesn't kiss me, he doesn't move. His mouth holds soft and steady there. "Don't," he mumbles against my skin. I start to pull away. "Don't. Please."

His voice is full of pain and heartbreak. Finally, he places a hard kiss against my forehead and then leaves me, standing alone and confused, in the snow.

CHAPTER NINETEEN

Christmas morning doesn't hold quite the normal splendor. The colors of the world are dull without the sparkle I'm used to. Jonah and my father call early to wish me a merry Christmas with grins and matching pajamas. My mother stays off camera, opting to wish me well from afar. It hurts my heart, but I can't blame her. I should never have gone this long without speaking to her. After we hang up, I get dressed in a well worn, lazy day outfit and brush out my hair. I'm ready for nothing but leftovers and Christmas movies. My phone buzzes with messages, each a picture of one of my friends with their family members. I respond to all with a bright and cheery "Merry Christmas!" with a long line of emojis and smile at the fact that they thought of me first thing on Christmas morning.

I find my spot on my comfy living room chair after flipping on the tree lights. I grab the massive remote, of which I'm now an expert, and click on the television. To my delight, *A Christmas Story* is on. It wouldn't be December 25th if I didn't start my day with this movie. I consider getting a cup of tea or something for breakfast, but I'm glued to the screen.

Of course I'm not alone in the house. The moment I feel completely at ease and absorbed in my movie, Conrad appears in front of me, dressed in his normal attire, gray sweatpants and black hoodie. He moves across the room like I don't exist and flops onto the couch. I'm not sure what to do. I sit stiffly in my seat, a blanket clutched around my shoulders. I keep waiting for him to say something, but he doesn't. It takes a while to relax again. I let my attention refocus on the TV. At one point I start to mouth the words with the movie and I swear I feel him smile. That instantly stops my lip synch. We watch the rest in silence until the credits roll. That's when he stands and my tongue slides down the back of my throat. I'm sure he's about to say something, make this more awkward, or maybe try to clear the air, but he doesn't. In fact, he leaves. I shake it off and change the channel to another movie.

Only when I start to push Conrad from my brain, he reappears with a few things tucked under his arm. He pushes my feet off the ottoman and pulls the little table between us, sitting a box on top of it. "Scrabble", America's favorite board game, stares back at me. He sets up the game and distributes the tiles, playing his first word and scribbling down his points. Those blue eyes stare at me, challenging and waiting. I decide that if he wants to play, we'll play. His wheelhouse may be calculus, but mine is the written word. I lay down "A-M-B-U-L-A-T-O-R-Y" through a triple word and raise a challenging eyebrow before picking out new letter tiles, my quiet smugness filling the room. Conrad smiles and writes down my total, then takes his turn.

We play like this for a while, with the musical stylings of Bing Crosby crooning in the background from *White Christmas* and blending into Judy Garland in *Meet Me In Saint Louis*. I'm grateful for the movies because Conrad and I never speak a word and that silence is booming.

As our second game which of course I'm winning, begins to close, I'm surprised to hear him talk. I figured we weren't doing that anymore.

"There's something I'd like to do today," he announces, laying down a sad "R-U-G" for an equally sad number of points.

"What's that?" I ask. His presence makes my stomach flutter. I need to get over myself because it hurts my heart that he doesn't feel the same way and we can't coexist in that manner.

The corner of his lips twitched and he said, "I want to make a pie."

"What?" is all that seems able to come out of my mouth.

He motions to my shirt with the pie shop logo across the chest and says, "You must know how to bake a pie if you work there. Teach me."

I personally think it's a little presumptuous to assume that I know how to make a pie because I happen to work in a pie shop. As if Rosie would ever let me touch her baking supplies.

"Okay," I croak out, like I have any idea what I'm doing.

"Great, I'm going to go jump in the shower and then we can raid the pantry and get to work."

As soon as he's out of earshot, I scramble to my phone and immediately call Rosie. The four rings it takes for her to pick up are the longest of my life.

"Ho, ho, ho, Merry Christmas, Hells Bells!" she exclaims when she picks up. In the background, I can hear her aunts singing carols at the top of their lungs in the background and I feel guilty for calling, but I'm desperate.

"Merry Christmas." I hurry through so I don't seem like a complete jerk. "Listen, I need your help with something."

"What's up? You okay?"

"Yes, I promise I'm all good. I just need you to send me your pecan pie recipe." The line is eerily silent, but I can hear Aunt Shawna singing again. I know I didn't lose her.

"Rose?" I question, making sure she didn't drop the phone.

"I don't share my recipes," she whines.

"Rosaline, I'm not trying to steal your recipe. I only need it for today and today only. I will let you watch me delete it from my phone when I'm home if that makes you feel better."

"I will demand the full story as to why you needed this recipe when you come home. We'll drink hot cocoa and you'll explain everything in great detail." I love this side of Rosie. She meddles with the best of them, but only when the time is right.

"I am dying to tell you everything."

I can hear the smile in her voice when she says, "I'll type it up and send it to you."

When Conrad finally joins me in the kitchen, I'm laying the last of the ingredients on the counter from Rosie's recipe.

"What kind of pie did you choose?" he asks, sounding nervous.

"Pecan. It's my favorite. I can't believe that all the ingredients are here. Even the pecans."

Conrad laughs and rubs the back of his neck. "Yeah, I think Potter is actually a doomsday prepper. You should see what's in the storage in the basement."

"There's a basement?" I say in shock. This place is a labyrinth of mysteries.

"Yeah, it's nothing special, just row after row of shelves."

It's like yesterday never happened and we're back to our old selves. I'm equal parts relieved and heartbroken. The rollercoaster that is Conrad Baxter is bumpy and nauseating. I want to get off.

I start pulling aside the ingredients for the crust.

"Any idea where I could find a pie dish?"

Conrad's lips purse and he starts opening cabinets. He finds a light blue dish covered in daisies and raises it above his head with a smile. "Success!" he exclaims, placing it beside me. "Okay, where do we start?"

"Preheat the oven to three hundred fifty degrees," I read off my phone, only to have him stare blankly back at me.

"You don't know how to preheat an oven, do you?" His head drops in defeat. I have no idea where we stand, and as uneasy as that makes me, I find it in me to laugh.

"I've never had to cook anything for myself. I've always had people for that," he admits. I set the oven myself.

"Well, that stops today. You're helping me do this." I point to ingredients and Conrad measures and dumps them into a mixing bowl with the focus and intensity of a nuclear physicist. There's a boyish glee to his demeanor as he does. It's adorable.

When all of the ingredients are in the bowl, mixed together like crumbs, I start to stir as he adds the water. His arm brushes mine, sending that familiar electricity through my skin. I focus all my energy into mixing and remind myself over and over that he does not feel the same.

"Bella, I think you've stirred it enough," he says softly. I can feel his body heat radiating off him, warm and welcoming. He's right there. All I'd have to do is turn into him, but I can't.

I throw a bit of flour onto the counter and grab the marble rolling pin. "You're going to roll this out so that it's in a circle about an inch thick," I read off my screen.

He starts to roll back and forth, proving incredibly difficult on his left side. The pin keeps slipping from his hand. He grits his teeth and grips the pin hard. "I can't do this Bella."

"Hey," I encourage, placing my hand on his. "This is a peCAN pie, not a peCAN'T." A gentle snort escapes him at my punny line. "We'll do it together."

Reaching across him, I place my left hand over his putting my weight on his wrist. He chuckles under his breath, enveloping me in his arms with his hands over mine on the rolling pin. Back and forth we move it, the only sound between us is the rolling mechanism inside. The silence is thick and tense. We over roll the dough, to the point that it's falling off the counter. Neither of us stop. We just keep rolling.

I realize I may never have this opportunity again. Pressed up against this boy I feel so deeply for, I memorize every detail of this moment. My back molded against his front, the sound of his heart pounding near my ear. His chin and cheek against the side of my hair, his arms against mine and his fingers flexing over my own. Suddenly the pin stops, but neither of us move. I stop breathing and wait. I feel completely out of control and yet never safer. His face turns and his nose and lips press against my hair. He whispers, "Bella." The sound of my name is all it takes to melt my last resolve. "This is a bad idea." His voice is sad, broken, and so hopeless.

"Why?" I ask the question that's plagued me all along. What about me isn't worth the risk? What part of me isn't worthy?

"I'm a mess," he mutters, with pure sorrow rushing through his words. "I put on a good face when we're together, at least I try, but I'm a disaster. When I say I'm a monster, I don't just mean my skin. I'm a dark pit on the inside and you don't deserve what's there." The tip of his nose brushes the shell of my ear and a pleasant shiver rushes through my whole body.

I pull my fingers out from under his and turn around to face him, my palms behind me on the counter. His hands remain on either side, his fingers splayed out, almost like he's afraid to touch me. Our faces are so close, I can feel his breath on my skin.

"What are you trying to say, Conrad?" I demand, not settling for anything less than a straight answer. He tries to pull himself away, but I hold him the way he always seems to hold me. His chin trembles, vulnerability rippling off him.

"Bella, I'm not good, definitely not good enough for you," he admits, his voice breaking with his truth. "You're going to an Ivy League school. You're brilliant, funny, beautiful, full of life. You have a family that cares about you. You're everything and I'm this abyss that will consume you and I can't do that. I won't."

What happens next isn't about being brave. It's about being the person I've always been, the girl my parents raised me to be. I release my hands from the counter and rest my fingers against his cheeks, one side stubbly and coarse and the other smooth and glassy. His eyes close and two perfect tears roll fast down his cheeks.

"Conrad, look at me." He does as I ask and I can see the pain that plagues him. He's opened a wound that bleeds in front of me and I know I'm holding his fragile self in my hands.

"I see you."

The words are simple and soft as they leave my lips. I've said them before, but they mean more now. I flex my fingers against his skin, my thumbs moving back and forth.

"I see you," I say again with more force. I need him to hear me. "I see you and you are not an abyss. I see who you are. You are not a monster. You are someone who has been through so much pain, and I see you."

His hands reach up and cover my wrists, holding my hands in place. "Don't you dare ever say you aren't good enough. I wouldn't step forward if I didn't think it was worth it."

"Bella," he begins, but I'm not done.

"What do you feel for me? Forget everything else, every ounce of doubt you have about yourself. What do you feel when you look at me?"

He doesn't hesitate to say, "The second night you were here, the night I covered you with a blanket after you went to that party with Pollie, I knew I would be no good where you were concerned from that day forward."

I pull him toward me, letting my eyes close as our lips touch. My hands slide down to his chest when he kisses me back, his hands digging into my hair. I wrap my arms around his neck and pull him closer, kneading my fingers into the back of his neck. A low growl sounds in his throat. His tongue enters my mouth and that fear I had when Gatty did the same is gone this time. It's different when you love someone.

He abruptly pulls his mouth away, his body remaining in place as he kisses both my cheeks and wraps his arms around my back to crush me against him in a hug.

"I need to pause," he admits against my ear and I smile like a little girl. "I can't go too far with you. I won't let myself. I need to pause." I'm not sure how long we stay like that, wrapped up together on the ruined beginnings of our pie, but I know I could happily stay here forever.

We clean up the kitchen, abandoning our poor sad pecan pie, and since I'm covered in flour, I run upstairs to change my clothes. When I return, he's on the couch waiting for me. I snuggle up beside him and the afternoon falls away and we watch movie after movie. I can't remember a merrier Christmas in all my life. It feels so adult, like we've finished with our families for the day and are spending some private time together. I wonder if that's what it will feel like, when I finally grow up.

"I was thinking," he says after our fourth movie. "Maybe we could go see *Antony and Cleopatra*."

"Seriously?" The mere idea that he would voluntarily go out amongst the human race is enough to knock me off my feet. He laughs humorlessly, clearly undervaluing the extremeness of this revelation.

"You made a good point when you brought it up. We can get there right before it starts, sit in the back, and leave right when it ends. I'll wear a hat and long sleeves, all that good stuff. It would probably be a good start."

"Really?" I say, with a grin that makes my cheeks hurt. He's talking about a date, a real life date with Conrad Baxter.

He takes my hand and squeezes. "Really."

I'm about to lean over and kiss him again, happy that I can when my phone starts buzzing in my sweater pocket. I pull it out and a smiling picture of Elle comes up on screen.

"Do you mind if I take this?"

"Not at all," he says as he unwinds himself from me and moves to the far end of the couch.

I swipe my finger across the screen and Finn and Elle come into frame. "Merry Christmas, Bella," Finn says with a wave.

"Hey Finn, Merry Christmas. How's the holiday, folks?"

"It's been a good day. Miss you!" Elle responds. "How are you doing, honey? I was kind of hoping to see that boy there with you!"

It hits me that I haven't told any of them what happened with Gatty. My stomach sits like a heavy stone in my torso and pulls me out of the bubble of my merry Christmas.

"Well, um, well-"

Before I stumble over my words anymore, Conrad moves next to me. Putting his arm over my shoulders, he says to them, "She actually decided to go another way," and I have never been more grateful for someone to speak for me.

CHAPTER TWENTY

The next morning we're back to work in the greenhouse. "You know, most people take at least a few days off after Christmas before getting back to school," he says with a huff.

"Well, most people aren't trying to cram almost two years of work into a few months. We work now," I tease.

Instead of getting back to studying, he keeps watching me. I shut my book with a delicious force that snaps in my hand.

"Mr. Baxter, I have been hired to do a job and your staring is making that difficult for me."

His finger traces a figure eight on my knee, trying to distract me further. "And how can I make this up to you, Miss Southland," he asks in a way that makes my stomach flip. I lean forward and kiss him on the lips. He hums his approval. I pull back slightly, leaving him in a bit of a haze.

"Get your diploma, that's how you can make it up to me."

"Wow, you're tough," he mocks, flipping back to a condensed history of Abraham Lincoln.

"As nails. Study, please."

When his continued attempts to distract me are ignored, he accepts his defeat and settles into reading. There's something so calm and comforting about the silence, the only thing I can hear is my internal voice reading the words on the pages of the book in my hands.

"Mind if I put on some music?" he asks, scrolling through his phone to find a song. Not everyone works best in the quiet, I guess.

When Dolly Parton starts to sing through the speakers of his phone, my brain short circuits. "Seriously?" I laugh.

"When I was in the hospital, Pollie made me a playlist of songs she thought I'd find soothing. Most of them are Dolly Parton. I still find it oddly comforting," he says, his thumb running along the edge of his screen.

"That was a nice thing for her to do," I say.

"She was amazing when I was there. I spent most of the first month screaming for my parents. My mom was dead, my dad couldn't deal, and Pollie took all that on herself. She thought the music would help, because in her eyes, music can fix anything."

He drifts far away for a moment, lost in thought. "I don't thank her enough for all she's done."

Unsure of what else to do, I take his hand and tell him, "I think she knows."

After kissing me on the forehead, he leans back, returning to his book. "That's enough of my sadness for one day." Desperate to switch gears, he flips his phone around to me. "I got tickets for Friday to see that play."

"Really?" I ask, waiting for the punchline. I want it to be true that we could do this, but I never thought he'd actually go through with it.

"Did you change your mind about going?" he asks, hopeful.

"Oh, we're going!" I've never been more excited to see a show.

The next few days pass in a blur of homework, movies, food, laughs, and too many kisses to count. In a word, heaven. Conrad only grows slightly moody on the day of the actual show.

"There's probably a movie version we can stream," he whines from the passenger seat of my car. "I could probably get someone to go and stream this exact show for us."

I know this is hard for him, but he's being too dramatic.

"We both know this has nothing to do with Shakespeare," I respond.

"There's still time to call Pollie and have her go with you," he murmurs, fiddling with the Orioles baseball cap I loaned him.

"Listen, if you're really not ready, we do not have to do this. I can turn this car around and go home." This isn't a doctor's appointment or a hospital visit. This isn't something he has to do.

"No, no, we should go. Let's hope no one confuses me with the *Phantom of the Opera*," he laughs, but fear lies under the words. He stares out the window, quiet as a mouse, and I wish I knew what he was thinking. As sure as I am that everything is going to be okay, I find myself gripping the steering wheel a little tighter than necessary. Apprehension fills me from the tips of my toes to the ends of my hair. I want to protect him, even though we are walking right into a situation where I will have no control.

I pick a spot in the back of the lot as people leave their cars and meander into the theater. He slouches down in his seat even though it's dark enough that no one could possibly see him. At five minutes to eight the parking lot is quiet, but Conrad still makes no motions toward getting out of the car.

"You okay?" I ask. Our window for an unnoticed entrance is quickly closing.

"Let's go," he mutters, his fingers white-knuckled on the door handle. "I'm ready." I think he's trying to convince himself more than me.

He rounds the car and waits for me to get out to hold my hand. He tucks his chin down to his collarbone and I direct us to the entrance. His stance never changes when I hand the usher our tickets. While the man does take a look or two over at Conrad, I think it's more because Conrad is trying so hard not to make any eye contact.

We claim our seats in the very back row as the lights fade to black and spotlights illuminate the stage. The immortal words of William Shakespeare float through the speakers toward us. For a while I forget about worrying for Conrad. In what seems like the blink of an eye, the lights go dark on the stage and the house lights come up. People stand and stretch in their seats, gearing up for the second half of the play. A few pass us and make their way out of the theater. Conrad turns completely toward me, his hand, deep in the sleeve of his jacket, up against the burned side of his face.

"You doing okay?"

"Better than I thought I would be," he mumbles. I run the pad of my thumb over his knuckles, trying to calm us both.

"It'll be dark again soon."

The play ends and the cast begins to line up for their curtain call. I nudge Conrad with my elbow.

"You want to go?" I ask, knowing that we planned to miss the crowd.

A confident smile stretches across his face as he applauds with the group. "It's okay, we can watch the curtain call and then bolt."

I sit back in my seat and clap, but the little hairs stand up on the back of my neck. This wasn't the plan.

After Cleopatra makes a deep, dramatic curtsey, signifying the finale, Conrad says, "All right let's go."

People are already leaving their seats and funnel through the exits. This is more public than we wanted. He places our clasped hands into his pocket, keeping his head down as we take a handful of steps to the back of the theater. Conrad's strides become faster and longer when it sinks in how many people are around. He's clearly forgotten how much taller he is than me as he pulls me behind him.

We're almost home free to the safety of the darkness outside when a little girl zooms into our path and Conrad nearly falls over her, stuttering to a stop. His hat falls off his head and he lets go of my hand. The two lock eyes like people who have never encountered another human before. The little girl's already pale skin blanches. The seconds tick away like hours. Neither of them move. A sob ripples from the little girl's throat when she cries "Mommy!"

A small red headed woman zips through the crowd. I want to reach out and touch him, make sure he knows that I'm here, but he seems too far away to notice me. As soon as the mother sees him, the glassiness of his skin and the milkiness of his eye, her expression falls. Her mouth remains agape, but the rest of her demeanor softens with maternal pity as she stares at him. His chest rises and falls with ragged breath.

"Oh," she mumbles, tucking her sniffling daughter behind her. "Oh, I'm so sorry."

A sea of people has formed around us while we stand in the bubble at the center. Whispers echo off the walls and people point and stare. No one laughs from what I can tell, but the looks of disgust and pity are much worse. My brain clicks back on and I lunge forward and take his hand.

"Conrad, let's go."

I'm losing him to every bad thing he's thought about himself. Maybe this was a mistake. I place the palm of my hand on his left cheek and he noticeably cringes under my touch. It breaks my heart.

"Let's go," I repeat and pull him behind me toward the doors. He follows in robotic fashion, his body going through the motions but his brain detached. People part to let us through. I'm sure my harsh expression has something to do with it. I keep hold of him until we make it to the car. I open his door and let him inside, closing it behind him. The car ride home is dead silent, my fingers locked at ten and two on the steering wheel. The only sound is Conrad's knuckles cracking one by one as he releases the tension in the only way he has.

I park in my normal spot at the house and I've barely stopped the car before he's stepping out into the cold all alone. By the time we cross the threshold I've reached the point of tears.

"Conrad?"

He places his hands on my cheeks and kisses me hard on the forehead, holding me there for a long time. When he releases me, his voice is soft and so very sad.

"I just need to go to bed Bella. I can't talk about this right now. Tomorrow, okay?"

And then he's gone, leaving me standing alone by the front door. I try not to blame myself for what happened, because it wasn't my fault. It tears me apart wondering if he blames me. As I climb the steps to my bedroom, my phone buzzes in my purse. It's a text from Blanche.

Hey Hells Bells! Just checking in, miss you!

I hug my phone to my chest, too exhausted to answer. It eases my heart to know that they're there.

I begrudgingly make my way down to the kitchen the next morning, throwing my own private pity party. I'm surprised to see Conrad at the kitchen table. I had assumed he would want to hide away today. Mr. Potter and Lusta both lean against the counter by the sink.

Mr. Potter hands me a steaming mug of tea and I ask, "What's going on?"

"You tell me. What happened last night?" Lusta inquires.

Mr. Potter places his hand on my shoulder and whispers in my ear, "He's been sitting there for two hours. He's gone through two boxes of cereal and hasn't moved other than to pour and chew."

As I'm about to unload the whole disastrous story, Conrad comes up behind me and kisses the top of my head. He hands his bowl to Lusta who gawks like he's a ghost come back to life.

"You ready to study?" he asks, his voice hoarse like he hasn't used it in weeks.

"Su-sure," I stammer.

He takes me up to the greenhouse, pulling the door shut behind us. As soon as it clicks, he pulls me in, crushing me against him. He buries his good hand in my hair and the other grabs me behind my back. At first, I'm not sure how to react. I don't understand what is happening. But when he nuzzles his nose against my ear I get it. He just wants me.

"You okay?" I murmur, my words lost against his burly chest. He nods against the top of my head.

After many long, blissful moments pass, he pulls back enough to lift my chin and kiss me.

"Better?" I ask.

He smiles and says, "Better. Sorry if I scared you. I didn't sleep much last night."

"I'm okay. I'm sorry, I dropped the ball."

"What are you talking about?" he asks, twirling a strand of my hair around his finger.

"I knew we needed to leave sooner. I should have pushed, I'm sorry. I feel like I let you down."

"You didn't do anything wrong. If I remember correctly, I was the one who wanted to stay for the curtain call. At least there weren't any rioting villagers with pitchforks," he jokes, a smirk on that perfectly imperfect face. "It wasn't great and if given the choice I wouldn't repeat it, but it won't be the last time. Now I know I can survive it, even when it's unpleasant."

He pulls out his phone and hands it over to me. On the screen is a picture of Conrad before, deeply tan with curly, honey colored hair and a scruff of a beard growing on his chin. His blue eyes sparkle with laughter as he hugs his sister, his broad form consuming her. He looks happy.

"I looked at that picture for hours last night. I am not that guy anymore. It's time to face that fact," he says with a sorrowful yet poignant finality. He looks down his left arm, scarred from blistered burns to the hand with its missing fingers and I refuse to let him fall back down that black spiral.

"Thank God. I'm not really into pretty boys," I joke and his eyes twinkle with that same amusement from the picture.

I pull out my books and get to work. Conrad has made incredible strides. If he can keep this pace, he might actually be able to graduate by the end of the summer.

We fall into a lull, both of us absorbed in our reading. The lone sound, a consistent buzzing, hums from Conrad's phone on the table between us. Every now and then, Conrad picks up the phone to stare at the screen before ignoring the call. I let it go for as long as I can stand it.

"Should you get that? Might be important."

"I know who it is. It's Pollie. she's calling about Gatty," he says, snapping his book shut. I try to remain unaffected, but the mere mention of his name throws my body into high alert.

"What?"

"Pollie filled me in on what she did, confronting the Gattmans," he says. I wondered if he knew. I certainly wasn't going to bring it up to him.

"What does this have to do with right now?" If I don't have to ever think of him again, I don't want to.

"Pollie heard through the grapevine at school today that his parents sent him off to military school. He's gone."

I know he spoke the words in English, but they make about as much sense to me as if he'd said them in Greek.

"I don't understand."

Conrad turns off his phone to stop the vibrating. "I'd like to tell you that it was all because of you, what he did, but I think it was a 'last straw' kind of thing. Gatty and I used to get into a lot of trouble together and even though they don't have all of the specifics, I think they know he was involved in my accident. They've had enough."

I wish it brought me more comfort, but it doesn't. He should have to face real justice. I know that. I also know we live in a world where this outcome is far more than I'd normally get. Most girls live in silence without anyone knowing their stories or whether the people who hurt them faced any consequences. I should feel better, this is something after all. Then I realize, I don't have to feel anything. Whatever I'm experiencing is valid. I have to keep reminding myself that just because other people have had it worse, doesn't determine how I get to feel about what's happened to me. Justice and healing are a spectrum and grieving this lost part of my innocence will take time.

"Bella? Are you okay?" Conrad asks. I've been sitting here, silent, lost in my own head far too long.

"I think I need a break."

Conrad recognizes my need to be alone for a minute and heads down to the kitchen to make us a snack. I start counting flowers growing up from the pots on the tables hoping that if I distract my brain with a mundane task, it might keep me from breaking down.

My brain is running in a thousand different directions at the same time. My body feels like it's trying to rip its way out of my skin. Everything is on fire. I run out the back door into the garden, hoping the shock of the cold will calm me down. My breathing rushes in and out in icy puffs. I place my hands over my heart and press down, taking comfort in the beats that prove I'm still alive.

The anger starts to brew down in my feet and works its way up my body to where it meets the sorrow in my stomach, the pain in my heart, the fear in my throat, and the relief behind my eyes. All the emotions mix and twist together and come barrelling out of my mouth in an alien scream that doesn't stop coming until I run out of air. When it's done, my hands shake and I expect the world to be different, because it's all out now, but I'm still hurting. I take another deep breath and let it out again, screaming with every ounce of my being, and stomping in a circle. Shaking my arms and legs, letting it all go. In the distance, I hear birds chirping and the wind rushing overhead. The grayish blue sky of winter comforts me in its blankness and it brings me peace. This is enough for now.

The knot in my stomach has significantly lessened by the time I reach the kitchen and my hands have nearly stopped shaking.

"I'm calling on behalf of your father sir," Colin says through the tablet and the calmness I had just found rushes away.

"Of course you are," Conrad hisses, his hands on either side of the screen. Lusta and Mr. Potter hover in the doorway of the pantry. I can't seem to move past where they stand.

"I'm very sorry sir, but it seems as though your father won't be able-" Colin begins before Conrad smashes his good fist against the wall.

"Enough," Conrad lets out, gruff and pained. "It is enough, Colin! I don't want to play this game with him anymore. I am exhausted," he confesses and the words flow from him like a dam finally burst. He smacks the palm of his left hand against the wall and a shudder runs through me.

"If he wants to treat me like some creature that he has to hide away from the world, then fine. I can't change his mind. But he has to drop this charade that I'm still his son. He has to stop acting like I haven't been dead to him since the day my mother passed away and my injuries weren't the excuse he needed to put me away. I don't want to play anymore. You tell him that."

I expect a smart remark to leave Colin's lips, but it doesn't. The old man sniffs hard and says, "I will tell him that, sir."

When the call ends, the room falls silent, and I don't know what to do. Only Conrad can dictate what happens next. My blood runs cold when he begins to punch the wall in rapid succession, breaking through the plaster and his hand in the process. Mr. Potter links his arms through Conrad's to pull him away from the wall.

"You're okay. You're okay, son," Mr. Potter soothes and Conrad screams out in pain that has nothing to do with his bones. Lusta places her palms on his cheeks and pushes his tears away with the pads of her thumbs. I take a step back. He doesn't need me right now. He needs the only parents he's had in a long time and they've got him. I feel like I have to do something. My calm resolve returns and I know what I can do to help.

"Wait, walk us through this, babe," Blanche demands through the phone. She and Rosie watch as I search through my bedroom to find any clothes that could resemble professionalism.

"Conrad's mom died when he was younger and his dad's a jerk. He hurts Conrad nonstop," I explain. I find a pair of pants that, while stretchy, don't look like sweatpants. Maybe I can make them dressy.

"Okay, that's not enough information," Rosie exclaims as they try to rein me in.

"Hells Bells!" Blanche shouts at the phone. "Focus!"

"I'm dating, seeing, hanging out with Conrad," I begin, unsure of what our definition is yet.

"Right," Blanche responds. "Finnegan and Michelle informed us of that after Christmas."

"Anyway," I start again. "His dad is horrible to him. Pollie told me they were never close, but after his mom died and after his accident, it's like he's cut his son out completely. I can't take it. Conrad pretends like it doesn't bother him, but I know that's not true."

"Okay," Blanche begins, trying to reel me in. "You still haven't told us what you're doing and I'm getting concerned."

I let out a sputtering breath that ruffles my hair up out of my eyes. "I kind of have this new persona I call Brave Bella. She's stronger than I have ever been and she protects the people she cares about. I don't think that Mr. Baxter knows or cares how much he's hurting Conrad. That doesn't sit right with me. I'm going to talk to him."

Rosie's head starts to shake back and forth.

"Abort! Abort! Danger Will Robinson! That is a horrendous idea!" she exclaims, waving her hands back and forth at me.

Blanche's thumb juts in Rosie's direction and the sides of her mouth turn down, saying, "Yeah Bells, I'm with Rosie. This sounds like a really bad plan."

"It's not a bad plan! Conrad needs the people who care to stand up for him. I'm the only person who can do this. Lusta and Mr. Potter rely on their jobs to live and I'm sure Pollie doesn't want to completely destroy her relationship with her dad. That leaves me."

"Is this even something he'd want you to do? Have you talked to him about it?" Rosie questions.

"No," I begin, running my tongue along the bumpy edge of my teeth. "He would tell me not to get involved. He has this strong, stoic nature about him and he'd rather suffer. He shouldn't have to. He should know people are there for him. I'm here for him," I explain in one overrun breath.

"Bella, if there is already a tiny bit of doubt in your brain that he wouldn't be okay with this, you shouldn't do it," Rosie says.

"Why can't you just support me?" I moan, my teeth grinding together.

"Why did you call us if you didn't want our opinions?" Blanche bites back, her hands waving at the camera. Rosie gently pats her knee to bring her back down. "If you want to know what we think, we don't think you should do it."

I should probably absorb what they're saying, at least take it under consideration, but my brain won't hear it. My momentum's going and I've already decided.

"I have to go," I snap, clicking off the call in normal fashion without saying goodbye. I look up at my reflection in the mirror and consider my options. I really care about Conrad and I don't like that anyone could be hurting him.

"This is the right thing," I say to my reflection, but I'm not sure which one of us I'm trying to convince.

CHAPTER TWENTY ONE

The building that holds Baxter Industries is an intimidating structure of glass and steel that reaches up into the clouds. It gives new meaning to the term skyscraper. My hodge podge outfit doesn't scream strong, executive female. The first thing I'm doing upon getting home is buying a suit. A pair of security guards in matching black attire sit behind a sleek black desk in the lobby. They eye me skeptically, ready to throw out the hooligan that clearly doesn't belong.

"Can I help you?" one of the guards asks me.

"Yes, I'm here to see Mr. Lionel Baxter."

The two men trade a glance. The one I'm speaking with raises his eyebrow at the ridiculous concept that this little girl would be here to meet with an international mogul.

"Do you have an appointment?" his voice mocking as he taps his fingers against the smooth surface of his desk.

"No I do not," I begin and the guard immediately opens his mouth to shoo me away. "But I work for him. I'm his son's tutor."

The other guard sits forward and says, "Your name please."

"Isabella Southland."

The second man extends his hand with thin, long fingers and asks for my identification. He motions to the waiting area and invites me to have a seat.

I sit on one of the leather chairs that line the floor to ceiling window of the lobby. The perfectly fanned pile of *Architectural Digest* feel welcoming, but I'm too wound up right now to consider opening one. My fingers drum against my thigh as I wait.

"Miss Southland," the security guard calls out. "The elevator on the right will take you to the top floor."

Piano music plays softly in the background of the elevator in a way that's meant to be soothing, but I find it unnerving. My stomach flutters and apprehension tickles on the back of my neck. The elevator glides to a stop and doors slide open.

The office is stark white, from the carpet to the walls to the single desk. It feels like if heaven had a waiting room. There's a woman sitting behind the desk, dressed in a red suit and lipstick to match. She stands as I enter and offers me a kind smile.

"Miss Southland," she begins, "Mr. Baxter will be with you in a few moments. Can I offer you some water with cucumber?"

My brain skipping like a broken record. I can't make a coherent thought. Instead I nod my head with my mouth a little agape. She hands me a tall thin glass and I take a seat on the white couch and sip the crisp deliciousness. The lady in red goes back to her desk and I realize how much I don't belong here. I only get to take a few sips of my water before she announces, "Mr. Baxter will see you now."

I return my glass and head through the heavy wooden doors. Inside, the walls are lined with books that look like they've never been opened with sensible art hanging on the blue-gray painted walls. There is a black leather couch between the two shelving units and a massive, almost regal, black wooden desk by the far window. Seated in the high wingback chair is an older version of Conrad. The sandy hair that I know well is speckled with gray at the temples. A pair of thin, wire-rimmed glasses perch on the bridge of his nose as he reads the lines of the paper in front of him at a lightning speed.

"What did he do?" Lionel Baxter's voice booms across the room. It hits me like a wave.

"I'm-I'm sorry?" I stutter, suddenly feeling very small in this big office. With utter annoyance, he abandons the pages in front of him and locks me with his gaze in that way I thought only Conrad could. Mr. Baxter, however, is much colder. A chill runs through my body.

"What. Did. He. Do?" he snaps in staccato fashion. When I make no quick move to answer, he tosses his glasses onto the tall stack of papers. "I'm a busy man, Miss Southland, and I know you're smart enough to realize that. If you're here interrupting my day I'm assuming it's because my son has done something to warrant it."

Be brave. Be brave. Be brave.

I take the seat opposite his desk and sit as tall as I can.

"He's done nothing wrong sir. I came to speak with you," the final word is barely out of my mouth before he interrupts me.

"Then you must be here for more money. Not that I can blame you. I know how challenging Conrad can be. God knows you've made it longer than any of the others."

"No!" I exclaim, shocked that he'd think I was trolling for a raise. "I'm not looking to get paid more. It's nothing like that."

"Then what do you want? I don't find this guessing game amusing," he demands.

"Conrad is a wonderful person, Mr. Baxter," I start, sitting even straighter, to the point that I'm nearly lifting off the chair. I need to be Jessica Southland's daughter. No one pushes around my mother and I won't allow him to do it to me either.

"But I'm troubled, sir, because of the way you hurt him. You hurt him every, single day. He feels like an orphan because of how you treat him. How can you abandon him at that house and never visit him? Never call? You didn't even see him for Christmas. What kind of father does that?" My level-headed demeanor and prepared speech have fled my brain. I immediately sense that I have stepped out of bounds, but the words are out and I can't un-ring the bell.

Mr. Baxter sits forward in his seat, his mouth set in a thin line and his elbows balanced on the desk. "You forget yourself young lady. The affairs of my family have nothing to do with you," he bellows.

"I love him sir," I admit out loud for the first time. I expected it to be hard to say, but it's as natural to me as breathing.

"Oh, of course you do." He picks his glasses up, dismissing me like gum on the bottom of his shoe.

"What is that supposed to mean?"

"Of course some childhood crush would convince you that you have any right to come here and speak to me this way. You're my employee, Miss Southland."

Without hesitation, I stood up from my chair. "Not right now, Mr. Baxter," I responded, holding my chin high. "Right now I am a person who loves your son. I won't let you belittle how I feel because I'm young or a girl. Besides, that's not the point."

He crosses his arms over his chest and waits.

"One day sir, you're going to wake up and you're going to be an old man who will be all alone. Pollie will only put up with you for so long before she moves far enough away that she can make excuses never to see you. And Conrad? One day you're going to realize that you did everything in your power to push him away. You'll convince him that he never mattered to you and keeping him hidden was the best thing for you. He'll want nothing to do with you. One day you're going to count your piles of money all alone and realize that they are all you have. Conrad is going to get through this, Mr. Baxter. He's going to survive all of this and he'll be the better for it, and that will be in spite of you."

His righteous layers start to crack a little. His eyes soften.

"You have no idea how wonderful he is and I feel sorry for you because at the rate you're going, you never will." A few tears spill over and I quickly wipe them away under my glasses. "What kind of father isn't at his son's bedside after he survives burning alive? He told me he screamed for you and you weren't there."

Genuine surprise flashes across his face like I had physically struck him. I continue, "I'm ashamed of you. I don't even know you, but I am ashamed. You don't deserve him!" I practically shout, sniffling back my tears. I reach down and grab my purse.

I hoped to make a dramatic exit. Leave like an old Hollywood starlet through slamming doors, but Mr. Baxter's voice booms through the silence, halting me where I stand.

"Miss Southland." I peer over my shoulder, too paralyzed to turn. "You're fired," he says with absolute finality as he readjusts his glasses and returns to his work.

"Good. I don't want your money anyway," I hissed, doing my best to ignore the shaking in my legs. It should bother me more.

I've never failed at anything in my life, but I don't feel sad or upset. I cross the white waiting room, past the lady in red to the elevator. An eerie sense of calm runs through my body on the ride back to the lobby. The shaking begins once I'm safely inside the car. My previous calm twists and changes into an infectious anxiety. There's no way I can avoid telling Conrad. While I don't regret it, and I still think it was the right thing to do, a nagging pain stabs at my heart that it will hurt him.

I remain in the parking lot until a burnt orange sunset starts to fall and I know I can't put this off forever. It's time to suck it up and face the music. I stay right at the speed limit and take my time getting back. I try to ignore the spooky silence of the empty house and my brain runs through the speech I rehearsed in the car to explain things to Conrad. My blood pressure drops in the doorway of the kitchen. At the glass table, facing me with his hands folded on top, eyes full of angry fire, is Conrad.

"Tell me you didn't," he utters through a clenched jaw, like it's taking everything in him not to scream.

"What?" I ask, an acidic taste burning the back of my throat and tongue.

"Tell me you didn't. Tell me he was lying and you did not go to my father's office and yell at him about me," he roars like a volcano ready to explode.

"I didn't yell," I defend, my voice meek and small.

His entire face twitches before he slams his fist, still red and bruised from this morning, into the table. I'm certain the glass will shatter.

"What were you thinking?" he yells.

"I'm sorry, I-I didn't mean to upset you. I did it for you."

"I didn't ask you to Isabella," he booms, smacking his palm into the glass again. "I'm not some broken bird for you to nurse back to health. You don't have to defend me against the world."

"But I want to," I cry. "You should know that you have people in your corner to help you."

"I don't want your help with this! You honestly think I want anyone to beg my father to want me?" he screams back, his face flushing an angry red. "How would you feel if someone did that to you?"

"I didn't do it *to* you, I did it *for* you. He's your father!"

He pushes up from his seat, knocking over his chair. The sound reverberates through the room. "Do you have any idea what it felt like to have the first words from my father in months be, 'Don't have your girlfriend fight your battles. Be a man'?"

A new fire rises up inside me. My heart isn't breaking for him and it's definitely not pity. I'm mad. My phone starts to buzz in my pocket, but I ignore it.

"That's what this is really about, isn't it? Some toxic masculinity crap because I was the one to stand up to your father and not you?"

"That has nothing to do with this and you know it. You do not get to make decisions for me," he hisses. I throw my arms up in the air and pivot away and back, like my body can't decide where to go.

"If I didn't, nothing would ever get done."

"What is that supposed to mean?" he demands.

"When I got here you were an angry hermit who only talked to his flowers. If I didn't push you nothing would ever change!" I exclaim. My phone starts to buzz again. It's Jonah.

"I knew this was a mistake," he says, pacing back and forth behind the breakfast bar.

"What?" I cry, my heart dropping to my feet.

"This," his finger flies between the two of us. "I knew this was a bad idea and I kept trying to turn you away, but you had to keep pushing and pushing like you do with everything." He turns towards the fridge and lays his forehead against the cool metal. "You and I are not going to work, Isabella. We come from completely different worlds. You do not know me."

Every part of me wants to run to his side, but my feet stay firmly in place. "Tell me what I don't know," I demand.

"Do you have any idea the kind of things I would have said about someone like you before the accident?"

"What do you mean?" I ask, even though I'm pretty sure that I already know. I finally break through that barrier, the physical distance between us and push him away from the fridge.

"What? Do you want to throw a fat joke or two out there?" I snap, venom dripping from my words. "Maybe moo or oink as you walk behind me?" Those blue eyes that I love so much are dead, nothing behind them. "Because I promise you, Conrad, I have heard them all."

His head shakes and he cracks the knuckles in his fingers. "You do not understand who I was, that guy-"

"Is not who you are anymore!" I scream loud enough for my throat to quiver. I should stop talking, nothing good can come from this, but I can't. "You are not that guy anymore, he is gone. You will never have the perfect face or body again. And yes people are going to point and stare and whisper when you go out in public and it's awful, but you'll get past it. Trust me, I know all to well."

Cruel amusement falls over his face as he starts pacing the room again. "God, are you serious, Isabella? Are you seriously trying to compare the fact that I'm Freddy Krueger to you being fat?" And there it is, the word that people have given so much power. "They are not the same thing. You can change yours and I can't do anything about mine."

Normally, I would start crying like I do in any emotional situation. Yet not a single tear forms. I'm mad, not heartbroken.

"You think I never tried? You think my mother hasn't put me on every diet and exercise plan that exists? This is my life Connie. This is how I am and maybe the public attention you'll receive will be worse than mine, but you're just beginning to receive what I have always gotten. And the real problem is, people will feel bad for you. I know pity isn't what you go for, but no one will blame you. Meanwhile, people look at me in disgust."

"So who resents who, exactly?"

"God! I don't resent you, I-" and I'm about to tell him what I told his father, but I can't think of a worse time to tell someone you love them. "I don't resent you. You matter to me."

He raises his hand to silence me, "Just stop, Bella. Stop."

"Tell me one thing. Why did you think it was okay for Pollie to go behind my back and stand up to the Gattmans for me, but it's not okay that I went to your father for you? Explain that."

"It's not the same thing." He pinches the space between his eyes and lets out a sigh that will surely deflate him. It's like I've suddenly become the most exhausting creature in the world.

I try to speak when my phone starts buzzing again. I pick it up in my rage and Jonah enters the screen. It's obvious he's been crying by the puffiness in his eyes, but I'm so angry that I don't see it.

"What?" I snap.

"Bella, you need to come home," he responds with a sniffle.

"What? Why? Isn't the snow still bad? It's not time for me to come home yet. I haven't talked to Mom and Dad," I ramble, my mind drifting to the fact that Conrad is taking steps away from me.

"Bella!" Jonah exclaims with his voice, grabbing my attention and centering me. He waits a moment before he continues and I finally notice how upset he is.

"Bella," he begins and dread starts to creep in. "Mom had a heart attack this morning. You need to come home."

All I can hear is my own breathing as the world melts away.

"I'm coming," I sign back before clicking off the call, no time for goodbyes. I didn't ask if she was okay or how bad the situation is because I don't think my heart can take the answer. She has to be okay, she's Mom. The screen goes black and for one moment that lasts days, my body refuses to move.

"My mom had a heart attack. I have to go," I finally say aloud.

Conrad is already miles away when he says, "Maybe that's for the best." There's a shattering finality to it that hurts worse than anything else he's said.

CHAPTER TWENTY TWO

After he loads the last of my things into my car, Mr. Potter asks, "Do you want me to drive with you? I'm sure I could find a bus or grab a train after you get settled back with your folks. I don't feel good about you driving all the way home by yourself, especially when you're this upset."

I wrap my arms around his middle. "I will think of you every time I eat a potato," I mutter against his shirt. His body vibrates with that deep chocolatey laughter that I've grown so accustomed to. I make sure to absorb it, remember it.

Next to him is the hardest goodbye. Wrapped in her purple coat, hat, and scarf, Lottie stands crying with Lusta's hands on her shoulders. Some comforts only a mother can provide. I kneel down to her level.

"Hey," I say, tilting her face up to mine. "This isn't goodbye forever. I promise you we will talk again soon." She throws her arms around my neck and plants a loud smacking kiss against my cheek. She doesn't need words and I'm so grateful to her.

Mr. Potter hands me a paper bag, heavy with snacks inside I'm sure, before I let myself into my car. I roll down my window and say, "Thank you all for everything."

Lusta pulls her daughter against her and says, "You make sure you call me when you get there."

I wave to my little adopted family and can feel in my bones the glaring absence amongst the group. I'll call Pollie on the way to let her know what happened with my mom. I don't have time to wait for her to get here, but Conrad is only a few floors away. I let myself steal a final glance at the window where I can always find him and instantly wish I hadn't. Not a single curtain rustles or moves. He's not watching me leave. He doesn't want to say goodbye.

I try to focus only on my driving and how furious my parents would be if I got in an accident. I drive without stopping until I arrive at the hospital in New Shiloh. She has to be okay. I take the first available parking spot and run across the icy lot to the main entrance. A nice older woman in pink scrubs and a red cardigan takes my information and hands me a visitor badge before giving me directions to my mom.

The elevator ride to the fourth floor is the longest in my life, the dings between floors aging me. I finally arrive and pause briefly before walking through the entrance that leads to my mom. She has to be okay. I'm too young and unprepared for her not to be. I palm the button that opens the doors into the waiting room and tears fill my eyes. They're all here, sitting together in a line. Nixie, Elle, Blanche, Rosie, Goldie, and Beattie. My mom has always said that the true definition of a friend is someone that shows up when you need them, without you having to ask. And here they are, my people, my tribe.

When they see me they all rise to their feet and Nixie runs to me full force, colliding with me and bursting into tears. My entire body freezes in a panic at her reaction and I'm pretty sure I'm going to faint. It must be bad, really bad. Rosie can sense my dread and steps forward, placing a strong hand on my shoulder and firmly declaring, "She's okay."

It's all I've wanted to hear, but I'm not ready and my knees buckle beneath me. Thank God for Nixie's strong swimmer body holding me up. The others quickly surround me and take some of the load while I cry and put all my weight and every problem onto them. And just as they always have, they hold me up.

Beattie leaves to get my dad. Blanche sits me down on her lap like a little girl who needs comforting and I snuggle right into place. My entire body is heavy with exhaustion and fear and all I want to do is sleep. Goldie and Nixie in the chairs on either side and Rosie and Elle on the floor in front.

"I can't believe you're all here," I hiccup when the sobs subside.

"Jonah texted me immediately. He told me you were on the way and I rallied the troops," Rosie explains, rubbing my knee through my leggings.

"Beattie agreed this is a good reason to close the shop for the afternoon," Blanche continues and I throw my arm around her neck, inhaling a deep whiff of her vanilla shampoo.

"I missed you girls," I cry out and no sentiment has ever been truer.

Elle and Rosie exchange a look before Elle says, "We kind of expected to see Conrad walk in with you."

"I messed it up," I admit. In reality, we both did. We fired words like missiles at each other, shattering whatever we had into pieces small enough to pass through the eye of a needle. I don't know how we come back from that.

"I can not believe I didn't know you had a boyfriend," Goldie whines, an attempt to lighten the mood. Her long hair sits on the top of her head like a bow atop a Christmas present.

"I can't believe I didn't know *you* did!" I exclaim remembering that she and I still have a fight ahead of us for her not telling me about Dubuque Reyes. Goldie is about to open her mouth and say more when the doors open back up and my father rounds the corner. I run to him like he's oxygen and I'm suffocating. There is no man in this world that a girl needs more than her daddy.

"Oh, Peanut," he murmurs, his voice sad. He lifts me off the floor like I'm four years old again and it's everything I need.

"Is she okay?" I ask into the weathered cotton of his shirt. It won't be real until he says it. He nods against the top of my head.

"She's weak and a bit groggy, but she's going to be okay." Relief rushes through every limb. "Let's go see her," he says.

I can't move. My dad looks tired and older than the last time I saw him. I wonder if he's slept.

"I was awful to her," I lament, the pain ripping through my chest. "She doesn't want to see me." He leans down, placing his hands on my cheeks and looking into my eyes.

"I don't often speak in absolutes, you know this. But I swear to you, I promise you," he begins, his voice strong and sure, "there is no one in this world she wants to see more."

I cast a glance back to my friends who offer me comforting smiles. They'll be waiting. I hold my father's hand while he navigates the halls like he's done it a thousand times.

"Go on in, and send you brother out." He's going to make me do this alone.

I push the curtain aside and there she is, my perfect mother, in a hospital gown. Her hair is in a ponytail and she's not wearing any makeup. It barely looks like her and she seems small in the bed, frail. My mother is the epitome of strength, nothing can break her. Her smile stretches across her face and I remember that Dad said she would be a little groggy.

"There's my favorite girl!" she exclaims.

"I'll give you two a minute." As Jonah passes me, he squeezes my shoulder hard enough that it hurts.

I look back to my mom, unsure of what to do.

"I got into Brown." I blurt it out knowing it's the most important thing I've wanted to tell her. I never would have been able to forgive myself if I didn't get the chance. She got me there after all. Her smile holds steady and she opens her arms to me, a welcome homecoming. I cry against her cheek and she pets my hair, shushing me sweetly. Ever the mother, comforting me when she's the one in the hospital.

"I should have called!" I wail, digging my fingers into her bed. "I should have called you. I'm so sorry, Mommy."

I realize how foolish it's all been. If my mother had died, her last memory of me would have been my hanging up on her while I was shopping for a Christmas tree.

"Oh, my baby," she whispers. "I'm sorry, too. I didn't call you either." I pull myself back a little and wipe under my eyes, taking my glasses off.

"Did you hear me, Mama? I got into Brown!" I exclaim.

"I know you did."

"What? How?" I scan my brain for some explanation.

"Well," she begins, a soft smile spreading to her lips. "I suppose I didn't know officially, but I had no doubt. I can't act surprised because I'm not. I knew you could do it." My number one fan always. My personal cheering section. My eternal best friend. I lay my head on her shoulder and we talk until she falls asleep.

They send Mom home from the hospital the next day, despite my many protests to her doctors. My father finally had to give me the parental death stare to get me to stop. I personally don't think anyone should go home the day after a heart attack, no matter how "minor" it is. Alas, I'm outvoted. No one listens to teenagers.

I surround myself with all things related to my mother. I wake up promptly the next morning at seven a.m. to make her breakfast. The sheer level of confusion when I rise before either of my parents is extreme. My dad descends into the kitchen, his tie still undone and hanging around his neck, glasses on the bridge of his nose.

"Hi?" he questions, fiddling with the collar of his pale blue dress shirt.

My tea bag bobs up and down in my pale yellow mug as I wait for the coffee machine to brew. In front of me, beside my mug, I cut a Honeycrisp apple into thin slices. I remember Blanche telling me a story about how apple seeds are basically cyanide. I make sure to cut around those. When she's awake I'll make her some egg whites. For a moment I am Mr. Potter. While his speciality seems to be pancakes and breakfast meats, I'm sure he makes a mean egg white too.

"You okay?" Dad asks.

I nod, keeping my attention on the sharp knife in my hand.

"Yeah, I kind of got into the habit of getting up early. I figured I'd help keep mom on track with healthy food."

"That's nice of you, Peanut, I'm sure she'll appreciate it," he says, dumping half of the sugar bowl into his travel mug. He has to seize every opportunity while Mom isn't watching over his shoulder.

"How are you really doing?" he asks sincerely. "We haven't had a chance to sit down and talk about everything that happened."

"Mom's okay Dad, what's there to talk about?" I ask. I finish cutting the apple into lopsided sections.

"You know very well young lady that's not what I mean," he continues, his voice a little harsher than I'm used to hearing. I expected I'd have some time to prep for this conversation. "Tell me about what happened up there."

How am I supposed to approach this? Do I lie and say it just didn't work out? The simple thought of not telling my dad the whole truth twists my stomach.

"It got complicated," is the most honest yet vague I can seem to be. He stays quiet and waits. I've always been able to tell my dad anything. Not speaking to him much the last few weeks has been torture. I push myself away from the counter and begin to pace in front of him. He pulls out one of the stools at the breakfast bar and settles in. It doesn't matter that this is normally when he leaves for work. If I needed him to, I know he'd sit there all day.

"Here's what happened," I begin before unloading every ounce of weight on my shoulders. I tell him everything. When I'm finally done, I hop up on the counter, a big no-no by my own standards, but I worry my feet won't hold me up much longer.

"And to think," he begins with a chuckle. "We thought we were sending you up there for a tutoring job."

I crack a smile, letting my head lay back against one of the smooth kitchen cabinets.

"It's such a mess, Dad. I don't know what to do."

"What do you want to do?" he asks.

"I want to fix it, but I don't know how to do that. Maybe he's a little too broken."

"Could be," he says, smoothing his hand over his beard. "He certainly has been through a lot. I can't offer the most objective opinion without knowing the young man personally. But there are two sides to every story. Can you see his?"

I give myself a moment to really run through it. I saw it simply as me defending Conrad's honor with his father because no one else could; but to Conrad I stuck myself in a place I didn't belong. I could have talked to him about what I was planning to do. I also could have thought it through a little better and not run out the door to confront Mr. Baxter the moment the idea crossed my mind. Maybe we were both wrong.

"I think I can," I mutter, my voice small, ashamed of the way I acted. "I made some big mistakes, but I really care about him and he hurt me." I feel like a little girl when I say it, but it's the truest description I have for what I'm feeling.

My dad's eyes never waver from my face. "As your father, the idea that anyone could hurt you in any way makes me insane and I'd love to tell you to forget him and he's not worthy of you…" His voice trails away.

"But?" I finished for him.

"But," he begins again, taking time to choose his words wisely. "Do you think he's worthy of you, Peanut?"

I think back to our failed attempt to bake a pie in his kitchen and I realize how little Conrad sees in himself. He thinks he's a gargoyle, an unredeemable demon, and he's wrong. He's so wrong. I love that stupid gargoyle.

"He is, Dad. He really is."

A smile forms on his lips. I doubt any father really wants to hear that his little girl has any other man in her life, but my daddy is always genuine.

"Then maybe don't give up on him just yet."

After a long hug with my dad, I send him off to work with coffee in hand and set about finishing breakfast for my mother. I lay out a tray of the healthiest food I could think of and take it up to her bedroom. She looks so small in her bed wrapped in her favorite Brown University sweatshirt.

"There's my girl," she sings, the corners of her eyes crinkling with her smile. Multiple days of no makeup is out of character for my mom, but there's a part that's nice to really see her look her age. I hold up the mug and plate, hovering around the doorway. It's still strange to be home, I feel like a visitor.

"I made you some breakfast."

She pats the spot beside her and it takes everything in me not to take a running leap onto the bed like I did as a little girl. I hand her the mug before scooting up across the blanket and placing the plate on her lap. Her nose scrunches up when she sniffs the bland eggs.

"Is there any salt on these?" she asks.

"Mom, you had a heart attack, of course there's no salt!"

She nibbles on one of the apple slices with a disappointed pout. "I mean, a little salt wouldn't kill me. Ooo, or bacon!" she exclaims with a giddy expression.

Holy role reversal! Am I the one who has to push healthy eating habits on Mom? That's a first.

She takes a sip of her coffee and shudders with the full force of an earthquake.

"No sugar!" she gasps. "I thought you loved me!"

"I do love you!" I cry. "That's why you're not allowed to leave me any time soon."

Abandoning her breakfast on her nightstand, she picks up the book she'd been reading before I came in. "Your brother found this next to the TV downstairs." I glance over her shoulder to see the notebook I'd been scribbling in at the hospital. I try to snatch it back, but her reflexes are much faster than mine.

"Relax," she laughs, opening the book. "It's not a bad thing."

"Just embarrassing," I mumble.

"The Perfect Love Story," my mother reads after clearing her throat. I had meant for this to be nothing more than a passive stream of consciousness, pondering to pass the hours by her bedside. No one was ever supposed to see it. She reads down the list, settling on my final choice of Wuthering Heights. "Hmm," she hums when she gets there.

"Oh, come on Mom! You love this book!" It horrifies me that the woman who introduced me to the Brontes could possibly disagree with my love of Catherine and Heathcliff.

"Yes, Lambchop, I do love the book and I do think it's one of the best love stories. I'm surprised that you thought it was the best, though."

My head cocks to the side. "Really? It's all about passion."

She smiles and pulls a different book off her bedside table. She hands me an old, weathered copy of Pride and Prejudice. "You're no Catherine Earnshaw, honey. You're all Lizzy Bennett."

Does that make Conrad Mr. Darcy or Mr. Wickham? Or is he neither?

"Why do you say that?" I ask her.

She leans over and plants a kiss on my forehead. "'Till this moment I never knew myself,'" my mother quotes. "I think you've discovered a lot about what makes you *you* over these last few weeks. I noticed it the second I saw you and it makes me feel so much better about you going off to school by yourself." She proceeds to boop me on the tip of my nose. "I've been worried about it."

"Me too," I mumble, plucking at the end of her sweatshirt sleeve. In a few months I'll get my own Brown sweatshirt to hold onto forever.

She folds the cover of the Austen over and begins reading to herself, humming rather than reading aloud. I could fall asleep to that sound. "So," she begins, flipping the page. "Eventually you're going to tell me all the details, right? Your father seemed to hint at something revolving around a boy?" Knowing my mother, she's already obtained every detail she can from my dad, Jonah, and possibly all of my friends.

"I'd rather not right now if that's okay. I'm still figuring out how I feel about it." What happened with Gatty is over and I'd rather not reopen that chapter. I still don't know where I stand with Conrad and as good as my mother's intentions are, I'm not ready to analyze it the way she'd want to.

Her gaze never leaves the book, but I doubt she's actually reading it now. "Promise me you're okay?" she asks.

I prop myself up on my elbow and take in my mother's full image. Her petite bone structure makes her look fragile from the tip of her sharp nose to her delicate ankles crossed under her blanket. And yet I know that if I were to tell her I was even the slightest bit not okay, she would hop right in the car and drive herself to New York to strangle them both with her own two hands. "I'm all right, mom," I say instead.

"Do you promise, whether it's tomorrow or twenty years from now, you'll tell me?"

I know how hard it is for her to not know every detail of my life. She's nosy because she cares. This boundary is more than a huge step for her. I stretch up and kiss her on the cheek before nuzzling back into her side. "I promise," I respond, my voice soft, but I know she hears me.

And just like that, the conversation is over and she's onto the next. "Last night your father and I got a very interesting phone call." When I don't take the bait, she continues all on her own. "It appears you've been awarded the Baxter Industries Scholarship."

A nervous and acidic lump forms in the back of my throat. I told Lionel Baxter I didn't want any of his money. I wonder if he's purposefully disrespecting my wishes or if he thinks this is some clever way around them. I certainly believe that Mr. Baxter is not a man who's told what to do by anyone.

"What do you think about that?" she asks. "I'll tell you what I think. No matter what happened with his son, you have worked incredibly hard and deserve that money. It would really help out a lot. But," she says, interrupting my train of thought. "If it's too difficult for you to take it, whatever the reason, I won't force you. You have the right to decide."

From unilateral decisions about my future, to letting me make my own choices. Quite the flip.

"I did work for it. I earned that money."

I can feel a grin, probably from relief, spread across her lips before she kisses my forehead again.

"You most definitely did."

After a week of driving her insane, my mother forces me back to work at the pie shop. The chaos of being in charge again is a welcome distraction from all the garbage in my head. I talk to Pollie occasionally on the phone, but we avoid all conversations related to Conrad. I'm grateful for that.

The first Saturday night after I return, I find a happy, steady rhythm in folding pie boxes while my friends scramble around to close the shop as quickly as possible.

"Is that it?" Goldie booms to the empty store when we seal the final box.

"Looks like it is," I say, tucking my hands in the pockets of my coat. As always, I'm bundled up for the tundra and Goldie skips around in a thin, long sleeved shirt. I'm far more insulated than she is; something is backwards.

"Excellent!" Elle exclaims, grabbing her duffle bag from behind the counter. "We have like an hour to get ready."

"What time are we supposed to be at this stupid thing?" Blanche shouts from the bathroom. A curling iron in her hand she swirls her short raven hair into tight curls at the sides of her head.

"No one forced you to come to New Shiloh," Goldie says, taking the curling iron from Blanche to help with the back of her head. She tsks and mumbles, "I cannot comprehend why anyone would cut their hair this short."

"I'm an athlete thank you," Blanche responds. "And are you really giving me an out from this thing tonight?"

"Oh, no you don't!" Elle shouts, scurrying around the corner from the kitchen. "Blanche Fa Summers, you promised me!"

"What's happening?"

"Dub and I got invited to a party and I invited Finn and Elle to join us," Goldie explains. Ah yes, the boyfriend we've still yet to discuss.

"Where's the party?" I ask, wedging my trusty screwdriver into the cash drawer, ready to count out of the register.

Goldie reapplies her already perfect lipgloss. She snaps the mirror shut with a loud click and leans toward me. "You know Harpersgrove is a really small town. Everybody kinda goes to the same house for one big party."

"Sure, Gold," I laugh as the drawer springs open on my nemesis of a machine.

She looks for help from her cohorts, but they're still fighting over curls in the bathroom. Realizing she's alone, Goldie finally says, "The party is at Lucy Wilcox's house. I'm really sorry. I'm sure it sounds like we're going to the house of the enemy. Her house is big and Dub really wants to go, and I'm sorry."

I reach out and place my hands on her cheeks, glad she hasn't applied much makeup yet. "It's okay," I say with a smile and her entire body relaxes. "Do you think maybe I could come?"

"What? Are you serious?" Blanche demands, emerging from the bathroom, fully curled. She and Elle sit on stools beside Goldie at the counter, all of them watching me.

"I would like to come with you to the party."

Elle and Goldie trade a nervous look that, now, I find kind of insulting. But I know that Brave Bella would enjoy going, even if it is hosted by the devil.

"You did hear her say it's at Lucy Wilcox's house, right?" Elle reiterates.

Ever the hero, Blanche hops to my side. "Hells Bells, don't listen to them. You can be my date!"

I smile and move out from behind the counter to grab my purse and coat. "Would you guys mind closing up? I'd like to run home and get ready. I'll meet you back here in an hour."

CHAPTER TWENTY THREE

Here I stand, in Lucy Wilcox's living room with a red solo cup of beer and dancing drunk children on all sides of me. Children who I've grown up beside but never really known. It's honestly not all that different from Gatty's party. The DJ is set up with a laptop and two ancient speakers on either side plugged into this phone. Some of the details might be a little different, but one thing remains the same. I do not belong here. The most glaring difference is that in the crowd in New York I went unnoticed and here I'm the parasite that doesn't belong. They don't know me, but they're actively aware of it. These people have all been coming to the same parties since the eighth grade, or at least that's how Goldie explained it to me.

"I still can't believe you're here," Blanche yells to me over the music. We've lost the other girls to their boyfriends and the crowd. This whole scene makes me miss Pollie.

"Conrad's sister took me to a few parties. I didn't totally hate it."

332 | KATELYN BRAWN

Blanche gulps down the last of her second beer. "I'm going to get another drink. Do you want anything?" She's gone before I can answer. Not even ten seconds go by before someone takes her place.

"You've got to be kidding," a voice I'd been hoping to avoid says from behind. I turn around to find Lucy Wilcox in all her intimidating glory.

"What the hell are you doing here?" she demands.

As if summoned by radar, Goldie rounds the corner at a speed that defies physics, her boyfriend close on her heels.

"Listen here, Satan," she begins, but I step in front to stop her.

"Don't worry, Gold," I say with a smile, placing my hands on her arms. "I got it."

Goldie looks far from convinced. My girl is ready to pounce.

"I think someone said I had to start standing up for myself," I say, echoing what Goldie told me the day before I left for New York. Her shoulders relax a little, but her eyes never lose their scowl.

"I will be standing right over there. Signal if you need me and I'll punch her." Dub wraps his arms around his girlfriend to hold the girl at bay. I'm hoping for zero bloodshed.

I think, *It's now or never. Be brave, Bella.* I square my shoulders at Lucy, standing tall and ready. I've spent enough of my life being afraid of the Lucys and the Parkers and the Gattys of the world. It's enough already.

My hands lift up from my sides. "Isn't this exhausting for you?" Her normal stone face cracks ever so slightly as she tries to blink away her surprise. "I don't think I've actually done anything to you. Our interactions have been few and far between to say the least, and yet you go out of your way to make fun of me. Aren't you tired of keeping up the same mean girl crap all the time? In a few months we're all going to be away at college and who knows if or when we'll see each other again. You don't have to like me, but wouldn't it be a more peaceful existence for everyone if you weren't so angry all the time?" A hush falls over the room.

"You're going to come into my house and talk to me like that?" she yells, gearing up for a fight. I don't need her theatrics. I'm not here to play her games.

"Oh, Lucy, you're just hopeless aren't you?" I sigh. A hushed gasp sounds around us. No one disrespects the Queen Bee. Lucy's expression sharpens. She opens her mouth to yell again, but the words turn to cotton. Her attention shifts, moving behind me, and her eyes go wide instead.

"Oh my God," she mutters and the crowd focuses on the same place.

I turn to see what all the fuss could possibly be about. My heart drops to my feet. The energy in the room switches from loud, raucous party to whispers and giggles. But I can't hear any of it. Standing just inside the front door is Conrad. My Connie. In his hand he holds a bouquet of his mother's roses. A few steps behind him I notice an all too familiar head of black curls belonging to his baby sister. I know Pollie well enough by now to be certain that hanging back is killing her. Conrad may be bigger and older, but Pollie is the protector. The room is silenced. This is the main event now.

"What in the literal hell is this freakshow?" Lucy snaps and it's more than I can take.

I whip around, my hair smacking me in the face and snarl, "Shut up Lucinda." Her jaw snaps closed with such force I hear her teeth clink. If a grown up conversation doesn't reach her, maybe sheer strength will. At the end of it all, let Lucy Wilcox have her miniscule amount of power now. How sad it must be to peak in high school. A part of me feels bad for her.

When I come back to Conrad, I fear I'm dreaming. There's no way he can possibly be standing here, in Harpersgrove, in the middle of Lucy Wilcox's party.

"Hi," he says simply and all the chaos around us fades away. I suddenly realize that my friends have all moved in closer, ready to save me.

"Hi," I hear myself say. "What are you doing here?"

He pushes the sleeves up of his shirt and I notice that he's not trying to hide. No hat, or sunglasses, or hood. I know that everyone is staring, but he doesn't seem to notice or care.

"I wanted to come sooner, but Pollie said I needed to wait and do some real thinking first." At the mention of her name, Pollie's hand shoots up behind her brother to wave to me. She must have driven him here. Without prompting, Blanche wiggles through the crowd of staring drunkards to pull Pollie into the small Bella cheering squad.

I hate how much distance is between us, but I can't move. For the first time Conrad seems to notice the people around us, especially Lucy Wilcox with her hip popped and arms folded stiffly across her chest. His breathing labors, but he never loses focus.

"How did you know I'd be here?" I ask, taking that first step forward. My brain's lost the battle. My heart seems to be in charge. A grin flashes across his face and just as quickly, it's gone.

"Well, I had this whole epic romantic gesture planned and went to your house to see it through, but of course, you weren't there." Imagining Conrad coming face to face with the likes of Jessica and Silas Southland without any backup fills me with dread. "Your mother was every bit as intimidating as I expected."

Internally, every muscle in my body shudders.

"Sorry, she can be a bit much."

"No, no, I was impressed. Like I'd expect anything less from the woman who raised you," he chuckles. He's not wrong of course.

"Your brother was the one to tell me where to find you," he says with his mouth, but that's not the language I'm focused on. No, it's the way his fingers form the words, *brother*, *where*, and *you*. An airy giggle sounds between us as I motion to his hands with my own.

"Did you learn super secret spy language?" I ask.

"The little one's been helping me out."

"What are you doing here, Conrad?" I ask again, refusing to abandon my ground. Brave Bella is here to stay. People start to move back to the party. There's still a decent crowd invested in what's happening with us, but I don't care who's looking and neither does Conrad.

"Bella, I will never be more sorry for anything than I am for how I handled the situation with your mom. You needed me and I wasn't there for you. I will never forgive myself for that or for everything that happened that day."

Be brave Bella. "But why are you here?"

"A few days after you left, my father came to my house. We stood in the foyer and he said that no one has ever stood up to him like you did and I was a fool if I let you go. He apologized for how he's treated me. I'm pretty sure my father has never apologized in his life. I seriously doubt anything will change, but an apology alone is huge for him. And then," he starts, but his voice falls away, leaving the ghost of a smile left on his face with words unsaid.

"What?" I ask, taking another step toward him, close enough now that I could reach out and grab him if I wanted. Not yet.

His expression softens and he says, "He said you told him you loved me. Is that true?"

Everything with my mom has taught me that life is too short to stay mad for the sake of being mad.

I nod my head and say, "Yeah, a little bit."

An enormous grin stretches across his mouth. He exclaims, his voice booming loud enough for all to hear, "Well good, because I love you a lot!"

I close the distance, I can't take it. "While we're apologizing for things," I begin, running fingers up the lapels of his jacket. "I'm sorry I overstepped. It was selfish of me to go to your dad without talking to you. I'm sorry."

"Maybe we can forgive each other?" He places his fingers under my chin, tilting my head up.

I motion to the flowers in his hand and say, "No books this time?" Maybe they aren't such a bad romantic gesture after all.

"I thought we might do things my way this time."

A compromise. I can handle that. Reaching down, he laces our fingers together and squeezes. "I'm still a mess, Bella, and I'm going to mess this up again, but I've never wanted to work harder at anything in my life. I want to be better. Better for you and better for me." He runs his hand over his hair, and says, "It's not like there is some magic spell that's going to lift and make me different. I will always be Conrad after the accident."

I place the flowers in Lucy Wilcox's arms and she gawks like I've handed her a poisonous snake.

"Thank God," I exclaim before leaping into his arms and kissing him with all the love I feel. The party erupts in applause like it would in my favorite chick flick. Out of the corner of my eye I see Blanche embrace Pollie, old friends meeting new, and I know everything's going to be okay.

It's in this moment, when I'm kissing the boy that I love, that I realize maybe the ideal love story isn't about two perfect people, in a perfect situation, finding the perfect happily ever after. Perhaps it's two imperfect people finding their reflection in one another.

And I like the way I look through Conrad's eyes.

CPSIA information can be obtained
at www.ICGtesting.com
Printed in the USA
LVHW081253250222
712017LV00021B/196